The Club

THE CLUB

A Novel

ELLERY LLOYD

THORNDIKE PRESS
A part of Gale, a Cengage Company

GALE
A Cengage Company

Thorndike Press® Large Print Thriller, Adventure, and Suspense.
The text of this Large Print edition is unabridged.
Other aspects of the book may vary from the original edition.
Set in 16 pt. Plantin.

LIBRARY OF CONGRESS CIP DATA ON FILE.
CATALOGUING IN PUBLICATION FOR THIS BOOK
IS AVAILABLE FROM THE LIBRARY OF CONGRESS.

ISBN-13: 979-8-8857-8145-9 (hardcover alk. paper)

Published in 2022 by arrangement with Harper, an imprint of HarperCollins Publishers.

Printed in Mexico
Print Number : 1   Print Year : 2022

THE CLUB

The Club

By the time the Land Rover was halfway across the causeway it must have been obvious they were never going to make it. Not at the speed that tide was coming in. Not with that distance still to go. At which point, what do you do? One spot about halfway across at which careful passing is possible aside, even at its broadest the road linking the island to the mainland is only ever about a vehicle and a half wide. Even at its highest, at the lowest tide, the road is only a foot or two above the level of the surrounding mudflats. There is nowhere even to attempt a three-point turn. There is no way you are going to get back to the island in reverse, blind drunk, in the middle of the night, in a borrowed and unfamiliar vehicle.

Behind you, on the island, the party is still going strong, fireworks popping and fizzing. A mile or so ahead you can just make out the silhouette of the village — the orange glow of

7

the harbor front, a light or two still on here and there in an upstairs window. So what do you decide? Your first instinct is to keep going, to put your foot down. To take your chances at forty, at forty-five, fifty, on this unfamiliar, sinuous track in the pitch dark, the headlights illuminating just one unpredictably curved stretch of the causeway in front of you at a time, black waves already lapping across it, the road ahead rapidly narrowing, disappearing. You could sound the horn, flash your lights wildly — but even if you did manage to attract someone's attention, even if somebody on shore did see you or hear you and call the coast guard, what could the coast guard possibly do, given the speed things are progressing, considering the distances involved?

And then the horror becomes not just what is happening, but how easy it is, numbed and jumbled and fuzzy as you are, to imagine what will happen next. The grimly dawning realization that within minutes the water will be up to your axles, up to your headlights. That at some point, probably sooner rather than later, the engine will suck in water and choke, and the whole vehicle will grind to a halt.

And all this time, the Land Rover's other occupant is screaming at you from the passenger seat, telling you this is all your fault, demanding you do something, flailing around, panicking.

And it occurs to you that you should call someone, call anyone, but then of course you realize your phone is still on the island; they took your phone, and even if they hadn't, there probably wouldn't be any reception out here anyway.

And you wonder how long you would survive out there, in the cold water, in the darkness, if you tried to swim for it, given the time of the year, and the strength of the currents, and how far you are from the shore.

And at some point it dawns on you that whatever you do now, the result is inevitable.

And at some point it dawns on you that the media are going to have an absolute field day with this.

And perhaps at that moment — but only perhaps, and only for a moment — it dawns on you that this is no more and no less than the ending you so richly deserve.

Vanity Fair
Murder on the Island

It was the club you'd kill to join; the launch event to which the A-list were dying to be invited. What no one could have anticipated was how tragically things were about to go wrong. In this exclusive investigation, Ian Shields cuts to the heart of the case that baffled the world . . .

The party on the island had been going on for days.

All Friday morning, all Friday afternoon, helicopters had been arriving, departing, circling. Speedboats thumping back and forth across the glittering waves. A steady stream of blacked-out SUVs making their way down hedgerowed Essex lanes, past bare brown fields and damp black trees, through the narrow streets of the village of Littlesea. At around midday someone counted three Model S Teslas driving past, one after another.

10

A celebrity wedding, you might have said, if you didn't know better. Some millionaire's fiftieth birthday.

All Saturday afternoon, all Saturday evening, from across the water, sometimes louder, sometimes fainter, came drifting the steady *doof-doof-doof* of distant bass. Here and there, over the course of the weekend, in the late mornings, in the afternoons, if your eyesight was good enough or you had a pair of binoculars, you could just make out from the mainland where people had laid big blue-and-white-striped blankets on the foreshore. A head bobbing in the water. A horse kicking through the sand, its rider bouncing along in the saddle.

Now and again, in the evenings, you could make out through the trees the flicker of huge flaming Tiki torches, the front of the Manor illuminated in yellow or green or blue. There were even times, if the wind was in the right direction, when it was possible to imagine you could hear the crowd: their cheers, their whoops, their laughter. Their screams.

As well as celebrating Island Home's grand opening, the lavish party also marked thirty years since the company's CEO, Ned Groom — one of hospitality's great visionaries — had inherited the Home Club in Covent Garden from his grandfather and boldly set to work transforming it from a dusty and undersubscribed private drinking den for "actors, performers, and other stage professionals" into the modishly renamed Home, the most exclusive and talked-about London nightspot of the decade (that decade being the 1990s), whose famous front-door superstars stumbled out of and straight onto the pages of the next day's tabloids. Kate Moss had her birthday party there several years in a row. Kiefer Sutherland and his entourage were famously turned away one night. The entire cast of *Friends* took over the roof terrace for their final London press junket.

It was now almost twenty-five years since Ned and his right-hand man, his brother Adam Groom, had crossed the Atlantic to launch their second club, the now-iconic Manhattan Home.

In the years and decades since, the Home Group had become a genuine global brand, a collection of eleven members' clubs with attached hotel suites, all offering — for a hefty annual fee — the same comforting combination of down-to-earth luxury, effortfully understated cool, and absolute privacy to the chosen few. There was Santa Monica Home. Highland Home. Country Home. Cannes Home. Hamptons Home. Venice Home. Shanghai Home. There were Homes in Malibu, in Paris, in Upstate New York. Each one in a jaw-dropping setting: a former embassy (Shanghai), a grand palazzo (Venice), a deconsecrated cathedral (Cannes), a restored country pile (Country Home, in Northamptonshire; Highland Home, in Perthshire).

Even so, nothing that Ned Groom had ever attempted was on anything like the scale of Island Home. A whole island, two miles across, two and a half miles long, ninety minutes' drive from London, complete with neo-Palladian manor, acres of woodland and miles of beaches, ninety-seven individual guest cabins, five restaurants, three bars, several gyms, tennis courts, spin studio, spa, sauna, helipad, screening rooms, stables, and heated natural outdoor swimming pool. All of it private property, accessible by land only at low tide along a twisting mile-and-a-half-long causeway. Despite the five-thousand-pound-plus-per-night price tag, before a single member had ever set foot on the sand, Island Home was booked solid for an entire year.

It was perhaps only to be expected, given the size of the place, given the ambition of what Ned Groom and his team were attempting, not to mention Ned's legendary perfectionism, that not everything had gone quite according to schedule. First it had been due to open in the early spring, then the late spring, then the summer, then autumn.

For months, Home had been hiring staff — kitchen staff, front-desk staff, maintenance staff, waiters, housekeepers, a thirty-person events team, an eighty-person security team — and training them all in the particularities and peculiarities of working for one of the world's most exclusive and discreet cliques, dealing with some of the world's most particular and precious people.

For weeks, all hands had been on deck, inspecting and testing and double-checking, to make certain that the cabins scattered around the island — each one composed of vintage timber reclaimed from hundreds of historical wooden barns, huts, and sheds the design team had spent years sourcing and acquiring from as far afield as Bulgaria, Slovakia, Estonia — were ready to receive their first overnight guests. To certify that the log burners were correctly ventilated and weren't going to suffocate anyone in their sleep. To ensure that all the lights switched on, all the toilets flushed, all the baths ran at the correct, thunderous water pressure, filling each cast-iron, claw-foot tub in under three minutes. To confirm that the winding gravel paths were clear and navigable, whether on foot or by bicycle, electric scooter or chauffeur-driven golf cart. That sudden sharp drops and deep water and other natural hazards were clearly sign-posted. That, by the time the first members arrived, all the paint was dry, patches of splintered wood sanded, exposed wires tucked away, and that no one was going to get electrocuted or accidentally impaled.

In retrospect, perhaps any tragedy seems to acquire a sense of inevitability.

"The final event of the launch, Sunday morning's brunch, was meant to be the surprise highlight of the entire weekend," reports Josh Macdonald, one of six successive head architects to have worked on the Island Home project over the course of its eight-year gestation. "Ned was in an expensive arms race with himself — each new Home club had to outdo the last, with at least one extraordinary feature that

15

made it unique: the Perspex-bottomed rooftop pool in Shanghai, the glass cube bar inside the ruined chapel at Highland Home. This time it was the underwater restaurant, Poseidon."

The idea, says Macdonald, was inspired by a place where Ned had dined in the Maldives. "There's a bar and an entrance at beach level with a view out across the water, over toward the mainland. When it's time to eat, you cross a polished concrete bridge and then walk through a tunnel and down some steps and find yourself emerging into this vast room, like a giant fishbowl. In the middle of the room is the kitchen and bar, surrounded by tables and chairs, and out through the windows all you can see is the sea," Macdonald explains. "Shoals of mackerel. Clouds of blue jellyfish. The undersides of boats. The sunlight playing on the waves overhead. Ned wanted all that to be the last thing that guests saw before leaving the party, to ensure a truly lasting impression of Island Home that everyone would be talking about for weeks to come."

He certainly achieved that.

According to those who were there, the question most members were asking as they filed into breakfast on that final morning of the three-day party, nursing their hangovers, was, Where was Ned? Usually at a launch like this he was omnipresent, telling jokes, making sure everybody was having a good time. Six foot four and solidly built, a former rugby player, a qualified barrister, he had a booming voice and a raucous laugh you could hear wherever you were standing in the room. Now, remarking on his absence, guests found themselves wondering aloud about the last time they had spoken to him. Speculating about where Ned might be, gossiping about the events of the night before and the night before that, tucking into their egg-white omelets, green juices, and turmeric lattes, on the lookout for familiar faces, it was some time before anyone noticed anything peculiar out there in the water, beyond the curved plate-glass windows.

It was the sun breaking through the clouds for the first time that gray, late-autumn morning that did it, sending a shaft of light into the gloom of the seabed, illuminating what had previously looked like a cluster of rocks, an indistinct shape in the water.

"That was when diners began leaving their tables, started wandering over to the window, pointing at it," recalls one Home member and party guest, who has asked not to be named. "People were laughing and joking. We thought it was a Land Rover publicity stunt and people were impressed, especially as the car was upside down, and about twenty feet underwater, wedged against a big rock. What a way to get us to sit up and take notice! Everyone was asking how they had got it down there, how long it had been submerged." Then, she says, people started to realize what was inside the car. Then, she says, someone started sobbing.

Shortly afterward it was announced that a body had been found on the island.

And that was when the party of the year turned into the murder mystery of the decade.

CHAPTER ONE:
THURSDAY AFTERNOON

JESS

She had made it.

That was what Jess kept catching herself thinking.

Head of housekeeping, Island Home. Her name was Jess Wilson and she was the new head of housekeeping for Island Home.

She still couldn't quite believe it.

It had all been a bit like a dream, the past week. First the phone call from Home's head office, offering her an interview — after all those years of applying. All those years of hoping. All those years of being told they would keep her CV on file.

Then the interview itself, down in London, with Adam Groom, Home Group's director of special projects, the second-most-important person in the whole company. Her sudden panic about what to wear, what to say.

It would be hard to exaggerate how much

she had wanted this, or for how long. Growing up where she had, in Northamptonshire, just down the road from Country Home, she could remember driving with her parents past that long drystone wall, glimpsing through the trees the glinting waters of the estate's private lake, peeking through the front gates at the long straight drive up to the Elizabethan manor house, experiencing a little thrill every time, trying to guess what it looked like inside. Hearing a helicopter passing overhead and wondering who was on board. Reading about Home in magazines, as a teenager, imagining what it would be like to work there, to be part of something like that.

There was still a very small part of Jess that worried this was all going to turn out to have been a terrible mistake. That she was going to get to Island Home only to be told they'd looked into her references and discovered her to be an imposter. That as soon as she opened her mouth everyone would immediately know — new haircut and new clothes notwithstanding — that she was just not cool enough to work somewhere like this, would never fit in, was not what they had been looking for at all.

That was certainly the impression she had carried away from her interview.

It had taken place at Covent Garden Home, Jess shifting forward and backward in an armchair that was slightly too low for the table, conscious that the straining button on her new blouse was in serious danger of popping open, trying to assume a position that looked relaxed yet eager, trying to work out what to do with her elbows. All the advice her friends had given her about this interview and all the pep talks she had given herself on the journey felt suddenly irrelevant and absurd when faced with an obviously hungover Adam Groom eating a full English breakfast.

Between wincing sips from a Bloody Mary, he had squinted at her printed-out CV for what was evidently the first time, telling her random things about himself whenever he glanced up from his scrappy bit of paper and addressing her chest throughout. The only mention made of the distance she'd traveled down from Northamptonshire to meet him in person was when Adam remarked that the hotel she currently worked at — the Grange — was just down the road from Country Home. "I know," she had told him, smiling. "I've actually applied for jobs there quite a few times . . ." Eight, to be precise. She would have said more about why, perhaps added something about how much she admired all that Adam and his brother had achieved with Home, what a once-in-a-lifetime opportunity working at the launch of one of their clubs would be, but as she was in the middle of talking, Adam had called the waitress (young, slim, pretty) over to ask for a bit more ketchup, and Jess had trailed off.

All the way home on the train — that long, expensive, unreimbursed train journey — she'd kicked herself for all the stupid things she'd said, all the opportunities she'd missed to sell herself, thought about all the things she would say to Adam if she were being interviewed again now. All the things she would not say. Knowing that this had been her big chance and she had fluffed it.

That night she had received a phone call asking her whether she was available to start immediately.

"Of course," she'd told them, not even really thinking until she got off the phone — it was so unexpected, the whole thing — what a bombshell this was going to be to her current employers, her colleagues, her friends. Not until even later did it occur to her that she had never asked why her predecessor had left so suddenly, what kind of arrangements, if any, had been made for the handover.

It was hard to believe that had only been a week ago. The past few days had been manic. Frantic shopping expeditions, the last-minute haircut she was not quite sure about (a feathery shoulder-length bob the hairdresser told her would be easy to manage but was actually impossible to style into anything other than a bird's nest by herself), a moment of panic late the previous evening when it had looked as if her suitcase wasn't going to close. A couple of days' induction at Home's head office in London. The kind of restless night you always have before a big day, waking before your alarm goes off.

And now here she was, having waited on the mainland for the causeway to become passable, crossing it in a chauffeur-driven electric Land Rover Defender with two other new arrivals, both Littlesea locals, all daunted, all trying very hard not to show it. She would surely never forget that first sight of the road emerging from the sea, surprisingly winding, alarmingly narrow, the way the piles of rocks on either side of the track appeared first; then within minutes the wet surface of the road itself was shining in the early-afternoon sunlight, clumps of seaweed still stranded across it in inky scribbles, the island a hulking outline on the horizon.

She would have been a fool not to be a little nervous. How different all this would be from the Grange, the hotel at which she had worked for so long, with its acres of tartan carpets, its formal dining room complete with bow-tied waiters, the saloon bar with its golfing prints, the little plastic bottles of lily-of-the-valley toiletries, the lingering smell of disinfectant in the corridors. How weird it was going to be to move from somewhere so familiar, where she knew everybody, where everybody knew her, to somewhere completely new, completely strange.

It was a bright October afternoon, the cloudless blue sky crisscrossed with vapor trails.

As the wooded island ahead of them loomed ever larger and wider and darker, Jess tried to make out all the different buildings and features that had just been described in their induction. The Manor, or at least a windowed turret of it, was visible first, peeking out among the tips of the pines. Then, as they got closer, she could make out their destination: the Boathouse, a two-story weathered wooden building a hundred meters from the end of the causeway, with an adjoining large parking lot full of glossy black SUVs next to a glass-fronted

24

reception area where members collected their cabin keys, deposited their phones for the duration of the stay, and sipped champagne in front of a blazing fire while they waited for a porter in a golf cart. Next to that, farther down the pine-lined beach, was a concrete and cedar single-story building jutting out into the water — this, Jess supposed, was the underwater restaurant, Poseidon. Beyond that she could make out a steep road disappearing up a sharp slope into the woods.

This was not the landscape she'd grown up with, but she could see its beauty, even — or perhaps especially — at this time of year. The pale slender trunks of the silver birches. The fierce glow of the beeches. The yellow of gorse and broom. The dark pebble beaches. The white-blond stretches of sand. Springy thickets of sea buckthorn. Banks of browning bracken. The late-autumn sunlight sparkling on the waves.

For the most part — and for obvious reasons — the cabins and their terraces were arranged so they weren't easy to spot from a distance, from the water. The spa and tennis courts were on the far side of the island, close to the old water tower that was now a revolving Italian restaurant, near the sailing and water-sports facilities and the staff accommodations (not visible from the water either, and where about half the island's employees — Jess included — would be based, the other half arriving each morning from the mainland). It was funny to think how strange all this felt to her now, and how familiar it all would be in just a few days' time. Her Home.

The people were going to take a bit of adjusting to as well. The head of membership, Annie Spark, for instance, an extraordinary vision with waist-length Jessica Rabbit–red hair, in a bright pink jumpsuit, high-top sneakers, and huge gold hoop earrings, who had greeted her at the Causeway Inn, the seventeenth-century harbor-side pub overlooking the exact point the causeway met the mainland, acquired by the Home Group (Annie had explained) as somewhere members could sit and enjoy one of a range of fifteen local ales and ciders or a bite to eat while they waited for the tide to turn and the road across to the island to become passable.

In one of the downstairs bars — a room with a sea view, arranged with low, mismatched vintage armchairs, a pair of crossed logs smoldering in the fireplace — Annie had talked them all through the itinerary for the weekend.

Tonight, Thursday, there would be an intimate dinner for a select five guests (and four very senior members of Home staff) in the Manor, hosted by Ned Groom. Annie had listed the members invited. Jess felt her heart jump. All around her, fellow newbies tried to keep their expressions neutral. It had already been underlined, both at the interview and in a stern aside from Annie, that you would not last long at Home if you were the kind of person who was easily starstruck.

It had also been made very clear, when she had accepted the job, what a privilege it was as a senior member of the team to be allowed to keep a phone on her while she was working. Indeed, on her arrival at the head office, she had been given a brandnew work iPhone and instructed to keep it with her, charged and on at all times, in case she was needed. She had also been told, very firmly, never to take it out when a guest was there — just as all the arriving staff had been instructed to keep an eye out for any member who'd failed to surrender theirs on arrival.

"This is one of the few places in the world," Annie had reminded them, "that most of these people can eat a meal or have a drink or just sit around doing nothing and

27

be absolutely confident no one is going to snap a picture of them doing it. Try to imagine what that feels like. Just try to imagine how much you'd be willing to pay for it. And that's why any member you see with a phone in their hand — because, believe it or not, they're not immune to the urge — is off the island, immediately, their membership canceled. And that's why none of our waiters, waitresses, bar staff, or housekeeping crews are allowed mobiles either."

She could do this, Jess told herself. She had been in hospitality ever since she left school — before, if you counted that first weekend job, making beds in a local B&B. She'd spent ten years at the Grange, steadily working her way up to housekeeping manager. She had always got on with her team, always taken pride in her job. She could do this. People were people. Guests were guests.

The rest of the invitees — Annie had reeled off more names, some familiar, some Annie obviously expected to be — would arrive in carefully coordinated waves from Friday morning onward, and there was a packed schedule to keep them occupied all the way through to Sunday afternoon: boat trips, horse rides, brunches, lunches, dinners, movie screenings. Every cabin would be occupied, every guest one of Home's most valued members. Nothing — Annie's tone was gently emphatic, her expression encouraging — would be too much trouble.

While she spoke, Annie's phone kept pinging and ringing. Every so often she would inspect it and smirk or frown. The instant the induction was over, she had it clamped to her ear and was talking loudly in a bright voice before she was even out of the room.

How Jess envied Annie her confidence, her air of unflappability, the boldness of her style. All that scarlet hair, gathered in a twist over one shoulder, the heavily kohled and fringe-framed eyes. Those great crimson talons. Perhaps it was easier to be confident when you were as tall as Annie was — six foot something, easily. Jess wished she had introduced herself a bit more forcefully, or that she had been brave enough to put her hand up during Annie's talk and ask just one of the hundreds of questions she had about this island, this weekend, this job.

She was going to need all the confidence and boldness she could muster to get through the next few days.

"Nearly there now," their driver — he wore a tight blue polo shirt and mirrored sunglasses — announced over his shoulder.

He gave a little tap on the horn as they neared the end of the causeway. Someone emerged from the glass-fronted Boathouse holding a clipboard, and waved.

This was it.

If only her parents could see her now, Jess thought. All those girls at school.

There was no doubt that this was the opportunity of a lifetime.

Now all she had to do was stick to the plan.

ANNIE

It could be brutal, this job.

"My darling, my angel, *my love.* You know if there was space, I would have you here in a heartbeat! No, no, don't cry . . ."

For months now Annie Spark had been having conversations like this, or avoiding them. For the past week her phone had literally not stopped ringing from the moment she got up in the morning until she crawled into bed at night. The texts. The Instagram DMs. The voice-mail messages. The texts to see if you had got their DM or had a chance to listen to their voice-mail message yet. The emails to see if they still had your mobile number right.

At the last count, there were 5,761 Home members worldwide. There could only ever be 150 of them, give or take, at a launch.

The invitation to Island Home's Halloween weekend opening party had been couriered to the chosen few on August 14. For weeks before that, Annie had been adding names, rethinking, removing, making the final adjustments. As soon as the coveted gilt-edged cards had been sent out, nestled in custom monogrammed cashmere bathrobes and silk pajamas, she braced herself for the onslaught. Annie occupied an odd space in members' minds — a hybrid of superfixer, paid best friend, and put-upon PA. Somebody you could stay up until 2:00 a.m. drinking espresso martinis with, someone on whose shoulder you might cry in the midst of a bitter divorce. But also the person you'd bitch to if you couldn't get three extra friends into Malibu Home for drinks on Labor Day. Or shout at if the roses in your room were droopy, or the table you'd been given on the rooftop in Venice Home was drafty.

When people began to realize they hadn't made the guest list, they went into overdrive: unexpected dinner invites, insistent suggestions of a quick drink, questions about when it would be a good time for a quick phone catch-up, all started to roll in. PAs — or lower-tier members pretending to be the

PAs she knew they couldn't afford — began emailing ten times a day just to check there had not been an administrative error, some sort of oversight.

She did have sympathy for these people. She couldn't have done her job if she didn't. But equally she couldn't have done her job if she let herself be swayed by that sympathy. Her loyalty was to Ned and she knew that he trusted her implicitly to make decisions in Home's best interests. Take, for instance, this actress Annie was on the phone with now, as she paced up and down the cobbled harbor front outside the Causeway Inn, huge emerald-green down coat pulled tight around her against the chill October air, smoking first one cigarette and then another.

At the other end of the line? Ava Huxley. British actress, auburn-haired, startlingly thin, teeny-tiny, next-level posh. Once widely regarded as a very big star in the making, she had been in one well-regarded Sunday-night costume drama on the BBC, then a couple of British thrillers that had not done much at the box office, then starred as a lady serial killer in an HBO series in which she murdered, among other things, an American accent. If Ava had applied these days, she probably wouldn't even have been accepted for Home membership — not that anyone who applied to be a member ever really got rejected. Those who did not quite make the cut instead got placed on a permanent waiting list, queueing in a line that never moved, stuck (as Annie thought of it) in celebrity purgatory. And why was that? Because if this job had taught Annie anything, it was that you could never tell when a career might take off or be revived, and you didn't want anyone holding a grudge as well as an Oscar.

Even with all that in mind, Ava Huxley was currently nowhere near the level of success that would get her invited. This was not Annie being mean; it was simply the harsh reality of the situation.

Although she would never have remembered it, neither did it help Ava's cause that she'd been the last person Annie had profiled before she chucked in her job as a celebrity writer to join Home. In granting the interview, a cover feature for *OK!,* Ava had grudgingly fulfilled a contractual obligation to a perfume brand she was the face of. The actress had arrived late and flustered for the fifteen-minute slot, answered every question in a snotty monosyllable, and then stormed out angrily muttering something about feminism, after Annie, scratching around for a topic that might engage her, had inquired where her shoes were from. Annie had then been forced to craft a twelve-hundred-word piece with precisely thirty-two words from the talent, twenty-three of which were no. "Not your finest work, Spark," was her editor's offhand verdict, before she cut it down to a single paragraph and ran an AVA HUXLEY IN ONE HUNDRED DRESSES picture special instead.

Ned had offered Annie the job as Home's head of membership just a few days after the debacle, and it is no exaggeration to say Ava was the reason she'd accepted.

Annie had always been obsessed with shrugging off her utterly unspecial, perfectly pleasant, suffocatingly suburban upbringing and accessing the glossy world of the beautiful, talented, famous few. She had never really interrogated why proximity to celebrity was so appealing — in fact, the only thing she had ever really questioned was why you would *not* want to be surrounded by stars. But with no discernible skills in that direction — she couldn't act, dance, sing, or play anything at all, although she had tried her best — she decided simply being around them would do. *Now* she knew there were any number of jobs that got you close — agent, assistant, stylist, florist, massage therapist, clairvoyant, life coach, dog walker — but since she had been brought up on a diet of *Heat* and *Hello!,* journalism was the only way in that she could think of with the talents she had available. What nobody had told her — what was not at all obvious from the outside — was that although an interviewer *did* get within touching distance of the beautiful people, the beautiful people considered the press an ugly, irritating imposition, to be grimly tolerated at best.

At first it had winded her, how mean they could be. That instead of hanging out on red carpets and being on first-name terms with her subjects, Annie was patronized and ignored, reprimanded and ranted at, treated as if they'd just peeled her off the bottom of their high heels, as if she *personally* had been following them around shoving a camera in their faces, rifling through their bins or hacking their phones. All those junkets she'd been sent on back in the late nineties at the start of her career, often in a suite at Covent Garden Home, those awful awkward chats, with the agent or press officer lurking in a corner the entire time, ears pricked (*Oh don't mind me, I'll just be here on my laptop, hardly even listening . . . Excuse me, NO! That topic's off-limits. And that one. And that one*). It had shocked her how dull they were too — that people with such astonishing lives were so crushingly bland, had so little to say, so few opinions and anecdotes and interesting quirks (now she knew, of course, that the person she met was often as much of an invention as the one she'd seen on screen).

By the time Ned called to offer her the job, *this job,* she'd simply had enough — the idea of being the person calling the shots, of being the one *they* sucked up to, or bothered to engage in conversation with at the very least, was simply too tempting. Ava clearly had zero recollection of an event that had changed Annie's career path entirely. Funny how life turns out, she thought as she listened to Ava explain, between sobs, that she'd had lunch with a gang of other actresses and they'd got talking about what they were going to wear to the Island Home launch and she had somehow, mistakenly, could-you-believe-it, how-did-it-happen, given the impression she'd be there too.

"I mean, I don't know what I was thinking, of course I was never even expecting to be invited in the first place, why would *anyone* invite me to something like this, I would be embarrassed to be invited probably, assume you had made some terrible mistake, but — I'm such an idiot — I think

36

I might have accidentally given them the idea I was coming — please, please, *please* could you just make an exception as I am just so mortified?"

Annie suppressed a sigh. At least the Americans were up-front. Brits could be absolute torture. Was this an all-girls boarding school thing, this performative self-flagellation? Or was it somehow part of your contract with the public, as a British actor or musician, that if you did make it big you had to pretend like the whole thing was some sort of embarrassing accident?

Ava was still talking.

Passing one of the bow windows of the Causeway Inn, Annie glanced in at the lounge bar, where three of her team were sitting around on sofas, hunched over their laptops. She tapped on the window. They all looked up, saw her, and smiled. Annie crossed her eyes, pulled a face, and gestured at her phone. Then she cleared her throat, firmly.

"I'm sorry, Ava. There's nothing I can do. But do let me take you out for lunch next week and I promise to give you *all* the gossip."

There was no need to be any ruder than the situation demanded. After all, there was still some slim possibility that, via some hard-to-imagine sequence of events, Ava Huxley might succeed in reigniting her career, that she might even become one of those members Annie spent her time chasing after and buttering up, rather than vice versa. Ava had better hurry, though, Annie thought. If she remembered rightly, Ava would turn forty next month.

No sooner had Annie hung up than another incoming call appeared on her screen.

Fuck's sake. Jackson Crane's PA. No doubt calling — for the third time that day — to update Annie on her very famous, very important client's progress, his estimated time of arrival, to confirm when dinner was scheduled that evening, to triple-check that Jackson and his wife Georgia had been given separate cabins (they were always given separate accommodations when they stayed at Home, with no questions asked or eyebrows raised). And just as she had on the first and second calls, Annie reassured the PA that both Jackson's and Georgia's rooms would be set up to precisely the specifications outlined, down to the exact number and type of bottles in Jackson's drinks cabinet and the exact brand of activated charcoal on Georgia's bedside table.

She would get all of this right, as she

always did, as Home always did — but there was more to a successful launch party than inviting the Very Important People and making sure they had everything they needed. There was an alchemy to it, just as there was an alchemy to who was accepted as a Home member in the first place. In some ways this was very complicated. In some ways it was very simple.

No wankers.

That was Ned's sole directive, the sole criterion he had offered Annie when she accepted this position, when it came to how to decide who ought or ought not to be accepted for membership. *No wankers.* On Ned's confidence in her ability to understand that instruction — to recognize the sort of jerk, the manner of dickhead he meant — had rested Annie's entire career at Home. *Wankers* was, for Ned, a broad and varied category. It included — for starters — all bankers, all consultants, all lawyers (even though he had for several years worked as a barrister himself). Nobody barking into their phone about being the CEO of an app while tapping away ostentatiously on their laptop. Bad behavior in the clubs was fine, encouraged actually; it just couldn't be *uncool bad behavior.* He never wanted to see an oligarch waving a platinum

Amex, ordering a bottle of Chablis from the bottom of the wine list, and asking for a few ice cubes in it. Because even though that would undoubtedly have kept huge amounts of cash ringing through the tills, those sorts of overpriced hot-right-now joints had a built-in expiry date. Home's long-term reputation lived or died on an ineffable, unforced cool — and on the quality of its members.

Obviously, one needed to be at a certain level of wealth to consider joining — but essentially, although a good deal plusher than its original dusty incarnation, Home was still intended as a place for artists, dreamers, creators, performers. That was Ned's vision. Just look at the five members he'd invited for dinner tonight. One major Hollywood star and his highly successful actress wife. One of the most recognizable (and expensive) artists in Britain. A transatlantically visible talk-show host. A hot young film producer, and son of one of the most famous directors of all time. Forget Gandhi, Jesus, and Oscar Wilde. *This* was the stuff of which dinner-party dreams were made. And she, Annie, had arranged it, got to sit in, make small talk. Instead of pre-agreed monosyllables spat out at junkets by celebrities who would rather be *anywhere* else, she got to hear what Jackson Crane really thought about working with Christopher Nolan. To hear what Georgia's guest appearance on the Chanel Haute Couture catwalk felt like. To understand firsthand how hard it was to coax an entertaining anecdote on live TV out of, say, a professional golfer. What Elton really asked for in his dressing-room rider.

And all five of them, no matter how celebrated, were probably a little bit excited about it too. But not one of them had any idea yet, the slightest inkling, what was in store for them tonight, what Ned was planning.

It could be pretty brutal, this job.

Annie absolutely loved it.

NIKKI

It had been clear that Ned Groom was revving up for a tantrum from the moment he'd arrived at breakfast.

"Big day today! This lot had better not fuck it up," he'd barked, with a jut of the chin in the direction of the waiters bustling nearby in stiff denim aprons. "Got that?" he added, to the one nearest to him, smiling warmly when the boy nodded in answer, clapping him on the arm, telling him he was sure *he* wouldn't be letting anyone down.

41

Joking. Joking. Not joking. Joking. That was how it worked, with Ned. Everything was a joke until it was serious. Everything was serious until it was a joke.

Their table — their regular table — was right next to the building's vast picture window. Ned sat down. He glanced briefly through it to the wildflower meadow beyond, the grass still frosted where the shadows of the trees fell, the mist still lingering in the hollows of the ground. He adjusted his napkin on his lap.

"Now then, Nikki, what's on the agenda?"

Nikki ran her boss through the morning's diary between sips of green tea — final meetings, before the first members were due, with the head chef, head bartender, head gardener, spa manager, design director, and events team. When Ned's attention turned briefly to the menu, she discreetly dashed off a three-word email with them all on cc: *Warning! Bad mood.*

"I want everyone to be match fit. Biggest opening in the history of Home, this. Certainly the most bloody expensive. It needs to be perfect," he said, draining the first of many coffees, dabbing at his lips with a folded napkin. "Any word from my brother this morning?"

Nikki looked at her watch. It was 6:45 a.m.

"En route by now, I think. I've asked him to call and let me know when he's on the causeway."

Adam *should* be on his way, even if he had not yet texted to tell her so. Or replied to either of her texts checking in. She had booked the cab for him, put the pickup and the driver's number in his diary, texted last night and again this morning to remind him when it was coming. All he had to do was wake up and clamber into it and fall asleep again. Adam could surely manage that, couldn't he, on a weekend as important as this one?

Just as every morning for the past month, Ned and Nikki were the only diners in the Barn — the most casual and relaxed restaurant on the island, with its rustic-luxe decor, its couches, its all-day breakfast menu from which you could order a bacon sandwich for dinner should you so desire. Nikki had ordered the Bircher muesli, Ned the eggs Florentine. Alerted by their snotty wobble, Nikki could tell from about ten feet away (easily) that Ned's yolks were undercooked. She tried to signal to the waitress bringing over the plate — with a quick grimace, a sidelong glance, a meaningfully raised eyebrow — that she should abort her mission, but the waitress was oblivious. She placed the plate in front of Ned. Without even bothering to prod the eggs with a fork, let alone take a bite, Ned wordlessly lifted up his breakfast with both hands, rotated his torso ninety degrees, and let the plate drop to the floor. He was very particular about his eggs, Ned Groom. He was very particular about lots of things, although Nikki was sure it had never been *quite* this bad before.

"Why don't we head over to the Orangery?" Nikki had suggested, gently shooing the shell-shocked waitress away from the mess before Ned could stand up and start the inevitable dressing-down. "You have a meeting with the head chef over there in fifteen minutes — he makes the best poached eggs anyway . . ."

As personal assistant to the CEO of the Home Group for nearly a quarter of a century, Nikki Hayes could always tell when her boss was taking a leisurely run-up at a screaming rage. The jerks in his neck muscles, the involuntary jaw twitches, the way he fiddled with the bezel of his platinum Rolex. When it *was* finally unleashed, that temper of his, he could change the air pressure in a room so quickly it would give you the bends.

In the end it was the design team who really got it.

Their 9:00 a.m. meeting was *meant* to be Ned's final tweaks for the island's refurbished neo-Palladian manor: this lampshade is wonky, that bolster would look better over there, swap those Damien Hirst spots for this Tracey Emin squiggle, that sort of thing. Instead, it had turned into a ceremonial defenestration of underwhelming antiques. Nikki winced when — as his opening gambit — Ned lobbed an art deco vase out of the open first-floor window, then watched open-mouthed as he jumped up and swung on the crystal chandelier to demonstrate that it was hung two inches too low.

"Where did you get all this stuff?" Ned demanded to know. "Are you all just lazy and stupid, or are you fucking joking? *Contemporary vintage,* that was the brief. What have you come up with? Third-tier National Trust property. Suburban hoarder's front room. Your dead grandmother's house. How much did all this crap cost me and what fucking idiot signed off the spend on it?"

Nikki took a deep breath. He wasn't expecting an answer, of course, but all seventeen pairs of eyes were silently pleading with her to say something, *anything.* "Well, actually Ned," she replied, scrolling through emails on her iPad. "It says here it was *you* . . . About a week ago, I'm sure you said this was your favorite room on the island . . . Perhaps the light in here looks different today? I think that armchair might have been over there . . ."

She trailed off. Ned, as usual, continued as if no one had said anything at all.

"I asked for statement pieces. STATE-MENT PIE-CES. What statement is this fucking thing making, exactly?" Ned yelled at the top of his voice, wrestling an oval gilt-framed oil portrait from the wall, holding it at arm's length for inspection, pulling a reasonable facsimile of the expression worn by the scowling dowager it depicted, and sending it sailing out the window with a flourish and a shrug.

How many of these scenes had she witnessed? Nikki wondered. How many of these little performances?

All of this gone, that was what he wanted. These knickknacks. That rubbish. Move this Louis Vuitton trunk-cum-coffee table over there. Get rid of all the art, put a Keith Little nude over the fireplace. Think about the overall effect you're trying to achieve here, for God's sake. It's not rocket science. Do I have to do everything myself?

The director of design, a slight man with a silver-white ponytail and cricket sweater

46

knotted around his shoulders, was discreetly rubbing his jaw where he had, some moments earlier, taken a leather-bound volume of botanical prints to the chin. Nikki had watched as he silently picked it up and gently placed it back on the coffee table while Ned continued his rant.

She felt for all of them, gathered in the Manor's drawing room, then kept waiting for an hour and a half, excited and nervous to show him their handiwork, this being their job, their career, something they had spent years working toward and dreaming about, only for Ned to storm in and immediately start screaming — literally screaming, little flecks of spittle arcing through the air, face puce. Screaming at people who had worked with him for a decade. Designers whose first project at Home this was. Underpaid assistants who had been working evenings, weekends, developing ulcers trying to keep up with Ned's demands, his brain waves, his abrupt reversals of opinion. Seventeen professional people who seemed unsure whether it would be better to jump forward and assist with the casual vandalism, or remain where they were and avoid making eye contact.

Nikki did respect her boss, but it could be exhausting, all this. Just because Ned's rages were frequent, short-lived, and utterly indiscriminate — as likely to be triggered by an undercooked egg as a million-pound overspend — it did not mean they did not also upset people. Because really, isn't that what power is? A middle-aged Rumpelstiltskin, jumping up and down, visibly out of breath, swinging on a chandelier, and no one daring to laugh. A grown man so cross with an oil painting of an old lady he looks as if he is about to burst the buttons off his shirt, and nobody daring to suggest he might be overreacting *just a little.*

There was one poor girl at the back, nibbling away on the skin of her already-gnawed cuticles, pulling with her teeth a single strand of nail on the edge of her little finger in an effort to stem the tears. She must be new, poor love, to be taking it all to heart like that. If you worked at Home for any length of time, after a while you became accustomed to the outbursts, got used to not letting it get to you, stopped taking any of it personally. The rages, the rants, the rows? It was all part of the legend, wasn't it? Ned Groom the visionary stickler. The volatile genius who had built an empire on taste. The man who could make a career if he chose to (or kill it stone dead on a whim). Nikki had seen him throw a decora-

48

tive paperweight through a plate-glass window, three feet from a cleaner's head (days before the launch of Country Home). She had seen him waving a kitchen knife within a few inches of a porter's face (Highland Home's opening night). On her own first shift at Covent Garden Home all those years ago, as a timid little coat-check girl, she had watched him literally roar at a receptionist for fluffing a member's last name.

The thing you had to admit, though his delivery could do with some softening, was that he usually had a point. If those yolks had landed on a member's table, they would have been sent back. Once the details in this room were tweaked to his exact specification, it would undoubtedly look a million times better. And Nikki also knew — they all did, with the possible exception of the poor girl at the back of the room — that after he had vented, Ned would forget about the chandelier and the vase and the art. Everyone would get their slap on the back and their bonus, and get complimented for being a good sport.

"You!" Ned hissed, looming over the terrified five-foot-nothing assistant. "You look like you've got some taste — *unlike this fucking guy.*" He jabbed his finger accusingly at her boss. "Did you not at any stage feel compelled to point out that this looks like the aftermath of a bar brawl in a junk shop?" She looked pleadingly over at her superior, who simply shrugged apologetically. Ned looked from one to the other, then back again. No one spoke.

"Right," said Ned, shaking his head, a slight smirk playing around his lips. "Who's going to show me the library, then?"

Nobody looked very keen to show Ned the library.

Nikki excused herself at that point, pointing at her phone and miming making a call. The first floor of the Manor was a series of high-ceilinged rooms with sweeping views out to sea, with restaurants and bars and a glass-roofed orangery on the floor below. She walked along the oak-paneled corridor, peering as she went into the various opulent dining rooms and lounges, then down the sweeping central staircase. In the soaring entrance hall, a few of Annie's membership team were huddled around the front desk, flicking through members' headshots on their iPads and giggling, while bartenders crisscrossed the room carrying boxes of vintage Krug, doing their best to dodge housekeeping who were enthusiastically vacuuming the Persian rugs and dusting the pair of stuffed flamingos that flanked the entrance.

It was slightly chillier outside than the brightness of the morning sunshine suggested. Nikki checked the time. Was it too soon to text Adam again? Or to call him? He was Ned's actual brother. He should be there, dealing with all this stuff too, soaking it up, helping smooth ruffled feathers. "Adam," she sighed into his voice mail, the third message she had left this morning. "Adam, can you text me an ETA, please? Ned was expecting you an hour ago and he is . . . not in the best mood."

Turning back toward the Manor and surveying the smashed and scattered antiques on the lawn and in the flowerbeds and on the gravel path beneath the window, she sighed. Well at least that was out of the way now — on a day such as today, it was not a question of *if* Ned was going to explode, it was when and how much damage the blast would do. Exactly, Nikki often thought, like her mother — which was probably why it simply washed over her most of the time.

What a revelation, what a relief it had been to realize, at the age of about twelve perhaps, that her mother's tempers were not actually something you could prevent. That no matter how quietly you walked or how carefully you cleaned up after yourself, or how studiously you tried to avoid attracting her attention, she would always be able to find something to lose her temper about. That did not make it any more pleasant to be in the eye of the storm of course, but what it did mean was that you stopped internalizing any of it.

She heard a slam, looking up to see the girl who had been blinking back tears upstairs run out of the Manor's front door, skidding to a halt when they locked eyes. Nikki smiled and beckoned her over. "I'm sorry, I should know this, but there are so many people on this island — what is your name?"

"It's Chloe," she said, almost whispering. "I'm sorry. I'm really sorry. This is only my first month here. I was so excited. I thought I would be really good at this." She sniffed. "Do you think he's going to fire me? Should I try to apologize?" Nikki put an arm around Chloe's shaking shoulders and gave her a squeeze. No, she thought, you're safe. He doesn't often sack the pretty ones. He even joked about it, paraphrasing a pretentious and long-sacked Home architect: "It's like William Morris said, Nikki, right? Have nobody in your Home you do not know to be beautiful or believe to be useful."

As it happened, Nikki was quite aware that her own looks were one of the reasons she'd been a fixture at Home so long. That wasn't arrogance; it was simply a fact. Because if there was one thing a modeling career — even one as short-lived as Nikki's — gave you, it was independent confirmation of your attractiveness, a clear-eyed sense of the doors that it opens and the problems it brings with it.

Nikki was also extremely good at her job.

She enjoyed it too, mostly.

Because if Ned could be vicious sometimes, he could also be incredibly generous, remarkably thoughtful. Some of the birthday and Christmas presents he had given her — "Sorry for being such an arsehole the last twelve months" — had been ludicrous. The wardrobe in her little Victorian terrace in south London was stuffed with expensive apologies: Celine bags, Louis Vuitton boots, Hermès bangles. Ned could be funny and charismatic too. His impressions. His turns of phrase. He was the kind of person you had to literally beg to stop, because you were laughing so hard you couldn't catch your breath. Chloe would see all that eventually, if she stayed at Home.

"Oh sweetheart, don't cry. You've done an

incredible job, your team — I mean, look at this place! It's beautiful." They both looked up at the perfectly symmetrical house with its imposing Corinthian columns, the honey-colored stone dripping with the wisteria that Ned demanded be stapled to the front a week ago, at astonishing expense.

"Deep breaths now though, back in the room — go and ask one of the bartenders for a brandy to calm your nerves — Ned will notice if you're gone a long time and he won't like it. He wants people who work for him to have a thick skin, to be able to take a joke. We're all tired, all on a short fuse. It's nothing personal. He's always like this in the run-up to a new club," she reassured Chloe, the usual platitudes, the familiar excuses, tripping easily off her tongue.

But even as Nikki was saying it, she knew that wasn't quite true. Ned *was* different this time. His anger less focused. His triggers less predictable. His patterns of behavior, the swoop and swerve of his annoyances, far more erratic.

Maybe that was what it did to you, buying an island.

Maybe he was squirming, mentally, under the pressure of how much this place and its redevelopment had cost, how much it had been delayed. The endless emails from contractors demanding payment, the legal letters they'd started getting from suppliers, Ned the perfectionist ignoring them all and spending more money Home did not seem to have getting the details *just so.*

Maybe.

What Nikki was sure of, when it came to Ned, was that something was spiraling seriously out of control.

ADAM

Me or the job, that was the ultimatum. In other words: either Adam Groom told his brother Ned by the end of this weekend that he was quitting, that he wanted to be bought out of his share in the Home Group, that a working partnership that had lasted a quarter of a century was over — or his marriage would be.

"Am I being unreasonable?" Laura had asked him.

She was not, he had told her. She was not an unreasonable woman, his wife. She had been very patient. He could remember telling Laura on their very first date — dinner at the Ivy (back when it was still cool) followed by a nightcap on the roof terrace at Covent Garden Home — that he was keen to strike out on his own eventually, emerge from Ned's shadow, cash in his stake in the business and start up his own place: a little gastropub somewhere, near the river maybe. Perhaps a local wine shop, with a couple of candlelit tables for evening bookings. Get fitter maybe. Take up golf, or tennis.

That was the vision. That was the dream. That was fifteen years ago.

Ten years ago, on holiday, he could remember them sitting up late with a bottle of wine one warm evening and discussing how much his share of the business might now be worth, who might buy it, what they could do with the money, getting excited about the possibilities. The great thing about life coaching, she had pointed out, was that she could practice anywhere. The restaurant scene back home in Melbourne was amazing. She still had contacts who could help her set up over there, find clients. Why not start up something of his own, out of Ned's shadow — or if Adam wanted to be farther away from her parents, maybe Sydney?

It was now a decade later, a decade in which Home had been steadily opening clubs all over the world, and he still had not extricated himself. Adam could understand why Laura was starting to get impatient. He could understand why she was annoyed. She had also been woken up at seven that morning by a grumpy taxi driver ringing their doorbell. "Adam Groom?" the man had asked. He'd been waiting outside for half an hour, he said. He had been calling and calling. The problem was that the phone he had been calling was Adam's phone, and Adam's phone was in the pocket of Adam's jacket, which was hanging on the back of a chair in the suite nine miles away in Covent Garden where Adam was still fast asleep.

"Where are you?" Laura had asked, angrily, when eventually Adam had answered his phone.

"Home," he said, not meaning for it to sound like a joke. "Look," he told Laura, reflexively checking the time on his watch and flinching as he did so, "it got late. I didn't even sit down to eat until almost ten thirty, and then people wanted one more drink afterward. I know. I'm sorry. I did promise, and I'm really sorry."

He had let her down. He had let himself down. He had no excuses, really, or at least none he had not worn out already, years ago. Could he not have called? Could he not have sent a text? He pictured Laura waiting up, reading in bed, checking her phone, alternately anxious and annoyed. Probably mostly the latter.

"I'm sorry," said Adam again.

And he was. He really was. But she knew

the drill by now, surely, how stressful a new launch got on the eve of opening.

With Ned on the island — as he had been nonstop for the past month — Adam was not only in charge of signing off every aspect of the still-ballooning budget for the biggest party in Home's history, he was also making decisions for the whole company. It was a lot of responsibility. It was a lot of pressure. Not to mention that he'd had just three days to find a new head of housekeeping for Island Home because Ned had taken it upon himself to sack the old one ten days before they were due to open. And all the time, constantly, he was getting calls from around the world asking for his approval for this expense or that arrangement, calls from Nikki making sure he knew where he was supposed to be next and how to get there.

One of the downsides of having a role as ill-defined as director of special projects was that he never quite knew what special project his brother would foist on him next, or who was going to be on the other end of the line with a request, a question, or a problem. Who would suddenly turn up in town and need to be taken out to dinner, or want to discuss something over a drink.

How he used to love this job, back in the early days. How delighted he had been to

58

work alongside Ned, the older brother he had always adored. How privileged he'd felt, being the first person, often the only person, with whom Ned shared his plans, his schemes, his ambitions for the club. How he used to enjoy all the parties, the dinners, the impromptu midweek all-nighters. Celebrating with some band their first number one single. Dancing on tables on a Tuesday evening. Leading the midnight charge to the rooftop pool. Now it was with a distinct sense of dread that Adam forced himself into an ironed shirt, dragged a razor across his crumpled face, forced an affable expression onto it, steeled himself for yet another evening of shouting and drinking, grinning his way through conversations he could only partly hear.

Laura was right. Things could not go on like this. *He* could not go on like this. He was forty-nine years old. What was it Laura told her clients? That if you really wanted to do it, it was never too late to change your life. To follow your dreams. To be a better person. To start treating the people around you the way they deserved to be treated. That was what Adam wanted. To be. To do. All of those things.

When Adam caught a glimpse of himself sometimes late at night or on a morning like this, in an unfamiliar mirror from an unfamiliar angle, he felt a genuine jolt of horror and pity, concern and revulsion. At the thinness of his hair, the shine of his scalp under a direct overhead light. At the sort of piggy look his eyes got as the evening wore on. At the vacancy of his own expression, the slouch of his mouth. At the realization his fly was open and his shirt half untucked and he had spilled either several drinks or one drink several times down the front of himself. At the thought of all the things he had said and done, or not done and not said. At how unwell, how unhappy, how bloody middle-aged he looked.

It was literally going to kill him one day, this job.

By the time Laura had called, the cab driver had already departed in a huff. Which was a shame because otherwise he could have brought Adam's ready-packed weekend bag into town and picked him up at the club. Instead, Adam had to order another cab to take him out to Richmond (precisely the wrong direction) and then proceed with him and his bag to the island. In solid traffic, both ways.

By the time he got to Island Home, waking in the back seat of the car with a jolt, Adam had thirty-two missed calls — most

of them from Nikki, some of them from Annie — and was very late indeed. *Tell him the
cab company fucked up,* he texted Nikki.
Tell him I'll be there in a minute.

There was also a text from Laura. It
simply read *Good luck.*

He was going to need it. He very much
doubted it was going to be a pleasant one,
this conversation with Ned. There were
good reasons — not all of which his wife
was aware of — for why he had been putting it off for so long.

Every time Adam crossed this causeway
he remembered his first visit to the island,
on a freezing February morning in the early
2000s, thinking at the time how ridiculous
the idea of buying this place was, how even
if the Home Group had been able to afford
it, what would they do with it? This huge,
beautiful, overgrown, practically uninhab-
ited island, thickly wooded for the most
part, the grass and weeds waist-high when
you did pass a stretch of open ground, only
one real road, the landscape dotted with
abandoned farm buildings and moss-
covered, sea-facing concrete pillboxes and
roofless cottages and glassless greenhouses,
half the manor house derelict, the rest occupied by one eccentric old couple, most of
the furniture under dust covers, the whole

place a melancholy study in brown and gray. And just look at it all now. Say what you liked about Ned, it took a certain kind of person to create what he had created.

It was as Adam was removing his weekend bag from the boot of the taxi outside the Boathouse that he heard the helicopter approaching. He turned to scan the horizon in search of it and spotted it coming in low — concerningly low — over the causeway, a private chopper. Almost too quickly to be believed it went from being a speck in the distance to a great thing thundering overhead, rotor blades spinning, its downdraft bringing faces to the windows, scattering clouds of dust across the gravel. Paparazzi? he wondered, then reminded himself that if anyone was trying to get pictures of the arriving guests, they would hardly have wanted to make their presence so obvious. No, Adam realized, there was only one guest likely to arrive this early and this conspicuously.

Freddie Hunter.

Why is it the person you least want to see who always turns up first at a party?

CONTINUED FROM PAGE 8

Even before the body on the island was
officially identified, even before the divers
had arrived and attempts to access and
recover the submerged car and its grim
contents had started, the overheated
media coverage had begun.

All around the country, all over the world,
people watched and rewatched as news
channels replayed the same footage:
blurry drone shots of the incident tent amid
the trees; the forensics team in their
ghostly hooded jumpsuits; the same short
video clip over and over of Ned Groom,
shot a few years earlier for *GQ*'s Men of
the Year awards, demonstrating how to
mix the perfect old-fashioned ("This is
what I get all my guys to make before I
hire them — Home's bartender test . . . so
you get your sugar, bitters, whiskey, and
an orange slice . . ."), talking to the camera

63

about what made a great party ("It's about making people feel welcome, creating an environment where you can kick back and be completely yourself — we are called Home, after all . . .").

That jerky footage of the first boats arriving back on the mainland, the first party-goers huddled against the cold spray of the waves, the gray shell-shocked faces of those being helped up onto the dock. People swaddled in foil blankets on the harbor front. People crying. The weirdness of spotting, among those tearstained, anxious faces, one that you recognized, someone famous, then another, then another. That actress. That singer. And having to force your brain to understand that this was not a movie, that this was really happening, and happening now.

All around the world, people who, a few days earlier, had barely heard of Home, sat glued to their phones, strangely unsettled, oddly excited, waiting for the identities of the deceased to be confirmed.

It didn't take long for the online sleuths to spring into action and the conspiracy theories to start and spread. Confident claims appeared almost instantly on Reddit about who was on the island. Wild assertions circulated on 4chan about who

64

was in the sunken vehicle. YouTubers pored over leaked autopsy reports, scrutinizing new footage for evidence of fakery. Unsubstantiated stories emerged about unmarked helicopters sighted approaching the island, leaving it. People thousands of miles away were preemptively furious that there was going to be a cover-up. Suddenly everyone on Twitter was well versed on the safety features of the Defender 2020 Electric Land Rover, everyone on Facebook was an expert on the Blackwater Estuary's currents and tides. Several actors felt compelled to announce publicly, via social media, that they were still alive. In several cases they were asked immediately by hundreds of people to prove it.

Even now, six months later, many of the party guests pictured shivering on the dock in that first grainy footage still can't post anything online — a picture of themselves on the red carpet at some premiere, say, or hiking in the Hollywood Hills — without being immediately bombarded by questions about what they saw on the island that weekend, what they told the police, messages demanding they clarify this or that supposed incongruity in the official version of events.

"They can get a bit upsetting, the Instagram comments. I posted a picture of my daughter Lyra's eighth birthday party last week and instantly someone was ranting underneath about a pedophile ring, demanding to know what really went on at Island Home. Like I would have the first clue!" Kyra Highway shakes her head at the ridiculousness of the suggestion. "The thing is," she points out, "I wasn't even meant to be there. I'm a member, sure, but I was never going to be on the list for a launch like that, not anymore. I think the last one I went to was Venice Home, and when would that have been? Early 2014?" The singer shrugs.

Anyone with a memory for celebrity scandal will recall that 2014 was not a good year for singer Kyra Highway. She had only recently married professional soccer player Keiran James — *Hello!* spent a seven-figure sum securing the print exclusive on their lavish wedding, where their then one-year-old daughter Lyra was an adorable flower girl in a pink glitter tutu — when their family life imploded. The *News of the World* ran a front-page story on Kyra's affair with James's best friend and teammate, Sean Nicholl, and it turned into a months-long tabloid feeding frenzy, each headline more sensational and intrusive than the last. Their subsequent divorce played out publicly and bitterly, her music career in the UK never quite recovering from the fallout, with her breakup single "Free Again" stalling at number forty-one in the charts (although it was a top-ten hit in Germany and number one in the Philippines for a week).

Sitting cross-legged on the cream leather corner sofa in her Primrose Hill home, Highway has her curly hair pinned back in a messy bun; her doll-like, heart-shaped face is glowing but entirely makeup free. Apologizing profusely for not being dressed-up enough, she is still elegant in a pale gray cashmere tracksuit with bare, perfectly pedicured feet. "What happened was, a few nights before the opening party, I was at Covent Garden Home and bumped into Freddie. I was so happy to see him, because I'd completely forgotten he was even in town . . ."

Freddie, of course, is Freddie Hunter, the angelic all-American former choirboy who found early fame back home Stateside in chart-topping pop trio Sideways (you may recall the coordinated denim outfits, the gelled spiky hair), before walking out on the band at the height of their success and moving to the UK to escape the spotlight. Now, of course, Anglophile Freddie is best known as the top-rated late-night talk-show host in the US — a gig landed after several stints in rehab and a good few years bouncing around his adopted home, presenting British prime-time TV (hence the occasional cockney inflection to his Californian accent). Famously fun, faultlessly charming, unfailingly flattering to his talk-show guests, Freddie was the one who hatched the plan to smuggle his old friend onto Island Home in the helicopter he keeps at his Surrey mansion (one of several palatial properties he owns around the world), the same make and model as the one he keeps at his Montecito house and pilots (or pretends to pilot, for insurance reasons) while singing with guests in the Mile-High Duets segment of his show.

"Home clubs are like that," Kyra explains. "Even if you're just dropping in for a quick drink on a Tuesday night, it feels like a house party where you know everyone. Anyway, Freddie and me have been friends forever," she continues, pointing to a framed photo on the sideboard of them both, obviously in their teens, on stage at

Madison Square Garden. "That was back when I was trying to break out in the USA." She laughs and shakes her head. "That never happened, did it? Anyway, Freddie and I got on like a house on fire from the first time we met, and when he quit the band and moved over here, we had an absolute riot. Possibly too much fun actually . . ." She winks.

"We've had this tradition since he moved back to the US for his show, that once a year we go away somewhere to just hang out." She gives her trademark cackle. "Clubbing in Ibiza, a week in the Maldives if we're feeling flush. We've done Vegas, a detox retreat in Hawaii — we lasted two nights on a juice fast there before we escaped to drink piña coladas . . ." She points to another framed photo of them grinning, clutching bucket-sized cocktails in a beach bar, flushed with rum and sunburn.

"Anyway, that night, after a drink or three, we did a few songs on the piano in the upstairs bar, and then we had a few more drinks. And he said he was going to Island Home on Thursday, he was flying himself down. Because we hadn't had our trip yet that year and it was already October, he said that I should come." She gives

69

a little shrug. "I didn't have anything on, so I said yes. We didn't really think it through, I guess."

For someone who, if this five-floor north London townhouse is any indicator, made serious money during her recording career, with three UK number ones, two top-ten UK albums, and sold-out stadium shows across Europe under her belt, Kyra Highway is astonishingly modest. So self-effacing that it's easy to overlook the scale of her success, how big a star she actually was at the peak of her career. Given her composure, it is also easy to forget how far she has come — how much she has overcome — to get here, something she details with brutal honesty in her best-selling autobiography *My Way, the Highway.* The abusive teenage boyfriend. The bullying at school. The sudden ascent to pop fame aged fourteen. All those jokes on *Never Mind the Buzzcocks* about her Birmingham accent. The paparazzi harassment. The tabloid stings. That divorce. When you think how long ago she had her first hit, how solid a presence she has been in the public consciousness since, it is hard to believe the singer is still only in her midthirties.

"I did briefly question if they'd actually

want me there, but Freddie was adamant Annie Spark would be thrilled — or at least if she wasn't, then she wouldn't cause a scene," Kyra recalls. "And he was right about that. You should have seen their faces, though, as they walked up the lawn to meet us and it wasn't just Freddie standing there waving. My God, their expressions. The panic. Especially after they realized I'd brought Lyra too, when she hopped out of the chopper behind me." She half smiles at the memory, then shakes her head, grows thoughtful.

"You know," she says, quietly, "when I think about what happened, the decision I regret most in my entire life — and if you've read my memoir or the newspapers you'll know I have made some really bad ones in my time — is bringing my little girl with me. My second-biggest regret is not leaving sooner. It was chaos, that Sunday morning. Really scary. Drones circling. Everybody attempting to get off the island, trying to work out who was missing, desperate to get their phones back — squeezing their way through the crowd into the Boathouse, shoving, shouting — to call their agents, their PAs, their publicists, their mothers. I'll never forget it. Wandering around the island with my daughter —

the only child in the whole place —
clinging to my hand and crying, people
pushing past us, the two of us trying to
find anyone in a position of authority, to
tell them what Lyra had told me. What Lyra
had seen."

CHAPTER TWO:
THURSDAY EVENING

JESS

This was not how Jess had envisaged her first evening on the island: babysitting a tiny gate-crasher.

There was so much to do. *So much to do.* That was the panicky thought that kept gripping her. Under normal circumstances someone in her job would have been in place a year in advance for a launch like this. Choosing her team, getting to know their foibles. Understanding the island and its quirks, figuring out the quickest ways from one cabin to the next.

Her tour of Island Home had been whistle-stop, conducted by a recently arrived, crumpled, and quite put-out-seeming Adam Groom, the golf cart barely stopping as they looped its wood-chip paths, rattling here and there across little wooden bridges over streams and gullies, squeezing half off the track into the bushes or onto grass whenever they encountered a buggy coming in the opposite direction, Adam pointing out through the trees, as they hurried by, the outdoor pool, the yoga pavilion, the breakfast barn, the lake, the concrete track down to the water-sports center (not yet quite finished, not that anyone was likely to want to go paddleboarding this late in October, even if the sun was shining), the turn for Ned's own personal residence on the island (the road up to it was clearly marked private), the big jetty where all the island's supplies were unloaded, the staff canteen, their accommodations (a long two-story brick building with tiny windows, adjacent to a generator) — which was where he had dropped her off, so that she could check out her room (single bed, wardrobe, sink, mirror, view of the corrugated and pine-cone-covered roof of the staff bike shed) and freshen up (there were showers at the end of the corridor on each floor) before she met her team.

A handover document? Sadly not, Adam said with a glance at his watch. Sorry. Her team would let her know anything she couldn't work out for herself. He was sure she was going to be absolutely great. He gave her a reasonable imitation of an encouraging smile, looked for a moment as if he might be about to say something else; then two young waitresses (one a redhead, the other blond) emerged from the accommodation block in their uniforms, and Adam tapped his horn and called out to see if they needed a lift anywhere. One climbed in next to him and one hopped up onto the back as Jess was lifting her bag down and Adam said something and they both laughed; then, with barely a goodbye over his shoulder, off he went.

Jess hoped she had made a good impression, with her team. She hadn't made a big speech, just said a few words about how excited she was about working with them all, explaining who she was and a bit about her previous experience. Her attempt at a joke had garnered a couple of scattered laughs and quite a few smiles. At the end, she had asked if anyone wanted to ask anything and — predictably — two people with questions regarding their work schedules immediately shot up their hands.

It often felt a bit odd, telling people how much of her career she had spent working at a hotel — the Grange — where her father had once been general manager, trying to decide whether to mention the family connection. Not that she wasn't proud to have followed in his footsteps. But unless you'd grown up in the kind of village she had, it was hard to convey how limited the employment options were — unless you were lucky enough, pretty enough, to land a job at Country Home — if you had caring responsibilities as Jess had and couldn't just move away.

It was amazing to be here, she'd told them all, and she had not been exaggerating. The scale of the place, the distances between the cabins, that was one of the things it was hard to get your head around. This was not somewhere you walked out on your balcony and there was your neighbor on his balcony in his bathrobe eating breakfast, and you both had to ignore each other. Here, on the island, by careful design, you would never really be aware of your neighbor or the other cabins. Members could feel perfectly comfortable having a bath with the curtains open, watching the sun going down over the ocean, log burner blazing. Nor had Jess been expecting how far away the rest of the world would feel here, especially when you knew the tide was in, that the only way on or off this place for the next twelve hours was by boat or helicopter. Their nearest neighbors — the village, out there on the horizon in one direction (a vague impression of distant gray buildings and white-hulled boats, even on a clear day like today, and presumably no more than a tiny cluster of distant orange lights at night), the bird sanctuary on the far side of the estuary on the other.

All the time, as Adam gave her the tour, Jess was thinking about what this would mean, for her, practically speaking. Given the size of her team. Given what was being asked of them. Given how long it would take two people to turn one of those huge cabins around. This had always been the aspect of her job she enjoyed most, the logistics. Finding ways of making everything more efficient, saving her team time and effort. Working out who would have to be where and when and how. Not just meeting people's expectations but surpassing them. Figuring out what was going to need to happen in what exact sequence to ensure it all worked perfectly. That was the sort of thing — problem solving — she enjoyed. That was how she would have loved to spend her first night on Island Home.

Instead, here she was, stuck for the evening looking after an extremely precocious seven-year-old.

It had been about 6:00 p.m. when Annie had called — just as Jess had been about to make herself a cup of tea and take the weight off her feet for five minutes.

"How are you with kids?" Annie had asked.

Obviously Jess had hesitated too long before giving her an answer — which would probably have been something like "I'm not sure, to be honest" — because before she knew what was happening, Annie was explaining which cabin she should present herself at, and when.

"It'll be easy," Annie had promised. "Order some room service, watch a couple of films, read a story or two, put her to bed. I've met Lyra a few times, very sweet girl, very mature. She'll be no trouble at all, I promise."

Naturally, Jess remembered Kyra Highway, Lyra's mother. Once upon a time she had been absolutely everywhere. Pepsi ads. Panel shows. Magazine covers. The front page of the *News of the World* . . .

Despite herself, Jess had been a little nervous on the way over, all Annie's instructions from that afternoon ringing in her head.

It was perhaps only as she was walking along the cabin's front path — the lights on either side just beginning to glimmer into life in the dusk, a wood pigeon cooing nearby — that it really hit her where she was, and what she was doing, and how real all of this suddenly felt.

It was perhaps only as she was readying herself to knock on the cabin door (having failed to locate the bell, if there was one) that it had occurred to Jess how she might turn this whole situation to her advantage — if she dared.

Slightly to Jess's surprise — what had she been expecting? A butler? — Kyra Highway herself had opened the cabin door. Still only half-ready, still only half-dressed, she had waved Jess inside, called through to Lyra to come and introduce herself, told Jess to chuck everything off any of the chairs and sit down, then apologized profusely for having put everyone in this awkward position. She really could not have been friendlier, more apologetic, more charming. There was a nanny coming, she promised Jess — Home had found one and she would be here in the morning.

"God knows what I would have done about tonight if it wasn't for you, though, Jess," she said. "We hadn't really thought this through . . ." She trailed off, distracted by rifling through her suitcase.

There was a strange kind of buzz in hearing your name in the mouth of someone famous. There was something strange too, something quite dreamlike, about finding yourself face-to-face with someone you had seen bantering on Freddie Hunter's televised couch, someone whose wedding photos you had pored over at the doctor's, whose divorce you had read about in the *Mail Online.* Especially when they were still somewhere between outfits, and wandering around in just their underwear and tattoos for quite a long stretch of the conversation.

Jess did wonder, as she listened to Kyra chattering away, talking about the helicopter flight down, explaining how she knew Freddie, if she had any idea quite how much chaos and consternation her unexpected arrival had caused. The debates about whether she was to be allowed to come to that night's dinner. The anxious discussions about where on earth, if they did stay, she and Lyra were going to sleep. It was lucky for Kyra, Jess thought, that another member had been forced to cancel their attendance at the party last minute, calling midafternoon from a hospital in the Pyrenees with a broken leg.

"I won't be late," Kyra had promised as she was leaving, with a big hug for Lyra, a kiss on both cheeks for Jess. "I promise. I'm just going to meet Freddie for a drink in the bar, then we're all going for dinner. I doubt it'll be much after ten when I get back here."

The time was now almost half eleven. Even if Kyra got back in the next five minutes, it would still be after midnight by the time Jess got to bed. A bit rude, that. A bit inconsiderate.

To be fair, just as promised, Lyra Highway had really not been any trouble at all.

The first thing she had asked Jess was how many of the different Home clubs around the world she had been to. Two, said Jess — if you included this place and the one in London where she had been interviewed. Lyra had been to all of them. Paris Home was the one she liked the best, she thought. She then began to rank all the others, in order.

"I like the Malibu Home pool most," she had informed Jess, breezily. "But the water is a bit too cold." At Shanghai Home they let you watch as they prepared the dim sum. The view from the cabins at Upstate Home in New York were pretty amazing, but these cabins here on this island were a bit bigger, and a lot nicer. "The burgers there are better though," she'd said, eyeing her uneaten room-service order.

Jess tried to remember if she'd had such confident opinions about anything when she was Lyra's age. Ice-cream flavors, possibly. Her favorite member of Sideways, perhaps. It was also quite unsettling to be babysitting a child who was objectively a lot cooler than you were.

After they'd played *Candy Crush* on Lyra's iPad for almost an hour, Jess had tried and failed to teach Lyra chess with the ornate set on the coffee table, realizing in the process that she couldn't remember the rules all that well herself. Jess had called reception to see if there was anything to draw or color with — but with under eighteens not technically allowed on the island, there was nothing in stock to entertain them so they'd sent an ice bucket full of silver fountain pens and some Home-branded notepaper instead. Jess had used the paper as kindling for the wood burner in the corner of the cabin, which quickly made the room so hot they had to open the balcony doors.

Lyra had asked for a Wagyu burger and a bottle of Badoit for dinner but it had been unclear to Jess whether she should order something to eat as well, so she had decided against it. This was a decision that, as the hours passed, she had come to regret.

After Jess spent some time fumbling with it, Lyra had shown her how to open the TV cabinet, on the cabin wall opposite the enormous bed with its scalloped rust-colored velvet headboard. About eighty channels — movies, news, lots of lifestyle and travel stuff — she had scrolled through without finding anything quite suitable for a seven-year-old. They had ended up watching some kind of endless information loop about the island — the different places to eat, the spa menu, plus a video about the art here, which incorporated an interview with Keith Little.

"Do you know Keith?" asked Lyra from the bed, chin resting on her upturned palms, her tumbling curls, hazel eyes, and heart-shaped face an exact facsimile of her mother's, but in perfect miniature. The question was seemingly a genuine one — perhaps it simply didn't occur to her that there were other social circles to move in.

Jess, in her armchair, shook her head. She knew the name, of course, and vaguely recognized the face on the screen — the grizzled stubble, the earring, the jet-black hair tied back in a ponytail, the striking pale blue eyes. There was a clip they always showed of him, from the nineties, drunk on some late-night BBC Two talk show, slowly slipping down in his chair, gradually getting growlier and growlier until eventually he ripped his microphone from the front of his shirt and stormed off set "to get a pint of Guinness."

"I've met him about *ten* times," said Lyra, counting on her fingers and nodding along as she mentally checked off the occasions. "But he still never remembers my name. He always kisses on both cheeks and his stubble scratches. And he stinks of cigarettes."

Jess checked the time again.

It was now nearly a quarter to midnight.

She had suggested, more than once, that it might be time for Lyra to brush her teeth and go to sleep.

"No point," said Lyra. "Mum will wake me up when she turns all the lights on or falls over something. Don't worry, you won't get in trouble. I don't have a bedtime."

Nevertheless, Jess insisted Lyra at least try to close her eyes. Grumbling, yawning, Lyra did so.

Only after she was certain Lyra was properly asleep did Jess turn off the bedside lamps and make her way to the bathroom. It took her a moment to find the light switch — or rather a cluster of brass dimmers, which she then made her way through, illuminating the lights under the sink first, then the overhead light in the enormous frosted-glass shower, then a shaded light hanging directly over the claw-foot bathtub, then finally the one she wanted. All across the polished concrete floor were scattered clothes from several suitcases. Against one antique-delft-tiled wall stood a double sink, and next to the sink sat a child's travel wash kit, and next to that a bag of makeup the size of something you might expect a professional to turn up at a photo shoot with.

It didn't take her long to find what she was looking for, tucked away in the corner of one of Kyra's monogrammed cases. Given the length of time Kyra Highway was due to be staying on the island, it was extraordinary how many different kinds of pills she had brought. Had you found this see-through, Ziploc bag on the street, you would have assumed it had been discarded by someone who had just robbed a pharmacy.

Here we go, thought Jess.

Sleeping pills. Strong pills too from the looks of it, and several types.

She found herself wondering how many she could pocket without Kyra noticing. Ten? Twenty? There were three large bottles. She settled on fifteen, counted them out, wrapped them up in some toilet paper, and slipped them into one of her pockets. Then, recalculating things in her mind, she went back and tipped another half dozen into her palm.

In the other room, Lyra Highway was still fast asleep in bed, her mouth slightly open. Jess lay down on the couch and decided to try to get a little bit of sleep as well.

It didn't take her much time at all to drop off. It was a warm cabin. It had been a long day.

It always begins the same way, the dream.

She is six years old, not much younger than Lyra. She is lying under a blanket on the back seat of her parents' car. They are driving at night down a country road, the headlights illuminating the hedgerows on either side of them, the overhanging branches. Her father is in the driver's seat. Her mother is looking for something — a different CD, perhaps? — in the glove compartment. Hearing Jess stir in the back, her father mutters something softly to her mother, glances at Jess over his shoulder, smiles. And even in the dream she always knows that this is a dream she has had many times before.

Sometimes, although she knows this is not how dreams or memories work, she will notice something, some detail — the pattern on the blanket, the way her mother rests her hand gently for a moment on the back of Jess's father's hand and gives it a squeeze — and think, Oh, I've never spotted that before. Other times there are glitches, incongruities, little logical gaps, that even in the dream she is capable of noting and being irked by, like the way she is suddenly sitting upright in her seat belt without ever being able to remember how or why; like the way the radio is often playing not the song she actually remembers it playing but a song they played at her father's funeral; like the way she always knows what is going to happen next. And she keeps trying to warn her parents, keeps trying to attract their attention, but her mother just keeps groping around for whatever it is in the glove compartment and her dad keeps driving and it is never the moment of impact that jolts Jess awake but the moment at which she realizes that however loud she screams, he cannot hear her, will never hear her.

It would not be until almost two in the morning that Kyra would come stumbling through the door of the cabin, shushing herself, and then turn every single light in the whole place on full glare by mistake.

"A toast," said Annie Spark, indicating to the table to raise their glasses, "to the birthday boy!"

Due to the tightness of the dress she was wearing, the sharpness of her shoulder pads, and how aggressively they appeared to pin her arms to her sides, Annie didn't seem able to raise her own champagne coupe much above waist height. This didn't escape Ned's attention, or that of Jackson Crane. Even though the two men were sitting on either side of her, Nikki could sense without turning her head that both were wearing sly smirks.

"Did I miss the dress code, Sparky?" Ned had laughed when he strode into the room before dinner, looking her up and down. "Let me guess . . . space pirate? But then what do I know about clothes? You're Home's resident fashionista." Annie had giggled as if she were in on the joke, but Nikki could tell that if her shoulders had not been buttressed by the dress, they would have dropped three inches in embarrassment. It was not an entirely unreasonable jibe, though. Even Nikki had done a double take and briefly questioned her own low-key outfit choice, a black halterneck Stella McCartney jumpsuit (80 percent off, the last size eight left, bought with the Net-a-Porter five-thousand-pound voucher Ned had given her two Christmases ago, which she had been chipping away at in the sales ever since).

She should not have been surprised. As these launch weekends had grown ever more overblown, so too had Annie's ensembles for them. Even for her, though, this one was over the top: a skin-tight, ankle-length, gold pleated gown, simultaneously retro and futuristic. With the fake tan, fire-engine-red dye job and bum-length extensions, it added up to quite the look (Nikki could barely keep track of Annie's hair color and style from month to month — from blond crop to chestnut bob to pale pink curls). The unfathomable thing was that Annie didn't *need* to try this hard — when she'd started at Home, she was a porcelain-skinned willowy brunette with poker-straight hair down to her waist, so striking she was often mistaken for an actress herself, was constantly being asked out by the members. Nikki could not quite recall the moment Annie Spark had started dressing like her own drag-tribute act, but she hadn't seen her in jeans and a sweater for a very long time.

It must be absolutely exhausting being

Annie Spark all the time. It was definitely exhausting working with her. The shouting. The showing off. The pathological need to be noticed, as if she thought she might actually evaporate if ignored for thirty seconds. Despite being her colleague for nearly two decades, Nikki had never really understood her. Or wanted to understand her, particularly. Or liked her very much. The members? *They* all loved her. At the start of this evening, she had watched Annie slink around the table, rearranging her gown as she crouched behind chairs, resting her chin on the seat backs, complimenting Georgia's highlights while twirling a lock of the actress's hair, laughing as Jackson whispered something into her ear, lustily fingering Freddie's garish paisley velvet smoking jacket.

Nikki wondered if it was only she who secretly found her colleague so annoying, so brittle. The fact that she called everyone in her orbit some version of darling, lovely, dearest, gorgeous, beautiful. The whoops. The jarring brightness of her lipstick (a trademark acid-orange Chanel, ostentatiously and frequently reapplied). On the one hand, it was impossible to imagine Home without her — she made sure the club was always packed with the right people, had an astonishing knack that Ned valued above all else for knowing who was about to be the next big thing. She seemed to smell the faint whiff of gunpowder when a career was about to explode, whether it was an actor on the cusp of being offered a plum role in a major franchise, a singer with a surefire hit, or a model secretly dating Hollywood (or actual) royalty. And when she got the scent, she made it her absolute mission to understand everything about them, bring them into the fold, like some sort of benevolent stalker.

As valuable as Annie was, Nikki thought, she should still be treading very carefully right now, with Ned so on edge. Because if there was one thing Ned Groom could not abide, it was being upstaged.

Tonight, it was as if Annie had deliberately dressed to outshine not only the guests but the soft furnishings too. The heavy silk drapes, fringed kilims, the hand-painted de Gournay wallpaper, and mustard-yellow velvet chairs made this one of the most opulent rooms in the Manor. Logs crackled and spat in the stone fireplace and, as Annie turned the electric lights off, bathed the room in a warm glow while she gave a toast.

"To Kurt! The birthday boy!" voices repeated around the table, to the clink of cut crystal.

On Annie's signal, a very slight nod in the direction of the doorway, two aproned waitresses carried in an ornate chocolate cake lit with sparklers and candles — far too large for nine guests, a wedding cake practically — and placed it at the center of the table. Freddie Hunter and Kyra Highway, arms around each other, wineglasses aloft with their contents sloshing on the table, burst into a surprisingly competent two-part harmony, encouraging the rest of the room to join in. They had spent the evening so far hooting with laughter at nonsense in-jokes and making friends with the waiters, who had all ensured they were constantly topped up. If you wanted to know the measure of a member, Nikki knew, just watch how they speak to the staff. Kyra and Freddie were on first-name terms with every single server within five minutes.

The birthday boy — wunderkind film producer Kurt Cox — seemed a little flushed, a little embarrassed by the attention. Thanks to the boyish mop of dark curly hair, the sweet, doughy features that did not look quite yet cooked, it was hard to guess an exact age. Film school student, you might think, if you saw him out on the street in New York or London in his usual parka and unlaced boots. Aspiring screenwriter, you might assume, if you spotted him earnestly hunched over his laptop in any coffee shop in the Western world. He looked like the kind of young man you'd overhear enthusiastically explaining the film he wanted to make to a not-especially-interested girl in the kitchen at a party, getting in the way of everyone trying to grab a beer from the fridge.

In fact, Kurt Cox had produced — in *Swipe Right* — one of the most critically and commercially successful small-budget psychological thrillers of the decade so far. His follow-up, *The Roommate,* was the surprise hit comedy of last year. Only a week or two ago he had announced a deal with Netflix so big that Nikki had read about it in the *Financial Times.*

Even though this success was his own, Hollywood must surely have given Kurt Cox a friendly leg up — as the son of a movie actress mother and film director father he was hardly coming to the industry cold. There were distinctive similarities between father and son, Nikki noticed; small mannerisms, if you watched the young man closely. The little flutters of the hands as he said something self-deprecating. The way he tilted his head slightly to the side for emphasis. The warm, toothy smile that started off as a twitch on the right-hand corner of his mouth.

"Oh you guys, you really shouldn't have, but thank you. We were never that big on birthdays in our house, so I honestly forget when mine is most years. But it means a lot that you care — Ned, Jackson, especially you both, as I know how close you were to Dad . . . *are,* I guess it's still are . . ." Kurt trailed off slightly and blinked. Was it Nikki's imagination, or were his eyes glistening slightly in the candlelight?

"He's a good man, your father," Jackson said solemnly, lifting his glass and giving *that* lopsided grin. "Best I ever worked with. Truly, one of the greats."

It was always weird, Nikki found, when she accidentally stumbled across one of Jackson's films on the TV or on a plane — one of his comedies from the eighties (the time-traveling one, the one about a house party in a borrowed mansion) or his action roles from the nineties, or the more recent serious issues-y stuff — to observe how many of his own mannerisms found their way on-screen. Or was it perhaps the other way around? That smile, that trademark knowing smirk, for instance — had he always done that in real life, at dinner, or had some director once suggested it to him for a long-ago role?

"You mean a lot to him, Jackson. You too, Ned — Home feels like a true home to me, my dad spent so much time in the clubs. I can remember watching cartoons in the Manhattan Home screening room when I was a kid. And the chocolate ice cream in Santa Monica Home." Kurt grinned.

Nikki could remember it too — the chubby little boy in a Mickey Mouse T-shirt, reading his comics. It seemed impossible to Nikki that anyone born in the nineties could be a fully grown adult now, someone with a house, a driver's license, let alone a production deal in the hundreds of millions. How strange to think that Ned, a friend of Kurt's father since the very earliest days of Home — although of course they rarely met since dementia had really taken hold — had literally known this young man his entire life.

She wondered what it must do to your sense of reality to be one of the Coxes. To be Ron Cox, someone whose films everyone who was a child or teenager between about 1979 and 1993 grew up quoting and reenacting. To be Marianne, perhaps the funniest, most beautiful comedy actress of her generation, to go in the space of a very few years from being one of the most bankable

95

female stars of the late eighties to being the full-time mother of six on an isolated 250-acre New Mexico ranch. To be one of those children.

"Go on, make us all feel ancient — how old *are* you?" laughed Kyra.

"I'm a 1996 vintage, ma'am. Twenty-five years old," he said sheepishly.

"And is it actually today, your birthday?" inquired Georgia Crane, in her strangely LA-inflected British public-school accent.

Kurt Cox shook his head.

"Not quite. It was a few days ago — the twenty-fifth of October," he said, as Annie made a big performance of cutting into the cake, before waving at the waitress to finish her botched job.

"Well done for remembering, Annie — and Kurt, very many happy returns to you, young man, from all of us!" said Ned. "Next year, drop Nikki here a line and we'll book you a weekend at Home for your celebrations — the club of your choice! Right, Nikki? Make a note in your calendar so we don't forget: October twenty-fifth."

Nikki nodded blankly and picked up her phone, hand shaking slightly, although really, she did not need to write it down. That date was not one she was ever going to struggle to remember, or one that she would ever be able to forget.

ADAM

He'd been set up to fail, of course. Disaster had always been a foregone conclusion. At no point, as Ned was explaining the task he needed Adam to perform that night — Annie in her usual clown makeup and weird gold dress, pulling faces of faux commiseration in the background — had there been any real pretense on anyone's part that this was anything other than his punishment for turning up late. Although if he'd made it to the island on time, he would still have had to do it, this job; it just would have been his punishment for some other misdemeanor, real or perceived.

It was going to be strange for Ned, after this weekend, not having his little brother around to palm off all the shittiest jobs on.

"Listen," he'd told Adam. "I wouldn't ask you if it wasn't important. You've met them all before, you know what they're like. All I need you to do is pop over to the Causeway Inn, have a couple of drinks, crack a few jokes, answer a few questions. I would do it myself, but you know . . ."

Adam did know.

Ned would be having dinner with the

chosen few, showing them his island, soaking up their admiration, dispensing largesse. Adam, meanwhile, would be hosting an emergency last-minute summit, dealing with the latest round of complaints and protests from their neighbors on the mainland.

"Sure thing, Ned," he told his brother. "Leave it to me."

All the usual suspects would be there, no doubt. Not just local nut-jobs either, like the man with the porridge in his beard who had stood most afternoons for months outside the front gates of Highland Home, waving a rain-spattered sign about newts. These people *actually* had some influence; some even had a bit of money. The angry man who put together the village newsletter. The grumpy landlord of the other pub with the brassy, busty barmaid who always wore those low-cut T-shirts. A load of old codgers from the parish council. The same people who had tried to kill off every planning application they'd made, from their very first attempts to tart up the Causeway Inn onward. Ramblers. Bird-watchers. The sort of people who called Noise Prevention every time a truck drove through the village, and the Civil Aviation Authority every time a helicopter flew overhead, and had photocopied signs reading HOME GO HOME in their front windows. None of whom were at all happy about the prospect of a three-day party to which they were not invited. Some of whom had been threatening a sit-in on the causeway the following morning just as guests were due to start arriving. None of whom — the ungrateful bastards — were appeased by the fact that the value of property in Littlesea had shot up 25 percent since Home had acquired the island. All of whom would be immediately annoyed that instead of Ned himself they were getting his little brother.

"Don't be late," Nikki had reminded him, at least five times that afternoon.

"Knock 'em dead, superstar," Annie had called with a cackle as she had waved him off outside the Boathouse, the wind whipping her scarlet fright wig across her face.

The whole thing went even worse than Adam had been expecting.

On their arrival at the Causeway Inn, people had been directed into the Boot Room and invited to order a drink at the bar, above which was a neon piece by Keith Little: *I Love You, Now Fuck Off* in a three-foot-high illuminated scrawl. A great start? Probably not. Nor had it been a great sign, in retrospect, that they had all arrived en masse on the dot of seven thirty wearing the same aggrieved expression.

When Ned made the previous landlord an offer he could not refuse, the Causeway Inn was one of those run-down, pint-and-pork-scratchings pubs — swollen-nosed old-timers sitting alone at the bar, sticky carpet, toilet doors that didn't lock — that London-ers dream of buying, sloshing a few tins of Farrow & Ball paint on the walls of and serving scallops and samphire in. But the bones of the place, its wooden beams and oak paneling, thatched roof, leadlight win-dows, were solid — and then of course there was that view out over the water: the island a mysterious silhouette in the distance, the causeway a winding silver squiggle in the foreground, the whole thing framed by the gently clinking masts of the sailing boats on the old quay. The design team's very first task on this whole project had been to give the Causeway Inn a Home makeover, and so now, with its chestnut leather button-back benches, brass sconce lights, ornate etched mirrors, and parquet floor, it looked like the kind of ersatz British boozer a suc-cessful expat actor might build for himself at the end of his LA garden. An expensive, knowing, parody of itself.

The locals had not been impressed. Not

by the refurb, not by the discovery that from now on, entry to the Causeway Inn was restricted to Home members and their guests.

Nor was it easy to think of anything else that he and Ned and the Home Group had done since they'd come to town that had attracted the approval of any of this lot.

Clearly there had been a lot of back-and-forth in advance about how they were all going to play things tonight, who was going to say what, the points they wanted to get across. They were a sea of suspicious frowns and folded arms. Adam had not even finished introducing himself before someone in the front row who seemed to think he should know who she was — which of course he didn't because why *would* he remember every frumpy middle-aged woman he met — demanded to know where his brother was.

"Is Ned Groom planning to make an appearance at all? Or are we not famous enough to be graced with his presence?" harrumphed someone from farther back.

Adam apologized, tried to explain. The woman sat there with her mouth pursed, her arms still crossed, intermittently shaking her head at him. There were a couple of other head shakers behind her, one man in the back row who kept half raising his hand to interject.

Adam pretended not to see him, took someone's point from the other side of the room.

As it turned out, this was a big mistake, because the lady he picked — "Yes, you, um, please, with the, uh, purple . . . is that a cardigan, would you say?" — proceeded to give him a very thorough dressing-down about everything from Island Home's impact on the traffic to the way she had been spoken to by a receptionist when she had called to complain.

Adam frowned, he nodded, he looked contrite. Several times as someone was berating him, he would begin to respond to one of the points raised — "Well, if I could just . . ." — only to be glared down for interrupting. Occasionally he would jot a note on a piece of paper — a note he had no intention of ever reading on a piece of paper he planned to chuck as soon as this meeting was over. He kept telling people how sorry he was to hear they felt that way, how disappointed he was at what they were telling him. About their dog, and how much all the building work had upset it. About the damage done by one of his construction vehicles to the verge on their lane. About the impact this was all going to have on the *character* of the village.

He glanced at his watch and his heart sank. Already they had gone way over the hour originally agreed. Every time one person finished speaking, or even paused for breath, a sudden forest of insistent, indignant hands would shoot up around the room. Every point someone made, someone else would announce, "Exactly!" or turn half around in their chair to nod along vigorously with the person speaking. Every time Adam said anything, someone would announce, "Not good enough," or demand to know why they should believe him.

They had a point. It was a pretty village, Littlesea. Nice green, nice pub (the one the locals were still allowed in), nice church, nice tea shop. If he'd lived here all his life, if he'd retired here to concentrate on his gardening, he would probably resent exactly the same things they did. "What should I tell them?" he had asked his brother. "Tell them anything you fucking want" had been the answer.

The thing was, once upon a time, Adam would have thought of this kind of assignment, this sort of special bloody project, as a chance to impress his brother, to show how useful he could be. And he had made himself consistently useful, he hoped. On several occasions he could name, he had made himself very useful indeed. But then something had changed. And instead of getting ever bigger, the tasks, the responsibilities, had started getting smaller, more demeaning. It was something he found hard to talk about, even with Laura. It was something he wondered how much Ned himself was conscious of. How consistently now the sensitive assignments, the delicate stuff, went to someone else. How often the jobs he got were the ones that either no one could fuck up or it didn't really matter if they did.

Tell them anything you fucking want.

Once upon a time he might have taken Ned's words as a vote of confidence, an offer to back him whatever terms he wanted to offer, a gesture of faith in his ability to respond to the situation on the ground. Adam was a shareholder, a director of the company, after all, even if no one including himself was ever quite able to explain concisely what exactly he was directing.

Nowadays? Well, the whole point of sending Adam — as half these people had clearly surmised — was that he could say anything because nothing he said had any weight behind it. He was not here as a negotiator.

He was here as a punching bag. He was here as a fucking piñata.

Adam Groom did not want to be a piñata anymore.

"I have an idea . . ." he heard himself saying. Then again, louder, in a firmer voice, which prompted a few more of the people to stop talking.

Ned was going to hate this. The one thing Ned had always been completely obsessed with was not letting people from the village onto the island for any reason — not for a placatory Sunday afternoon film screening, not for a monthly ramble even along set routes, not to count salamanders in the pond. And yet, before Adam had even had a chance to think about it, before he had even had a chance to finish the thought, he was inviting everyone in the room over on Saturday evening to watch the fireworks from the Boathouse.

"Of course," he added immediately, seeing at least five hands already creeping up, "if there are things we haven't got around to discussing tonight then *please,* do put them in an email . . ."

Sure, they would come, and being the kind of people they were, they would make a point of not being impressed or overawed by anything about Island Home. But if they were watching the fireworks from the Boathouse, glass of champagne in hand, at least they would not be calling the police with noise complaints, hassling the fire brigade. At least they would not be blockading the causeway or picketing the jetty or circling the island in boats, with bullhorns. First thing tomorrow Adam was going to find out whether it was possible to order ear defenders for dogs.

All in all, under the circumstances, Adam was proud of how he had acquitted himself this evening. This might not please or impress Ned, but maybe that was not always the most important thing in the world.

It was at precisely the moment Adam was thinking this that the brick came through the window.

ANNIE

This was it, surely. She checked the time. Nearly two in the morning. It had to be soon. There were only four members left now, still drinking, still talking — most of them slurring, really — sunk deep into sofas and sprawled across armchairs in front of the library's blazing fire. Annie, as always, found reasons to constantly shift position — Ned didn't like her talking to one member for too long, playing favorites, so she

106

was perching on the sofa arm one minute, then jumping up to order a drink the next, then crouching down (with difficulty, given the dress) to throw another log on the fire.

Jackson and Freddie were knocking back Ned's famously strong old-fashioneds; Keith was slumped with his crystal tumbler resting on his chest; Kurt was sipping on sparkling water. None of them had the slightest idea of what was about to take place, the turn the evening was about to take.

Ned was talking about the paintings that had come with the house when he'd bought it, the supposed Stubbs, the disputed Gainsborough. Keith had stirred himself up onto his elbows briefly to announce that "all great art is either about sex or death, yeah?" and then when this failed to produce much response sank down into his armchair once more.

"I fuckin' hate Gainsborough," he could then be heard muttering into his chest.

It was surely going to happen soon.

Nikki and Georgia were probably fast asleep by now, tucked into their emperor-sized beds with the thousand-thread-count sheets, both having yawned and made their excuses almost as soon as dinner was over.

It was half an hour since Kyra — who had

been sitting staring at the fire in silence for quite some time — had suddenly shaken herself out of her reverie, announced it was past her bedtime, and tottered off down the hall to relieve the babysitter.

Was it the shallow breaths this too-tight dress was forcing her to take that were making her feel light-headed or was it the anticipation? What was Ned waiting for, exactly?

All evening he had been laying the groundwork for this moment. Making a big deal about what very special friends of Home they all were — avoiding eye contact with Kyra, at this point — what remarkable, important people they were, to the clubs, to Ned himself personally, how much it meant to him that they had all been able to make it tonight . . .

At which point Keith had snorted, as if at the very idea that anyone would turn an invitation like this down. As if it were conceivable that somebody given the option of being in this room, sitting around this table, could choose to be anywhere else in the world tonight.

Annie smiled to herself.

It was one of her old editors, back in her journalist days, who had outlined to her his five-rooms theory of fame — which she had loved explaining to people and then name-dropping the person who had come up with it, until he published his memoirs and now everyone knew it too. The theory was this: that to the public, the general public, it looks as if being famous is like being in one big room, the Oscars or the Grammys or something, a room full of familiar, beloved faces all huddling together for selfies, all smiling, all the best of friends. Whereas, in fact, Annie's editor had explained, leaning in slightly closer, what fame more closely resembles is a series of roped-off rooms, each more exclusive than the last, the whole thing as hierarchical as high school.

Picture a nightclub, he had told her. If you're on the outside, queueing to try to get in, all you can see is a bunch of people having what appears to be a good time. And then you get inside. And for a while you think you've made it. And then you realize that in the club there is a VIP area, behind another velvet rope that, actually, is where all the really exciting people are. And maybe you manage to get in there, eventually. And you get a drink, and you see who's around, and you feel pretty pleased with yourself. And then you realize there is another velvet rope, and another door, and beyond that there is a VVIP area and your name's not on the list. And even if you manage to get in there you realize . . .

"You get the point," he had concluded, with a wave of his hand.

She had got the point. It was also a pretty accurate explanation of how Home worked, except the velvet ropes were invisible. Most civilians had never even heard of it. Few who had would ever dream of applying. Most who did wouldn't be accepted. Those few who were would not imagine for a moment that they'd be invited to a launch party. None of those excited guests who would be arriving later this morning would suspect there had been a dinner the night before. And that was what Ned had been telling them all, Jackson and Keith and Freddie and Kurt, with varying degrees of subtlety, all evening. That they had made it. That this was it. Right now. They were past the last velvet rope, they were in that final room, the one that people spend their whole lives, their whole careers, trying to reach, that people sacrifice everything — marriages, friendships, sanity — trying to get into.

For the past twenty minutes Keith had been explaining to Jackson Crane his philosophy of art, and how this was reflected in his own creative practice.

110

"I would say I don't really have a *medium,* you know? Painting, photography, poetry, sculpture — I've mastered them all. It's not for me to call myself a Renaissance man, but . . ." He shrugged. "It has been said. Really if I had to say what my art was *about,* though, it's a celebration of the female form but also a rumination on the gaze. That's why I only use the body, not the head, so they're not looking back at you — there's a purity there, you know? *In the looking.* Power in anonymity. I want to confront the viewer — but I'm posing questions. The viewer has to answer those questions themselves . . ."

Jackson Crane, his head on a cushion, drink still in his hand, appeared to be briefly resting his eyes.

Ned, standing by the fire, one elbow on the mantelpiece, the buttons on his shirt straining slightly to reveal little tufts of gray chest hair, was telling the story of how he'd first heard about this island, how he'd fallen in love with the idea of buying it. Freddie — Annie knew how thrilled and surprised he must be, to find himself in this company, to be able to tell people he was here — was sitting bolt upright in his chair, nodding along.

"Wow," he kept saying. "Golly."

Kurt, having wandered around the library and inspected some of the decorative books, was now perched on the end of one of the couches, listening to Ned, occasionally asking a question about how old something was.

Down at the far end of the library, a grandfather clock let out a whirr and a creak, gathered itself, and then clanked flatly twice.

"This house itself dates from 1723," Ned continued. "Modeled on Chiswick House, but without the dome, built by the family who used to own the whole place."

"One family owned an entire island?" asked Freddie. "Wow."

"Yep — although from 1941 to 1991 half of it was leased to the Ministry of Defence. You should have seen the state of it when we first came down. The Boathouse really was a boathouse — a shed full of rotten hulls and broken oars. This place was half boarded up. I think the Bouchers — spelled B-o-u-c-h-e-r, pronounced Butcher, this is all Boucher's Island, officially — lived in about three rooms. It was freezing, obviously. Damp. Holes in the roof. They showed us all these pictures of when it was a hospital in the First World War, of costume balls on the lawn in the twenties — and the

112

wife served us incredibly strong gin and tonics, half gin, half tonic, the flat supermarket stuff, no lemon, no ice. Adam wandered off to find a loo at one point and I wasn't sure he was ever going to find his way back. And then we had a drive around the island in their old Range Rover. Only one road, back then, of course. Deer crashing around in the woods. Crows starting. Now this is something that might interest *you*, actually, Kurt, if history's your thing . . .."

As Ned took Kurt out of the room for a moment, Annie briskly suggested something to perk them all up a little.

"None for me, thanks," announced Keith, who nevertheless swung himself up into a sitting position, as did Jackson Crane. Freddie eagerly pulled in his armchair closer to the table.

"Wouldn't want everyone falling asleep now, would we?" observed Annie, producing a clutch of short silver straws from her handbag, a little glass vial, and a matte-gold Home membership card.

By the time Kurt and Ned returned, the atmosphere had livened up considerably. Annie had called over the waiter — he had remembered something important to do at the far end of the room at around the time the silver straws had come out and remained there discreetly until summoned back — to order another round of drinks. Freddie was telling the same meandering story about himself for the second time in short succession, Keith was smirking, Jackson chortling loudly well before the punch line.

Nobody seemed to notice the look on Kurt's face, the way he simply dropped back into his chair, in silence.

And over the course of the next three-quarters of an hour, Annie watched as in different ways, Ned discreetly managed to draw each of the remaining three men in the room aside one by one — up to the other end of the library to look at a painting, down the stairs to admire a suit of armor, along to the window at the end of the hall to see the moonlit view down the lawn to the sea.

And one by one, Annie watched as they returned. All night Freddie Hunter had been cracking jokes, pulling faces, clowning around. He was not cracking jokes or pulling faces now. He looked as though he were about to burst into tears.

Keith came back looking absolutely furious.

It was Jackson who got taken aside last, and it was Jackson who seemed to take what Ned had said to him worst. He barely seemed aware of his surroundings as he drifted back into the room alone, whacking straight into the corner of a table with his hip, stumbling over the edge of the carpet, glancing up at Annie — and starting as if he'd seen a ghost.

None of them seemed in the mood to speak much. Nobody seemed inclined to make eye contact with anyone else.

For someone who claimed this was all a necessity he took no pleasure in, Ned looked very much like a man having the time of his life. When he had told Annie how much he was planning to hike the membership fees for this lot, she thought he was joking. Of course she knew how much Island Home had cost the company, but even people as successful as Jackson Crane, Keith Little, or Kurt Cox didn't have that kind of money lying around — and as for Freddie Hunter . . .

"I think I'm going to be sick," Freddie announced, and made a dash for the corridor, the toilets.

Keith crunched an ice cube between his teeth and glared into the fire.

Kurt Cox looked as if he were about to say something, then changed his mind.

"What you'll find, on your dressers, when you return to your rooms," Annie informed

115

them, "is a letter about your new membership status, and a statement about the new fees, a contract to sign."

Jackson slammed down his empty tumbler on the low table next to where he was sitting, hard enough to set the other glasses on it rattling. Kurt jumped. Keith flinched. No one seemed to know quite whom to make eye contact with, or how to look.

There was a reason — she realized — Ned was doing this in stages, separating his special guests to spring that first surprise on them, setting them up to wonder whether they were all getting gouged equally, sowing the seeds of mutual suspicion and distrust. Once that had been done, he could bring them all back together, ever the showman, to deliver his next surprise.

"And by the way," Ned told them, face uplit by the flickering flames. "Just in case any of you are thinking about leaving the island early, or planning to turn this offer down, there's one more thing I should mention, about this weekend. At some point over the next three days, each of you is going to have something else delivered to your cabin . . ."

CONTINUED FROM PAGE 43

"I *was* invited, of course," explains Ava Huxley, the British actress, best known to US audiences for her role as Lexi Glass, consulting psychiatrist by day and serial killer by night, in HBO's *Seven Bullets* and as Lady Daphne in the BBC's acclaimed Sunday-night period drama *Mannersby.* "The truth is, I just had a sixth sense from the start that I shouldn't go. And thank God I followed that instinct. I couldn't have processed it, being so close to . . ." She trails off, shakes her head and shudders, taking a sip from her cup of orange pekoe tea. "I pity my friends who did go — I remember us excitedly talking about what we were going to wear. Even then, I had a really bad feeling about the whole thing."

"I resigned my membership when I heard about it all — too much bad karma in those clubs now. I haven't stepped inside one

117

since. Although actually," she says conspir-atorially, "if you ask me, something hadn't felt right at Home for a while." That's certainly a sentiment echoed by some former members from Home's earlier days. There are even those who would trace the start of this perceived rot — a certain sense that among all the glamour and opulence something valuable had been lost, that the rot had set in — to the very start of the Ned Groom era.

Certainly nobody has ever accused Ned of having an exaggerated respect for the past.

Founded in 1887, named after the great Victorian actor-manager Henry Home, intended as a place where theatrical professionals (performing and nonperform-ing) could meet, drink, attend to their cor-respondence, play cards, and dine, the Home Club (as it was known until 1994) has owned and occupied the same five-story townhouse on Bedford Street in London's Covent Garden almost continu-ously now for 135 years. For all that time the building, and the club, have remained under the same line of ownership, handed down through the Groom family — bar the occasional skipped generation — from son to son to son.

Less stuffy, less prestigious, than the Garrick (from which Home himself had been famously blackballed in 1874), the Home Club saw its membership peak in the 1920s at almost fifteen hundred people. Then and well into the 1930s it was a favorite for actors appearing in the West End to retire to for a post-show nightcap. The kind of place where you might find Ivor Novello settling down behind the piano, or brush past the young Olivier, the young Gielgud, on the dark, steep, narrow stairs. All through the war, all through the Blitz, it remained open, albeit with the curtains closed. In the 1950s John Osborne came in as a guest for dinner a few months after the opening of *Look Back in Anger* and called everyone fossils and mummies. In the 1960s Oliver Reed drank there, famously urinating — mid-anecdote, brandy glass in hand — into the fireplace. By 1992, when Ned Groom inherited the club from his grandfather, its active membership had fallen to seventy-one people, the joke in circulation being that was also pretty close to their average age.

Part of the appeal of the Home Club, for its long-standing members, had always been its idiosyncrasies. For example, because the original head bartender from the 1880s was named George, all subsequent head bartenders were, by convention, also referred to by members as George: there were photographs on the central stairwell of all the Georges, numbered I to XI. George III was notoriously rude to Americans. George IV was notoriously rude to women. George VII was notoriously rude to everybody. The walls of the library were decorated with lithographs and drawings and paintings of Henry Home in the roles that had made him famous — as Shylock, as Othello, playing the world's oldest Hamlet at fifty-five. Food, famously bad, from a galley kitchen in the basement, was not served after 8:00 p.m. Spirits were not served in the afternoon. Those who had not mastered the knack of catching George's eye often found it difficult to get served anything at all.

"The Home Club," Ned Groom told an interviewer for the *Daily Telegraph* in 2004, on the occasion of the tenth anniversary of the club's big reopening as Home under his management, "was the kind of place that everyone gets nostalgic about now, but you would feel less misty-eyed if you'd been there at the time. Often I used to be up on the top floor, late at night, curtains drawn, candle on the table, having a drink with my grandfather as he went through the accounts, and all of a sudden there would be a squeak and something furry would run across your foot. You also have to remember, I used to see that place in the daylight. The dust on the wineglasses. The stains on the carpet. And he loved the place, my grandfather, just as I loved it, and just as I loved him, but he never had the resources or the energy to turn things around. You know, it's funny, and I always tell this story, but when we did that big refurb, the big re-launch, all these journalists — from the *Times,* from the *Observer* — did their pieces about their one magical night at the Home Club, the night some jolly raconteur at the bar told them the most wonderful stories all evening about Sir Ralph Richardson or whoever, and what a wonderful slice of the old West End it all was — and I tell you, if they had come in the next night, exactly the same guy would have been telling exactly the same stories to whoever happened to be sitting on that same stool. And every time you tried to do anything to get anyone under eighty in, all the other members would be up in arms about it. And there wasn't a thing you could do with the building, because it was Grade I listed. And every month, on top of all the hours I spent in chambers or in court, I was hanging up my wig and then haggling with suppliers, negotiating with creditors. It was impossible to keep running it the way it had been — we'd have been shuttered within a year, sold off as a London pad to some bloody banker or turned into luxury apartments. It simply was not financially sustainable."

The chambers to which Groom is referring is One Knight's Court, Lincoln's Inn, a private family practice specializing in high-profile divorces where he was a barrister until shortly after the club was left to him, aged twenty-nine.

On the death of his grandfather in 1992, Ned and his younger brother Adam inherited — in unequal shares — the business and title deeds to the building. A long-running family dispute is alleged to have been the reason their father, Richard Groom, was passed over. Some have suggested that this came as rather a shock to Ned's father. There are some who believe it was a shock to Ned too.

"I think we were all a bit surprised, at the time, when he decided to give up the law," says Sebastian Shaw QC, a commercial litigation barrister from Blackwell Row, a neighboring chambers. "He loved the law, and he was bloody good at it too. Bloody good. The number of cases Ned Groom won before he left the bar — celebrities, CEOs, oligarchs — was almost unheard of at his age. Juicy stuff, that — not like the dull contracts most of us deal with," he says, self-deprecatingly. "That memory, that quick wit, that single-mindedness. Anyone who ever got in an argument with the man knows he's like a dog with a bone. Even in those days he was the most tremendous show-off. Loved to be up there in court, the center of attention. They call politics show business for ugly people — well, you can add the professional bar to that too." He chuckles. "I remember a lot of people being completely gob-smacked that he would give all that up to go off and take over what was a pretty dingy and uninspiring sort of place back then."

Ned wasted no time in trying to shake things up. He rewrote the menus, deep-cleaned the dusty old spaces, and shut the guest bedrooms entirely after an outbreak of bedbugs. He approached banks for loans, applied for planning permission to gut and refurbish the old building, the top three floors to be taken up with luxurious suites designed to attract the right sort of clientele. He decided to rename it Home: simple, elegant, modern. He repeatedly clashed with English Heritage, trying to convince them to permit his vision: a twenty-first-century club in a late-eighteenth-century shell. The drinks prices were hiked, monthly fees increased. Existing members struggled to pay and, some felt, were compelled to leave. Every time someone started telling a story about the old days Ned was said to insist the bartender turn the music up a notch.

Then, in the small hours of September 16, 1993, the first news reports began to emerge of a fire in Covent Garden, smoke billowing in great grimy clouds above Bedford Street, which had seemingly started in the Home Club's basement kitchen — a fuse box was later identified as the most likely culprit — but quickly spread to the first, then second, then third floors and prompted the evacuation of much of the street. Over the course of the next few hours, despite the best efforts of several teams of firefighters, it spread to consume the entire building, leaving it a smoldering shell.

There were those who found it a bit

convenient, that fire. There were those —
Private Eye's Piloti among them — who
found Ned's plans for how he intended to
rebuild the club just as horrifying.

There were many who found Ned's at-
titude to the natural and architectural
heritage of Boucher's Island equally van-
dalistic. The Victorian rookery bulldozed.
Acres of woodland cleared for cabins.
Natural habitats destroyed. Noise pollution. Light pollution. And even those who
worked for him found his methods ques-
tionable. A year on from the opening of
Island Home, there are still local contractors — plumbers, builders, electricians —
who claim not to have received payment.
As terrible events on the Island were
unfolding that Sunday, former employees
had begun posting on social media under
the hashtag #HomeTruths about behavior
they'd witnessed or had been subjected
to. The rages. The rants. The bullying. At
least one person, identifying themselves
on Twitter as a former member of the front-
of-house team at Manhattan Home,
claimed that in light of Ned's temper and
the way they had seen him behave, they
had always suspected he was going to
end up killing someone, one of these days.

Then came the news that Ned Groom
had disappeared.

CHAPTER THREE:
FRIDAY MORNING

NIKKI

When she set off, the 6:00 a.m. light was a hazy pink, purple, and gold, like a bruise spreading slowly upward across the sky. This was always her favorite hour, before her phone started pinging and the to-do list gobbled up all her attention. On waking, Nikki — a naturally early riser further conditioned by a boss who averaged four hours' sleep a night — had, as usual, pulled on her running stuff and headed straight out for a brisk circuit of the island's sandy six-mile circumference. Normally this was the hour that set her up to deal with the other twenty-three. Normally — with the wind whistling in her ears, the running trails almost entirely to herself — this was when the shape of the day ahead came into focus for her, the time when, as her feet pounded away below her and the bushes blurred past, her brain began numbering and ordering

127

the tasks ahead, the things that should be avoided or must not be forgotten. This morning, instead of feeling sharper, she still felt foggy and dazed, as if she had sucked in the morning mist and it was now billowing inside her head.

The cabins were illuminated by the warm glow of their porch lights, a look that was intended to be cozy and quaint, but today felt eerie and uninviting, especially with most of them still unoccupied. For the past few weeks, the team had been running the whole operation as if at full capacity to make sure that when guests checked in, Island Home was a well-oiled machine. This time of the morning — when only members who hadn't yet been to bed would be stumbling drunkenly around — was when all the invisible activity happened. The people who made things work — the ant farm of porters and cleaners and maids and prep chefs — crisscrossing the paths. Passing the staff block, she spotted a nervous-looking new recruit hovering at the door — and judging by her lack of apron and the phone in her hand, quite a senior one at that.

"I'm guessing you're Jess — I'm Nikki, Ned's PA. Lovely to meet you. I hear you got drafted in to babysit last night," she said apologetically, still jogging lightly on the spot. "I'm sorry — if I'd known that was Annie's plan, I'd have tried to step in. You must be exhausted."

"Oh, don't worry, I wouldn't have slept well anyway, never do." Jess gave a nervous laugh; then her eyebrows knitted as if she'd said something she shouldn't have. "Sorry, you didn't need to know that."

"I had a terrible night's sleep too, if that's any consolation. Look, if you need anything — have any questions — try to come to me. It's best not to distract Ned or Adam this weekend. The same with Annie — she's got a lot on her plate, so don't worry if you find her a bit brusque and snappy. You can imagine what it's like. I've really only got one person to organize on a weekend like this. Annie's got to run around after hundreds! I don't know how she does it."

Nor do I quite get why she wants to, Nikki added in her head.

Then again, being parachuted in as head of housekeeping on an opening weekend must be pretty terrifying too.

Once upon a time, Nikki might have gently tried to offer Jess a few pointers to help these first few days run a little smoother. Whom to ask about this. Whom to avoid asking about that. She did not tend to bother anymore. After all, in the end, it made no difference really — you either intuited how all of this worked pretty quickly or you were out within the month. Or sooner, if you managed to attract Ned's attention in the wrong way somehow.

"Thank you, I appreciate the offer, that's really kind." Jess smiled. Nikki noticed her hands were shaking from the cold. "But I know what I'm here to do and there's nothing like being thrown in at the deep end. Oh look, here's my lift!" she pointed at the housekeeping van that had just pulled up. "I'm shadowing a couple of my girls this morning — there's so much I still need to find out about this place!"

Sweet girl, thought Nikki, as the van drove away, and mentally wished Jess luck.

She was probably going to last about five minutes.

A bit delayed by the encounter, Nikki sprinted the last hundred meters to Island Home's spa, arriving dripping sweat and hammering on the vast oak door to alert a bleary-eyed therapist to her presence. As a breather before the island became overrun with members, Ned had suggested Nikki take some time off this morning for a spa treatment — she'd selected an IV vitamin drip in the hope it would help power her through the day.

She slipped through to the changing room and undressed, placing her sneakers exactly parallel at the bottom of the locker, folding her damp gym kit into a neat pile on the shelf. After a steaming-hot shower, she slipped into a gray cashmere sweater, ballet pumps, and skinny black jeans. Her close bleach-blond crop — cut short to kill her mousy curls — took approximately six minutes to blow-dry and her face, as always, got just a veil of moisturizer and a slick of mascara. She surveyed her reflection in the mirror, tugging at her jawline and the corners of her eyes, inspecting her skin for signs of her forty-one years and any trace of the girl that had started on the coat check all those years ago. She could find neither.

By 6:30 a.m. Nikki was sunk in an over-stuffed armchair in the spa reception and, just like every morning for as long as she could remember, was scanning on autopilot through Home's new press clippings, an eye out for anything that should be brought to Ned's attention. A lot of what dropped into her in-box each day was just fluff — a fifty-word gossip piece in *People* about who had been seen canoodling with whom by the rooftop pool at Malibu Home. An article in the *Sunday Times*'s *Style* magazine about how the Home design team had lent a touch of casual chic to the knocked-through conglomeration of Grade II-listed historical farm buildings that some rock star and his wife were in the process of turning into their dream home in the Cotswolds. It was amazing how gentle the coverage of the Home Group mostly was — or perhaps not amazing at all, if you considered how many editors were members.

This morning, naturally, there was rather more coverage than usual to sift through, the press salivating over every leaked detail of the opening party — who their sources said was coming (Jackson and Georgia, naturally — they had never skipped a single launch — as well as some people she knew would definitely *not* be on the island; Nikki wondered how many fed their own names to the press, invading their own privacy for a single paragraph in *Heat*). There was also a scattering of details of the island itself, salivating descriptions of the cabins with their enamel Agas, wood burners, sheepskin rugs, roll-top baths, and rain-forest showers accompanied by some grainy photos, presumably leaked by a contractor. This would infuriate Ned since the whole point of Home was that it stayed firmly out of the press — its suites and bars and spas were for members' eyes only — but it wasn't the photos that stopped her in her tracks.

It was the interview Annie Spark had given to the *Evening Standard*'s *ES Magazine*.

"Oh, Annie. Annie, Annie, Annie," Nikki muttered aloud, shaking her head.

If Ned read this, yesterday's explosion was going to look like a polite fart — in fact, Annie would be lucky if he didn't try to throw *her* out of a window. When she had reached the end of the article, Nikki scrolled back to the start and began to read again. Frowning. Wincing. Letting an *uurgh* escape loudly enough to give the white-coated receptionist a start.

"Is everything okay? Can I get you another ginger tea?" she asked.

"I'm fine but actually, yes, that would be lovely, thank you." Nikki smiled.

A simple puff piece, that was all that Ned had signed off on — she'd read the email chain. He was too busy, so could Annie just give them a couple of quotes to tie in with the thirtieth anniversary of his inheriting the Covent Garden club, something to mark the opening of Island Home? Instead here was Annie talking about what *she* thought made an ideal member, about *her* vision for the future of Home. Here was Annie talking about what *she* had planned for the launch weekend, the many surprises *she* had lined up for their guests. Here was Annie completely and utterly overestimating her spot in Home's hierarchy (which was actually very easy to understand: Ned at the top, everyone else underneath), dressed like a Fraggle on a Friday night out, in a series of sequined evening gowns and extravagant fake-fur coats.

Nikki had seen this play out with so many Home employees so many times. People she had liked, whom Ned had loved at first — head bartenders, architects, finance directors — who got comfortable, thought their positions were so secure, their opinions respected enough, to step out of line, say what they really thought even though it clashed directly with Ned's own opinion, or — worse — claim credit for something Ned thought was his own idea. And Ned thought every good idea was his own idea.

It never ended well.

She used to try to warn people she could see getting too big for their boots but it was remarkable how little some people thought of a PA, that it didn't always occur to them she might have insight to offer. The inner circle — she, Annie, Adam — were the only ones who remained after a quarter of a century of this endless conveyor belt.

What was completely baffling about this interview was that Annie had watched the same thing play out on repeat too.

But the article itself wasn't the worst of it.

On the cover of the magazine — the actual cover — there was Annie, standing outside the famous black front door of the original Covent Garden club, the pop of paparazzi flashbulbs reflected in the glossy paint, her head thrown back in laughter.

Its big cover line? HONEY, I'M HOME!

She considered deleting it, but Ned would inevitably find out and it would become her problem. She started typing an email to prime him before his eyes alighted on the piece, stopped, started again. But there was nothing to say that would save the situation. Nikki took a deep breath and hit forward, then set her laptop down on the coffee table in front of her, picking up her mug and cradling it in both hands, looking out the window at the tranquil landscape.

Working for Ned, even when you knew there was going to be a tantrum, you had to get on with your life as if you did not. You simply had to make the most of whatever moments of peace and quiet and restfulness were available to you. This was the perfect setting for that — it was, for one thing, one of the very few places on the island where you could be guaranteed not to bump into Ned. He did not like to sweat or swim; still less was he interested in lying down for long enough to enjoy a hot-stone massage or a healing quartz facial.

A shame really, as it was a beautiful place to be, even for treadmill-phobes. Housed in a U-shaped collection of outbuildings set in a dip in the island, it had a freshwater pond in the center that had been transformed into a heated natural swimming pool that belched clouds of steam into the cold air. The pool was half-covered by a wrought-iron greenhouse from the twenties, repurposed from another part of the island, which dripped with clematis, still flowering in October, with swaying reeds lining the banks and weeping willows trailing their branches into the water. Surrounding the pool, what had formerly been stone barns and corrugated-iron sheds had been transformed into a gym, yoga studio, nail bar, cryotherapy chamber, meditation room, hair salon, and treatment rooms with one-way picture windows perched out on an overwater deck.

"We're ready for you now," the therapist whispered as she ushered Nikki into one, which felt like it was floating out above the pool.

"This shouldn't hurt," she said as she unsheathed the needle from its tube, tapped the inside of Nikki's elbow, and inserted it into her arm. "The infusion will take half an hour, and I'll give you a head and shoulder massage while it does."

Nikki allowed her breathing to slow and focused on the scene outside — the one-way glass protecting the privacy of those being pampered was framed in brass, making the whole scene look like an oil painting. Tomorrow, the pool would be packed with members posing in Lycra and swimming off their hangovers but right now, it was as still as a mirror.

The therapist made awkward conversation about how excited she was for guests to start arriving, asking how dinner had gone last night, if Nikki had been there, expressing her excitement at the news that Jackson Crane — Jackson Crane! — was on the island. Had Nikki met him? What was he really like? Nikki pondered a variety of answers before settling upon an enigmatic smile.

As the cocktail of vitamins flowed into her bloodstream, she started to let her vision slip into an unfocused haze. She hadn't slept well, after dinner. Perhaps it was the rich food so close to bedtime. Perhaps it was the knowledge of how intense this weekend was going to be. But all night she had been thinking about the past, thinking about Ned, thinking terrible, impossible thoughts, feeling as though her brain were just on the cusp of solving a problem, of fitting everything together, and just as she was about to do so, the pieces would scatter or change shape.

Everyone was feeling a little frayed. That was what she had to keep reminding herself. It was just the stress getting to her. Her eyes still half-closed, her lashes clouding her vision, Nikki noticed movement outside.

Kurt Cox had wandered out onto the deck and, unaware that anyone was watching, had stopped, dropped his towel, slipped off his robe, and stepped out of the Home monogrammed sheepskin slippers — to reveal a pair of terrible knee-length Bermuda swimming shorts. Carefully, with his feet, Kurt arranged his discarded slippers so they were precisely aligned. Then he placed his neatly folded towel and robe next to them on a wooden bench.

Nikki allowed herself a gentle smile.

It was then she noticed Kurt's tattoo — just one, unusual for someone of his age in his line of work, in her experience: his parents' initials, RC and MC, in copperplate — on his shoulder blade. Directly underneath it, a large darker patch of skin, which the script wrapped around. The same kind of dark brown patch crept around his left shin.

"Hey, are you okay?" asked the therapist. "Pressure too firm?"

"No, no. Keep going, I'm fine," Nikki answered.

It wasn't the firmness of the massage that had caused her to gasp, or set the tears quivering in her eyes.

JESS

When you had worked in hotels for as long as Jess had, after a while you got used to how thoughtless people could be. How weird. How disgusting. It wasn't designed to give you a rosy view of human nature, witnessing morning after morning the sorts of things some guests thought it was okay to expect somebody else to clean up.

She had never seen anything like this.

It wasn't long after everyone had departed on a yacht trip around the island — the very first official event of the launch-party weekend — that the call had come in, something about an incident in cabin ten.

"An incident?" she had asked.

"You're going to need to come and see this for yourself," they'd told her.

They were not joking.

When she got to cabin ten, two of her team were standing outside on the wooden veranda, next to the stand of upturned pristine navy-blue Wellington boots, looking faintly shell-shocked. One of them — Bex — was a local girl from Littlesea. They had spoken yesterday in the staff room, and Bex had said something about how keen her boyfriend was to get a job here (he was going to keep applying; he worked in the kitchen of the other pub in the village). The other, Ella, was an old Home hand who had spent three years at Highland Home, then a year with the company in London. She'd been one of the girls with a question about changing her work schedule. The closer Jess got, the more upset they looked. Bex was blowing her nose into a little scrap of tissue. Ella was shaking her head, muttering, pacing up and down the deck.

"Everything all right?" she asked.

Neither quite seemed to know how to answer.

One glance inside cabin ten and Jess did not blame them.

The place looked like a crime scene.

"It's okay, guys," Jess told them. "You did the right thing, calling me. We'll sort this out."

Picking her way carefully around the broken glass in the hallway, she made her way toward the living room.

All the bedding was in the bath, completely soaked. The mattress, also sodden, was on the back terrace. Half the antique books that had been on the bookshelf were now in the middle of the floor, shredded; the rest were in the log burner, scorched and ruined. None of the lights came on when you tried the switch. This turned out to be because all the light bulbs were on the bathroom floor, ground to shards and powder.

"My God," she said out loud.

Although the members would likely not realize this, not all of the cabins had been created equal on Island Home. There was a distinct variation not only in their size — number five was about half as large again as the cabin allocated to Kyra and Lyra, with two extra bedrooms and a balcony at least twice the size — but also in the private amenities associated with them. Cabin ten, for instance, had an outdoor fireplace, sunken lounge, and copper bathtub, as well as its own hedge-enclosed rose garden with a private beach at the end of it. It was by some distance, in every respect, the most impressive of all the island's accommodations.

It was no surprise to whom this particular cabin had been allocated for the launch weekend.

Jackson Crane.

There are some people in the world so famous it is quite hard to imagine a time when you did not know who they were. The sort of man who stars in movies rather than acting in them. Jess had not even been born when Jackson Crane had started out, back in the eighties, playing the bad boy in all those teen comedies. Nor had she been old enough in the nineties to watch him in action movies like *Max Velocity,* or playing an eco-conscious superhero in *Captain Aquatic.* Even so, Jess would have been very hard-pressed to recall a time in her life when Jackson Crane's face — on a billboard, on TV, on the front of a magazine, on the side of a bus — would have not prompted a little jolt of recognition. Even in his Captain Aquatic mask or goggles or whatever they were. Even with the dyed blond hair they'd given him in that movie — she could remember the posters for it everywhere, one of those films that somehow imprints itself on your consciousness as a kid without your ever having seen it. One of those faces.

She did wonder what it might feel like to be the owner of a face like that, global public property, to wander about on holiday and suddenly spot your own visage staring back at you from — say — the side of a bus in Istanbul, or a billboard in Dubai, or painted wonkily on the side of some fairground ride in Prague. Your actual face. To know that all around the world people were measuring their lives against yours, fantasizing about you, imagining what you or some character you played twenty years ago would think of a life decision they were considering making, asking: What would Jackson Crane do? To wander around the corridors of a hotel in Tokyo in search of your room and bump into yourself illuminated on the front of a machine selling little cans of iced coffee. To think about the number of times that a GIF of you shrugging in character had been tweeted in a single day. To smile good-naturedly on some — Irish? Belgian? Italian? — talk show as the host produced from behind the couch a boxed plastic toy figure of you in one of your action roles, and joked about the thickness of the neck, the absurdity of the torso they'd given you, your unremovable plastic pants, and then asked you what you thought the figure was going to say when they pressed the button on its back. To nod along, come-to-bed eyes crinkled in mirth, as you must have done at least a hundred times before, as someone like Freddie Hunter expressed their amusement at the fact that the character you played in *Max Velocity* was literally called Max Velocity.

Just the practicalities of being that famous, the impossibility of turning it off, all the normal everyday things — an uninterrupted meal in a restaurant, say; dropping off your dry cleaning or going to the dentist — you would never be able to do again. The fact that you could not get away with anything, ever, unless you were somewhere like Home. It must be quite the headfuck, she imagined, after a little while. Jackson Crane had been a star of that magnitude now for almost thirty years. He must feel a little like that boxed plastic toy at times.

That did not give him the right to behave however he liked.

An hour — that was how long her team had scheduled to clean up the occupied cabins, how long before the yacht where the guests were all currently sipping champagne would arrive at the jetty.

It would take an hour even to work out

144

where to start with cabin ten.

The scatter cushions were in the shower, spewing their feathery contents all over the tiles. Every pane of the Crittall shower screen was cracked or shattered. The lid was off the toilet. The big TV on the wall over the fireplace in the sitting room of the cabin was hanging by one wire from its bracket. It looked as if somebody had jumped on the radio, then stomped on the TV remote, then kicked in the coffee machine. Wherever the wiring was accessible, it had been pulled out, pulled down, left hanging. The iron chandelier was no longer attached to its overhead beam. You could see from a dent in the wall where the crystal bedside lamp had been thrown at it and had shattered. Every glass in the drinks cabinet, every bottle, had been smashed on the floor. There were red-wine stains, spatter marks, across the ceiling. At least she hoped it was red wine. It was as if Jackson Crane had come in the night before and set out, deliberately, systematically, and presumably single-handedly, to dismantle his entire cabin.

On the floor, next to a torn envelope, was a crumpled letter printed on Home notepaper. Jess stooped to pick both up, turning the letter over as she did so to see if it was important. Jesus, she thought. The letter was from the Home Group, welcoming him to some new exclusive level of top-tier global membership. At the bottom of the letter it said, in much smaller print, how much it was going to cost, annually, in perpetuity.

No wonder Jackson Crane was upset.

If she had received an invoice on that scale, she would probably have been quite tempted to start smashing things up herself.

Jess stooped to feel if a darkened patch of carpet by the drinks cabinet was stained or just damp. And then she noticed the memory stick.

ADAM

I can't do this anymore, Adam thought to himself, looking out from the yacht's prow across the choppy water. I just can't do it.

It had been almost eleven by the time the police had left the Causeway Inn, past midnight before he got back to the island, almost one by the time he got to bed, another hour and a half — brain churning over the events of the day, body unable to find any position it was comfortable in for more than three minutes at a time — before he finally managed to get to sleep.

They had been fucking lucky that brick had not hit anybody. He had been fucking

146

lucky it had not hit him. The thing had come straight through the window, right next to where Adam was standing, pretty much where his head would have been if he had taken a step back. Three times along the table it had bounced, smashing glasses, before coming to rest at the feet of a startled old lady in a green tweed jacket.

Then all at once everyone in the room seemed to be screaming or shouting or cowering on the floor or pushing forward to see what had happened.

From outside, from the lane on the other side of the wall that ran the length of the inn's garden, Adam could hear laughter, footsteps, a starting engine, a motorbike speeding off.

For some reason one of the men in the front row was staring at him, furious, as if this were something Adam himself had planned.

One of the women in the second row was holding up the sliver of glass she had just found embedded in the lapel of her coat.

Probably teenagers, the police said, when they eventually turned up. Young people often went down to the quay, to drink and smoke, via that lane, Adam was informed. The police would of course investigate whether CCTV had captured anything or if

147

there had been witnesses to the incident.

"Teenagers?" Adam had said. "Seriously?"

The police officers — there were two of them, one with very neatly trimmed stubble, one with blond hair tucked back in a bun, both pretty fresh-faced themselves — asked whether he could think of anyone who might dislike or resent Home's presence in the village or have a grudge against him or his brother.

"How long have you got?" he had replied.

Quite apart from all the disgruntled Little-sea locals, there were plenty of people Ned had hired and fired in the area, plenty of others he had refused to hire. Electricians, carpenters, plumbers, gardeners, scaffolders, roofers, you name it really. Their head of housekeeping, fired for asking for a day off the week of the launch — to attend her sister's funeral, it had come out during the row that followed, although of course even then Ned had not backed down. It was no wonder, really, that Island Home was opening far later than expected, or that it had gone over budget by so much. Adam had more than once tried to calculate how much it must have cost the company in total, Ned's perfectionism, Ned's unpredictability. There had been plenty of times he had been tempted to lob a chunk of masonry at his brother himself.

The brick had been wrapped in one of those photocopied signs some of the people in the village had in their windows, the ones that said HOME GO HOME, secured with elastic bands. Unsure if he should be handling it, unsure if it constituted evidence, Adam had nevertheless stooped to pick it up between a thumb and a forefinger before he noticed the thick brown smear next to the brick on the rug, another smear of a similar brown substance right across the flyer itself.

That was the bit of the story Ned kept insisting he repeat to people. To Annie. To Nikki. To every member of Home staff they'd bumped into all morning, in fact.

"Only Adam," Ned kept saying, struggling almost to get the words out, he was wheezing so hard with laughter, jabbing with a finger in Adam's direction. "Only my brother would actually pick up a shitty brick."

And of course they had all laughed along, Annie, Nikki, their waiter at breakfast, even if there wasn't actually a joke there, the way there would have been had he picked up a literal hot potato or the wrong end of an actual stick, even if half the staff Ned insisted he repeat the story to had never actually spoken to Adam before.

It was all part of the pattern, of course, a pattern that had gradually established itself over time.

And he deserved it, a little ribbing. Sometimes he had drunk too much at dinner, or lunch, been hungover in a morning meeting, said something stupid, done something stupid, nodded off. The thing with Ned was he never let you forget it. Never let *you* forget it, and never let anyone else forget it either. You were expected to simply sit there, nod, smile, take it. And somehow, somewhere along the line, without really noticing, he had gone from being a person to being a running joke. Somewhere along the line he had got so used to being shouted at and blamed for everything, called names, told he was useless, had got so used to just sitting there while other people were informed of his uselessness, that he barely noticed it, most of the time.

And then occasionally, the way some comment landed, the mood he was in that day, he really did mind. And minding about that comment meant he suddenly also minded about all the other comments, over the years, all at once. Or it could be days later, or even weeks later, and suddenly he would remember some snide remark, and he would suddenly be able to hear his breath whistling in his flared nostrils, suddenly feel himself gripped with real anger.

And the point Laura would always remind him of, when he had one of those moments, when he started brooding and frowning and snapping at her, was that he did not have to put up with it. He did not have to confront Ned; he did not need to lose his temper or start a fight. All Adam needed to do was calmly tell Ned what he had decided and make it clear this was serious.

I know it's scary, Laura had texted him that morning. *But I trust you and I know you can do it.*

He hadn't texted back. There was no point, not until he'd done what he'd promised. He knew Laura. They had been married a long time. She'd made herself absolutely clear on the phone the day before. She loved him. She would always love him. She believed in him. But what she was not able to do was to stick around and watch him destroy himself, to stay in this marriage and watch him making himself so unhappy. Just like the clients she coached, she said, once he had taken the decision to make a change, she could help him. Every inch of the way, she would be there to help him. But Adam had to take this first step alone.

It *was* scary. All his life, everywhere he went, he had always been Ned Groom's little brother. At school, where the first question every teacher asked him, year after year, the first time they took the register, was whether he was any relation. As a teenager, when he started noticing the way people's manner immediately shifted once they knew who he was — or rather whose little brother he was. It was hard to convey, to someone who had not been there, to Laura, just how big a deal Ned had been, even while they were growing up. His brother had always been magnetic, one of those people everyone seemed to know, everyone wanted to know. Not just at school. Every party Adam went to, someone would recognize his brother in him. Get on a bus and the driver would give him some message to pass on to Ned. The guy in the corner shop would ask how his brother was doing. Wherever he went, whomever he spoke to, Ned seemed to find a way of connecting with people, remembering something about them, leaving an impression.

Adam had probably been about twelve when someone had first asked him if it was weird for him, all that.

His answer had been: "I dunno really."

It was not just that his life would have

152

been different, if he had not been Ned's brother. *He* would have been different. Ever since he was a child, it had partly been Ned's eyes and ears he had been looking through and listening to the world with. Ned didn't like the taste of carrots? Adam wasn't going to eat them either. Ned hated swimming? For years, Adam had refused to learn too. He had absolutely idolized Ned, as a teenager. He could still recall how it used to thrill him when someone commented on how much he looked like his brother — more of a compliment then than it would be now. When Ned had gone off to study law at university, Adam had literally moved into his bedroom, started wearing his clothes. With music, books, even people, Ned's taste was his touchstone, Ned's imagined opinion the one he found himself triangulating his own against. Perhaps that was one of the reasons he had proved so consistently useful to his big brother, that ability to anticipate what Ned would think about something, what was going to excite or annoy him, how he was likely to react.

One of the things he had looked forward to most, going away to university, was not the chance to reinvent himself, but to meet people who would not realize quite how many of his mannerisms and interests and even turns of phrase were borrowed from someone else.

This was the sort of thing he had not really discussed with anyone, before he met Laura.

That his wife and his brother did not get on better had always pained him. The problem was, he supposed, that they both had very different perceptions of who Adam was, of what he could be, of what he was capable.

Adam was pretty sure he knew how Ned was going to react to the news that he was leaving. As for the idea that he wanted Ned to buy him out so he could be free of the place entirely? This was the part of the conversation Adam had been dreading. He was one of the few who knew how the whole operation functioned, because he was one of the few who had been with Ned right from the start. Extracting his share would be like unmaking an omelet.

The main thing was to choose his moment.

Kicking off Friday with a leisurely sail around the island on a 1930s motor yacht, bought and restored at astonishing expense, had always been part of Ned's plan for this weekend. It was an unrivaled opportunity to show off the size of the place, to underline the scale of what he had achieved. There was the old water tower, at the top of which was now an Italian restaurant, Torre dell'acqua. There was the little bay on the sheltered side of the island that, come summer, you'd be able to paddleboard around. There was the private jetty near the Manor, reserved for Ned himself.

It felt like as good an opportunity as he would have, this weekend, to get Ned on his own.

Nor would Adam ever be likely to catch Ned in a better mood.

"We did it," he kept muttering to Adam, every time they were the only people in earshot. "We actually fucking did it."

And for a moment it would feel like they were a team again, as it had in the old days.

"What do you reckon to my island?" he kept asking people, as he and Adam circulated. "Not bad, eh?"

His boat. His island. His party. Slapping backs, cracking jokes, exchanging nods of recognition across the room, scoffing canapés by the handful, the center of attention — this was Ned Groom in his element, at his happiest. Triumphant, that was probably the best word to describe his brother at that moment.

Then Ned checked his email.

It seemed to be going well, so far.

After they had all been ferried over on speedboats from the Causeway Inn, and been checked in at the Boathouse, Annie had welcomed the weekend's new arrivals up the gangplank and onto Island Home's very own yacht. As for the guests already on the island — Jackson and Georgia, Freddie and Keith, Kurt, Kyra and her daughter Lyra — Ned had insisted on riding along personally in the golf cart that had collected them from their cabins, just in case they tried to wriggle out of this cruise.

It had taken them about forty-five minutes to circle the island the first time. They were due to do so twice more before they all disembarked for lunch.

As guests mingled, chatted, tried to work out who was here and who was not, Annie had been circling the wraparound terrace making introductions, dropping in, as she always did, the flattering snippets of information she'd spent weeks researching and memorizing about every single guest ("You must meet Alicia — did you know this *angelic human* has just got back from a humanitarian mission in Syria?" or "Johnny, I hear you are ninety-five percent plant-based now — and positively glowing, if you don't mind me saying!").

They took themselves, their own celebrity, very seriously, Home's members, and they expected everyone around them to do the same. That was something you needed to remember. After all, these were people who, straight-faced, spent whole months in front of a green screen pretending to fight aliens. Thirty-year-old multimillionaires who sang to crowds of thousands love songs they'd written in their teenage bedrooms. And maybe you did need to believe in yourself, for all of this to happen, for other people to buy into you too.

From where she was now standing, leaning against the railing of the yacht's top deck, Annie — champagne coupe in hand, dressed in a diaphanous leopard-print caftan with a gem-encrusted neckline (thermal vest and leggings underneath, of course) — could look down and, in a single glance, take in pretty much the entire party.

Jake Price, an extravagantly eyebrowed, absurdly muscled actor with thick dark hair scraped back into a long plait — no doubt grown for his role as a bloodthirsty Viking in the HBO series he'd just started shooting — had already made the entire party audibly gasp by disrobing to reveal a tiny pair of pale pink Speedos, then executing a perfect twisting dive into the sea. There were barely concealed sniggers when, after floundering in the waves for a few minutes, he started shouting for assistance and was hauled back onto the boat, goose-pimpled and visibly shriveled, and handed a Home-branded bathrobe. Annie could hear the captain, standing a few feet away from her, muttering under his breath. "Action hero idiot — that undertow will drag you down in a second!"

The waiters ignored the drama as Annie had trained them to do, circulating with their trays, ever discreet, ever watchful for anyone trying to catch their attention. Casting her eyes around, all she could see were familiar faces, some catching sight of her and smiling, waving. Any direction you looked, members, probably fifty in total now, were checking — while trying not to look as if they were checking — who else had been invited, who that was over there.

"Champagne?" Annie gave a start as a waitress appeared behind her holding a bottle, its neck tightly wrapped in a crisp linen napkin.

"Thank you, darling girl, good work noticing me up here. Gold star for you," she smiled, proffering her glass. The girl tipped the bottle, her face falling as she and Annie watched the liquid dribble into the glass, refilling it by barely half an inch. Annie raised an eyebrow.

"Well that's not very good now, is it, sweetheart?" she said spikily. "Have we taught you nothing? Never ever pour from a practically empty bottle. Do these look like the sort of people who like to drink dregs?" Annie gestured down to the party. "Get someone who actually knows what they're doing to bring up another bottle, please. I think you should stay below deck and polish the glasses now, don't you?"

Harsh? Maybe a little. But Annie's *entire job* was making sure every member interaction was faultless, and it was something Ned trusted her implicitly with. Members had to feel as though their monthly fees bought them something special or else Home was just a fancy pub you paid to get into. In other words: she was a dick so the members didn't have to be.

With a deliberately audible sigh, Annie turned back to the balcony.

A neat visual illustration of Home's hierarchy, that's what she got from this vantage point. Observing who made a beeline for whom, noting who stood still and expected others to orbit around them. Watching who held forth, loudly and at length, about their latest philanthropic project without noticing eyes slowly glaze around them — it had been half an hour now, and Georgia Crane, waving her slender, manicured hands for emphasis, had barely drawn breath.

Seeing the members that hovered on the periphery of a group, shifting awkwardly from foot to foot and laughing a little too loudly (Freddie Hunter a major offender in this regard). Knowing that they all consumed the same media as the rest of the world and understanding the awkwardness around that — congratulate Jennifer on the engagement reported by BuzzFeed or Monica on her pregnancy leaked to the *Times,* or piously pretend not to read the papers? That was a dance Annie had to do herself. She could feel their excitement, understand their anxiety; she realized, from years of observation, that being famous yourself did not inoculate you against others' celebrity.

She did not like that word really. *Celebrity.* It irked her when people described Home as a club for celebrities, their events as celebrity parties. That interviewer from *ES Magazine* had used it repeatedly, and Annie had winced a little, internally, every time. It had been strange, that whole experience — she was not used to being the one asked the questions. She had corrected him on that point — she preferred to think of their members as *celebrated people.* Annie had read once, back in her journalist days, that was what it had meant, originally. Back in the nineteenth century, *celebrity* was simply used to describe someone recognized in their field. Charles Darwin was a celebrity; Florence Nightingale was a celebrity; George Eliot, just as much as an actress like Ellen Terry or an actor like Henry Home. It was only quite late in the twentieth century that the word had begun to take on negative connotations, to carry a suggestion of superficiality, to be associated increasingly with undeserved fame, someone to whom society paid unwarranted attention. All of which happened at exactly the same time as the word began increasingly to be used to describe young women in the public eye. Well I never, Annie had thought. What a coincidence.

Celebrity was not the word people used to describe Jackson Crane ever, was it? Look at him, Annie thought, smiling and waving and raising his eyebrow, holding court, looking as though he were lit by a slightly kinder cinematographer than everyone else. He was a *movie star.* Nor, interestingly, was *celebrity* a word people used much to talk about his wife. Was that perhaps partly due to her age

— she must be in her early forties now, although still a good decade younger than her husband. Was it — no interview failed to open with it — where she had gone to university? *Cambridge-educated actress and activist.* Or was it her specific type of beauty — her dark hair, sharp cheekbones, her striking green eyes, the kind of looks that saw her continually cast in films set during the war or as some poet's muse. The sort of elegantly, effortlessly expensive looks that someone like Annie — the same age, also tall, also naturally dark-haired — would never have the time, or money, or self-control, or access to the right people with the right needles, to maintain.

Celebrity was, however, the word people used to describe Kyra Highway — currently playing some version of hopscotch with her daughter, both of them doubled up in laughter, on the painted lines at the far end of the main deck, meant for passengers who wished to play shuffleboard. *Celebrity artist,* people called Keith Little, currently stretched out pouting on a striped daybed, sunglasses on, shirt open to his mahogany six-pack as usual, something silver glinting in his chest hair, making quite a show of observing everybody — but that too carried with it a strong hint of disapproval, didn't it? That he was a little *too* famous, and that he enjoyed his fame a bit too much.

He didn't look as though he were enjoying it very much this morning. Every time a waiter came near him, he would give them a scowl, flap them away with his hand if they got too close.

It was a key part of Ned's plan, to keep them all in suspense like this. To stagger the next stage, postpone the second turn of the screw, keep them at a disadvantage. After all, he couldn't have all four men blowing up at once, spoiling the party. From the looks of things, Keith was currently somewhere between taking the whole thing as a weird, off-color joke and convincing himself he would not pay Home an extra penny, and worrying a bit more seriously about what it was, this mysterious soon-to-be delivered package that would ensure Ned's was an offer he should not, could not, refuse.

It was clear just from looking that Freddie Hunter had not received his package yet. He seemed to be everywhere at this party — clowning around with little Lyra, letting out a cry of delight every time he ran into anyone he knew, which was constantly, making a beeline for people who had not been on his show yet to schmooze them, ensuring everybody there knew he was at the party too. Admittedly he did seem a bit more manic than usual, a little bit pale and sweaty — but the night before had been a late one and he'd been knocking back the drink. Maybe, with a bit of time to process it, he'd come to the conclusion that the whole thing was a wind-up.

Yes, Annie thought, it was safe to say that Freddie Hunter had not received his package yet.

As for Jackson Crane, it was impossible to tell.

Jackson was, after all, an actor — and not just any actor. Annie had once shared an elevator with Jackson and Georgia at Manhattan Home, all the way from the lobby to the rooftop bar, and the whole way up they had been tearing chunks out of each other. He stank of booze. She was a nagging bitch. On and on it went. At one point, Georgia had hit him right across the face with her clutch bag; he gingerly touched his lip with a forefinger, inspected it in the mirror on the wall, and looked as if he were considering whether to retaliate. It was as though they had forgotten Annie was even there — or perhaps that was the point, and all of this was part of some kind of performance too. And then the doors had opened and,

164

without missing a beat, Jackson had slipped his hand into Georgia's and out they had walked, all smiles, to join their friends for dinner.

It was Kurt Cox, currently standing alone near the bow of the boat, she felt most sorry for. Still, he was a twenty-five-year-old man with a multimillion-dollar Netflix production deal and an inheritance coming that would surely dwarf even that. He was not going to starve, no matter how much Ned squeezed him for. He would kick up a fuss, and go through all the usual phases, and then — like all the others — he would accept the inevitable.

Yes, it seemed to be going well.

And then she stepped inside to rejoin the throng. This deck of the yacht, the third and highest, was connected to the one below by an open-sided spiral staircase, and from the top looking down, she could see Ned and Adam, deep in conversation, Ned showing Adam something on his phone, Adam looking serious. She was tempted, for a second, to call down something silly, do something to startle them. Ned loved those little jokes.

Then she saw Ned's face.

Then she saw on his iPhone screen what he was showing Adam.

"Who the fuck does she think she is? I'm

165

Home? *I AM Home?* I'll tell you what she is. She's done. She's fucking done. Come the end of this weekend, come the end of this party, Annie Spark is fucking history at this company . . ."

CONTINUED FROM PAGE 79
It was former journalist and Home's long-serving head of membership Annie Spark — something of a celebrity herself among Home's regular clientele, with her flamboyant dress sense and constant changes of hair color (sea-green one week, peroxide-white the next) — who first raised the alarm that Ned Groom was missing, on Sunday morning. "She started asking all of us when we had last spoken to him, or heard from him, and no one could pinpoint it. And you always remember an interaction with Ned," says one former Island Home waiter, who has requested to remain anonymous. "We were all trying to work out what that meant and what was going on. But she was so completely calm that nobody panicked. Before that, I hadn't taken her seriously, because of the outfits probably, the air-kissing, but she really

stepped up. Someone had to — it was chaos. It wasn't just people on the island going crazy, we had calls coming in from the media, from all the other Homes. It was Annie who told us what to say, what not to say, who to hang up on, who to pass on to her. She was completely unflappable — it was like nothing that day could surprise her."

In fact, Annie's measured response is one thing on which everyone who experienced the panic and confusion of that Sunday on Island Home seems to agree. Freddie Hunter even went as far as thanking Annie personally in the solemn monologue he delivered at the start of his first *Freddie Hunter Show* after the tragedy.

"At first, in the underwater restaurant, none of the staff seemed to know what was happening, if there had been a security breach on the island, if we were all in danger. Bear in mind, most of us normally have a security detail, but that's never been the vibe at Home — you leave your bodyguard at the door along with your phone," recalls one party guest. "When the police turned up, they didn't seem to know quite who to speak to or what to do. But Annie was telling everyone where to go, explaining what had happened and was going to happen next, reassuring members that we were safe, that we would be escorted back to the mainland safely and soon."

It was not until every guest was off the island — a full thirty-six hours after the last confirmed sighting of him — that police began their full-scale search for Ned Groom. By that time it was established that if he had left Island Home, there were no witnesses who had seen him do so. He did not appear on CCTV at any time, in any kind of vehicle, leaving via the causeway. No unidentified boats had been seen approaching or leaving the shore. It appeared that his mobile had been switched off at some point early Saturday morning. Under the circumstances, it was clear his vanishing had to be treated as suspicious.

It takes a lot of time and a lot of people to search a 380-acre island, even with the assistance of local volunteers, and those Home staff who had chosen to remain, including Annie Spark herself. Days of tramping through the woods in the drizzle, traversing sodden fields. Of inspecting cabins, and peering under them. It was the wilder, more inaccessible part of the island, where Ned's private cottage was located — the side that had been rented

for decades by the Ministry of Defence —
that the police decided should be the focus
of their search efforts. The police officers
and volunteers had all been shown a
photograph of Ned, been issued a description of what he had been wearing when
last seen — a white shirt, blue trousers,
Gucci loafers, his uniform of sorts. They
had been told what make and model his
phone was. They had been reminded, if
they did find something, not to do anything
that might disrupt or contaminate a potential crime scene.

They searched in the driving rain, with
the biting wind whipping off the water.
They trekked through glades of soaked
ferns. They poked around in bramble-
clogged ditches. They tramped, heads
down, along wet pebble beaches. They
scrambled down wooded slopes, climbed
up muddy banks, slipping and sliding and
swearing. They searched all morning, they
searched all afternoon, even as the sky
grew dark, they continued to search, by
flashlight.

They found absolutely nothing.

CHAPTER FOUR:
FRIDAY AFTERNOON

ANNIE

"A few more bottles of that Vermentino!"
Ned barked at the waiter, with a side glance
at the empty glass in front of Jackson Crane.
"So what do you think of the island so far,
Georgia? I know it's October but if you
squint on a sunny afternoon like this I
reckon we could all be in the Med."

Annie did not catch the reply. She was sitting at the far end of the table, next to
Nikki, and Georgia Crane spoke quietly at
the best of times.

"And what do *you* think, Freddie?" Ned
asked.

Freddie, who had been halfway through
demonstrating to Lyra Highway some kind
of magic trick involving a glass and a
napkin, jumped a little in his seat.

"It sure is a pretty amazing view from up
here, Ned."

Jackson muttered something to which no

one at that end of the table responded.

The view *was* wonderful, from fifty feet up in the air, looking out from one of the highest points on the island, nothing to impede it in any direction. You really did get a sense of its size and shape — an elongated diamond with the still partly submerged causeway snaking from its tip — how much wilder and more closely wooded it got at one end, where Ned's cottage was, how much flatter and lower and more sheltered the other side was, the network of cycle tracks and running paths that cross-hatched the island, the relative locations of the spa and the log-cabin screening room and various restaurants, how exactly the Manor with its formal lawns and rose garden sat proudly at the center of things. The Mediterranean? Maybe not. But it was certainly some kind of achievement.

Perhaps most impressive of all was that almost everything on Island Home — apart from the slightly absurd neo-Palladian splendor of the Manor itself, its soaring portico and campy columns — had been either built from scratch or repurposed from corrugated sheds and tumbledown barns. This particular, inexplicably Grade II–listed, carbuncle of a water tower had been the design team's biggest headache, plans for what it would house shifting right up until the eleventh hour. First, it had been earmarked as a SoulCycle, then a climbing wall, then a spa suite complete with high-rise hot tub. They eventually settled on an industrial-chic terrace restaurant, with a wood-fired oven, accessed by an elevator that ran through the tower's core.

And then Ned had announced he wanted the whole thing to rotate, which was the absolute final straw for the fourth of the seven architects to have been involved in the project. It was ridiculous, he had told them. Impossible. Somehow, though, with a lot of head-scratching and even more money (not to mention a new architect), Ned got his way.

As the restaurant started to slowly turn, there was a soft coo from the diners around the room, little Lyra jumping up and down, some measured clapping, one whoop. The sea breeze was scented with the oak burning in the oven and the garlic from platters piled high with lobsters and langoustines. Jackson Crane, ignoring the food and already one more glass of wine down, for a moment seemed so disconcerted by the room having started to gently spin that he reached out to steady himself with both hands on the reclaimed driftwood table in front of him.

Annie knew that feeling. She was quite tempted to get a few stiff drinks inside her too. She fiddled with the fluorescent gems on her caftan's neckline, wishing that these launch events had not become her own personal Met Gala, everyone asking for months in advance what she would be wearing, reminiscing about outfits past. If only she could get away with the chic navy turtleneck dress that Nikki, as usual, was looking elfin and effortless in.

Apart from anything else — despite the thermals — Annie was fucking freezing. She ran a manicured hand over the soft ridges of the cable-knit blanket on her lap, identical to the monogrammed ones she'd placed on each member's chair, a place setting you could cuddle up in. It might look pretty at this time of year, the island, and it might still be just warm enough to get away without a coat in the sun, but once you were in the shade . . .

Which was pretty much a metaphor for how it was going, this weekend.

It was not just what Ned had said, on the boat, it was the way he'd said it. Spat it. Hissed it. Meant it. *Annie Spark is fucking history at this company.* For what? For an interview in which she had dared to suggest there might be more to Home than one fifty-nine-year-old man and his singular vision?

Throughout the rest of the yacht tour and on the trip up here to the restaurant, Ned had been ignoring her, apart from the eye roll he had aimed at her dress as she was climbing out of the golf cart, and the snort he gave when she was having trouble with her heels on the gravel as they were waiting for the elevator.

"Annie, Ned's trying to catch your attention." Nikki nudged her, gesturing toward him. "I think Jackson might need some . . . assistance over there."

For Nikki's benefit, Annie flashed a forced smile at Ned.

"I'll see what I can do to get Jackson out of here once everyone's eaten. He'll just make a scene if I try now, the state he's in." Annie beckoned the waiter over. "Pour slowly, okay?" she whispered to him, with a subtle nod in the extravagantly inebriated actor's direction.

Then she turned to face Nikki fully.

"You sent it to him, didn't you? That article. Flagged it up for his attention."

"I had to, Annie. It's literally my job to keep him in the loop. You must have known he'd see it this weekend. I mean, talk about a guaranteed way to wind Ned up . . . taking credit for his entire island in a magazine cover story? *Your* launch party? *Your* members? 'Honey, *I'm* Home?' What on earth were you thinking?"

What *had* she been thinking? Probably, in retrospect, that it was nice to be asked her opinion for once. On what she thought made Home so special. About how it was to work there and what she actually did all day. The delicate diplomacy of it all, the power dynamics, the practicalities. The things she had thoughtfully, painstakingly, planned for this weekend. She had not set out to boast. Annie had worked at Home long enough to understand that getting too big for your size sixes was a sackable offense. She felt stupid and ashamed for slipping up so badly, especially as someone who started her career posing the leading questions for exactly the same magazines. But it was the first time in a long time — ever, perhaps — that someone had asked a question and *listened to her answer.*

"You want to know why I told the journalist what my literal, day-to-day job is, Nikki? How hard I work? So hard that I haven't had a boyfriend in a decade because I'm married to oh, at the last count, five thousand, seven hundred and sixty-one paying

Home members? How vital my being on call, seven days a week, twenty-four hours a day, is to the basic functioning of this business? This business that pays your wages too? How, if I did not know the things I know, remember the things I remember, about all of these people," she shout-whispered, gesturing around the room, "the entire operation would have ground to a halt long ago? Just so I understand, you're asking why I told the *Evening Standard* that I am actually slightly more to Home than an overpromoted coat-check girl?"

She watched Nikki recoil and instantly realized she'd gone too far.

"Nobody thinks you're not important, Annie," Nikki said quietly, not meeting her eye. "But he's not going to let this go."

In some respects it was a mistake, as a woman especially, to be really efficient over a long period of time. Because if you made things seem easy, and people had no experience of things not running smoothly, it came to seem that anybody could do it. Especially if you were also as gregarious as Annie was, if your laugh was a boisterous shriek (it was helpful if whenever anyone needed her, they could hear her across a room — and someone always needed her, for something) and if you dressed for maxi-

177

mum impact (so you were similarly easy to spot — although in some ways the elaborate almost-costumes were also a cloak of invisibility, allowing the woman she really was to disappear under sequins and silly shoes).

When she thought of all she had sacrificed. When she thought of the stories she could tell. Except she could not tell any of those stories, and Ned knew that, and it was not just because of the legally binding agreement she had signed all those years ago.

It was just as her mind wandered to Jackson Crane that she heard a shout at the far end of the table, Jackson throwing his napkin onto his plate, waving a finger in Ned's face; Keith Little eye-rolling over his Aperol Spritz; Lyra huddling into Kyra; Freddie and Georgia and Adam all trying to placate Jackson, persuade him to sit down again. Other members at neighboring tables trying not to stare but desperate to see.

Jackson would not sit down again. He was not going to calm down. Georgia whispered something in his ear — he announced he did not give a *fuck* if people were staring.

Had Ned just glanced down to Annie's end of the table again, to see what she was going to do to sort this out, how she was going to sweep in and smooth the situation over? Well, forget it. What was the point?

Annie was history. She had heard the steel in those words. She had seen Ned's face. This was not the kind of thing about which he changed his mind. You can handle this one, boys, she thought.

Christ, Jackson was drunk, though. The eyes were gone. His balance was all over the place. Admittedly being in a revolving restaurant did not help.

In turning to go, brushing Georgia's hand from his arm as he did so, Jackson managed to catch the end of his shoe on his chair and send the latter screeching across the floor, then shin-barge the same chair across the Moorish-patterned encaustic tiles again as he stormed off in the direction of the elevator. Or what he took to be the direction of the elevator. Two or three times he did the circuit of the water tower's central shaft, muttering to himself, bumping into the backs of other people's chairs, actors and directors he'd worked with, all the while scowling and glaring, while the restaurant continued to turn. Even after he found the elevator doors, he could not find the buttons. There were no buttons. The elevator had a sensor and came automatically. Once inside, he stood there for several minutes, swaying, as the whole restaurant revolved past, before he realized there *was* a button you had to push to close the doors and go down.

Annie checked the time. It was two fifteen in the afternoon.

At least she now knew which of last night's diners had been the first to receive their package.

JESS

Three hours, it had taken them. By "them" Jess meant not just herself and her team — although Bex and Ella had both been incredible, totally unfazed, even cracking jokes once the initial shock of seeing the smashed-up cabin had worn off — but the squad of handymen in their Home-branded blue boiler suits and baseball caps in a Home-branded blue van who got to work on replacing all the broken glass in the cabin. The similarly clad guys — she could not even remember calling them — with three new TVs of varying sizes who immediately set about installing them on the walls. The team with a pickup truck full of furniture who started dragging out and replacing everything that was unfixable, the guy who had driven over in a Land Rover with a new set of identical, unsoiled curtains. It was amazing. It was all so practiced; it was like watching ballet. The speed, the efficiency, the lack of fuss, the level of preparedness. The striking absence of chit-chat. You would have thought one of the guys would at least have asked them whose room it was, or if anyone knew what had happened. It made you wonder how often things like this did happen, at Home.

Would Jackson Crane be as impressed by it all as she was? If you stood in the doorway of the cabin — she had sent the girls off to get lunch, told them she would follow after one last check of everything — it genuinely looked as if someone had waved a magic wand and returned things to exactly the way they had been before he'd gone on his rampage. Even the book on his bedside table — the original she had found floating spineless in the Jacuzzi — had been re-placed. When he saw that, when he imagined how much effort and time on the part of multiple people must have gone into doing that, on an island, in three hours, would he feel embarrassed, regretful, a little sheepish? Somehow Jess doubted it.

Obviously when you were as rich and suc-cessful as Jackson Crane, this was just the way things went in life. Someone else always there to make sure you had whatever you wanted within reach, the instant you needed it. Someone else always there to tidy up your mess.

The last three hours had not been simply a matter of returning the room to its factory settings, so to speak. Just as with every other guest on the island, Jackson Crane's Home records contained detailed instructions on how a room was to be prepared for his arrival. For every member there were notes specifying their preferred ambient air temperature, their favorite flower, their preferred brand of soap and shampoo and moisturizer and hand sanitizer. All their requirements, all their requests, everything from scented candles to blackout blinds, salt lamps to charged crystals (whatever they were). Some of these lists went on for pages.

Jackson's and Georgia Crane's had been the very first Jess had read.

The note on Jackson Crane's specified that any room in which he was staying was always to be provided with one bottle of Midleton Very Rare Irish whiskey, decanted into heavy crystal; one bottle of Rhum Clément; two bottles of Dom Pérignon Vintage 2008; a half dozen Diet Cokes. It also noted that the room should be kept at a temperature of thirteen degrees Celsius at all times, that his pillow should be rock-hard, that there should be a copy of *The Catcher in the*

Rye on the bedside table, and that unless he had issued specific instructions to the contrary, he was under no circumstances ever to be disturbed.

According to Georgia's notes, she liked a medium-strength massage, hated flowers in her room (the pollen), and required there to be twelve large bottles of Tasmanian Rain mineral water in her fridge at all times. A weighted cashmere face mask was to be left on the dresser, her pillowcases made of silk. Three sets of size-two Lululemon workout gear were to be left in her wardrobe, along with a cushioned yoga mat. The notes also specified that she was always to be given separate accommodation from her husband — and that she was never to be asked about his whereabouts.

Jess had been expecting that.

Working at the Grange all these years, living just down the road from Country Home, she had heard all sorts of rumors about Jackson and Georgia Crane. About his drinking. About their marriage. While their house in London was being refurbished, a few years back — by the same designer who had revamped Venice Home, naturally — they had actually lived at Country Home.

"We were so excited," Jess could remember one of their bar staff — a girl she had vaguely known at primary school and had bumped into at the supermarket and invited for a catch-up drink — telling her over a bottle of wine one evening. "I mean we were used to famous members, but both of them at once, staying for months? That was different."

"So what are they really like?" Jess had asked.

Georgia, apparently, was even more beautiful than she looked on-screen, very down to earth, surprisingly friendly.

"And Jackson?"

The girl's expression had wavered slightly.

"He's very charming too, the first time you meet him. Then charming in the exact same way the second time. And the third. Same jokes. Same questions. I mean, I get that. I know he meets a lot of people. Still, by about day three, it got . . . kind of weird."

Jess had topped both their wineglasses up, pressed for more details. What about the Cranes as a couple, she had asked. Did they seem happy? Was it true they never actually shared a room?

"I mean, it's not unusual for married members to have separate suites. I sort of think you would, if you could afford it. I would. We all kind of got the impression they were going through a bit of a bad

184

patch, though. They hardly seemed to spend any time together at all. She would jog around the lake every morning, he would go for a run in the gym. She would go for a swim and learn some lines by the pool in the afternoon, he would go for a horse ride or use one of the meeting rooms to make calls in."

It was the same childhood acquaintance who told Jess about the precision and care with which every guest's personal preferences were catered to at Home. About the whiskey and the champagne and the Diet Cokes, all of which needed replacing every single day. The bottle of rum that needed replacing every two. All this on top of the wine Jackson would put away with dinner, sometimes with Georgia but more often alone, the drinks he would get through in the bar afterward, sitting there alone in a corner of the room in his baseball cap, his dark glasses, night after night.

It was strange to think that conversation — how many years ago now? — had planted the seed in her mind that was on the cusp of germinating now.

Jess checked the time on her watch. She was now the last person left in the spotless cabin. If everything was running according to schedule, everyone should be at lunch now. She inspected the drinks cabinet. She inspected the fridge. She tested the pillows with her hand, smoothed the ironed-in creases. She adjusted the lighting slightly, rechecked the room temperature, and allowed herself a little rush of excitement. It was hard not to feel excited, the way things seemed to be falling into place.

From one of her pockets she removed the plastic sachet into which earlier that morning she had ground, not just the sleeping pills she had taken from Kyra Highway's room, but the various — and numerous — tablets and capsules she had obtained before coming to the island. Combined, they had produced a surprising amount of white powder, but it was a new bottle of Midleton and there was more than enough whiskey to dissolve it all.

Only as the last spinning crystalline crumbs in the bottom of the decanter vanished and her vision began going spotty did Jess realize she had been holding her breath.

Oh God, she found herself thinking, her mood suddenly wilting, this is not going to work, this is never going to work. Not in real life. Not a chance. Even with all the research she had done, the trouble she had gone to, getting hold of everything, all this planning. Jackson would notice something off, the first sip he tasted. He might be in the mood tonight for the rum or the champagne. Would it be too obvious to set out a whiskey glass next to the decanter? To put both on a little tray next to the bed?

At the sound of footsteps on the cabin porch, Jess started with such force that her feet literally jumped in her shoes. He was back. Jackson Crane was here, scratching at the door of the cabin with his key, mumbling and muttering to himself as he did so, breathing so heavily through his nose that she could hear it all the way from where she was standing.

Finally, after several minutes, he managed to get his key into the lock and turn it, and — apparently surprised at how easily the door swung open — advanced into the room with a three-step stumble. If he was shocked to find his cabin restored to its former pristine condition, he did not show it. If he was surprised to find one of the housekeeping team standing with a weird nervous smile on their face in the corner of his room, he gave no sign.

The first thing Jackson Crane did was to try to turn the lights on despite the fact they were already on. Only as he was looking for the light switch did he realize he had left

the front door open with the key still hanging from it. Only after he had managed to
slam the door — on his second attempt,
after experiencing considerable difficulty
extricating the key — and missed by about
three feet when endeavoring to toss the key
into a bowl on the table, and stumbled on
the lip of the carpet, and bashed the coffee
table out of the way with his shin without
even noticing, did he finally acknowledge
Jess's presence.

"Hnnh," he said.

Even from here Jess could smell his breath.
It was him. It was him. It was him.

Jackson Crane squinted at her, attempted
a smile, took a couple of sudden unexpected
steps sideways, then steadied himself. And
for a second, the years dropped away, and
Jess found herself staring into his eyes, and
he was staring into her eyes, and his brow
furrowed, and for a moment she found
herself wondering if he had recognized her.

Looking down at her hands, which seemed
somehow a long way away, Jess realized she
was still holding a glass and the whiskey.
"Sorry, sir," she said, her gaze abruptly
lowered, her voice husky in her ears. "May I
offer you . . . ?"

It was the decanter he took, grabbing it
and twisting the stopper and chucking it

188

onto the sofa and necking down at least a fifth of the liquid before he even paused for breath. Then he wiped his lips with his fingers, a sort of pinching gesture.

And for a moment, just a moment, as he passed her, Jess could feel his appraising gaze sweep over her, his eyes pausing fleetingly on her chest, his interest briefly flickering — and then switching off again as his brain ruled the possibility out, as she stopped being a potential person of interest and reverted to being something else, like furniture.

Still holding the whiskey, with a slightly stagy flourish of his free hand, Jackson Crane allowed himself to fall backward onto the bed. Jess put the glass down and headed for the door. Having reached it she paused, turned to look back at him.

Sitting up against the head of the bed, still wearing his shoes although his jacket was now in a tangle on the floor, several shirt buttons undone and the bottom of his shirt untucked on one side, Jackson Crane glowered at her and then, with an air of somewhat vague defiance, lifted the decanter to his lips.

Glug glug glug. Glug glug glug.

By the time he lowered it this time, it was almost half-empty.

As she was closing the door behind her, she could hear him grumbling something to himself about fucking. Whether it was addressed to her, whether it was addressed to himself, whether it was addressed to anyone at all, it was hard to say.

Glug glug glug.

She had already added a note to the cabin ten cleaning work schedule, making it emphatically clear that Jackson Crane was not to be disturbed until further notice, under any circumstances. That had not felt like murdering someone. But in a way it was. In a way, ticking that box had been as much an act of murder as grinding up those pills, as putting them in that whiskey, as handing it to him.

She hoped the producers of whatever film Jackson Crane was working on at the moment were paid up on their insurance.

Probably the sleeping pills alone would have done for him, the number she had ground up, the amount he had just ingested. Given what else there had been in that plastic sachet, though — all the stuff she had brought with her, everything she had helped herself to from the other cabins — half the contents of that decanter would have been enough to kill an elephant. Just a decent-sized glass of it would have been enough for a human being.

She had done it. She had actually done it. Even now she could not quite believe it.

It was not until she was halfway back to the staff block that she realized she still had Jackson Crane's memory stick in her pocket.

NIKKI

The giant firepit on the back lawn had been nonnegotiable, another one of those ideas Ned was determined to make happen even if everyone else told him it was crazy, or impossible, or actively dangerous. Even Annie, whose enthusiasm for Ned's plans was usually immediate and absolute, had tried to steer him away from this one. "Hmmm," was the way she had put it, when he had first floated the thought. "Is that wise? Do we really want an enormous permanent bonfire, in a giant metal bowl on legs, spewing three-foot-high flames, within stumbling distance of the bar? Best-case scenario, a member will try to light a cigarette off it and lose their eyebrows."

"Or set their hair on fire," Adam had added.

It was a very Adam move, in meetings, just to repeat or closely paraphrase what the previous person had said. What the previous *woman* had said, usually, as if he were

191

translating from the original Estrogen. For years, Nikki had watched him do it, generally blunting the joke or missing the point or demonstrating he had not understood either the problem or the proposed solution. And for years, Nikki had wondered what was going through his head as he did so. Because she was always taking the minutes, writing his words down, and therefore giving them a weight they did not often deserve. She could count on one hand the number of times, in her twenty-five years there, that he had made an insightful comment or useful suggestion. She did not dislike Adam Groom — not especially — but it was hard to see the point of the man, professionally speaking. Nor was it any wonder, in career terms, that he had never left Home.

"And what do you think?" Ned had asked her. Nikki checked the minutes she had been typing on autopilot for what he was actually proposing, then waited a beat. She told him she loved the idea.

And sitting here on a bright October afternoon, sunk into one of the circle of low outdoor sofas surrounding the firepit at a safe-ish distance, watching the sparks spiral upward, the great logs creak and glow and settle, she had to admit once again that when Ned was right about something, Ned was right about something. And she had always thought herself lucky in life to have the benefit of that, the proximity to it. Little could she have imagined, when she landed a job behind the coat check of Covent Garden Home, where it would take her, how it would end up.

A movement caught the corner of her eye and Nikki became aware that she was not the only person to have drifted down to the lawn in this brief lull in the afternoon's activities. Someone else had already been sitting here when she arrived, staring into the flames, their blanket pulled up around their shoulders and over their head, like a shawl. Only now that the figure coughed, and raised a closed fist to catch it, letting the blanket slip, did she realize it was Kurt Cox.

He looked just as startled to see Nikki as she was to see him. Evidently, his first reaction was to get up, to get away, but as she half rose to her feet at exactly the same time as he did, he then sat back down again — and she did the exact same thing.

"Sorry," he said.

"No, no, I'm sorry."

She rose to leave and did so, gesturing with her hand for him to remain seated. He

193

was, after all, the guest.

Nikki neatly folded her blanket and placed it back where she had found it.

Kurt glanced up at her.

"My head was somewhere else — that was rude of me." He shook his head as if to wake himself out of a daydream and gave her an apologetic look. "I wasn't ignoring you. Nikki, isn't it?"

"Yes, and don't worry! I'm sorry for intruding. It's hard to get a second to yourself on one of these weekends. I should know, I've been to all of them. Look, I hope you don't mind if I ask you this — it must have been hard, listening to people talk about your father last night and now you seem . . . it's just . . . are you okay?" she asked.

"To be honest, I was thinking about my mother," he said.

"Oh, I'm sorry . . ." she said again. "I shouldn't have . . ."

"That's okay," he said softly. "It was, you know . . . She was . . ." He rubbed his nose with the back of his sleeve, stared into the fire. "Pretty amazing, actually." Kurt took a deep sniff. "Sometimes it's hard."

One of the things Nikki always found disarming about people who had lived their entire lives in the public eye was how open

194

they seemed, how swiftly someone like Kurt slipped into talking about his mother, telling you about his feelings. It was something that had struck her the first time she'd met Kurt's father too, the way his anecdotes were peppered with references to things Robin had told him, or his friend Jack, as if you also knew Robin Williams and Jack Nicholson. And of course in a sense you did. It would be disingenuous, tiresome, kind of creepy, to pretend that you did *not* know who Ron's wife, Kurt's mum was, had been. That you had not seen her films and watched her interviewed and knew the whole story, how she had given it all up to raise the children, all six of them, on that ranch. The refusal ever to confirm to the media — some said even to the kids themselves — who was and who was not a biological Cox, the denial that it mattered. And what a gift they had been given, considering the challenges and pressures that came with having those parents, that life — how normal they'd turned out, how down to earth, perhaps because they did grow up entirely out of the limelight.

Not that she'd ever been a recluse, Marianne; that was a common misconception. She had always continued to give interviews about the conservation issues close to her heart, talked about life on the ranch. Nikki could still remember a *Time* magazine cover, Marianne on horseback, the morning light on her face, her golden hair. Those wonderful pictures of all the kids sitting around a bonfire under the stars, Kurt and his brothers and sisters splashing one another in a stream, all of them watching a movie together on a proper projector under the stars, various enormous shaggy dogs lolling around. And of course Nikki also knew — no pretending she didn't — how Marianne had died, so young, the precise type of cancer, the rapidity of her decline.

"Did you ever meet my mom?" Kurt asked Nikki.

Nikki shook her head.

"It was mostly my dad who stayed at the clubs, huh?"

Nikki felt herself stiffen a little.

"Yes, he was a huge supporter of Home, even early on. Everyone loved him, your dad."

She was not lying. Not just a member but an early investor in Home as well, Ron Cox was the rare kind of superstar who knew your name, your pets' names, had running jokes with the receptionists, always asked after someone when he did not see them on a visit. It was terrible to think of that person and know — from what Kurt had said at dinner, from interviews with the other children she had caught snatches of — how diminished that memory was, how far advanced his dementia. To think of that glimpse of him on the news, at an awards ceremony, frail and hesitant in his tuxedo, clapping and nodding along and smiling, rising like everyone else around him to his feet, seemingly totally unaware that he was the person being honored.

"What's in the package, Nikki?" he asked, earnestly. "I don't know what game it is we're playing, and it's making me really anxious."

For the first time in their conversation, Kurt took his eyes off the flames and looked up at her.

Nikki frowned, confused.

"The package," Kurt repeated. "Last night after you left, Ned takes me aside and tells me he's hiking my membership fees, gives me a figure so crazy I think I'm hearing things, right? My first reaction is to laugh, like this is some sort of initiation, a prank he's cooked up. Because obviously this place is great but I wouldn't pay *that* much to be a member, every single year. Nobody would, right? But Ned's not laughing. No one else is laughing either. And he tells us all to expect a package, some sort of delivery. And I feel like everyone else in the room — Freddie, Jackson, Keith, Annie — understands something that I'm just not getting. Then this morning I get back from a swim and there it is, on my bed. And there's something about this whole thing that makes me scared to open it — like it's Pandora's padded envelope, you know? Like I open this and things, I don't know . . . change somehow. I'm probably being silly but . . . I just want to know what's in it, Nikki? Can you tell me?"

There was a pleading look in his eyes.

"I don't know," she said quietly.

Kurt raised his eyebrows at her response and she gave him a weak smile. She didn't know, but she had a horrifying feeling she could guess. "I honestly have no idea what's in the package — but I will find out for you." She glanced at her watch. "I'm meeting Ned in ten minutes. I'll speak to him. I'm sorry, I have to go."

Nikki set off at a pace toward the Manor, calling up a number on her phone as she went.

It rang a couple of times before a slightly disengaged-sounding receptionist picked up.

"Blackwell Row, to whom may I connect you?"

"The office of Sebastian Shaw QC please," Nikki said.

There followed a momentary silence before the clerk picked up.

"Hello? Hello, it's Nikki Hayes here, from Ned Groom's office at the Home Group. Look, I'm sorry to call on a Friday afternoon but I just need you to pull up a contract for him — it's from quite a while ago. The Manhattan Home investment is what he's after, from Ron Cox? Sorry, you know what he's like — that's all the detail I got, he just barks an instruction and expects me to guess the rest. Happy to wait while you look."

She circled the Manor twice while she listened to filing-cabinet drawers being opened and shut on the other end of the line, her shoes crunching on the gravel.

"Do you mean the loan agreement for eleven million dollars dated the seventh of August 1996? Or the termination of the loan dated the thirty-first of October 1996?" he asked. She stopped, her feet suddenly feeling like lead. "Oh God, I'm not sure which he means and if I double-check he'll go mad. What does a termination of loan actually mean?"

"I'm not the expert, and I'm afraid Sebastian's not here," he explained. "But essentially it means that although the loan monies have been received, any repayment is effectively canceled. It's quite unusual in general, but something that Ned does fairly regularly, and is certainly the case with all of Ron Cox's contracts." She could hear him flicking through paperwork. "There are five or six here, almost identical."

"You know what, maybe if you could send them all, please, to be on the safe side," she said. "I'll just have to ask him."

ADAM

Even as the words were coming out of his mouth, Adam knew that he had fucked it.

All afternoon he had been trying to corner Ned, get him alone, to engineer a situation in which he might have something like his brother's full attention, find a moment at which Ned was not greeting someone or other, bellowing with amiable ferocity down the length of the lawn at some new arrival, demanding to know why someone else didn't have a drink in their hand, roaring at someone's joke, or convulsing with laughter at one of his own. All afternoon Adam had been ignoring texts and phone calls from Laura. Was the timing right for the bomb-shell he was about to drop on Ned — the first afternoon of the biggest launch party

200

they had ever thrown at the most expensive club they had ever opened? Almost certainly not. Would there ever be a better time? Adam was not sure about that either. He had, after all, spent several decades waiting for the perfect moment to do this.

At one point, it had looked as if Ned were going to take it surprisingly well.

It was only when guests started drifting off to their cabins before dinner that Adam had finally managed to catch five minutes with his brother, and only then by offering to drive Ned back to his own cottage so he could freshen up too. Even so, for half the journey Ned had been on his phone, staring out the window and barking instructions about tonight.

It was funny, Adam thought. When the magazines and newspapers wrote about Home they always focused on the stupid row between their grandfather and father, prompted by some of the latter's ideas for modernizing the club and shaking up its membership policy, a row that had been temporarily resolved and then crackled ablaze afresh at every family gathering for half a century. When they profiled Ned they always made such a big deal about how much of the father's vision was shared by the son — and it was always *son,* singular;

how much he had inherited from their father: his looks, his ambition, his quick-cutting wit, his temper. As if their grandfather had not left Adam a share of the club too, albeit a much smaller share than Ned's. As if their father had spent his life sitting around fuming about being cut out of his own father's will in this particular regard, rather than having pursued for several decades a highly successful and lucrative legal career.

As with most things you read in the media it was all completely garbled, of course, most of it based on a single interview that one of their father's estranged cousins — Ned said he had met him once or twice as a child, although Adam could not recall ever having encountered him — had given about twenty years ago and had been repeated as fact in every profile piece ever since.

Had his father expected to inherit the club? Yes, probably, eventually. But he would have been a fool to rely on it. Adam's grandfather's entire existence revolved around falling out with one relation, while bringing another temporarily back into the fold. Hinting at what his will might hold for this one, or that one, who might get this much share in the club, to whom he might leave the building: if you wanted to identify where Ned had inherited his love of game playing from, his delight in getting people to dance to his tune, there was one very obvious candidate.

But this nit-picking, this assumption on Ned's part that unless he did something himself, somebody else would fuck it up? It was their mother from whom he had acquired that particular trait. The way she would fuss. The way she would hover. The way, the afternoon of the Covent Garden Home relaunch, Ned had so proudly shown her around, and all the time, the entire fucking time, you could see her eyes flicking from this thing to this thing, that to that, looking for something misplaced to comment on, something slightly askew to point out, something — anything — so he would be absolutely clear she was not overawed by any of it. "That must have cost a pretty penny," she would say, jutting her chin at the carpet, or the curtains, or one of the gilt-framed mirrors in the lobby, making it obvious who she thought had been taken advantage of.

It was not until Adam had left home, he had once told Laura, that he realized how intense it had been, how pressured, growing up in the same house with his dad, with his mum, with Ned. The rows. The silences.

The continual tension, never knowing when things were all going to kick off.

They paused at a crossing for a Land Rover to pass in the other direction.

"I'm leaving," he told Ned, abruptly.

Ned had turned to look at him with a sudden frown.

"What I mean," said Adam, keeping his voice calm and nonconfrontational, his eyes on the road, "is that I want to hand in my notice. To exit the business."

"I see," said Ned. "And how long have you been thinking about this?"

"A long time."

"A long time."

There followed a pause.

"And you've talked about this with your wife?"

"I have."

Another silence. Adam glanced at Ned. Ned's eyes were on the road, his face thoughtful. They were over now on the wilder, less manicured side of the island. The trees overhung the road completely in places, branches of bushes slapping against the side-view mirrors of the Land Rover as they passed. And all the time, as they drove in silence, as they turned onto the side road up to Ned's own cottage, past the Private sign, as he began weaving around the potholes that still remained on this stretch of thoroughfare, Adam was waiting for Ned to start screaming at him or pounding the dashboard and demanding he stop the car and fuck off and walk home.

It didn't happen. Instead Ned asked him quite calmly why he had decided he wanted out. Was it more responsibility he needed? Less responsibility? A different role? Projects that were slightly more *special*? Adam shook his head.

"So what *do* you want?" Ned had asked him, and Adam had told him: something of his own, somewhere. Maybe in Melbourne — Ned had registered this, nodded — maybe somewhere else. Ned had asked about the menu, about the concept, made a couple of approving remarks, made a couple of suggestions. Ned had asked how he was going to afford all this. Adam had explained he wanted to be bought out. His was, after all, only a 10 percent share. He had done a few rough calculations.

He was still mentally bracing himself for an explosion.

It still didn't come.

Instead Ned had asked Adam what he calculated his share of the Home Group to be worth, at this precise moment, the logic behind his figures, what kind of arrangements and time frame he would consider, whether he had any particular buyer in mind. He had listened with the appearance of thoughtfulness while Adam tried to explain how much he had learned, working alongside his brother all these years: "And I've enjoyed it too, obviously, and it has been wonderful, there's nothing I regret or resent."

One corner of Ned's mouth twitched very slightly at this.

"It's just that, the thing is, I need to see what I'm capable of myself now, you know? What I can make, what I can do. And if I don't do it now then I don't think I'm ever going to do it. I guess the truth is I just need to find out who I really am."

Ned cleared his throat at this, glanced aside to check the side-view mirror, turned his face very slightly away from his brother.

And, instantly, Adam wished he could take those words back. What a stupid, weak thing to say. Like he was going on his gap year. Like he was one of Laura's fucking floundering idiot clients. What a gift to Ned, to start gushing like that, to make everything he had been secretly thinking about and planning and dreaming of for years sound so flimsy and pathetic.

Ned hadn't had to say much, barely

needed to say anything, to make it clear who he thought was really behind this, whose idea he thought it all was, what he thought about that. And because he hadn't said anything directly there was no way to jump on it, except to insist that he, Adam, was not just parroting Laura. How could he attempt at this point to convey to Ned what it might be like to be in a relationship, a serious long-term relationship; how could he explain the need to compromise sometimes, and how that could be a sign of maturity rather than weakness?

They were nearly at the cottage now. Through the trees up ahead Adam could see the slates of its roof, the brick of its chimney, the white of its painted stone walls. The Cottage, everyone called it, or Ned's Cottage, but it was more like a farmhouse, really, on two floors, with a porch at the front, a high surrounding hedge, a walled-in flagstone forecourt. It was as they were turning in at the gate that Adam — keen to get back on the front foot in this conversation — said the thing that he knew immediately he would regret forever.

"I mean, I don't think what I'm asking for is unreasonable, given what I've done for this company."

207

The atmosphere in the car changed so fast he could practically feel his ears pop.

Their tires crunched to a halt on the gravel.

Something under the hood, cooling, pinged.

Ned unbuckled his seat belt, opened the Land Rover door, climbed out, and slammed it. Then he turned, as if to check he had not forgotten someone. Then he tapped on the window and gestured for Adam to wind it down. Adam did so. Ned leaned in. Adam leaned over.

"Is that some kind of threat, Adam?"

Already Adam was shaking his head, smiling as widely as he could, holding his hands up. He really had not meant it as such. He really had not.

Ned's expression did not soften. His face was taut with anger.

"What you've done for this company? Is that what you want to talk about?"

Adam said nothing.

"Who you really are? Is that what you want to know?"

"Listen, Ned, I didn't mean —"

"I can tell you who you really are," said Ned. "I can tell Laura who you really are, as well, if you'd like. If you're sure that's what you want. That's definitely what you

208

both want, is it? To find out who *you* really are. Do you want me to tell you? Do you want me to tell *her*?"

Adam did not answer. Somewhere in the distance another car was crunching along another track.

"Tell her what?" said Adam, flatly, although of course he knew.

"Tell her what you're like, of course, Adam. What you're really like. It's funny, isn't it, the way we go through life, curating the version of ourselves we show to the world, editing it oh so carefully, that version of ourselves we share with our friends, with our family. Maybe even with ourselves. Maybe most of all with ourselves, actually. Do you know what I mean, Adam?"

"Ned, you don't —"

Ned made as if to press the call button on his phone. Adam reached to undo his seat belt. Ned laughed. He took a step backward. A smile spread across his face.

"I'll do it, Adam. You know I'll do it. I don't care about you leaving. Go ahead. Knock yourself out. You can go your own way. Start a shit wine bar in Melbourne. Run a crappy gastropub in Richmond. Spend the rest of your life pushing sticky toffee puddings and thinking up promotions to get people in on a Tuesday night and worrying about your Tripadvisor reviews. Do what the fuck you like. We're both grown-ups. We'll still be brothers. I'll see you at Christmas. I'm sure Home will survive."

Ned's smile, which had already grown faint, now disappeared entirely.

"But if you ever start dropping hints to me again about what you think you've done for this company, what that's worth, how much of my money you think I owe you . . . I'll do more than drop hints, Adam. I'll tell her. Laura. Your wife. I'll tell her what you're like. I'll tell her exactly what you're really like. And you know what else I'll do? I'll fucking show her."

Ned took a step back, turned, and walked away across the gravel. He stabbed his key-code into the door with an angry forefinger, waited for the code to register, checked the time on his watch, opened the door, then turned again in the doorway. There was a smile on his face once more.

"I'll fucking *show* her, Adam."

CONTINUED FROM PAGE 108
Within hours of the announcement, the internet was awash with rumors and counterrumors, accusations and theories about the whereabouts of Ned Groom. That he was dead. That he was in hiding. He was on the run. He had been kidnapped. That he had faked his own kidnapping. That for some unknown reason Freddie Hunter had thrown Ned out of his helicopter and into the North Sea.

Freddie Hunter shakes his head, rubs the back of his neck. "I think sometimes people forget that you can see it, the stuff they write online. That they forget you're a human being — a human being grieving your friends, an actual person processing trauma, who is quite capable, against your own better judgment, of googling yourself," he says, his usually bouncy London-slash-California delivery noticeably subdued. "Or maybe they don't. Maybe they don't forget. Maybe you seeing it, being hurt by it, is the whole point . . . Know what I mean?"

For anyone expecting the wry patter of one of his opening monologues, the goofy sycophancy of his celebrity interviews, Hunter is surprisingly softly spoken, thoughtful, in one-to-one conversation. He gives the impression of someone picking his words carefully, acutely aware that what he says will be endlessly analyzed by the ghouls he describes, understanding that this is not his tragedy to own.

Speaking from his elegantly appointed Montecito house, in his open-necked white linen shirt, with his golden tan, Freddie does, on the other hand, look every inch the slick talk-show host. Long gone is the gawky awkwardness, the puppy fat and floppy hair of his boy-band days. Similarly distant is the stubble and bloat of his wilderness years, a period during which he has described himself as practically living at Covent Garden Home, having relocated to London in a bid to escape the harsh glare of the US spotlight, come to terms with everything he'd been through during his stint in Sideways, wrestling with his sexuality ("often very enjoyably"), taking acting lessons and auditioning, in his own words, "for awful parts in terrible movies and never once getting them." All of this peppered with several extended stays at the Priory for addiction issues, something that he has always been open about. ("Look, addicts are addicts," he once explained. "It's something I constantly have to be careful of. When I left Sideways, I replaced adoration with drugs, drugs with drink, drink with food, then food with buying disgustingly expensive stuff I didn't need.")

He is now very much a well-paid, well-loved member of the Hollywood establishment, frequently photographed by the paparazzi shopping at Fred Segal with a supermodel friend, grabbing a Starbucks and giggling with a hot new starlet. What people forget, he suggests, is quite how long it took, quite how hard he had to work, and quite how resilient he had to be to get here. "One of the things Kyra and I always say is, thank God we got famous before everyone had smartphones. Although perhaps if I had been on Instagram someone might have done me a favor and mentioned those leather chaps on stage were a bad idea . . ." He smiles, to show he is joking.

"Look, I had five years of almost constant

touring in Sideways, fans screaming every night that they loved me, opening the hotel curtains in the morning to see them all still out there with handmade banners with hearts all over them. But I woke up one morning and I just couldn't do it anymore. I was exhausted, couldn't sleep, was continually having panic attacks. Never saw my family. Didn't have any friends apart from the other guys in the band. So I quit and sacked my management. I'm not sure I thought through the implications — that I'd have nobody I trusted to help or advise me, that I would instantly become a person who used to be famous, a no-body. But at least back then it took a bit of effort to find out what people were saying about you. The cruel comments. The jokes. These days? It's always there, in your pocket. If there's something bad you think about yourself, within ten seconds you can find someone who has already said it online but ten times worse."

He stops to take a sip of water, eyes flicking left as if someone — perhaps, given the size of the immaculate house sprawling behind him, a housekeeper — has walked into the room. "I thought the worst it could get," he continues, "was just after I landed the gig back over here —

214

my own show, the thing I'd been working so hard toward. All these people — most of them with four followers and a cartoon character for a profile picture — speculating about how bad I was going to be before we'd even taped an episode. It did sting, and it did get to me, because I really wasn't sure I could pull it off myself at that point. And you're trying to make something good, and all the time part of your brain is obsessing about all those people out there you've never met, are never going to meet, hating you, priding themselves on how much they hate you, all waiting for you to fall on your face. And I really thought when I got through that, well at least it can never get that bad again."

Freddie once more pauses, to take another sip of water.

"I had no idea," he says, shaking his head.

The news that two bodies had been recovered from the submerged Land Rover had been circulating online for forty-eight hours before the police confirmed their identity. Until that point, the persistent rumor had been that one of those bodies was that of Freddie Hunter. "I should have just gone on social media and told everyone immediately, but I felt paralyzed," he explains. "It was always something I used to imagine, actually. Looking down at my own funeral, seeing how upset everyone was, how much they regretted every unkind thing they had ever done to me, hearing all the nice things they had to say. Instead, I look on social media and it's all people laughing. Cracking Freddie Hunter jokes. Cutting and pasting my face into the poster for *Finding Nemo.*"

In the end, it was his agent who released a statement. "I asked her to tell people I wasn't dead. That I had left on the chopper well before anyone knew anything was even amiss. She says it was one of the weirdest things she's ever had to draft." The internet reacted quickly to the confirmation. "About eight hundred people immediately tweeted something like: 'You're not dead, but your career is.' And then it went from bad to worse, because then word got out that Ned Groom had disappeared too, and all the online conspiracy theories started: that I killed Ned and disposed of his body out at sea, or that Ned killed someone else and I helped smuggle him off the island. People were posting memes of me behind bars." He looks wide-eyed at the idea.

By this stage, he explains, he was in his

Surrey mansion, wondering if he would even have a job to go back to in the US. "I remember sitting in my kitchen, due on a flight back to LAX in six hours' time, supposed to be on TV interviewing Jennifer Lopez the next night, and thinking what the hell are the networks going to make of all this, half expecting a call telling me not to bother coming back, that I was somehow tainted, could no longer front a prime-time show. And then I turn on the news and they're saying they've found another body on the island."

Freddie takes a moment, glances at something off-screen again, adjusts the hem of his shirt. "Three people dead, three people I knew, three people with friends and families and people who loved them," he says, shaking his head. "And someone else I know is missing. And still all these keyboard detectives are treating it like it's a game of bloody Clue."

CHAPTER FIVE:
FRIDAY EVENING

JESS

It was one of those afternoons when time seems not just to be moving quicker than usual, but vanishing in great unexplained leaps and jumps.

When Jess had returned to the staff block from Jackson Crane's cabin, Bex and Ella were still there, waiting outside the building for one of the housekeeping vans to pick them up for the next round of cleans and turndowns.

"Everything okay?" Ella had asked.

Jess gave them a double thumbs-up, her biggest smile. She was not sure she quite trusted herself to speak.

She could still save him, probably, perhaps. Pick up the phone and call reception and tell them she was a bit worried about Jackson Crane, or send one of her girls over to knock and check if he needed anything. Even if he had managed to finish that bottle

218

of whiskey, there might still be time — assuming the causeway was passable — to send for an ambulance, have his stomach pumped. Even now she could change her mind. Even now this might not work anyway.

Which was exactly what she had been telling herself every step of the way, of course. Ever since that night a few years back, listening to her old school friend talking about Jackson Crane and telling her about Country Home, when the whole thing had first occurred to her — and her horrified brain had dismissed it immediately as impossible. All the times she had thought about it since, turning over the practicalities, telling herself it was just a sort of weird mental exercise she was doing, a way of dealing with her hurt, her anger, her trauma. The number of jobs she'd applied for at Home, in the almost complete confidence that she was never even going to receive a response, that the universe would ensure she was unable to test her resolve. All this week, in a slight state of shock, as she had been packing hastily for the island. Even as she had been grinding those sleeping pills up this morning, the ones she had brought and the ones she had stolen. Even now.

Jess had checked her watch.

She could still save him, maybe.

Instead she had waved Bex and Ella off and gone inside to double-check that the strict "Do Not Disturb" notice on the staff instructions relating to Jackson Crane's cabin was still in place.

She had often wondered what it might feel like, to know you had killed someone. She had often wondered what it would feel like, to have someone's life in your hands.

It did not feel like she had expected at all.

None of the language people use to talk about death or revenge or regret seemed particularly pertinent to what she was feeling now. In fact, if anything, it all seemed rather abstract and artificial. Perhaps, she thought, it was the fact that nobody else knew about it yet that made the whole thing so hard to process, to take seriously. Perhaps it was the strangeness of the situation itself, the wondering every time she checked her watch what was going on in that cabin, knowing that at some point she was going to have to steel herself to return and confirm, to close the curtains, to wipe down all the surfaces, to make sure everything was in its right place.

Perhaps it might have made a difference if there had been a single moment in the past few hours when she hadn't been trying to do one thing while simultaneously conducting a conversation with someone — over text, on a walkie-talkie, across the room — about something else. Island Home was now operating at full occupancy and all afternoon the complaints, the queries, just kept coming. Was there a seamstress on the island, an acupuncturist available? What time did the spa open? Would it be possible to speak to someone about the hardness of the pillows, the softness of the beds, the water pressure? When the person asking was a member of Home, and the occasion was a weekend such as this, it had been made very clear to Jess that the answer was always yes.

The woman in cabin twenty-three — Jess owned two of her albums – had already called reception to complain that there were pine needles on her balcony. The man in cabin forty-six had rung to complain about the loudness of the birds. The couple in cabin eighty, he a director and she a producer, according to Jess's notes, wanted to know if there were dry-cleaning facilities on the island — if so, they wished to arrange a collection for two bags of clothes and a pair of curtains they'd brought with them. In all three cases Jess had promised to see what she could do.

The couple in cabin seventy-eight had

thrown a fit about their cabin being too gloomy. Jess had popped over personally to show them how to operate the dimmer switch. One she had recognized from the cover of a magazine, the other from an Evian ad on the tube back in London. Despite cabin eighty-four being at exactly the temperature specified in Jess's notes, the inhabitant hadn't been in there five minutes before he was complaining it was too cold. Jess had checked the thermostat and pointed out that the temperature was exactly the one he had specified. He said he was sure that could not be correct and asked her to come back with a thermometer.

And halfway through every conversation, all afternoon, she would remember something else she needed to do or confirm had been done. Had the magazines on the coffee table in cabin fourteen been triple-checked to ensure that none of them featured photographs of the wife from whom the occupant was going through a very messy, extremely public divorce? Had all the alchohol been removed as per instructions from cabin sixty-three?

And then she would remember cabin ten. She would remember the expression — first searching and lecherous, then defiant and contemptuous — on Jackson's face as he had chugged that whiskey down. And Jess would check the time again, and wonder how another three-quarters of an hour had passed so swiftly, and she would wonder: Is he dead yet? Are we past the point of no return now? And she would wait for a pang of guilt, a spasm of remorse, some impulse to save the life of the human being lying in that bed. Because he was still a human being, no matter what else he was, no matter what crimes he had committed and got away with, and he was dying, and it was her fault. Jess knew she should be feeling something, feeling bad. But she did not. She could not.

After all, Jackson and Georgia Crane had once done exactly the same thing to her.

ANNIE

It was a warm night for the time of year and large portions of the glass roof had been wound back on the Orangery, creating a smoking room open to the stars. Plumes of tobacco fog and sickly-sweet Juul vapor rose and mingled in the October air. From the stone steps on which she was standing, Annie could see right across the room, to the bar where Kyra Highway (dragging on a cigarette) was talking intently to a music producer (puffing away on a cigar), while

Freddie Hunter was hovering companionably about, eagerly eyeing a nearby piano. How many nights had Kyra and Freddie and whoever else was up for it gathered around to belt out show tunes and jazz standards at the baby grand in the Drawing Room at Country Home? Or at the knackered but irreplaceable old piano on the third floor of Covent Garden Home, with its sticky keys, its dodgy pedals; the one that Bowie was rumored to have played on once, that Jamie Cullum had been so rude about?

Someone waved at Annie. She smiled and waved distractedly back.

Maybe she could talk to Ned, she thought, coveting the champagne while grudgingly sipping her second Skinny Bitch (nobody actually *likes* vodka, soda, and fresh lime, but they were necessary if she wanted to fit into this weekend's wardrobe) and starting on her third circuit of the hour. She stopped every few steps, making introductions, laughing conspiratorially at jokes she could only half hear over the music, all the while wondering if maybe she phrased things carefully enough, flattered Ned just right, this situation could be fixable. Even to consider it, she knew, was a symptom of her desperation. Nevertheless, she had to try.

"Great party, Annie," someone else commented, as they were passing.

"What else were you expecting?" she asked them, with a grin. "Everything's always perfect when Annie's in charge, darling."

This was not just a job, to Annie. She had not been boasting when she talked to the *Evening Standard* journalist. She had simply, unguardedly, tried to give some sense of the dedication that went into making each Home club what it was. Annie had been head of membership for so long now that she wasn't sure she knew how to do anything else, be anything else, anymore. She had been invited to members' hen parties, their weddings, their children's christenings, film premieres, private views. Any Home in the world she walked into, members went out of their way to say hello, to see how she was doing, to make it clear to everyone else that she and they were on first-name terms. The flowers they sent on her birthday, the hampers, the presents. The endless stream of bribes from aspiring members.

Well, that was over now, wasn't it? She wasn't stupid — once she was no longer attached to a members' club with a hundred-thousand-strong waiting list, she was fully aware how abruptly it would all stop.

She had seen something like this happen

before, when she was a showbiz writer, and a glossy magazine editor she worked for got booted from her glamorous job. Just like that, the tap got turned off — no free handbags, no flower-filled suites at the Ritz for Paris Fashion Week, no tables in the inner circle of the Wolseley. First, her former editor was confused (Why is Kathy Lette not calling me back? Why did Karl Lagerfeld not respond to my tweet? Where's my invitation to the Met Gala?), then she was enraged (How dare Hermès not honor my 40 percent discount!), then it sent her quite, quite mad. The series of bitter broadsheet opinion pieces she wrote, fuming that her successor was not up to the job, then her novel *Back Row,* thinly veiled autofiction about an editor sidelined because she'd put on a stone and got crow's feet. The last Annie had heard of the woman, she was fronting a podcast about intermittent fasting.

That would be her. That would be Annie. Someone former colleagues laughed at, exchanged eye rolls over, then, eventually, forgot about entirely. Would Ned even let her keep her Home membership? Unlikely. With a sickening thud, she realized that she would instantly become a *wanker:* the gatekeeper no longer allowed past the gate. This rainbow jumpsuit, which Annie had taken great care in selecting, felt itchy and constricting. Its sequins reflected shimmying flecks of colored light onto the wall beside her as she tried to adjust it. Her heels had already started pinching and rubbing.

Perhaps what was going to hurt most of all was not that she would not be doing this anymore, but that someone else would. And though she was confident they would not be able to do half as good a job for anywhere near as long, the sad fact was that it was irrelevant. All that mattered at Home was not how effective you were, it was how much Ned wanted you around. And the obvious fact was that Ned no longer wanted her around. For an instant all the lights in the room flickered. Annie blinked, blinked again, sniffed.

Through the double doors, the Manor's ballroom had been transformed, with elaborate arrangements of roses and ivy, clusters of claret velvet sofas in the four corners, oversized gilt candelabras throwing warm light onto the trays of crystal champagne coupes.

On a leather banquette along one wall, Keith Little had positioned himself under one of his celebrated collage pieces: a giant black-and-white photograph of a headless nude, the nipples covered, bikini-fashion, with real tarantulas, the crotch area decorated with a shimmering Swarovski spider's web, multicolored gemstone insects trapped in its threads. He spotted Annie, gave a little ironic salute, and continued explaining the work enthusiastically to the group of young women surrounding him, constantly topping up their glasses with a bottle he must have commandeered from a waiter, occasionally tipping his own half-full glass into the champagne bucket when they weren't looking. Despite the hubbub, despite their distance, Annie knew exactly what Keith was saying, precisely what he was telling them his art was all about, raising, as he did so, both his hands and fondling a pair of imaginary breasts.

She stopped and, scanning the room, caught the eye of one of her team, also doing the rounds. "Darling, can you keep an eye on Keith for me tonight? And if you see him leave with anyone" — she gestured over at the crowd of women surrounding the artist — "make sure you find me and let me know right away. Okay?"

Her colleague, Andre, glanced in Keith's direction, appraised the situation, and nodded.

Even from across the room she could make out fragments of the anecdote (she had heard it before, many times) that Keith was currently recounting.

"And so I said to Damien — you can ask him this yourself, he'll tell you the same — I said to him, there just isn't enough *synergy* for us to collaborate, you know?"

My God, what did he think he looked like, these days? It was all part of the schtick, of course, but still. The silk Dolce & Gabbana shirt unbuttoned almost to the navel. The jet-black chest hair he obviously dyed. Wrinkled, crepey skin that had spent far too many summers lounging on one art collector's yacht or another. Whippet-thin but with Popeye muscles. The black leather trousers that bunched at the crotch. Maybe that was the point: that at a certain level, certainly as a man, it became a literal expression of your power, that you could wander around looking like that and people would still hang on your every word.

Despite appearances, he was no fool, Keith. A nasty piece of work, yes, but no fool. His art was no better and no worse than the kind you could pick up pretty reasonably at any graduation show. But he had been smart enough early on to realize that lending Ned work to hang on the walls at Home was the best advertising he could get, and falling out of the club with his

celebrity friends would help build his hell-
raiser brand. Success snowballed. And
snowballed. How much was he worth now?
Tens of millions, definitely. More, no doubt,
after the big retrospective of his work being
held at MoMA next spring.

Ned calibrated these things perfectly, and
his timing was impeccable. How much was
he squeezing Keith for? Annie wondered.
From Keith's general mood today, enough
for him to feel it. A couple of years ago,
she'd asked Ned what his policy was, with
this sort of thing, and he'd said that initially,
he used to think of a figure that they
wouldn't miss and ask for that. Because
nobody ever said no, however, he realized
he could double that figure, that even if it
stung, they still coughed up. It had dawned
on Annie then that what had started out as
a means to bolster Home's finances was
now as much about control as it was about
cash (although thanks to Island Home, he
certainly needed that right now too). It had
become a game — seeing how far he could
push members until they snapped. That was
why, this weekend, his grand wheeze was
letting the charade play out over days, and
in front of an audience. He wanted to watch
them realize, one by one, that he had them
completely at his mercy — each one under-

standing they were all in the same boat.

Keith reached the end of his story and all the girls laughed at once, throwing their heads back, shaking their shiny hair. She was never going to see him again, after this weekend. That was the truth. None of these people. Sure, maybe once or twice they would respond to a message, express surprise at her departure, vaguely wish her well, a week or a fortnight or a month after she had sent it. But now that she had nothing to offer them, would *anyone* in this room bother to keep in touch? Of course they wouldn't.

Ned was by the bar in the ballroom, drink in his hand. Annie made a beeline for him. From a velvet-lined DJ booth made entirely of refashioned wood from the pulpit of the island's tumbledown chapel, someone — was it Calvin Harris, or was he on later? — was attempting to enthuse the sluggish dance floor. It was always the same with Home members — it's hard to dance like no one's watching when everyone always is.

Maybe if she just swanned up to Ned and said sorry, the whole thing would defuse. Four and a half drinks in — where had she acquired this new one, she wondered, and how long had she been holding it, and where had the other half of it gone? — that

231

had started to seem like a plausible assumption.

Then, as she was approaching and her heel caught a little on the edge of a Persian rug, her hand shooting out to steady herself, Ned looked up.

And she saw the way he registered her stumble, an accident that might have happened to anyone. The quick glance up at her. The cruel flicker of a sneer. And it hit her that it did not matter, that an end had always been inevitable, that she could have been younger, older, quieter, louder, said too much to the press, said not enough to the press, and there would always have been a reason to get rid of her eventually.

And in that moment she realized there was really only one thing left for her to do.

NIKKI

It was almost midnight, and the elegant Powder Room — oak paneling, checkerboard floor, gilt-framed mirrors, and veined Carrara marble sinks — was more than living up to its nudge-nudge name. All around her, members lounged on pale pink sofas, retouching their lipstick or patting their nostrils in their mirrors, readjusting their dresses. Designer clutch bags were discarded everywhere — detritus left by drunk

232

girls so used to someone picking up after them that they could no longer be trusted to keep hold of an accessory for an entire evening.

Three actresses came stumbling out of one of the cubicles together, and Nikki slipped into it.

If she was honest, for all their glamour, these launch parties could be unbearable. All the air-kissing. All the arse-kissing. All the tedious, performative debauchery. Men shouting. Women cackling. Annie dressed as a disco ball. Adam eyeing up every woman under thirty.

Five minutes' peace, that was all she needed. Five minutes away from Ned, from having to hear his voice, see his face, pretend nothing was wrong, from every second wanting to hurl herself at him and demand to know the truth. What he had done. Why he had done it. How he could live with himself. Every time he'd smiled at her, every time he had rested his hand gently on her arm to move her out of the way of something, every time he had invited someone they were talking with to notice how fantastic she was looking tonight — "Home's staff supermodel!" — Nikki had felt her skin tighten.

Having locked the cubicle door, she removed her tuxedo jacket and hung it on the large brass hook. She felt flushed, shaky. Too hot even in only the thin, pale blue silk slip dress she was wearing. Ned would no doubt have something to say about the abrupt manner in which she had excused herself, the peculiar way she had dashed off when Ned beckoned Kurt over from across the room to join them. Not least since Georgia Crane had been in the middle of an endless anecdote, and one of the unspoken rules at Home was that you never interrupted or excused yourself or gave the slightest hint of your attention flagging when a member was talking. Even if it was a story you'd previously heard verbatim, recounted in the bored and detached style of an actress two years into a West End run, who had outgrown the role long ago.

The story Georgia had been halfway through telling was how she and Jackson had got together, what it had felt like to be on stage your very first night in your very first professional acting role after graduation (Cassandra in a modern-dress version of *The Oresteia* at the Almeida) and to look up and see someone you'd admired so much for so long sitting right there looking up at you from the front row. About the flowers he had sent her backstage, the note.

About their first date, at the River Café, and how nervous she had been, her panic about what to wear. Nikki wondered how rude it had looked, just turning and walking away while Georgia was still talking.

She didn't usually drink, but the first thing she had done this evening was stride straight up to the bar, order a double brandy, and gulp it down in one. She hadn't taken drugs for decades either — when she'd started at Home, the girl she did shifts with on the coat check would offer her a little bump to help her stay awake — but there was pretty much nothing she wanted so much in the world now as a fat white line of coke to sharpen her senses.

She couldn't stay in here all night, she knew that. Taking a deep breath, then letting it out slowly, she rose to her feet and reached for her jacket.

She was just about to open the door when she heard Lily McAlister's voice outside. *Oh God. Of all the people.*

Of course, Nikki had known she would be here. Lily McAlister was always at Home's parties, always did that thing of frowning and pretending initially to have to think where she knew Nikki from. Always — if someone important was there too — then told the story of how she and Nikki knew

235

each other as if that fact itself was innately comic, that one of them had ended up as a PA and the other one . . . well, the other one was Lily McAlister.

How often, back in the nineties, when they were both teenagers (Nikki was sure she was once a year or two younger than Lily, even if Lily's Wikipedia page now claimed the opposite), had they bumped into each other, each with a portfolio clutched under one arm, at the same model castings? Not that they had exactly bonded, even then. It was a solitary job, modeling, so there was rarely a lot of small talk, but even by model standards, Lily was icy — barely nodding in acknowledgment on the stairs of walk-up magazine offices, occasionally deigning to borrow-steal a Marlboro Light as they waited outside some self-consciously edgy designer's Clerkenwell studio, perhaps inquiring whom Nikki had seen that week while working at Covent Garden Home. Both scouted for the same agency by the same guy (Nikki in McDonald's on Oxford Street, Lily shopping in Fenwick with her mum); both tall (although only Lily quite tall enough for a catwalk career), flat-chested, and narrow-hipped; both dark-haired; both similarly pillow-lipped and high cheekboned; it was no wonder they had crossed paths so often, had frequently found themselves in direct competition for the same jobs. *That* was a strange thought. It was almost always Lily who actually got the jobs. Who had just got back from a shoot in Budapest or Tokyo or Berlin. Who was heading off straight after the casting to be in a music video.

It was also true that their lives had followed very different trajectories since. The thing was, whatever Lily or anyone else assumed, never once had Nikki felt the slightest sliver of envy of her — or of any of them, really, these members, the famous ones. What more obvious proof did you want of how horrible life in the public eye must be, how happy they were to avoid that harsh glare, than the very existence of somewhere like Home? No, she had never envied Lily any of that. The phone taps. The cloud hacks. The guy who'd got over the wall of her Brooklyn brownstone and into her backyard with a backpack full of duct tape and cable ties.

Given all the creeps and crooks and slimeballs that Lily had spent her career dealing with — the photographers, the managers, the bookers, all those other middle-aged men who made your scalp tingle and on whose approval the careers of young, hungry, hopeful girls depended — Nikki had always thought she was pretty lucky, only having to put up with Ned. She had certainly felt lucky he'd taken a chance on an unqualified teenager whose only proven professional ability was putting coats on hangers and handing them back — had always wondered what it was about her that had made her seem perfect for the job.

People often joked about Ned being married to the club, and it was striking how few of his inner circle had partners, children. But it did also mean something, to have watched Home grow from one club to two, from two to ten, each new project better, more ambitious, than the last. Also just to have worked for so long, at such a high degree of intensity, with these people. No one would ever have been cheesy enough to compare Home to a family, but there were similarities. Not similarities with her own family, of course — the mother she hadn't spoken to since she'd been kicked out of home aged fourteen, for daring, finally, to hit her back, her bags drunkenly packed and furiously thrown over the concrete balcony of their tenth-floor Margate flat with the farewell: "Fuck off then, Nicola. Let's just see if you can make more of your life than I did." No, her own family was the sort where nobody cared if you ran away and sofa surfed with people you barely knew, spent weekdays shoplifting in Topshop just for something to wear. In comparison, Home felt like the sort of big, complicated family you saw on TV and there had always been something comforting about that. The weird intimacy of it. The shared jokes. The ebb and flow of warmth and resentment. The way you felt you knew exactly how everybody's brains worked — even though it turned out she had been very wrong about that.

Nikki slid back the bolt and accidentally threw the cubicle door open with such force that it hit the wall before juddering closed again.

She stopped it with her hand.

"Hi, Lily," she said, across the room, perhaps just a little bit too loudly. Over by the sinks, Lily interrupted the conversation she had been having with a slight lift of the hand and shifted her gaze to Nikki. She smiled about as faintly as it is possible to smile.

"Lily, darling," said Nikki, making a point of the familiarity, grinning more broadly than she would usually have allowed herself. "I don't suppose you happen to have any . . ." She tapped her nose. "Do you?"

Because she was going to need something to get her through this evening.

Because she was going to need something to talk to Ned, to confront him. Something to give her the confidence, the fearlessness, to ask Ned what she needed to ask him, and to hear his answers.

But because, also, *fuck it.*

It's not every day that you discover your whole adult life has been built around an elaborate practical joke.

ADAM

Just before midnight, Adam slipped away.

He passed Nikki in the corridor, and they exchanged nods, and just after they passed, it sounded as if she had shouted something but he did not catch what, and when he turned she did not look back, just kept walking.

Upstairs, behind him, he could hear Ned holding forth, his brother's booming voice unmistakable and clearly audible even over the general hubbub, the clatter of heels on marble, the chinking of glasses, the bursts of laughter and shrieks of delight.

It was a relief to be out in the cool air. He descended the front steps of the Manor two at a time, unlocking his Land Rover with a press of the button on the key — *dip dip —*

240

and correcting his angle of travel toward the third of the three identical vehicles lined up in a row.

I'll fucking show *her, Adam.*

All the way to Ned's cottage those were the words ringing in his ears. As he turned onto the private road. As he pulled in at the gate. As he typed Ned's keycode into Ned's door and waited for it to click open.

The interior of the cottage was not what anyone would have expected from the outside. Even compared to his penthouse suite at Manhattan Home, even compared to his cabana with its own pool on the roof in the club in Santa Monica, Ned had done himself proud with this place. If the Home aesthetic was a certain lived-in chic, this was the real deal, super luxe. Three separate teams of builders, not to mention all those different head architects it had taken to get it right, to transform it into a study in chilly minimalism, part art gallery, part hotel lobby, all white walls and veined marble, an open-plan multilayered interior like something M. C. Escher might have come up with after bingeing on too many copies of *Architectural Digest,* complete with private screening room (a cedar-clad cube suspended from the roof and accessed via a stainless-steel ladder), a kitchen that would

241

not have disgraced a professional restaurant (and in which Adam was pretty sure Ned had never attempted anything more ambitious than toast), an enormous brightly lit bathroom upstairs with a shower that in itself was almost as big as the bathroom in the house they had grown up in.

Adam closed the front door behind him and stepped into the living room.

Once, this had been a simple coastal cottage, inhabited by tenants of the Bouchers. During the Ministry of Defence era, up until the early nineties, it had ostensibly served as the officers' mess. When he and Ned had first inspected the place, all the windows had been smashed, all the frames were rotten, daylight was visible through the gaps in the roof slates, and a layer of pigeon shit covered everything.

Adam found himself thinking once again of that first visit to the island more than a quarter century ago, just after they had refurbished the Covent Garden club. They had driven down together, Ned at the wheel of his Bentley, a pub lunch en route in front of a roaring fire, a drizzly afternoon, one February. All the way Ned had been telling him about the island, its history, how much it was worth, and what he was prepared to pay. And still Adam had been not quite sure how seriously to take any of it, how Ned thought he was going to get together anything like the amounts of money he was so casually talking about, even if the present owners were interested in selling, which by all accounts they were not.

"We could probably just about afford this place, at a stretch," Adam had joked, as they had their pints at the bar of the Causeway Inn and waited for the tide to retreat. Ned had glanced around at the room, looking thoughtful.

Adam could think of few occasions on which he had seen Ned as deferential to anyone — no member, no star, no potential investor — as he was to the Bouchers that afternoon, the old man in his Barbour and the old woman in her purple fleece who had been waiting for them next to a very old Range Rover on the other side of the water. The way he had listened to their stories, patted and chatted to their stinking labradors, sat for what felt like hours in their freezing house on their sagging, dog-hair-plastered sofas going through old pictures of the island then and now. Album after album of photographs Norman Boucher had dug out for them, opened up for them, while from an actual trolley Veronica Boucher served them crustless cucumber sandwiches on slightly stale and stiffening white bread, to go with their turbo-strength gin and tonics. Adam still had vague memories of a very long walk along several gloomy corridors, up and down several sets of stairs, to the toilet, where he had sat for a period of time he subsequently worried had been conspicuous, swaying slightly, just drunk enough to realize how drunk he was, slightly anxious about how he was going to find his way back.

After Adam had eventually rejoined the company, in the hour and a half (or an hour and twenty, to be on the safe side) remaining to them, they had all piled into a Range Rover — "Just throw the dogs' blankets onto the floor, that's it," Norman had instructed him — for the grand tour, shaking and jolting over the unsurfaced road around the perimeter of the island, Norman pointing out where his land ended and the section of the island he had leased to the MOD began, pointing out areas you could see where the wire had been, the various radio masts. Then, at an unmarked crossroads, with a glance at his watch, he had brought the vehicle to a halt and turned in his seat to face them.

"Now then," he had told them. "We've probably still got time, if you want to see the bunker."

The bunker, of course, was the real reason Ned was so obsessed with this place, why he had chosen to buy an island off this stretch of rainy coast and turn it into a Home, why Ned had always smirked when Adam asked whether it might not be more sensible to buy an island and build a club somewhere a bit sunnier. Like the Caribbean. Like the Maldives. Like the Balearics.

Adam could still remember the eerie feeling he'd had as they had made their flashlight-lit way down a narrow, spiral staircase all the way to the bottom, waited for Norman to fumble the metal tumblers of the lock into place and then to open the three-foot-thick steel door. Adam could remember thinking, what is this place? Late forties was when Norman assumed it had been built. Or the early fifties. Sometime early in the Cold War anyway — and in such secrecy that not even the Bouchers had known about it until after the land reverted to their ownership in '91.

The sheer size of it, that was what Adam could not get over. Here was a bunk room, still with green-painted metal bunk beds in it, still with a table and chairs in the corner. Here were the latrines, a room full of what looked like old radio equipment, a kitchen, a storeroom. Here was a boiler room, a room of sinks and shower stalls, a room with a table-tennis table in it. Here was another, slightly larger sleeping area with two single beds in it. Perhaps the eeriest thing was that apart from Veronica, waiting up in the Range Rover for their return, not a single soul knew they were there or that this place even existed.

"So what do you reckon?" Adam had asked Ned. "Turn it into a nightclub? Put some decks here, see what we can do about ventilation?"

The look that Ned had given him was genuinely pitying.

Now, crossing past the open fireplace to the far end of the living room, Adam pressed once on a narrow handleless door, painted so as to be totally unnoticeable unless you were looking for it. It opened to reveal a narrow space with a single broom in it. Once inside it, he stepped around the broom and pushed in the same way on a second door at the end of the cupboard.

He thumbed the code into the metal tumblers and spun the handle. Just as he had watched Norman Boucher do all those years before, just as he had watched Ned do so often in the past few months. The door opened to reveal a familiar room of whirring servers and blinking lights. Wires and cables snaked up and down the walls, across the ceiling, along the various corridors that ran from this central room in all directions. In the center of the room sat a huge leather couch — on top of which, Adam noted, was Ned's open laptop. Next to the couch at one end was a fully stocked drinks cabinet, in front of it a long leather footstool.

Home Cinema, Ned called it. There was one of them in every club, somewhere only accessible via Ned's private accommodation, but this was the largest, their most ambitious to date. No need ever, really, to turn on the lights in here, thanks to the constant glow of the bank of screens — twenty screens by twenty, each at least as big as the TV in the living room overhead — a TV that covered an entire wall of the place. How far they had come, since the early days, technologically, from the time when the thought of bugging the suites had first occurred to Ned, back when Covent Garden had been their only club, back before the refurb, when it was just a single microphone in each room, stuck behind a big mirror or the rear of a heavy wardrobe, when the whole thing had seemed more of a weird voyeuristic prank for Ned's personal amusement than anything else, and at the end of the week he and Ned would sit and listen to some of it with a drink and it would be hours and hours of Keith Little taking coke, and farting, and telling someone out of a minor Britpop band the same anecdote on repeat until the tape ran out.

Now you could sit here with your little remote and look into any room in any suite in any Home club anywhere in the world, and zoom in if you wanted, or rewind, choose your angle from the multiple options, all strategically placed. That was always a strange rush, a peculiar feeling. Being able to check instantly on the booking system who was in, where they were staying, whom they had signed into the club that night and at what time, what they'd ordered in the bar even, and then just call the suite up instantly. Being able to scroll back through the day and watch as Freddie Hunter — say — carefully rubbed himself wet with a damp towel, winked at himself in the bathroom mirror, and then hopped backward into the shower. To be able to flick the sound up on cabin twenty and hear Kyra Highway's raspy snoring. In cabin seventy-nine — the name of the single occupant appeared in the bottom left-hand corner of the screen — there were movements under the blankets and immediately in the same corner of the screen the little indicator came on to note that this was being flagged and filed, automatically, because the system had identified one of its key words or detected a certain pattern of activity, and that this was footage that would find its way somehow along one of these bundles of wires into one of the banks and banks of servers that filled the other rooms of the temperature-controlled bunker, footage that would join in the annals of Home the decades of carefully labeled memory sticks and disks stored in the other rooms down here, all those other rooms, down all those long, pipe-lined corridors.

How many hours of footage were there down here, all in all? Thousands, probably. Enough footage to end hundreds of careers, at least. To ruin hundreds of lives, end hundreds of marriages.

Among them, according to Ned, Adam's own.

CONTINUED FROM PAGE 139

How could Home's security have let it happen? That was the question people kept asking, shocked members, the media. How could the eighty-strong team tasked with safeguarding guests allow a car to be driven onto a waterlogged causeway? To fail to prevent a murder? To have no explanation for the fact a man had vanished, seemingly, into thin air?

The explanation, according to John McBride, former head of security for Island Home, is simple: "We were far more concerned about people trying to get onto the island than about anyone leaving it. There had been an incident on the Thursday night, on the mainland, so we had more guys than usual over there, and we were prepped to respond if anyone caused more trouble." Asked if he thinks anyone did manage to get past his team in that

250

direction, McBride says he thinks it highly unlikely. "And I mean *highly* unlikely. We had security patrols circling on foot and two boats on a constant loop of the island's circumference. But you simply can't be everywhere at once, no matter how many of you there are." Under the circumstances, he believes his team did all they could.

"Members expect to feel safe, but they also expect discretion," he says. "They don't want to see a load of big blokes in Puffa coats standing around, muttering into walkie-talkies. It makes for a challenging setup. And just for the record, when you see members interviewed, talking about how upset they were that Sunday? In reality, all those people, those same people, were outraged that their weekend was being curtailed. Ringing and ringing reception to order room service, furious no one was answering. Hammering on the spa door for the massage they'd booked, outraged the clay-pigeon shoot had been canceled. Kicking off. Making a fuss. Home members are used to getting what they want, the second they want it."

McBride scratches at a grizzled side-burn. "Look, at the end of the day, those cars were meant for staff, not drunk members. Yes, perhaps the keys should not have been left in the ignitions, but they were all in a staff car park and Home members aren't notorious car thieves, are they?" He raises a bushy eyebrow. "And the causeway? There was a huge sign with the tide times on it. It was well lit. The only mystery is where the hell they thought they were going, and why it was so urgent." As for Ned Groom? He shakes his head. "I ask myself that. Only the perimeter of the island has CCTV — very deliberately, to ensure the privacy of Home's members — plus the lobby of the Boathouse and the reception area of the Causeway Inn. Nothing suspicious was seen on any of them." As for Freddie Hunter's helicopter? "Well, forensics checked it very thoroughly, more than once, but they found nothing at all to suggest Ned had ever been inside it. And anyway, have you met the man? Being attacked by Freddie would be like being mauled by a kitten. So, the last multiple-confirmed sighting of Ned is just after midnight on Friday night. A chap at the absolute apex of his career, shuffling a little shoe with Georgia Crane on the dance floor, a little stumbly maybe, a little flushed. Then he heads out, patting the pockets of his jacket for a lighter maybe, a cigar or a cigar cutter perhaps. And then he's gone. Just" — he makes a gesture with his fingers — "gone."

Chapter Six:
Saturday Morning

ADAM

"Not coming? What do you mean he's not coming?"

It was six thirty in the morning and Adam and Nikki were the only people in the Barn, apart from the thirty or so Home staff polishing glasses, laying tables, gossiping covertly in corners, waiting attentively for the slightest hint that he or Nikki wanted something. Soon members would start arriving — most of them for their first breakfast on the island — nursing their first hangovers of the weekend. Parts of the walk up from Adam's cabin had felt as though he were wandering through the aftermath of a music festival — an abandoned golf cart lay on its side by the path; empty champagne bottles and shards of a wineglass, stem still attached, littered the gravel; a single high heel sat upright in the mud. No doubt when members did start emerging for breakfast, some would look like they'd spent a rough weekend at Glastonbury Festival too.

For now, though, there was a hushed calm in this cavernous restaurant with its rustic flagstone floors and vast ropework chandeliers, as Adam faced down an eggs Benedict and drained his second Bloody Mary and Nikki nursed a cup of green tea. A working breakfast, just the three of them, Ned and Nikki and Adam, that's what this was meant to be — a chance to touch base, make sure everything was all set for the day ahead. Except Ned had not turned up. Which, given the time he had called this meeting for, was more than a little rude, Adam felt.

"How do you know he's not coming?" Adam asked, exasperated.

"He sent me an email, at half past two this morning." She gave a disinterested shrug, tapped her iPad two or three times, and held it out across the table. He squinted at it.

"Classic Ned email," he observed. "Terse. Cryptic. No fucking around."

It consisted of three words: *Gone to London.* Adam checked the time stamp, read it once more, and passed Nikki the iPad back. "And that's it? No other messages since?" Nikki made a show of checking her phone, then shook her head.

"You know he doesn't tell me everything. I have to guess what's going on from his inbox half the time." Was Adam imagining it, or was there a little bit of edge to her voice?

" 'Gone to London,' " Adam said. " 'Gone to London.' Well that's fucking convenient, isn't it, right in the middle of a launch weekend. That's just . . . great. Well don't tell anyone else, will you? Especially not Annie — she's already swanning around as if she owns the place, as per bloody usual. I doubt she'll even notice anyway — too busy fangirling the members. If anyone needs Ned urgently, pass them on to me. I don't want this lot" — he gestured around the restaurant — "slacking off, today of all days."

Of course, Ned fucking off was by no means out of character. In fact, it was a power play he'd been pulling since he was a teenager, agreeing to meet people and not turning up.

Everything Ned did, when he thought about it, was some kind of power play.

Two and a half hours. That was how long Adam had been down in that bunker last night, scrolling through lists of files, trying different passwords, getting absolutely nowhere. Turning the place upside down. Throat aching. Eyes red raw. Cursing himself for being an idiot.

So frequently he had watched as people who had seen up close how Ned behaved, how he fucked people over, how he let people dangle, how he messed them around — and how he loved to do all those things — how those people assumed that Ned, having let them see all this, would not do exactly the same thing to them.

That was the move, the classic move.

And Adam had fallen for it too, completely.

The footage from before he was married, Adam did not give a shit about, because Laura wouldn't either. As a single man, it wasn't hard to end up sort-of-accidentally sleeping with a couple of women a week, given that he was spending pretty much every night at Home, that any table at which he was sitting automatically had their bill waived and all he had to do to get a suite was to ask for a key. He had never abused his position — that was something he could definitely say with a clear conscience. He was still a fairly attractive man, and used to be far more so; had certainly never been a predator, never a creep. If anything he had usually been the drunker party, sometimes much the drunker, sometimes perhaps even to the extent that this had impacted detrimentally upon his performance. There had been plenty of occasions when he would just be having a drink on his own at the bar and he would feel a girl's eyes on him and he would know he was being appraised, and he would breathe an inward sigh and look up and his eyes would meet hers across the room.

But it turns out fucking a couple of women a week is not that easy a habit to break. He had tried. He had really, really tried. And of course he felt guilty. *Every single time* he felt guilty about it. Afterward, always. During, sometimes. Before, even, on occasion. He felt guilty when he thought Laura suspected something, and he felt even worse when he knew she didn't.

He had tried to reason himself out of it, unpack the compulsion. Certainly, a large part of the appeal was that sense of anticipation, of possibility. To be seeing someone else naked for the first time, all the surprises, all the little details. The tender imprint of a recently removed bra strap on someone's freckled shoulder. The peculiar intimacy of finding yourself looking into a person's eyes from that close, your faces practically touching, and it being someone whose last name you didn't know. All those things you took for granted when you were young, that was so much part of it all, and no one who was still young could imagine how much you would end up missing it.

When you put it that way, it was obvious that it was really something to do with his own vanishing youth he was chasing, that his cheating was a doomed attempt to recapture. Some lost sense of freedom.

It was also possible that he was just really terrible at exercising any kind of impulse control when he'd had a drink or two.

There had been long stretches when he had been good. *Really good.* When he had been home every night or, when he was away, in his suite and watching a film by ten. Even when he'd been less good, he always called Laura, listened as she told him about her day, offered advice, sympathy. He had always been absolutely conscientious about using condoms, getting tested when he did slip up.

But now he was really fucked.

It was an impossible situation Ned had put him in. That was the conclusion, down in the bunker, Adam had eventually reached. Fail to leave Home and he would lose Laura. Leave and Ned would make good on his promise and Adam's marriage would be over anyway. And Ned *would* make good on his promise. Of that Adam had no doubt.

And as the minutes passed, as the hours went by — he knew he had until two in the morning, that Ned would not leave the party until at least then, and that he would probably find some quiet corner of the gardens on his way and stop to smoke a cigar after that — it had become clearer and clearer that this was a fool's errand, that if whatever he was looking for was down here, it was filed in some special fashion that only Ned understood. Aside from the very expensive, very discreet, rather shady Caymans-based private intelligence agency that installed and maintained the cameras and the server in the clubs around the world, only three people (he, Ned, and Annie) even knew about Home's lucrative sideline — and only his brother had ever watched most of this stuff. How clever Adam had felt, making a mental note of the combination code to the bunker door. How pleased with himself, to have worked out that if he slipped off early from the party he would have a clear stretch of time to identify and locate what he was looking for.

The problem was, there was just so much of this stuff. Room after room of it. Corridor after corridor. Those early audio recordings, from the devices Ned had installed in some of the rooms of the Home

Club, before the refurb even, before the relaunch. The grainy footage from those early years at Covent Garden Home. The slightly crisper images and sound recordings from the multiple cameras at Manhattan Home, the first time Ned had shelled out to have the video- and audio-surveillance equipment professionally installed.

Was Adam a fool, knowing all this stuff was there, knowing how many of their suites were wired and bugged, to have done what he had done? Well of course he was. He was a fool to be fucking around at work in the first place. He was worse than a fool for cheating on his wife, the wife he adored. But in the heat of the moment somehow it was easy to forget about the cameras, the recording equipment, especially after a couple of drinks, especially in those early years when the technology was less sophisticated and there was none of the automatic triggering software they had now, and to go through what they had got took so much longer, and the stuff itself was so much grainier, visually, the audio so much cracklier. Never in a million years had he ever imagined Ned keeping any of that footage. Not of his own brother.

It was their guests that the cameras were

there to keep an eye on; Ned's plan — only hinted at to begin with, revealed to Adam only in stages — to build up an archive, to slowly acquire enough material on any given member (not just the established stars but the up-and-comers, the carefully selected next big things that Annie was so good at identifying) that all he had to do was pick the right moment to reveal its existence, to hint at the scale of what he had, and tell them how much — or what — he wanted from them to keep it all a secret.

And of course, the beauty of the whole business, as with all blackmail: there was no one you could go to for help without revealing to them exactly what it was you were so desperate to keep secret in the first place.

The dates were the thing that would screw him. The starkness of the dates, and times, that would make the indiscretions unforgivable. For Laura to cross-reference her diary and know that the evening of the day they'd had that lovely lunch at Claridge's, a belated birthday present, he'd screwed a soap actress at Covent Garden Home. To know that five minutes after getting off the phone from Laura in LA — a serious conversation, about her mum's diagnosis — he'd honked a fat white line from the glass coffee table and been huffing and snorting like a naked bull and doing that horn thing with his fingers and pretending to chase a twenty-one-year-old around his suite. Even if *he* knew that did not actually mean anything, it would be very hard to convince Laura of that.

Nor, he imagined, would it be any consolation to his wife that no matter how badly Adam had behaved, there were members who had done so much worse. Take Ron Cox, for example, hitting on girls young enough to be his daughter — God, young enough to be his granddaughter. A guy who had famously been married to the same woman for decades, nursed her as she was dying of cancer, spoken heartbreakingly in interviews about what it felt like to watch someone you love wither away before your eyes. A devoted husband. A beloved father. The director of the most popular family comedies of his time. His chat-up line? "What's your favorite Christmas movie?" Knowing that half the girls he asked, in the age range he targeted, would immediately name one he had directed. That guy you saw with his arm around his wife — the same wife, all these years — at all the premieres, all their kids in tow in matching plaid shirts and jeans. That guy who insisted on giving himself some goofy cameo in every movie — a bewildered Christmas shopper, a man being interviewed on local news about being saved by Captain Aquatic. One of the most recognizable directors in America. One of the nicest men in Hollywood . . .

She was also going to have questions, Laura. *How long have you known about all this?* she would ask. *How long has it been going on?* And he would tell her. Since the start, practically. Since before he had even known her. She would demand to know how he had persuaded himself to go along with it, whether he had ever tried to stop it. And none of his answers were going to satisfy her. And he was going to have to watch the look of disgust on her face deepen, with his every answer to her every question.

Because the truth was, there had never been any opportunity to stop it, because Ned never gave him advance warning when he was going to do something, or asked his opinion, or listened when he did offer it. Everything with Ned was always a fait accompli. And it wasn't the whole place bugged, back before the fire. It was a couple of bugs in a handful of suites, as far as Adam knew. It was not until long after the refurb that Ned had mentioned something about one of their members, and Adam had asked him how he could possibly know that, and Ned's smirk had given the game away. Adam had realized then he was now filming as well as recording people, and all the suites were wired up. Maybe he should have made more of a fuss then, and threatened to walk, or call the police. But the truth was he could not imagine himself ever having done either of those things, blowing his life up like that, back in those days. And Ned knew that. And Adam knew Ned knew that.

There had been one night, at Manhattan Home, when Ned had been needling him about something or other, when Adam had said something back about how fucking creepy it was, and his brother had gestured around them, indicated with a sweep of his hand the club in which they were sitting, and asked Adam where he thought the money for this place had come from. It had taken a moment to sink in. And somehow the bigger things had got, the larger the sums involved, the bigger the names, the easier it became to persuade himself that he and Ned were on the side of the angels, that these people were paying the price for behavior they would have otherwise got away with, found themselves over a barrel of their own construction. That there was some sort of justice involved, in watching some of these people — these terrible fucking human beings, these terrible fucking *men* — beg, grovel, face for the first time ever the consequences of their actions.

Now, it seemed, Adam himself was in exactly the same position.

It was like Ned said, really, wasn't it? We all have versions of ourselves we can bear to look at, versions we prepare for the world's consumption, that we hope will make ourselves loved, allow us to be forgiven. Versions of our real selves that allow us to live with the things we have done. Adam did it. Ron did it. Keith. People who did the most terrible things told themselves whatever they needed to tell themselves to carry on living their lives as before.

Jackson Crane? He had fucking killed two people.

JESS

It might not have been the biggest, but of all the cabins Jess had been inside so far this weekend, the view from forty-two was by far the most beautiful, especially at this time of the morning, with a mist still on the surface of the glassy sea, a dull pink orange starting to spread across the horizon, the whole island so still you could hear the gentle lapping of the waves on the pebble beach just below the balcony. Of all the cabins it was also the most remote, the least overlooked, surrounded by a twee picket fence and at the end of its own little track, lined with red-leaved Acers. It was no co-incidence that of all the cabins on Island Home, it was the farthest from Jackson Crane's.

Jess opened the fridge, confirmed that all twelve bottles of Tasmanian Rain mineral water were in place, and closed it again. She had already checked that the weighted cashmere eye mask was where it should be, that there would be a fresh set of Lululemon gear in the correct size waiting for Georgia in the wardrobe when she got back to her room — she was currently half an hour into a ninety-minute sunrise session in the yoga pavilion on the far side of the island — as well as a clean pair of Allbirds sneakers in case she had scuffed the ones she was cur-rently wearing.

What Jess was fairly confident Georgia would not spot when she came in for a shower, as she sat down in her room to the breakfast of porridge with oat milk, tur-meric, vanilla paste, hazelnuts, and goji ber-ries washed down with a vegan protein powder and a mug of PG Tips tea she had ordered for 9:00 a.m., were the various *other* items Jess had spent the past twenty minutes placing around her rooms. The pestle and mortar, borrowed from the kitchen shortly after Jess's arrival, now neatly stowed on top of the bedroom wardrobe. The various empty or half-empty bottles of pills she had tucked away around the bathroom: folded into the very bottom towel in a very large pile of towels in one of the bathroom cupboards, for instance, or thumbed down into the soil of one of the balcony planters.

The trick, of course, was for the items to be hidden well enough that Georgia or anyone popping in to do the turndown before dinner would not notice them either, but not well enough to elude a careful search by the police.

Would it work? It should work. She could not see any reason it would not work.

Nor could she think of any more fitting punishment for the pair of them, Jackson and Georgia Crane.

One of the saddest things about losing her parents so young was how few genuine memories Jess had of all three of them together. How much she would have given for just one more photograph of her and both her parents together, smiling. How she longed for just one more memory of them both holding one of her hands each and swinging her — *one, two, three, wheee!* — all the way down the high street. Of her mother gently plaiting her hair before school. Of her father hugging her, of the scrape of his stubble against her cheek as he kissed her good night. How she dreamed of just one adult conversation with them.

How much she would have given not to have been looking, not to have been awake, at the moment of impact that night, not to have seen that big car just a split second before her father did, that big sort of black Jeep, coming at them out of the darkness, not to have seen the way her father's body jerked around in its seat belt, the way his head snapped back, the way their car crumpled around him, the way his face smashed into the steering wheel not once, not twice, but three times as they spun in circles.

A HIT AND RUN HORROR CRASH the local paper had called it. The other vehicle's fault entirely — the other vehicle, which, given the damage, must have emerged without stopping from a side road at well over the speed limit and which, with no attempt whatsoever to slow down before it hit them, had crushed their car like a Coke can with Jess and her mother and her father inside it. Five and a half hours it had taken emergency services to extricate her mother's broken body from what remained of their little Peugeot. The other vehicle? As far as Jess could remember (or anyone had been able to determine since), it had driven away — she could recall the crunch of glass as it reversed then sped off — with barely a dent in its bumper.

Perhaps in some ways, Jess had often thought to herself, guiltily, it would have been better if her mum had been killed that night too. Killed outright, as her father had been. Then at least she would have been spared those weeks, those months, those years of waiting for her mother to wake up, to come out of the coma, to open her eyes and say something, to open her eyes and smile. Then at least she would have been spared all those weeks, all those months, all those years of false hope. Of her mother being simultaneously the funny, vibrant, enthusiastic woman she could remember in her head and the waxy, shrunken, intubated husk that she was now. Every day she used to go — with her aunt, after school — and sit with her mum, and talk to her, and tell her everything that had gone on that day, and hold her hand, and squeeze it. And she and her aunt would brush her mum's hair, or play her music, or do her nails, and her aunt would tell Jess what her mum had been like when she was little, and how proud she would be of her daughter, doing so well at school, being such a good girl. And every day they would have to gently prize Jess's fingers from her mother's at the end of visiting time and promise her they could come back tomorrow, and every day she would plead for just five more minutes, because those might be the five minutes when she was there to spot her mother's eyelids significantly flutter, when her lips would meaningfully twitch.

Keep talking. I can hear you. I can't respond but I am listening. Keep talking. I am here and I can hear you and I love you.

That was what she tried to make herself believe her mother was thinking, as she lay there. And every day Jess wrote in her diary everything that had happened at school, everything that had happened in the world, so that she could give it to her mum when her mum eventually woke up, so that even if she had not really been listening, even if she could not remember anything Jess had told her, she would be able to read it all, to catch up on everything she had missed. Occasionally, very occasionally, Jess's mum would let down a tear, and it was never clear if it meant anything or it was just her eyes leaking. Occasionally her hand would clench around Jess's, and Jess would tell herself it meant something. And there could never be any question, for her, while her mum was alive — or whatever this was — of moving away. There could never be any question of living more than an hour or so from the hospital.

And all those years, Jackson and Georgia Crane had just been getting on with their lives as if nothing had happened. Making films. Making money. Parading down red carpets. Lending their star power to worthy humanitarian causes. Bantering playfully on Twitter, sharing cute pictures of each other sleeping or curled up with one of their dogs on Instagram. Basking in the world's affection. How endearing everyone had found it when they had actually turned up in person at the MTV Movie Awards to collect their award for being the world's sexiest couple. How romantic when they had been pictured ice-skating together in New York at Christmas, or holding hands in Rome.

And all that time, as it turned out, the whole thing had been a lie.

And eventually the police had announced that they were closing the case, or rather that they would no longer be actively investigating the crash that had killed her father outright. Despite several public appeals for witnesses, despite repeated requests for anyone with any information they thought might be relevant to come forward, anyone who had been in the area on that night, seen a vehicle matching the highly distinctive one she had described to them, they reminded Jess they were still no closer to making a positive ID on the driver of the car, the passenger she claimed to have seen, or the vehicle itself. If new evidence arose, they promised, they would be very happy to reconsider their decision. But until then . . .

Jess had never told her mother about that. She could never get the words out.

Because they *did* have a witness, the police, to the incident that night, and they always had done. And she had told them, Jess had told them, what had happened. Described the vehicle for them. The color of it, the size of it; she had even drawn them a picture of it in felt tip. And she had told them what had happened after the collision, about the sound the big black car had made reversing, about the raised voices she could hear, a man's voice and a woman's voice, screaming at each other. She had described the woman's voice and told them everything she could about the woman herself, a beautiful woman, dark-haired, pale as a ghost. She had told them about the man too, about the way he had got out of his car and made his way over to theirs — *crunch crunch crunch,* the sound of the glass under the soles of his shoes — and the way he had looked in through the broken windshield and then made his way around the car, squatted down and squinted in at her father and her mother, and run a hand over his face, and wobbled a little on his haunches. And he had looked at her father, and he had looked at her mother, but he had not seen Jess there, in the back. Yet she had been there, holding her breath, not wanting him to see her, terrified of what he might do, absolutely paralyzed by fear and shock. And she had heard him swear to himself, under his breath. And she had watched him walk back to the car and say something to the woman. And then the car's engine had started up. And then the car had turned around and driven away.

They did have a witness and that witness might not have been able to give them a license plate or tell them what make of car had been involved in the collision, but she had been able to tell them who was driving.

Captain Aquatic. That was what Jess kept repeating, the man she kept insisting had been behind the wheel of the vehicle that killed her father. His hair was not dyed blond anymore. He wasn't wearing the costume, obviously. But she knew that face. The man who had looked in and glanced at her mother in the front seat, suspended in her seat belt and suffering the brain bleed that would condemn her to a seventeen-year coma from which she would never emerge, was Captain Aquatic. *Captain Aquatic? Captain Aquatic,* she had insisted. *Captain Aquatic,* she had told them and they had listened and she had seen them at least pretending to write it down. And then, she guessed, once her aunt — red-eyed, bewildered herself, still wearing her pajamas under her big woolly coat — had turned up to collect her and take her home, they had all sat around the station and scratched their chins and rolled their eyes and probably had a good old laugh about that.

ANNIE

Annie's horse whinnied and gave a start as a member wobbled past on a motorized scooter.

"Are you sure you're okay back there?" the riding instructor yelled to Annie, Keith, and Freddie, who had stopped in a clearing.

275

Freddie raised an arm, gave him a thumbs-up.

"We're fine," called Annie. "Carry on, carry on, we'll catch up."

This really was not going as smoothly as she had anticipated.

Annie had been hoping to catch the two men — and put her proposition to them — on their way down to the spa for a morning swim maybe, or having a cheeky cigarette by the firepit after breakfast. Annie herself had been up for hours — she had awoken with a start and a splitting headache at five thirty, the sky still moody outside her slightly open curtains — and asked house-keeping to let her know when the men left their respective cabins. Unfortunately for her, both had ordered room service and failed to emerge before midday. Keen to avoid Ned today as far as humanly possible, she had slumped back into bed and done the same herself.

As a result, she'd been forced to tag along to the one activity she knew they were signed up for and trot around the island on a horse, her stomach lurching with every sway of the saddle under her. Not to mention her headache, which this helmet (her normal size, but far too tight today — had her hair extensions added an inch to her

276

head's girth?) was doing nothing for, and her outfit (black leather leggings, leopard kitten-heel boots, and a red cape coat), which in this context made her look like a demented ringmaster, and this horse — a skinny, weird-looking creature with dappled gray hair and one blue eye — which was so jittery she felt it might bolt at any moment.

Neither Keith nor Freddie looked like he really wanted to be here either — even if Keith did look surprisingly comfortable in the saddle. Still, what else were they going to do? Sulk in their cabins all weekend like Jackson Crane? Presumably they were both hoping for a chance to talk to Ned at some point, to plead with him, to explain why it was literally impossible for them to pay, on a regular basis, the kind of money he was talking about. Even for a man as wealthy as Keith. Even for someone on the salary of Freddie Hunter. Annie tried to imagine them receiving their packages, opening them to find the unmarked memory stick within . . .

What would *she* do in their shoes, she wondered? Would she realize at once what this was, what was happening, what it meant? Would she scramble to detonate the tiny truth bomb, plugging it into the side of the TV to see exactly what she was dealing with, try to gauge if there was a way to just let the film leak and spin the fallout somehow? Or would she ignore it for as long as she could bear, book a facial, go for breakfast, refuse to pull the pin on the grenade?

And when they did watch it, forced themselves to watch it, how much would they have to get through before they realized exactly what they were looking at? How long before they realized they were screwed — that however much Ned asked of them, they were going to have to find some way to cough up. If they valued their careers. If they valued their reputations. Their families, their friends, their freedom.

The douchebag tax, that's what Ned called it.

You'd think that the members themselves would be the weak link in the operation — that they'd warn each other somehow, take their fellow douchebags aside for a quiet word, so *they* didn't get stung the same way. But what would they say — and more to the point, whom would they say it to? *By the way, person I have once shared a screen with, you know that thing the makeup artist indiscreetly told me you like doing, that you can't do in your own penthouse, the thing that requires a hotel suite and someone to clean up after you? Well, I wouldn't do it anymore, not at Home, not if I were you* . . . It was not a conversation she could imagine members rushing to have — there was nothing they could say without incriminating themselves: *I too have a nasty habit, a dirty secret, an unpleasant little career killer I need to hide at all costs, so I know that Home is not the place to do things you wouldn't at home* . . .

She wondered if either Freddie or Keith had any idea what the other one was on the hook for.

Freddie, clutching his reins tightly, back stiff, face slightly greenish, looked like he might be about to vomit. Or cry. She did not blame him.

It could be tricky for Keith, perhaps, raising that amount of money, every year, indefinitely. It would probably involve a complete reorganization of the way he worked, the way he sold his work and to whom, but it *was* possible. There was simply no way Freddie Hunter could pay up that amount of cash. Not with his debts. Not with his spending habits. His mortgages. His multiple fucking helicopters. He knew it. Ned knew it.

In fact, that was the whole point.

Ned had deliberately selected someone who could not pay, who did not have the option of paying, just to demonstrate to the

279

others that he was not messing around. To show them exactly what would happen if what he had on them went public. It would be swift, and it would be apocalyptic. Freddie Hunter would be this weekend's collateral damage.

The sad part was that — Ned had never showed her the actual footage, but she had pieced it together from hints he'd dropped — in the grand scheme of things, Freddie's showreel of shame was very mild indeed. But it would still be enough to end his career in the States instantly. The way he talked about the stars he'd had on his shows, his indiscretions, the cruel impressions he loved to do, late at night, back in his suite, among close friends (Annie herself in there many a time, howling with laughter). Calling people has-beens, alcoholics, drug addicts, dullards. Describing Georgia Crane as the most boring person on earth, comparing interviewing her to trying to have a conversation with a swan? Funny, maybe; true, of course — but not a great look for someone whose whole thing was being a puppyishly enthusiastic interviewer, a soft-soaper, a friend to the stars.

What Annie could not understand — what she had struggled even to imagine, when Ned had first told her about it — was the

280

other stuff. The shady meetings in Home suites to sell stories about his *actual friends* to a tabloid journalist was just so pathetic; it was impossible to understand why a household name would do it. Of course she knew that was often how front-page scoops were obtained — Ned had his own circle of hacks to which he leaked his little films on the odd occasion members didn't pay up. But Freddie? It surely couldn't just be the money — the risk to his career, to his nice-guy patter, would simply be too great.

She wondered if Kyra Highway already suspected how the affair that had blown up her entire life had made it onto the front pages, and if she'd forgive Freddie when it all came out.

Would Ned drop the whole tape at once, or would he drip feed bits to various outlets anonymously? And, as they watched, what would the media, the internet, do to Freddie? She could imagine the delight some people would feel in having a reason to justify their dislike, the pleasure people would take in his downfall. And of course beyond that, there was also the question of how Jackson and Keith and Kurt would be feeling, knowing that what was on their little films was so much worse.

So much worse, she thought with a

shudder.

"So what do you want, Annie?" Keith demanded, shading his eyes against the sun. "Has Ned sent you to tell us he wants more money? Or have you just come to gloat about what he's got on us?"

"Neither," she told them. "This is Ned's own personal business sideline — he's the only one who can access any of the . . . the material. I can't, not even his own brother can. And by the way, this is hard for me too. You're my friends, my family." She took a deep breath, closed her eyes. "Do you think I *like* being in any way involved in this?"

"This ain't a members' club, is it? It's a fucking racket with a reception desk." It was actually quite impressive, the righteous indignation in Keith's voice, when you thought what was on his memory stick.

When Freddie Hunter was publicly shamed, it would implode his life as he knew it. If Keith's dropped, he'd be lucky not to end up in prison. Although Ned was no avenging angel, there was something delicious about being able to redress the balance a little, Annie thought, and punish someone like Keith for the crimes Home had enabled.

"I expect you know what Ned has on both

of us. I expect you know I don't have a chance in hell of paying what Ned's asking," Freddie said quietly.

"And it's never going to stop, is it?" Keith pointed out. "Every time Ned takes a fancy to one of my paintings, or feels like I can pay a little bit more this year, well, who's going to stop him? No one. He owns us now. He fucking owns us. And there's nothing we can say, and there's nothing we can do about it. And *you,*" he spat, "playing nice with us all these years, sucking up. You know that nobody actually *likes* you, don't you? You know we laugh at all the air-kissing and the ego stroking? You know that you're not *one of us,* don't you? That we all think you're just a *fucking waitress* in fancy dress?"

Keith's horse whickered, shook its mane, took a few steps sideways into a gorse bush. Was it Annie's imagination, or was a waft of whiskey coming from him? She felt tears prickle in the corners of her eyes and blinked them back.

"I might as well fucking kill myself," Freddie said. "I'd rather fucking kill myself than live the rest of my life like that."

"I can think of a much better plan than that," said Annie, jaw setting, resolve stiffening.

283

Keith narrowed his eyes at her. Freddie looked up, expectantly.

"This better not be a joke," Keith said.

No joke, promised Annie. No trick. Instead, she had come to make them a proposal.

The look of forlorn hope on Freddie's face was almost heartbreaking.

"Which benefits you *how*?" asked Keith, still frowning.

"Let's just say I've also found myself in a bit of a dilemma."

"Yeah?"

"Yeah."

Keith sniffed, scratched at the inside of his nose, inspected the end of his thumb.

"Go on then, let's hear it."

"You two," said Annie, "are going to kill Ned Groom tonight. And I'm going to tell you how to get away with it."

NIKKI

When she had met him, Ron Cox would have been within a decade of the age Nikki was now. He had seemed not just older, back then, but someone from another era. She would never have encountered a man like that, were it not for Home.

Nikki had not quite been able to believe her luck when she landed the job there.

It used to impress people when she told them she was a model — it had been a plus for her in her interview with Ned, she was sure — but despite what the scout had said, what the agency had promised her, even after wearing out the soles of her Converse traipsing across London to castings, she was still no closer to making any actual money from it. Quite the reverse, in fact: she was still in debt to the agency for her portfolio and test shots, sleeping on the sofas of friends of friends, borrowing money here and there, asking the agency to subsidize the cost of her travelcard. And she certainly wasn't going to skulk home and ask her mother for money — not that there ever was any anyway.

Then she had seen the job at Home advertised in the back of the *Evening Standard,* a dog-eared copy she'd picked up and flicked through on the tube — a few shifts a week on the coat check, two pounds an hour plus tips; no minimum wage in those days, of course — phoned up about it and been asked in for a chat that afternoon. It hadn't been a long one. Ned had sized her up, decided she looked the part, and told her to start at 5:00 p.m.

That very first night she made about seventy pounds in tips. Someone left a fiver.

Someone left a tenner. The second night she worked there a man left a twenty, with his phone number scribbled on the back. She used it to buy some flowers and a packet of Marlboro Lights for the person whose couch she was crashing on. That Saturday night someone left a fifty, and it was the most money she'd ever had in her purse at any one time.

"Anyone gets a bit handsy, anyone creeps you out, it's important you let me know," Ned had told her. "I'll watch them for you."

For the most part, what had surprised her was how nice everyone was. How patient members seemed those first few nights when she was finding her feet, as she asked them to describe for the second or third time their coat, their bag. And it was exciting. To see a band whose music you liked all come bounding up the stairs in their porkpie hats, their parkas, their V-neck T-shirts. To see an actor from TV. To be talked to and smiled at by people at all, as opposed to being a model and just standing there in the corner of the room in your knickers and no bra while people talked *about* you at full volume.

Nikki had been working at Home for a fortnight, the first time Ron came in. She'd already heard from the girls she worked with that he was a regular, staying in a Home suite whenever he was in town alone (his wife preferred Claridge's when they traveled together). He was . . . unexpectedly charming. *Twinkly* is probably the word she'd use now. She had remarked on his Yankees baseball cap as he stuffed it into his coat pocket before handing it over. Said she'd like to go to New York one day, hoped she might get booked for a shoot or a show there, laughed that she'd have to ask Ned for time off. He told her that he'd been out for dinner at the Ivy with his wife, Marianne, that she'd gone back to the hotel and left him to the nightcap that Ned had invited him out for.

He had leaned in a little closer, pointedly lowered his voice.

"I think to tell the truth he wants me to invest in somewhere like this in Manhattan. What do you think? Good idea?"

Flustered, Nikki had confessed she had never actually eaten or drunk here.

"My God!" Ron had exclaimed, all but clutching his head. "Do you mean to tell me that this beautiful young lady is kept in a cupboard all night like Cinderella, without ever getting fed? What kind of monster is Ned Groom? Now just you tell me, young lady, what time do you get off tonight?

Because I want to treat you to dinner, and I want you to tell me — *honestly* now — what you think of it . . ."

And that was how, still somewhat flustered, at the end of her eight-hour shift, Nikki had found herself sitting at a corner table in the Dining Room with Ron Cox and her boss. Ron was nursing a crystal tumbler of whiskey and she sipped an Archers and lemonade — Nikki winced at the memory now, but she hadn't had a clue what she should order — while Ron told her all about his life, anecdote after anecdote, all of them hilarious, all of them (looking back) extremely well polished and rehearsed.

It was one of those occasions when it's clear nobody can work out why *you're* the one getting special treatment. She chose something from the middle of the menu — not the cheapest, definitely not the most expensive — politely polishing off the well-done steak and praising it enthusiastically. Ron had announced with a wink that in that case he should definitely think about investing in this Manhattan Home. Ned had seen someone across the room who needed his attention, gave her an unreadable look, and excused himself.

She and Ron had ended up talking until

three in the morning, that first night. His tone was genial; his charm seemed genuine. It was flattering, intoxicating even, to think that a man who had directed films — at all, let alone films *everyone* had seen, that even her mother would have heard of — was the man sitting across from you at the table, who had asked you to be there, who cared what you thought. She kept saying she should leave, he kept asking her what — or whom — she needed to get back to. She asked if his wife would be waiting up, annoyed when he got back so late.

"Oh baby," he had told her. "That's not the deal with me and Marianne *at all.*"

He was back the next night as well, having skipped the second act of something, and again he was waiting for her in the bar as she was leaving, eating alone. She smiled at him across the room. He patted the leather banquette next to him. She hesitated. He pulled a face. He held up a single finger. *One drink,* he mouthed.

She stayed for several, spent the whole time laughing. Most of his jokes were dad jokes, really. He had repeatedly made reference to his age, done an impression of the noise his knees made when he was going up stairs these days. At the end of the night he had told her, with a stagy sigh, that he was leaving for the States the next day. He talked about how special a time he'd enjoyed in London. He talked about how wonderful it had been to meet her. He wished her good luck with the modeling, said to look him up if she ever came to New York (although how she might even begin to think about affording that, she had no idea). As they parted in the lobby, he'd clasped her to his lapel in a hug that lasted longer than she'd been expecting it to.

For weeks, everywhere she went, she told everyone how lovely, how normal, Ron Cox was, that he was exactly how you'd hope. When you saw him interviewed on TV — down to earth, self-deprecating, goofy — that was exactly what he'd been like in person.

Their affair — as she had thought of it, at the time — had begun six months later.

Filming at Pinewood, leaving Marianne and the kids — three of them if she remembered right, at that point, although he never discussed them — at the ranch, Ron had booked the best suite for a solid six months. "And you know why I chose this place, don't you?" he had asked her that first night, as he was taking his gloves off and folding them, before he removed the coat too, tucked them into the pocket and handed it to her with a smile. "Our little secret though, baby."

Filming during the day, he spent most evenings at the bar, chatting with Ned, drinking with other members, charming the staff, telling them all the most indiscreet stories about the day's shooting. The nights Nikki was working, he would pass by on the way back to his suite, hand her a note, give her a wink.

The thing she had to understand, he had made clear, was that even if he and Marianne had an open relationship, it came with certain expectations, certain understandings. You could not rub what you did in each other's faces, you know? You had to be discreet. You had to be respectful. Especially when there were kids involved. It was the grown-up thing to do.

The first time they made love — his words — was the night she lost her virginity. Afterward, he had asked her how it was. "You enjoyed that, huh?" he had asked. "You liked that?" He used a condom but said that it might be fun if she got the pill, if they didn't have to use protection the next time. "I'm sorry if I got a little bit overexcited," he called through from the bed to the bathroom. "You okay?" She was fine, she had told him, trying to keep her voice normal, trying to ignore the stinging sensation between her legs.

Then he told her that because he had a big action sequence to shoot the next morning, he should probably sleep alone to make sure he was fresh, that he had a taxi coming at 4:30 a.m., so . . .

Slightly dazed still, it took her an embarrassing amount of time to get the hint she should leave.

And even now, she could remember it with such immediacy it was as though she were reliving it, that moment, the elevator back down to the ground floor, smiling at herself in the mirror but for some reason also wanting to cry, feeling her face start to crumple and being proud of how composed she kept herself as she quietly collected her coat and bag from the staff room.

Again and again she went back, over the course of that six months, and sat with him and drank with him — he let her choose the wine, and she had felt so sophisticated even though she rarely liked the taste — and watched movies on TV with him. And laughed with him. And joked with him. And basked in the way he seemed to study her, noticing things — the pale blue flecks in her eyes, her birthmarks, the way she chewed the inside of her mouth before answering a question or twirled a lock of hair around her little finger when she was nervous — in a way nobody else ever had. "It's what I do, baby," he would say. "I watch people for a living." And he'd make a little square with the thumb and forefinger of both hands, close one eye and peer through it with the other. "Although none of them are as pretty as you, of course."

She smiled inwardly to herself when people asked if she had a boyfriend. And understood when pressures on the set made him cranky, when he was being an asshole because Jackson Crane had been an asshole all day. And sometimes he would catch her looking sad and would chuck her chin and ask her what was the matter and she would tell him it was because she knew this could only last six months and then he would be gone, and he would be back with his family, back with Marianne. And he would smile and tell her she had her whole life ahead of her, not to get hung up on an old guy like him.

And all the time, her secret dread, the thing she was most worried about, was how angry he would be and how angry Ned would be when he told him, if they found out she had lied to them.

If they ever found out she was only fifteen.

CONTINUED FROM PAGE 163
It has always been a Home tradition to hold a spectacular performance on the Saturday night of a launch weekend. A surprise concert in an unexpected setting. A banquet above which acrobats perform on flowing silks, accompanied by a gospel choir. A solo performed by the Bolshoi Ballet's prima ballerina. For the launch of Island Home, the idea was to create an immersive theatrical experience for which the entire island was the stage.

"It was Annie Spark who called us, actually," explains Ian Underwood, founder of the site-specific performance company Coup de Théâtre. "Someone" — Coup de Théâtre have some very enthusiastic celebrity supporters, perhaps one of the reasons their shows always sell out so briskly — "had taken her to see *Painter of Death,* a piece we devised for the Camden

Catacombs, based on the life of the artist Walter Sickert and examining his links to the area, his obsession with Jack the Ripper. The idea that maybe he *was* Jack the Ripper. And she just loved it. That's very much our thing, you know, encouraging an audience to interact with a location, using theater to explore a place and its past."

Underwood admits, though, that he was not quite convinced when Spark first suggested he and his company do something for the opening of Island Home.

"It was a lot of work, and honestly for anyone else, we would probably have said no. But Annie is very persuasive. We asked for two months of research time and one month on the island. I told her right at the start, if Coup de Théâtre do this, we do it properly — there would be no sugarcoating what we discover in the archives, what we choose to work from. Because I do think," he says, in his soft northern English accent, "the local historical society pamphlets gloss over things, make life on Boucher's Island seem more romantic than it was, give you no sense of what it must have been like to live and work and spend your whole life on an isolated island like this one, in one of those little clapboard cottages, especially in the winter. And of course that was just the history we could access — the MOD records for half the island are still classified. All we know is that they had a lot of powerful radio equipment here, obviously something to do with what they were up to during the Cold War, monitoring transmissions. We did reference that in the performance — there was one scene in an old abandoned Nissen hut, someone listening for a signal, instead picking up ghostly voices from the past."

Those who experienced it have described the evening as an unforgettable experience — two hours of urgent, costumed actors leading the audience across the island, whispering secrets in their ears, muttering dark suggestions. Strange moments when you suddenly realize you are the only person to witness some extraordinary spectacle, whether that's dancers appearing from behind a cabin to execute a pas de deux or a ghostly singer performing a plaintive aria from an ivy-draped boat in the middle of the swimming pool. An evening that unfolded with the logic of a dream.

The idea of dressing all the audience alike, of having them conceal their identities, was one that had arisen early in the process of devising the piece. "I knew, because we've had this problem with shows before, given the caliber of our fans, that we had to find a way of preventing our actors being overshadowed by the audience." His solution? To provide every member with an identical costume. "Even though it was Halloween, we didn't want to do anything tacky. The hooded cloaks were eerily beautiful — heavy black silk velvet, lined in thick claret satin, with a gold-tipped rope tie at the neck. The white comedy and tragedy masks were all handmade too, from featherlight porcelain. The visual effect was nothing short of extraordinary," he explains. "It was Ned's idea, really — he loved the idea of taking people who spend their lives being recognized and rendering them invisible for the night."

He pauses, rubs the back of his neck thoughtfully, a little sadly.

"I guess what we hadn't reckoned with was that when you give people a mask, that's when they show you what they really are."

CHAPTER SEVEN:
SATURDAY AFTERNOON

ANNIE

They had both gone for it in the end, of course.

If Annie had not known their answers in advance with absolute certainty, she would never have asked.

Naturally, just like her, they needed time to acclimatize themselves to the idea. To poke and prod at their consciences. To question whether they could trust her. To consider the alternatives. To realize there were none.

Freddie had looked at Keith. Keith had looked at Freddie. Keith had sworn and spat and run his hands through his bottle-black, unwashed hair. Freddie had shifted in his saddle, and sighed, and looked around, and then sighed again.

"This is not right," said Freddie.

"I'm in," said Keith.

"This is not right," said Freddie again.

"Of course it's not fucking right!" Keith had exploded, loud enough to make all three of their horses twitch. "We're going to fucking kill the bloke, Freddie."

"But you're also going to get away with it," Annie reminded them.

"Also, it's fucking Ned," Keith added. "Ned Groom, with our balls in his hands, for the rest of our lives. Squeezing them every time he wants to see us jump. Giving them a twist every time he's decided he needs a couple of mill more."

Freddie rubbed his face with his hands and let out a little moan.

"Listen," said Keith. "I don't want to kill anyone either. But if I did have to kill someone, it would be someone I wasn't going to feel too bad about killing, and if I had to choose the person on this island who best fit that category, I know who it would be."

"We are talking about killing a man, yes. Taking a human life," admitted Annie. "But when it comes down to it, what other choices do you have?"

It had actually not been all that hard to persuade herself that Ned Groom deserved to die. When you added up all the slights, all the digs, all the hurtful comments she had put up with or tried to brush off or pretended to take as a joke. When you considered every time she had come up with a good idea, and he'd put his fucking brother in charge of actioning it, knowing that Adam did not really understand the idea in the first place, or why it was a good one, why they might be doing it, knowing that he was going to half-arse it and make a hash of the whole thing. When you thought of all the things he had done to other people. Had allowed other people to do. Home, not Ned, was what she loved, and Annie had absolute faith both in her ability to run the business and in his brother's lack of interest in doing so with Ned gone. She would be the natural choice to take the reins and there was no doubt in her mind that Adam would happily hand them over rather than actually have to do some work.

She imagined it was even easier to persuade yourself that Ned Groom had to die when he had the kind of material on you that he had on Keith Little or poor Freddie Hunter.

Annie looked at Keith with his chin jutting out defiantly, then over to Freddie, whose chin was starting to tremble.

There had been plenty of points over the course of both men's careers when Ned might have done this, but he liked to bide

300

his time until his mark had everything to lose. He waited for the moment a misdemeanor that may once have felt tenuously excusable, the kind of thing a profile piece might jokingly allude to, a biography could breeze over, became something defining, tarring, and utterly unforgivable.

"So go on then," said Keith. "What's this plan? And how are we getting away with it?"

Step by step, practicality by practicality, she told them.

In a sense, it was Ned's obsession with watching Home's most private spaces and all but ignoring the rest that made this whole plan a possibility. Cameras might be wired into every single cabin to spy on the members and trained around the island's shore to monitor any unwelcome guests, but Annie knew there was no other CCTV. Because unless you were one of the unlucky few, privacy was Home's main selling point.

Vital to her plan too was the fact that this evening, during the promenade performance around the island, every single guest would be wearing a hooded velvet cloak and blank-faced mask. So how Keith and Freddie would get away with the murder was obvious.

The problem was *how* they would actually kill him. Ned Groom was a big man, and even with two of them, he would be tricky to overpower without causing a commotion. That was where Keith came in.

A spiked drink — one of Keith's little bottles of what she presumed to be GHB — would help to subdue Ned just enough to make him unsteady on his feet, render him unable to fight back. And from what Ned had told her, Keith had a lot of practice when it came to getting the dose right, perfected over decades of spiking drinks.

It turned her stomach even to think about it.

Annie was astonished — and a little ashamed — that she'd never suspected what he was up to. For as long as he'd been a member, Keith had had a habit of turning up at Home clubs around the world, hanging around in his leather trousers under his own artwork in the bar or the lounge, asking people — beautiful young women, specifically — if they could guess the artist. Asking them if they knew how much it was worth. Singling one woman out. Buying her drinks. Ordering whiskey after whiskey for himself. Showing her the expensive Leica on a leather strap around his neck. Asking if she'd ever been photographed, been someone's muse. Buying her more drinks. Getting louder, more arrogant, playing up to his hell-raiser image. Striding out to the front desk, slightly unsteady on his feet, asking if there was a suite available because he was too pissed to hail a cab, inviting the girl up there for a nightcap.

That much everyone working at the clubs knew, laughed about: it was pretty much Home legend. What Annie had not known until a few days ago was what happened next.

They had been sitting on the leather banquette in the Manor's ballroom when Ned told her whom he was planning to extort this weekend. He had asked what she thought Keith did when he got a woman back to his suite. Annie had mock-shuddered at the thought of those leather trousers being peeled off. "I can guess," she'd said. Ned raised an eyebrow. "I'm not sure you can, Annie. What he does," Ned had told her then, "is he sticks something in their drink. It takes a little while for it to kick in, of course. He's clearly very careful about that — it wouldn't work if they were passing out at the bar. They're always fine when they get into the elevator. But by the time he's poured them another glass of champagne or two back in the suite, well, they're not awake for that much longer."

Annie had braced herself for what she was

about to hear — and what came next was in one sense not as bad as she had feared, and in many ways far worse. "He straightens up, sober as a judge. Keith Little the hell-raiser doesn't really drink, you see. Not as much as he pretends. Not when he's up to his tricks. He orders them, yes, nurses the glass, might take a sip or two even. But then he spills it, pours it away when he thinks nobody's looking." Annie's eyes had widened. "He doesn't touch them though, the women. Not like that anyway. I would have done something about it eventually, if he had. I'm not a monster. No, he tells them he wants to photograph them and that's exactly what he does. Once they're in his suite, comatose, he undresses them. Poses them, like a doll. Then he gets his camera out and *click*. Then he moves one arm a little, one leg a bit, stands back to survey his handiwork. *Click*. Leans in a little closer. *Click*. Then a lot closer. *Click*. Never touches them in that way. Never touches himself either — our flowerpots are safe, thank God." He'd laughed at his little joke.

"He just drugs them, poses them, and takes photos. And then he puts their clothes back on. And then he fucks off home and leaves them in the suite with a little note saying he was worried they wouldn't make

304

it home okay, so he just tucked them up and left them sleeping peacefully, along with enough cash for their cab home in the morning. They leave thinking he's the perfect gentleman."

Ned had smirked and gestured upward with his eyebrows to the blown-up photograph on the wall above their heads — the giant, headless nude, the one with the spiders pinned on top. She looked upward and let out an involuntary gasp, then slowly, exhaling, shook her head. Whose stolen modesty, she wondered, was being barely spared by stuffed arachnids.

She had thought of the curtain fabric Keith had created, commissioned by Ned, for the Dining Room at Country Home — that paisley pattern composed, when you got up close, of thousands of bare arses. And then she thought of the photo series he had done titled *All the Women I've Never Slept With,* in the mid-2000s, those huge blown-up crotch shots, black-and-white, onto which he'd scrawled his poems, several of which adorned the walls at Homes around the world.

She felt sick.

"You already have the cloaks and masks in your cabins, and all the men will be in black tie tonight, so you won't be able to

identify Ned by sight alone. There's no talking during the performance, so you can't
work out who he is that way either. But I'd
know him anywhere, so stick behind me and
at some point, when I can, I will hand him
an old-fashioned. With an extra ingredient,
courtesy of Keith here," Annie said, bringing her horse to a halt. "I assume you have
the stuff with you?"

Freddie looked confused. Keith pretended
to.

"Keith?"

"Yes. I do. Back in the cabin. I did bring
some . . . force of habit. But I wasn't planning on —"

"That's all I need to know, Keith."

Some other time, she promised herself, he
would get his comeuppance. Some other
time, when she did not need Keith's help
quite so badly, there would be a reckoning.

"So when does it happen?" Freddie asked.

"At the end of the evening we're all going
to end up back at the Manor for the finale.
I've already done a walk-through of the
performance with Coup de Théâtre — they
actively encourage everyone to wander off,
to explore and experience the actors and
dancers alone. So there should be a point
where you can get Ned's attention, pull him
aside and . . . I'm going to have to let you

come up with that part yourselves."

Keith nodded slowly and turned to Freddie, as did she. He looked from her to Keith, and back from Keith to her again. In his eyes she could still see a desperate hope that this was a joke, a prank, that suddenly Ned was going to jump out of a bush laughing.

"It's up to you, Freddie," she told him gently. "Only you know what's on that memory stick. Only you know if you can afford to pay what Ned is asking, every year. Every single year for the rest of your life."

"Okay," said Freddie, quickly, sharply. "I get it. I'm in. I'm in too."

NIKKI

She was six months pregnant before she realized.

Just turned sixteen and six months pregnant.

It had simply never occurred to her that it was a possibility. She had gone on the pill, as Ron had suggested. Had she forgotten to take it, ever? Absolutely not. He always asked her and the answer was always yes. Occasionally he even made her take it in front of him. "I'm only thinking of you, my darling."

She did not want a baby — not then. Not

ever, probably. Perhaps, looking back, that was probably a major part of the appeal of girls like her to men like him.

Ron would blame her, that was her first thought. Her second was, how would he ever find out? She hadn't heard from him since filming had wrapped and he'd handed back the key to his Home suite. He'd said something vague about looking him up, but even in her naivete she knew he hadn't meant it, and there was no way to actually do it even if he had. She didn't have a mobile phone, or an email address. She could hardly ask Ned. This was just the kind of situation her mother had warned her about getting into: *Don't fuck your life up at fifteen like I did. They ruin your life, kids.*

Six months, though? Thin as she was in those days, relentless as she was in her efforts to stay that way, her periods had always been irregular. Maybe she'd developed a tiny little bit of a tummy — a couple of casting directors had even mentioned it, her agent calling to relay the "helpful" feedback. But she'd put that down to the carbs — the handfuls of skinny fries, the thick slabs of bread and butter — she snatched standing up in the kitchens at Home.

When Nikki first went to the doctor — the walk-in, in Soho — it was because she

308

was feeling lethargic, headachy, bloated. He asked her if she might be, if there was any way she thought she could be, pregnant. She had said no, she was using contraception; they'd given it to her at that same clinic, so he took blood to check what else it might be. But she had peed on a stick when she got back to the friend's flat she was staying at, just to check. *I can't be.* That was what she kept telling herself, over and over. *I just can't be.* She had not felt nauseous; she had not had cravings. Apart from being a bit run-down she had not felt any different from usual.

She went back to the doctor, completely incredulous. "Did you have food poisoning at all?" he asked her. "If you threw up just after taking your pill, your body may not have had time to absorb it." She thought back to the nights she'd drunk too much in Ron's suite — she never had been able to stomach much alcohol — making herself sick to stop the room spinning, and using one of those little fold-out toothbrushes to freshen up after.

"You're having what we call a cryptic pregnancy," the doctor had said. "Some women don't know what's going on until they're in labor — at least we know now. It happens more often than you think, although you're the first I've seen." He asked if she had any questions — she had too many to know where to start — and then referred her to the maternity department of the local hospital. He *laughed* at one point, she remembered, as if he actually found it all quite funny, a medical curiosity. She remembered thinking quite clearly: this is a story he's going to tell his friends. She could even imagine just the way he would tell it. *Poor thing, just sixteen. Not a clue what was going on. It's the child I feel sorry for.*

It was one of those moments when a whole imagined future shatters. She was still sleeping on couches and in spare rooms. There was no way, at that point, she could tell anyone. Whom could she tell that would care? Not Ron. What would she have said — even if she had the first clue how to do so? *That baby you were so desperate for us not to make — well, I'm having it! I've got no choice now.* Just the thought of getting through the next three months — let alone anything beyond that, which she resolutely refused to even contemplate — sent her spiraling into a panic. She prayed that it would all go away of its own accord.

The one thing that never crossed her mind was to go back to her mother.

A week later, Ned found her in one of the

storerooms at Home, sobbing her eyes out, unable to speak, hardly able even to breathe. Daggers in the throat every time she tried to get a word out. At first he looked startled, as though he didn't know quite where to put himself. Then, probably sensing that she wasn't going to stop, he said: "Come here." Suddenly, she was sobbing against his chest, smearing snot and mascara down the front of his shirt as he occasionally thumped her gently on the back, like an awkward uncle.

And out it all came, in a torrent of words, about the pregnancy, about it being a shock, all her fears, all her panic, about it being too late to have any choice in the matter. That it would end her modeling career and there was nothing else, apart from being thin and pretty, she was qualified to do. About wondering if she should try to contact the baby's father — she stopped herself just in time from blurting out who that was, instead muttering something vague about a one-night stand — and realizing that she had no way to do it, that she was completely alone. Then she stuttered that she had only just turned sixteen and, having heard it escape from her own mouth, she wailed even louder, knowing that Ned would have no choice but to kick her out of the building there and then for lying.

Instead, he did something that shocked her so much, she instantly stopped crying and simply stared and hiccuped pathetically.

"It's okay," he told her, still patting her on the back. "It's going to be okay."

"This is Home," he told her. "We look after our own here."

Take the week off, on full pay, he said. He'd put extra in her account to make up for the lost tips. On her first day back, Ned had called her into his office.

"Come to New York," he'd said, matter-of-factly. "Come to Manhattan and help me launch Home there. I've had an idea. An idea that can make this," he gestured vaguely in the direction of her midriff, "all go away, if that's what you want."

It had been far too much to take in at once.

"You want me to move to Manhattan? And work in your club over there?"

"No, no, no," he had explained, apologizing for going too fast. "Well, yes and no." Did she need a seat, by the way?

What Ned was proposing was an immediate change of role to something office-based, so she didn't need to be on her feet. A promotion to admin assistant, something like that. That way, he said, she could work right up until the baby was due. Only later did it occur to her that it might be driven by self-interest — would a fifteen-year-old working in his club have been a scandal? As a former lawyer, Ned must have known that was a possibility. Did he sense that the whole situation might have been something to do with Home?

At the time, she was simply grateful someone cared. It was hard to comprehend the kindness of the man, his unsuspected thoughtfulness, his generosity. She had been unable to even speak to say yes, just nodded mutely, tears welling up in her eyes.

"And listen, when this baby comes, we will support you. Whether you want to be a mother or not is entirely up to you."

She remembered being shocked by that word. Getting pregnant she had perhaps started to come to terms with. Having a baby? Well yes, that was the obvious out-come of her mistake if she allowed herself to dwell on it for any length of time — which she had been trying her best not to. But becoming a mother? That was impos-sible. She forced it out of her mind im-mediately.

Manhattan had been exciting. Even at seven months pregnant it was exciting. Before she had arrived, she had not even really been sure of the relationship between New York and Manhattan, whether they were the same place, how they fit together. Now here she was, amazed at how much like the movies it all looked, young enough to be pleased with herself for that insight. She was never quite sure how he'd managed to get her a work visa so quickly, but Ned always had a way of getting the things he wanted.

A fortnight passed, a fortnight of long meetings and snatched lunches — great doorstop sandwiches, delivered to their rickety desks — and rides in yellow cabs.

And then late one afternoon as she left the office — it was just her, Adam, and Ned in that first-floor walk-up — for the apartment Ned had rented for her, Ned had called her over, glanced again at her midriff, and asked: "So, Nikki, are you planning to keep this baby?"

And in that moment, as if someone had flicked a switch, she realized both the full horror of her situation and the futility of her coping strategy. No, this was not just all going to miraculously go away and, yes, at some point this baby was actually going to come out. And be a person. With a mother. Who would eventually want to know who its father was.

No, she was not planning to keep this baby. She. Just. Could. Not.

Ned had arranged everything.

Renting a little house for her upstate when she was a few weeks away from her due date, booking the car that took her to the hospital. Sending those flowers, those enormous looming white lilies, for when she was discharged. He'd tried to sit down with her and go through all the paperwork. The agency was a private one, that was how it worked in America; he'd shown her the brochures — they promised to place the child with a family who could provide a safe, comfortable home, a loving and nurturing environment. There were pages he'd flicked through about their vetting procedures, their criteria. Pictures of beautiful homes, happy babies, on every glossy page. Her throat ached, turning the pages. Her heart ached, every time she thought about it. Inside her the baby kicked, and hiccuped, and wriggled.

A closed adoption, that was what she'd asked for, when the options were explained to her. Was that because Ned had made it sound like the most sensible thing for both of them, Nikki and her unborn baby? Afterward, although she'd been sore for a week or so, cried and slept at weird times of the day and night, it all started to feel fuzzy, as if it had all happened to someone else. She asked Ned if she could come back to work and was comforted by the fact she had something to return to, something she seemed to be good at.

None of them mentioned it again.

She did think about Ron — once or twice she had even seen him, across a crowded room in one of the clubs, at a launch party, on TV at some premiere, or stumbled upon one of his movies on TV, and felt a curious mixture of emotions.

She thought about the child too, her boy, out there somewhere, wondered which of the two of them he might look like. And then she told herself he was better off not knowing any of it. But sometimes, just sometimes, she saw someone out of the corner of her eye, a boy, a teenager, a young man, and it struck her that it could be him, that the chance was slim but it was not impossible that it actually *was* her son. And that even if that boy, teenager, young man, was not her son, he *was* out there somewhere. Someone with his life and his hopes and his dreams and perhaps even his own family now. Someone she would almost certainly never meet and who would almost certainly never meet her. And that was a strange feeling.

It was even stranger to think that she had no photograph, had never had a photograph of him, had never named him, could barely even remember him — a weight in her arms at the hospital, a howling red thing, born with a great thick head of dark hair slicked down against his scalp, chubby little legs. She could remember the nurse telling her not to worry about that little red mark on his eyelid, and those patches — the two dark patches, one on his calf and one on his shoulder — that they'd probably both fade with time. And she remembered wondering why the nurse would think that mattered to her, and then realizing that she did care, it did matter, and then wondering what that meant. And she remembered being exhausted, and sleeping. And she remembered waking, and the baby being gone.

There had never been a choice, for her. How could she have raised that child? What possible stories could she have told him about who he was, how he had come about? It was a gift, not knowing how stupid his mother was or how his father should have known better. A chance to invent himself, write his own story. Have a good life with people who loved him.

That was the best she had felt she was able to give him.

ADAM

Ever since breakfast, Adam had been looking for somewhere to be alone.

At points today he had felt as though he were genuinely on the cusp of a panic attack. That pressure behind the eyes. That weird, horrible fizzing in your veins. That awful sensation as if all of a sudden you could no longer remember how to breathe. All day, his phone buzzed and twitched incessantly in his pocket and he had been constantly trailed by one anxious Home employee or another seeking sign-off on the final details for tonight's party, all sent in his direction by Nikki. His mood had not been improved by the fact that no fewer than three people had mistaken him for Ned — from a distance, from behind, but still, it was not exactly flattering, given the age difference and how much stockier than Adam his elder brother had always been. By mid-afternoon, on about the fifteenth occasion someone had queried whether Adam was allowed to approve something or other (the color of the sun-lounger coverings for the roof of Manhattan Home, to be precise — and you could see quite how paralyzing it

318

was for everyone, for the company, Ned's insistence on always having the final say on everything), Adam had quite spectacularly lost his temper, asked them whether they knew how long he had been with this company, screamed that no, he did not need to check with his brother before signing off on five thousand dollars' worth of calico, who did they actually think they were speaking to? An hour later he had called back to apologize and to say he had looked again at the two options and maybe they should hold off on a decision just for a bit.

That was when it had occurred to him it might be a good idea to find somewhere quiet and dark to be alone with his thoughts for a little while.

There were two screening rooms on the island, both housed in the same purpose-built cabin, both equipped with top-of-the-line sound and projection equipment and seats as spacious and comfy as armchairs. This weekend, one screen was showing a program of self-consciously hip, trippy stuff (*El topo, Szindbád, Stalker, A Field in England*). The other, rather obsequiously, was showing the complete works of Jackson Crane in chronological order — and was currently, Adam saw on the blackboard in the foyer bar, up to 1997's *Captain Aquatic*.

There was, of course, no sign on the door about turning your phone off, because this was the island without phones. As the door bumped closed behind him, Adam switched his own phone off and slunk into the back row.

Captain Aquatic. That took him back. Oh boy, what a mess of a movie that had been. Of all the films either Ron Cox or Jackson Crane had ever made, it was comfortably the worst. The epitome of a bad 1990s superhero movie. The whole concept of the thing unpromising to begin with (surfer dude nipped by genetically altered dolphin gains increased strength, swimming abilities, and sonar, plus a heightened sense of mankind's environmental responsibilities). Jackson Crane with that terrible blond dye job, kicking henchmen through crates, running across rooftops, leaping off exploding speedboats, delivering laughable dialogue in a strange monotone. The endless fight scenes in smoky alleys, slow-motion roundhouse kicks. The terrible special effects throughout. The laughable plasticity of the dolphin. The deadly leaden irony of it all, the cheap cynicism, the joylessness. Perhaps that was just what happened, when you took a funny, fresh, playful comic and tried to use it to sell a million plastic toys. Perhaps it was something to do with the notorious on-set tension between Jackson and Ron, their simmering dislike for each other. *Captain Aquatic* was one of those films you always thought you'd be able to enjoy if you turned half your brain off, but which somehow even then felt strangely depressing.

Evidently this was also the conclusion that the two members in the front row had reached; they left noisily just after Adam arrived, tripping up the steps to the exit in the dark. Now, apart from Adam, only two people remained in the room. Adam couldn't see the person in the third row but could tell someone was there by the gentle, rhythmic snoring. The third, down at the far end of the row in front of him, was Georgia Crane. Had she noticed him come in? He thought not. She seemed intent on the car chase unfolding in front of them, Jackson Crane (or more likely his stunt double) dangling in latex from the side-view mirror of an eighteen-wheeler, the driver attempting to lean across and bang on his fingers with a tire iron. It was always strange watching someone you actually know up on the big screen, so much larger than life, both themselves and not. It must be even weirder with someone you were married to. How old would Georgia have been when this

321

movie came out? A student, certainly. Perhaps she had gone to see it with her college friends at the cinema. That was pretty strange to think about too.

Jackson Crane took a tire iron to the face and fell back with a cry. Georgia did not flinch. Now it was just Crane's fingertips on the open window frame keeping him from falling, from tumbling under the wheels of the juggernaut. There was blood in the corner of his mouth. There was a rip in the shoulder of his costume.

Adam had wondered at points if Georgia had had any idea what she was getting herself into when she married Jackson Crane. He didn't just mean the fame thing either, although it was easy enough to read the relationship cynically, to itemize the ways that being seen out on the bigger star's arm had boosted her visibility, how being his fiancée had brought her attention. Their marriage had helped a smart and ambitious young actress launch her career, and the lifestyle, the platform, the opportunities, she had gained in return were undeniable. It was also easy to imagine how often he was away filming, or she was, how little time they ever actually spent together.

What he really meant was how well she had actually known Jackson Crane when she had agreed to spend the rest of her life with him. The truth being that he was very good at presenting himself as exactly who the person with him wanted him to be. Adam could all too easily imagine him asking Georgia for book recommendations, frowning in heavy-rimmed spectacles at one of Beckett's novels, sitting with her (in a coat with the collar turned up) through some avant-garde poetry reading.

And Georgia had been young, much younger than him, only twenty-two when they met, only twenty-four when they married. How could you possibly imagine what it would be like, being married to someone like Jackson Crane, at that age? The relentless media glare, everywhere you went. The intensity with which people all around the world knew you, or thought they did, and held an opinion on your relationship, your clothes, your actions. All the things in life you'd be able to do — the doors your newfound fame would open — and yet, simultaneously, all the things you'd never be able to do again, or at least, not without someone lying in wait to photograph you, hoping to catch you in an unflattering outfit or from an unfortunate angle. The number of people with a financial stake in every aspect of your lives, every aspect of your marriage. What all that might do to your psyche. To both of your psyches.

He could remember Ned convincing Jackson to hold the wedding — this must have been the summer of 2000 — at the not-yet-open Highland Home, a brilliant PR coup given the guest list. He could still taste the panic of trying and not quite managing to get the place (over budget and delayed as usual) ready in time for their wedding, having to order five hundred box hedges to hide cement mixers and piles of bricks, laying acres of heather at eye-watering expense because it had fried in the extremely unexpected heat wave. Making sure that everything looked perfect. How happy they'd looked that day. How rapturously happy. How hard it was to imagine that Georgia had had any idea what the man she was marrying was capable of.

Adam had not either, then.

He would never forget it, that terrible night, only a year and a half later, that phone call.

Ned answering his mobile, frowning, covering his free ear with his hand, looking around for a quiet corner of the rooftop bar at Covent Garden Home, where he and Adam had been having dinner, not finding one, stepping into the cold December night to take the call outside. Ned pacing up and down the length of the pool, free hand waving as he barked into the handset, then gesturing through the window for Adam to join him. *You did what? Why the hell did you do that? Where are you now? Give me a second and I'll call you back.*

Both of them rushing down the fire escape to Ned's suite as his brother explained the situation: Jackson, pissed as a fart, on the wrong side of the road, driving that stupid fucking tank of a four-by-four at twice the speed limit, colliding head-on with some little tin-can car, and then driving off.

It was on speakerphone, from Ned's suite, that they'd called Jackson Crane back. On Ned's laptop, via the cameras in Jackson's cottage at Country Home, they'd watched as he flinched at the phone's sudden ring, stumbled over to it, picked it up, stood there listening and occasionally taking an impatient gulp from the tumbler of something in his hand as Ned had him talk them carefully through events once more to make sure he completely understood the situation — clarifying exactly what had happened, exactly where.

And what a damning confession it was. Not just in what Jackson was saying — his mumbled admission that he could not even

325

hazard a guess how many drinks he'd had since lunchtime, the frequency with which he repeated himself, the stark facts of the situation — but the tone in which he was saying it. His flashes of irritation at having to explain again what exactly had happened, and how. His increasingly obvious frustration that he was *still* the person having to deal with all this: wasn't this what he paid people for, after all? His complete lack of concern — or even curiosity, it seemed, about the people in that other car. His snappishness every time a familiar female voice — anxious, strained — from across the room reminded him of something or corrected something he was saying or simply asked a question.

Oh God, Adam had thought, had she been in the car too? Perhaps that was why Jackson had been all over the road — showing off, messing stupidly around, trying to impress or terrify her. He could just imagine her, screaming at him to slow down, Jackson laughing, Jackson waggling the wheel, clipping the hedgerows, Jackson speeding up.

When this hits the press, Adam thought, that will be it. The end. Not just of Jackson Crane's career, of her career, but all of it, all of this, Home itself. The whole brand irredeemably tainted. And even as he caught himself thinking this, he recognized what a horrible thing that was to focus on, at a time like this, and felt a fierce little stab of self-disgust.

And then Adam had seen his brother's face, the little smile playing around his lips. And that was when he realized that Ned was *not* trying to clarify the situation, or get to the bottom of it, or work out what to do next for the best — he was making sure they had all of this recorded on camera, making them go through everything out loud so that he could be sure it had been caught by the microphone. That was always the moment Adam found himself returning to, the moment of that realization. Because he could have called the police right then, but he hadn't, hoping that he would not need to, that the accident would be reported and they would trace the vehicle and it would be taken care of. Because up until that point it had still been just about possible to persuade himself that all this blackmail stuff was something that Ned and the business would grow out of, that once Home was on a stable financial footing, there would come a point at which they would be able to draw a line under all this. That was what Adam had told himself. They were only doing it once or twice a year, after all — blackmailing cheaters, shaking down coke fiends, putting the squeeze on creeps. Never had he foreseen anything like this. Never, he told himself, could either of them have foreseen anything as awful and terrifying and tragic happening as this.

Then he had seen the expression on Ned's face, seen that little smile, and that was when he knew. This was the plan. This had always been the plan. This or something like it — an accident, an incident, a crime — was exactly what Ned had been hoping for all along.

It was in that same instant Adam had realized just how deeply, inextricably entangled with all this he was too.

Then Ned's voice changed, and he had gone from offering consolation to taking charge of the situation, giving instructions.

And Adam could hear him saying: "Is she there? She's still there? Okay, okay, put her on the phone."

And he could hear his brother saying: "Okay, are you listening? You need to keep him in the room — lock him in the bathroom, put him to bed, it doesn't matter. I can fix this, we can fix this, but you need to do *exactly* what I say."

Perhaps in different ways they had all

discovered what they were truly capable of, that night.

JESS

One thing was for certain — this weekend had confirmed everything Jess had ever heard about Jackson and Georgia Crane living very separate lives. Since Thursday night, according to the system, Georgia had notched up three hours of yoga, four hours in the gym, several solo screening trips, at least three hour-long runs, and two separate facial treatments. She did not appear to have bothered to try to check in with her husband even once.

This hadn't gone unnoticed among Jess's team. Every so often, as they were looking over the job list, Ella would remark — with a slight smile, a gently raised eyebrow — that the "Do Not Disturb" instructions were still showing in the notes for Jackson's cabin, make some wry comment about it, and Jess would pretend to check this was still correct. Every so often Bex would express surprise that Jackson had been absent yet again from some event or activity Georgia had dutifully attended and would wonder aloud how she felt about that.

"Probably relieved," someone else commented.

Over the past two days, Jess had heard plenty of other stories about the Cranes, from her new colleagues, from people who had been with Home for a while. About someone once having knocked and come in to turn the beds down and found Georgia tucked into one of them, midafternoon, sobbing into the phone. About blazing rows behind closed doors, things thrown, things smashed, accusations howled. Ella had described one night she was working at Covent Garden Home when Georgia had been waiting in the lobby for ages for Jackson to come down and take her out to some premiere in Leicester Square, and he had not come down, and eventually she had gone up and knocked on his door, and there had been a huge argument, a vase broken, an ambulance discreetly called, and several stitches administered to a six-inch gash to the side of his head.

Would people really believe that Georgia Crane had killed her husband? Would the police? Once those sorts of rumors started swirling publicly, Jess had every reason to think they might. Soon enough she would be finding out.

Before that, though, there were still a few final things she needed to do. For several minutes now, as the late afternoon turned

330

to evening, she'd been standing, hesitating, on the gravel footpath leading up through the trees to cabin ten. "Okay," she told herself. "This is it." Still, she didn't move. She really didn't want to go into that cabin. To see that body.

The drizzle that had started as a fine mist was thickening into rain now, pattering all around her in the darkening woods on either side of the path, the light on the horizon turning a burnt orange. In the distance, she could see the headlights of one of the golf carts — someone heading off for dinner, or to get a last-minute blow-dry at the spa. Up ahead through the bushes she could see the light of the cabin's porch.

It would only take a minute to confirm he was dead. From the end of the path it was five or six steps to the front of the cabin, where the bicycles still sat upright in their stands, the electric scooters in the same place they'd been before. It seemed unlikely anyone had been here since she'd shut the door behind her, the housekeeping team, and everyone else, on strict instructions to stay away. She knocked quietly, unlocked the door with the master key, and opened it gently.

"Hello?" she whispered. Then more boldly: "Room service?"

Still no answer. Jess made her way slowly down the hall, noting that nobody seemed to have touched anything in the bathroom, that the pile of towels on the edge of the sink remained undisturbed, that everything hanging on the hooks in the hall — the waxed coats, the Home-branded umbrellas and Wellington boots — remained exactly where she'd left them. Then she popped her head around the bedroom door.

On his back in the middle of the bed lay Jackson Crane, the blankets and the duvet piled by his feet, a pillow over his face. The empty decanter lay cradled in the crook of one arm. His other arm had been flung out to the side. Jess cleared her throat. The body on the bed did not move. After she'd watched it for some time, counting in her head, counting the number of seconds and then minutes that passed without any sound or sign of movement from the bed, she took a couple of cautious steps into the room. The body on the bed did not stir. The body on the bed, Jess felt confident in stating, was never going to stir again.

She had expected to feel some kind of triumph at this moment, at the well-deserved death of the man who had killed her parents. She did not feel triumph. She certainly did not feel any kind of happiness, or that any kind of resolution had been reached. Instead all she felt was an overwhelming sadness, a crushing sense of universal regret, for everything, on behalf of everybody. For her parents. For herself. There was a horrifying instant at which she found herself imagining, were they alive, what her parents, who had loved her and known her as a child, a sweet and placid and innocent child, would think if they could see her now — and found herself wondering how she could even begin to explain to them how it had come to this. There was a moment, as she took one last look at the body on the bed, when despite everything and despite herself she almost found herself feeling sorry for Jackson Crane.

Then she remembered once again the final moments of her father's life, the final years of her mother's.

Then she noticed a dent in the wall they had not quite been able to get rid of, a patch of paint that had not fully dried yet.

Then she remembered the memory stick.

Each of the many large wall-mounted flatscreen TVs in the cabin had a USB socket at the side into which such a memory stick could be slotted. On the basis that it was the farthest room on the ground floor from the bedroom, it was into the side of the set in the lounge that she inserted it. What was she expecting? Jess did not know. All she knew was that ever since she had first found it, on the floor of this cabin, it had struck her as being out of place. If it was nothing, some films he had downloaded for the flight home, some audition clips of unknown actresses for his next project, then she could just tuck it into the pocket of a jacket hanging in the hallway and go. Her fingerprints would not matter — she was housekeeping; of course they were everywhere. Still, if it was nothing, there was no sense having it in her possession, just in case when the body was discovered and the police inevitably searched the island, they went through the staff accommodations too.

Jess turned the TV on and found that whatever was on the stick had already automatically begun playing. She pulled a leather footstool up to the screen and tucked her clasped hands under her chin. Just five minutes, she told herself she would give it, with a glance at her watch — that was all she really had anyway before her absence would be noted.

At first she wasn't sure what she was looking at and listening to at all. The footage, while it appeared to have been edited to a fairly professional standard, had been shot from a strange angle and under far from optimal lighting conditions. It began abruptly, without opening credits, just a black screen with some numbers in the corner, the crunch of a car stopping on gravel, some vague noises like muffled footsteps, distant voices. Then a door could be seen opening. Then a light could be seen coming on. Then two figures could be seen entering what was now clearly a living room, in a hotel perhaps — or at one of the other Homes, Jess guessed, although there was little to offer a definite clue. Some wall. Some carpet. Some curtains. A table. A drinks cabinet. A phone.

The woman — slim, pale, tall, dark-haired, strangely familiar — entered the room first, hugging herself with both arms, and strode across to the windows and closed the curtains. The man leaned out of the door, as if to check they had not been followed. He turned another light on, crossed the room on unsteady legs to a drinks cabinet, dropped awkwardly into a squat, and started rifling through it. The woman was now visible only intermittently, pacing up and down the room, still hugging herself, her face obscured by her long dark hair, for the most part only her legs and the lower

335

half of her in shot. She was young — twenty-something? That was what Jess would have guessed from what she was wearing — all black, nondescript. He looked a good dozen years older, at least. Then, in answer to a question that the mic hadn't quite captured, the man — still squatting in front of the drinks cabinet, a tall glass in one hand now — looked back over his shoulder.

That was when Jess realized she was looking at Jackson Crane. It might have been old and fuzzy footage but there was no mistaking that face. That was when — with a jolt of the heart, her hands instinctively now on her cheeks, her mouth open wide in shock — Jess registered that the numbers in the corner of the screen were a date and a year and a time, that what she was watching was not a movie outtake but real-life time-stamped footage. With another jolt, she realized exactly what date and time she was looking at.

How often, despite the police's dismissive reaction, had she tried to tell people what really happened that night, what she had seen, *whom* she had seen? Jess had long ago lost count. Her aunt. Her uncle. The nurses at the hospital. Her friends. Her teachers. Every time she had seen him on TV, on a magazine cover, on the side of a bus. "That's him, Captain Aquatic," she would tell people. "He was driving the car." And they would tell her about shock and how it affected our brains, our memories. They would tell her he was a Hollywood actor who lived in America. And she would see the looks her aunt and her uncle gave each other, the way that when she said it to other people, their faces froze a little and they tried to change the subject. And after a while her aunt and uncle had suggested that it was not something she ought to bring up all the time at school, or at least when she first met people.

What does it do to someone, to be repeatedly told that what you know to be true is a lie? How does it change the way you relate to the world, to other people? How you process your grief, how you carry your anger? All that pain, all that rage — she could literally feel it, like a weight pressing down on her heart, her lungs.

Jess had been maybe eight years old, the very first time she saw a picture of Jackson and Georgia Crane together, in their wedding photos, on the cover of an ancient, well-thumbed copy of *Hello!* at the hairdresser. She had known without a doubt that the slender woman in the ivory satin dress, gossamer-fine veil resting lightly on her sharp cheekbones, was the one who had been in the car that night. She had wanted to go to the police, and her uncle had promised her he would write to them. One of Jess's fantasies had been that she managed to get a letter to Georgia herself, that it snagged her conscience and she went to the police and confessed. And the older Jess got, the stronger and more compelling the fantasy got, in some ways. Because surely she had a guilty conscience, this woman who was always turning up as an ambassador for worthy causes, talking in interviews in magazines and on TV about trying to use her platform for good, to highlight injustice or oppression or inequality. But if she had a conscience, then why had she not done something already? Why had she not done *anything* at the time? That hypocrite. That nasty hypocrite. When she allowed herself to dwell on it, Jess's anger at Georgia Crane had burned almost as fiercely as the anger she felt toward Jackson Crane himself.

She was ten when they first got internet at home, dial-up, and the very first thing she did was to go on all the Jackson Crane fan sites and cross-reference the dates and try to work out where he had been at the time of the accident. It had taken a long time. And her uncle and aunt had kept calling up

to see what she was doing and she kept calling back: "It's homework." The dates *did*
work, though. That was what it took a ten-
year-old girl one evening to discover; something that the police had clearly never
bothered to check. That Jackson Crane *had*
been in England at the time of the accident,
filming that awful Christmas movie.

She'd run down the stairs so fast she had
literally bounced off the wall coming around
the bend halfway between floors, skidded
into the kitchen so fast her aunt and uncle
both jumped in their chairs. She was panting so hard she could hardly get the words
out to tell them. And in her head maybe, at
the time, even though it was all so real and
still so painful, maybe one of the ways she
dealt with it was by thinking of herself as
some kind of detective, Nancy Drew, solving the mystery, her parents' murder, like in
one of her books, and now that fantasy
seemed to be coming true. Except that they
didn't seem excited, her aunt or uncle.
Neither of them had immediately pushed
their dining chair back and strode to the
phone on the wall to call the police. Instead
they'd exchanged a look as eloquent as a
sigh, and her uncle had gone into the other
room without a word, and her aunt had sat
her down for a serious conversation about

how much this was upsetting everyone, and how she was too old for it now. And her aunt had rested a hand on the back of Jess's hand and looked her in the eyes, seriously, worriedly, and said, "Do you understand me, Jess? This has to stop now. It's not good for him, your uncle, all this stress, on his heart. For any of us. It's not healthy for *you*, love." And after that, every time she went online, within about five minutes one or the other of them would remember something they needed from one of the cupboards in the upstairs room where the computer was, or pop in to see if she wanted a squash or a biscuit.

By the time Jess started secondary school she had got used to the way people's faces changed when she started talking about "all that," the way their expressions stiffened, the absolute certainty with which she could guess what they were thinking; she'd heard all the reasons someone might give as to why it could not have been Jackson Crane driving, why it could not have been Georgia in the car. Because she had been shooting something else on the other side of the planet at the time. Because why, if he had been filming down at Pinewood, which was near London, would Jackson Crane have been zooming down some country lane in

Northamptonshire? Because what happened to the car he'd been driving? Because how on earth would someone as famous as Jackson Crane have got away with something like that without the press finding out, the whole world knowing?

And so, sick of people's reactions, unable to answer these questions, Jess had stopped mentioning Jackson Crane, stopped mentioning Georgia Crane, even to her closest friends. An anonymous hit-and-run driver, that was what she told people, when she told them anything about her parents. Because she could just imagine what they would say, how they would react, all those girls at school who loved Jackson Crane, had a poster of him on their locker, his picture encased in sticky-back plastic on the front of their ring binder, if she told them the truth about him, that he had killed her parents — and that Georgia Crane had done nothing to stop him or report it. Nuts, they would call her. Attention seeker.

And it was then, perhaps, that her fantasies had begun to darken. That her childish visions of bringing Jackson and Georgia to justice — all her clever, ludicrous plans to confront them and trick Jackson into a recorded confession or prick Georgia's conscience — had begun to fade, and other fantasies began to take their place. Of crueler comeuppances. Of more savage reprisals. It didn't matter why, or how, or even if she had any hand in it; she just wanted them to suffer. Their films to fail. Their marriage to founder. But they did not. And it did not. And none of the even worse things she had sometimes wished on them happened either. And instead she had to read and hear about how happy they were, and how successful. How much their respective latest films had made at the box office. How excited everyone was about the production company they were launching. And she had tried to forgive them, Jackson and Georgia. She had read with impressed fascination of those mothers who could bring themselves to forgive, to correspond with, their child's killer. She wished she could forgive them, the Cranes. She could feel what it was doing to her inside, all this anger. And maybe she might have been able to forgive them, to start to move on, if they were just normal people she could pretend did not exist, if one or other or both of them were not always there, every time you sat at a bus stop or went to the cinema or opened a magazine or logged on to the internet. It was like being stung, being scalded. Time and time again. Every time she saw one of them laughing, on some red carpet, say, it was as though they were laughing at her. At what they'd done. At what they had got away with.

Even if she still could not work out quite how Georgia Crane could have been in the car that night with Jackson.

Because as far as Jess could ascertain, Georgia had been filming in Tahiti at the time of the accident, for weeks beforehand and weeks afterward. You could watch videos online of Georgia on set, talking about how much she missed her husband, how hard it was to spend Christmas apart. You could watch her, in material that had presumably been intended originally for the DVD extras, being interviewed on the beach with her costars, visiting the Pearl Museum in Papeete, learning to jet-ski. She had a tattoo done in a traditional pattern on her ankle — she mentioned it on Freddie Hunter's show, pulled up her trouser leg and showed the audience — so that she would always remember her time on the island. Nevertheless, Jess knew what she had seen that night.

Occasionally, when Jess was tempted to go to the press with her story, or to post something online, she thought about the way those who loved her most had struggled

343

to believe her. It was not hard to imagine what would happen to the person who went public with a claim like that, the avalanche of ridicule that would have been leveled at her, before you even started to think about the legal ramifications of making that kind of public accusation against a man that wealthy, that powerful, that beloved, with no evidence to back it up.

Now, unfolding on-screen in front of her eyes, here it was. Jackson Crane and a woman who could only be his wife, Georgia, rowing in a hotel room on the night in question, a room she now, given the context, had no doubt was one of the suites at Country Home, just down the road from where the accident had happened, screaming at each other about a car crash. About whose fault it was. About what to do next. About whether to call the police or call an ambulance or a lawyer or call Ned. Evidence. That was what it was. Precisely the kind of hard, undeniable evidence Jess had fantasized about and hardly dared even to long for all her life.

It was thirty-four minutes long, the footage. When she had watched the whole thing, tears in her eyes, body shaking, Jess went back immediately to the start and began to watch it again. And then she went back to the start and watched it again.

watch it again. And then she went back to the start and watched it again.

CONTINUED FROM PAGE 193

"Gone to London."

Those three words, emailed by Ned Groom to his PA Nikki Hayes at 2:36 a.m. on Saturday, October 30, have prompted perhaps more speculation than almost any other single aspect of the events at Island Home.

According to Detective Superintendent Neil Forsyte, the senior investigating officer assigned by Essex Police to the investigation, in a statement seemingly designed to quell some of the wilder theories doing the rounds, there was absolutely nothing else in Ned Groom's in-box or sent messages that offered any clue as to why he might have wanted to leave the island so suddenly, whom he might have been going to meet, where he might have arranged to meet them, or even how he intended getting to the mainland.

That Friday night was clear and calm. The party had gone off without a hitch. Ned was not, according to eyewitnesses, visibly intoxicated when last seen — as one Island Home bartender said off the record: "We'd served him a few drinks — he had been at a party — but I've never seen Ned anything less than totally in control."

The Home Group — and their lawyers — have been swift to respond to rumors that the company was in any kind of financial difficulty, or that large sums of money have since been discovered missing from company accounts.

There is no indication that Ned Groom might have had reason to attempt self-harm, nor did anyone report seeing him acting upset or out of character in the days leading up to his disappearance. "He was," wrote Annie Spark in the short statement still up on Home's official Instagram feed, "a brilliant man at the apex of his career. An innovator, a disruptor, a visionary. A tastemaker, a rule breaker. A man always looking to the future, to the next challenge, the next adventure."

His body was recovered from the sea thirteen miles east of the island, seven days from the date of his disappearance. According to the crew of the fishing vessel that hauled the grim discovery onto their deck, it was his shirt they spotted, ballooning on the surface of the water — at first, one crew member said they took it to be "an old white plastic bag."

The temperature of the North Sea probably prevented the body from surfacing earlier. It had likely spent some time on the bottom before bloating and rising, drifting with the tides and currents to the location where it was discovered. Even though bodies recovered from water within a week are generally not in an advanced stage of decomposition, confirming the exact cause of death with any degree of certainty is often impossible. It was noted in the postmortem that there was no obvious sign of physical injury, save those inflicted by the fishing nets used to bring the body in. With no broken bones, it is extremely unlikely, despite the persistent online rumors, that he was at any stage thrown or jettisoned into the ocean from a helicopter. The subsequent inquest delivered an open verdict.

Whether he was alive or dead, conscious or in some way incapacitated when it happened, the findings of the autopsy suggested it was likely that Ned Groom entered the waters of the North Sea at some point in the early hours of Saturday morning — the contents of his stomach revealed the fillet steak served on Friday night, suggesting that he died after the party but before he had consumed a substantial meal (his usual breakfast was eggs Florentine) the next day. All of which makes that single email even more puzzling. The tense, after all, suggests the sender has already left the island. If Ned Groom did so, no one has yet come up with a completely plausible explanation of how — nor, if he had hoped to convince his brother and his PA that he had left the island when he had not, why that might be.

It is easy, as Freddie Hunter says, to let the events on Island Home turn us into armchair detectives. To plow doggedly through the newspaper long reads, listen to podcasts with all the glib clichés of true crime reports, and let such cheap little tricks of familiarity prompt us to treat the whole thing as light entertainment. It is perhaps harder to put ourselves in the shoes of Ned Groom's elderly parents, seventy-nine and eighty-four, driven from their home in Wiltshire to a morgue in Maldon to identify the body of their eldest son after a week in the water, warned in advance of the kinds of effects on the skin, on the flesh, that a length of time immersed in saltwater has, told about the damage done by crabs, fish, and sea lice to any edible object that has spent any length of time on the seabed. Confirming that yes, they did still want to see him, even in that terrible state. Shown a Rolex the body had still been wearing and asked if that object is familiar. Given a moment to prepare themselves, a moment spent already imagining what is behind that curtain, gripping tightly to their partner's hand. Being shown a lifeless, mottled, waxy object on a gurney and being asked: Is this your son? Being asked that question and nodding yes.

Then imagine having to go through that process twice.

CHAPTER EIGHT:
SATURDAY NIGHT

NIKKI

The unfamiliar sensation of her phone sitting still and silent in her pocket unnerved Nikki.

On any other day, it would have been buzzing with Ned's constant requests and everyone else asking for five minutes with the boss. But, with all their attention focused on the members, Ned's absence had gone almost unremarked among the staff.

Still, every hundred meters or so, from sheer force of habit, Nikki pulled it out of her pocket to check for messages. 5:32 p.m. Nothing. 5:52 p.m. Still nothing. It would be dark soon and she should get back to her cabin to dress for dinner.

Nikki had chosen the quieter side of the island for a walk, where the staff accommodations were located alongside the ugly concrete jetty that took delivery of supplies by boat. Feet sinking with each step into the shingle, hood up over her head against the drizzle, she felt a strange sort of calm staring out to sea. Up ahead, there was a small collection of pre-Home beach huts that Ned hadn't bothered to demolish because nobody important would see them, clumps of tall grass that shivered in the wind coming off the water.

It was starting to look a little strange now, Ned's absence. Last night, after all, he'd been everywhere: spot-checking espresso martinis and sending whole trays back if the crema was patchy, chivvying waiters to keep a constant stream of small plates coming from the kitchen. Was his constant interference necessary? Debatable. Was it helpful? No. A sensible use of a multimillionaire CEO's valuable time? Absolutely not. But it reminded everyone who was in charge here, whose party this was, whose club, whose company.

She had been walking this way for half an hour, into the wind, noticing little, as the colors of the landscape faded around her, still no closer to having her head together. It was strange, how your perspective on things changed over time, how gradually. Even after all that had happened, she had still felt a secret pride in her relationship with Ron, a certain self-satisfaction that he'd chosen *her.* She'd felt a little tingle still when she thought of some of his compliments — he had praised her sophistication; she had teased him that he just meant her English accent. Smart, he'd called her, repeatedly, even though she hadn't seen the inside of a classroom since she was fourteen. "Book learning isn't what life's all about," he had said, batting away her modesty. These were things she had accepted as truths, things that had gone to make up part of her sense of self, a sort of gift from him, she had thought.

And then she got a little wiser maybe, a bit more worldly. And she looked back at some of the things she'd done and realized she might have tried to act older, but *sophisticated* was hardly the word. She remembered some of the things she'd said and cringed, clenched her fists in embarrassment, because *smart* was *definitely* not the word.

Her feelings toward him had not shifted in one great flash of revelation, but gradually she had come to see it all in a more uncomfortable light. In her twenties she dated properly, men her own age, nothing ever very serious, but still she let stuff slip — no names, no mention of the baby of course — and was always shocked at their reactions to the things Ron used to like her to do. And now, when she looked at photographs of herself back then, she was struck not just by how pretty and how reed-thin she was, but by the fact that no one could actually have *believed* she was the age she had claimed to be.

She thought about things that Ron had said — how patronizing to repeat over and over how smart she was, how he must have been chuckling to himself at this child bursting with pride at the compliment. How you wouldn't do that to someone you thought had half a brain in her silly little head. How the things that had seemed sophisticated at the time — like lying in his suite in bed, drinking champagne, ordering room service, and watching black-and-white movies — came to feel less so when she remembered they had literally never left the building together, that he made her duck out of his room and bolt for the elevator after listening out to make sure there was no one in the corridor, that when room service arrived she had to hide in the bathroom, and when he took a call she had to promise not to make a sound.

And often she thought about him, the baby, and the decision she'd made for both of them. And she wondered, with a pang, where he was and what he was doing, and she reminded herself of all those happy families, all those smiling children in the brochures. And sometimes she was absolutely convinced she had made the right decision for everyone, and other times she questioned whether she had just made the right decision for herself. But one thing she had grown increasingly sure of as time passed was that wherever he was, her son, whoever he was growing up to be, was better off not knowing his father, never learning the kind of person his father was.

Then she looked up and saw him.

Her son.

A lone figure, dressed for a run, headphones around his neck, throwing stones angrily at the water, as hard and as far as he could into the waves.

It was as he stooped to pick up another handful of them that he realized she was there.

"Hi, Kurt," she said.

He let fly another stone, rubbed at his nose with the back of his sleeve. For a moment she thought he was going to ignore her.

Then he glanced up. Then he spoke.

"You didn't know, did you? About the filming?"

355

Nikki tried to keep her face from crumpling. Shook her head.

"I never suspected," she said. "Not until this weekend. Not until you asked me about the package yesterday, told me what had happened. I had no idea. I honestly had no idea. I thought I knew Ned inside out because I had to, for years, for work, for my job. He was someone I respected, someone I trusted. And then you find out —"

She broke off.

Kurt looked across at her. "I know exactly how that feels."

"You've . . . watched it then?" she asked.

"Not all of it. But I've seen enough, to get the picture. Heard enough. The same lines, the same patter, the same jokes. Dad pouring himself a drink, pouring them a drink, sitting on the bed next to them. And then a jump cut to the next girl, the next Home hotel room . . ." Kurt took a deep breath, shook his head. She searched Kurt's eyes, trying to gauge if her own fifteen-year-old face had featured on the film, if he had recognized her.

"And I guess Ned probably thinks he's done me a favor with that. Spared me from actually having to watch what happened next." Kurt rubbed with two fingers at a point between his eyebrows. "But now I'm left imagining it . . ."

"I'm so sorry," Nikki said.

"You know, it's funny, growing up in the family I did, being raised the way my parents raised all of us. We were all supposed to be equal, and no one ever talked about which of us were their biological children, which of us were adopted. We were told our whole lives never even to think about it, that it didn't matter. We were part of the tribe, Ron was Daddy, Marianne was Mommy, that was that. And our birth certificates have their names on them — we couldn't find out even if we wanted to, without a DNA test, and I doubt my father would even be able to tell us now. I didn't care but I think there was always a part of me that hoped they were my biological parents, that he was my father. Not because I thought it would make me better than any of the others, not because I thought he would love me any more. Just because I admired the man so much, you know? Just because part of me believed if I was related to him in that way I had more of a chance of inheriting his magic. Now I hope to God I don't have a drop of his blood in me."

Nikki swallowed the words that were bubbling up in her throat. "Who you are has got nothing to do with who your father was, or what happened in those Home suites."

Kurt looked down at his palm to select a stone to throw, then seemed to think better of it.

"I've spent my whole life trying to be like that man. Idolizing him. But I should have known — I should have seen it," he said. "It was just one of those things you take for granted, stuff that Dad and his friends used to say, that Mom would roll her eyes at. That if you were a successful man there would always be these women, this particular kind of woman, who would throw herself at you. That it was one of the embarrassments of success, one of the downsides. I guess I just believed them."

He paused for a moment.

"But that was not what I saw, on this. That was not what I saw at all." He produced the memory stick from his pocket.

A wave broke, surged up over the pebbles, fell back. It was really getting dark now. All around the island, people would be getting into the capes and masks that had been delivered to their cabins, wondering if there was any significance to the comedy or tragedy mask they had been given. Nikki would be glad to have something to hide behind.

"I've been wondering why Ned was so

sure I'd pay up. I mean he knows I'll have the money, knows I'll have even more when Dad dies and it won't be too long before that happens. It can't hurt my mum now either, because she's gone. But he's asking for a *lot* and he must realize that after seeing this, I won't think my father deserves his legacy. Ned thinks I'll pay to protect my brothers and sisters, doesn't he? That if I say no now, I'm making a decision on my own that will hurt all of us. But you know what — this isn't my fault, and it isn't my secret to keep. Give this back to Ned, and tell him no. Tell him I'm going to leave this island right now."

Kurt handed her the memory stick, turned on his heel, and disappeared off into the darkness. She took it, closed her fingers around it tightly.

Back in her cabin, Nikki flipped open her laptop and plugged the memory stick into the side of it. The footage began to play immediately. Twenty-seven minutes of it, all shot in such a way, at such an angle, that the suites could never be identified as Home, footage jerkier and grainier than she had imagined but still unmistakably Ron. Frozen in time, exactly how she remembered him: hair still dark; creases around his eyes still smile lines, not yet deep wrinkles; the girls next to him on the sofa, on the bed, remarkably similar to how she now imagined herself acting in that suite twenty-five years ago. Although none of them *were* her. Ned had spared Kurt that as well as the graphic detail — with the obvious threat that the unedited version was on file somewhere. An extended trailer for what would be leaked if Kurt failed to pay up.

"God, I never do this, but you're so pretty, you know that? And so smart, my God. So sophisticated . . ." That self-assured drawl. Those familiar words. "Come here, baby."

Nikki ran to the bathroom to be sick.

JESS

All the way from cabin forty-two Jess had followed Georgia's golf cart in her own, keeping always just a turn or so behind, swearing under her breath when another buggy cut in, furious when that buggy stopped at a junction to let another by. And thrilled when their little convoy made it to the circular drive in front of the Manor — where all the guests had been instructed to gather for the start of that evening's performance — to spot Georgia (and it was unmistakably Georgia, that long pale neck, those clavicles, that glossy dark hair), with her mask on but her hood back, being assisted onto the gravel by her driver.

Just a few feet away — just a few people away — from Georgia she had hovered, next to the fountain in the middle of the drive's turning circle, while they all waited expectantly for something to happen. Jess wrapped her own cloak more tightly around her chest — it was so long she was terrified she might trip and rip the whole thing off, instantly giving the game away — pulling the hood down over her hairline so it almost met the top of her mask.

And then the performance had finally begun, with a sudden screech of violin, an announcement, the appearance of a troupe of costumed footmen and ladies-in-waiting in the doorway of the Manor, who then proceeded down the steps and off in various directions, instructing groups of people to follow them as they passed, and Jess had needed to be quick off the mark to keep her in view as Georgia and the three or four people standing with her were steered off — "This way!" — through a brick arch into the old herb garden. All through the garden, up the path through the woods (the trees lit up a ghostly white), Jess had kept her eyes fixed on the back of Georgia's hood, picking up the pace when it looked as though

Georgia were pulling ahead of her, hanging back when Georgia paused or slowed.

You had to admit, it was quite the spectacle. The cloaks. The masks. The solemn, flashlight-lit procession through the gardens, the candles in the windows of the Manor, the spark-scattering braziers on the main lawn. The beckoning woman in the flowing white dress, bearing a lantern, who had suddenly appeared at the mouth of one of the paths into the woods. The mustached man in the three-piece vintage shooting suit, fob watch in hand, abruptly striding, head down, through the gathered guests, intent on his timepiece, muttering to himself. The whispering voices in the hedgerows, the glimpses of faces among the trees. The sudden scream from a nearby, suddenly illuminated, grove of trees.

From behind her mask, Jess kept her eyes pinned on the woman in front of her.

It had not come to her all at once, this plan. For a long time, when she imagined taking her revenge on Jackson Crane — and it was Jackson Crane who was always the focus of these fantasies — it was a simple, bloody, spectacular vengeance she had wreaked. In how many different vehicles had she run that man over in her head? How often in her dreams had she found herself

362

somehow serving him in a restaurant, perhaps the grillroom at the Grange, and realized as she looked down at the white tablecloth in front of him that there was a steak knife in her hands, a carving knife, a corkscrew. And it was always at the moment of that first stab that she woke up, always at the moment the car she was behind the steering wheel of hit him, that the fantasy faded, because that was all they were, dreams, fantasies. It was when her brain started working on specific, detailed ways of killing Jackson and getting away with it that she knew this was turning into something more.

It was the idea of the overdose that came to her first, the idea of spiking his drink. Then the idea of somehow planting the rest of the bottle of pills on Georgia. And that had seemed like the appropriate punishment, the fitting reward, for Georgia Crane.

This final touch had come to her only on the island itself. Only after she had seen that footage. Only when she had watched, over and over, as Jackson slurred his guilt, as in the background Georgia Crane — the woman she had always somehow imagined as bullied by her husband into silence, into complicity — took phone calls, made phone calls, took control of the situation. If Jackson was responsible for the crime, it was clear who was responsible for the cover-up.

There had been no problem getting her hands on a mask and cloak of her own, that afternoon. Jess had simply presented herself and requested one for a member who she said was running late and would have to join the performance on the lawn itself. All kinds of details she had worked out in case they asked her who had authorized that, who the member was. All the guy had actually asked was what size cloak was needed, and what kind of mask.

Evidently Jess had looked blank. Then for the first time he had glanced up at her.

"The mask — comedy or tragedy? Which one?"

"Doesn't matter," Jess had told him.

A little way up ahead through the woods Jess tried to move slightly closer to Georgia as their group merged with another larger group, people exchanging nods as they did so, calling out through the trees. How strange a sensation this must be, for some of them, to be moving through the world unrecognized. How convenient for her.

So focused was Jess's attention on Georgia that for the most part the performance itself — How much had all this cost? How much work had gone into it all? — hardly registered. At one point a young man — with a powdered face, in tights and breeches and a uniform covered in buttons — appeared around a corner of one of the greenhouses and slipped a wax-sealed letter into Jess's hand. A moment later a girl in a tall white wig had appeared from behind them and started asking whether anyone had a message for her; it had taken Jess another moment to work out why everyone was all of a sudden looking at her. At one point, in a glade — she had rather lost track of where they were on the island by this point — they watched a duel between two men in tricorne hats, saw one suddenly plant his blade deep into the other, heard the other let out an all-too-convincing grunt of pain, and crumple. In a corner of the sunken rose garden they had come upon a man with rope-bound hands and a sack on his head standing on the boards of a raised platform, a noose around his neck; listened as another man holding a scroll read from it his sentence; watched as the rope of the noose was thrown up — second attempt — over the branch of an oak tree that overhung the garden. Then they were hustled swiftly away.

Only once, and only for a moment, was Jess nearly separated from Georgia, as they were nearing the Manor for the grand finale, when someone stepped out from behind a bush ("Quickly! This way! We must hurry!") and laid a hand on Jess's forearm and tried to steer her and two or three of the people from their group off in a different direction, the *wrong* direction. Jess had only managed to break away and catch up with the others by ignoring the cast member, literally tugging her arm out of their grip, ignoring their calls as she forged off after the others, in pursuit of Georgia's departing back.

And now here they all were, gathered on the main lawn again, flashlights glimmering through the trees as, group by group, the audience were led back to where they had started, the wind setting the flames in the braziers jumping and skipping. The tragic masks looked more mournful than ever. The grins on the comic masks appeared maniacal and mocking.

Through the windows of the ballroom, the dim glow of candlelight was visible; through the ballroom's open doors the sound of instruments being tuned could be heard. Then they were all ushered up the stone steps from the lawn to the broad balustraded terrace and directed into the ballroom. There, a dozen musicians in evening dress and half masks occupied one corner, while a group of dancers all in cotton shifts or their shirtsleeves, all shoeless, all utterly expressionless, stood frozen in the center of the room — and she found herself (at last) right next to Georgia Crane, so close that she could have reached out and touched her, so close that when she muttered something it was only Georgia who turned around.

"I'm sorry?"

Their eyes met. Impossible to tell what expression was on Georgia's face, beneath that grinning mask. Her voice — that familiar, unmistakable voice — had sounded genuinely puzzled, genuinely confused.

Jess repeated herself.

"Murderers," she said.

No doubt under other circumstances Georgia would have moved away, would have made a fuss. For a moment, it was clear, she was wondering whether this was part of the performance. When she did take a discreet step back, away from Jess, she collided immediately with the person behind her, who shifted foot to foot and could be seen applying a little shoulder pressure back.

Jess leaned in even closer — until the foreheads of their masks were almost touching — and said it again, a third time.

It was the truth. Georgia and Jackson

Crane had murdered Jess's parents. One of her parents quickly, one of them slowly. They had murdered her parents and then they had driven back to Country Home, and he had wept and shouted and drunk himself into a stupor, while she had made and received phone calls and paced the room, her dark hair swinging. Calling whom? Receiving calls from whom? Their lawyers? Their agents? Some kind of fixer?

Because neither of them had called the police. Neither of them had called an ambulance. Neither of them had even bothered to look and see if there was anyone else in that car. A little girl with barely a scratch on her by some miracle, hanging upside down in her seat belt for hours and hours, talking to her parents and not getting any answer, in the freezing cold, screaming, crying, terrified, distraught. And when you watched that video, that footage on the memory stick, there was a whole hour, just over an hour — you could see the timer jump in the bottom of the screen, from 02:15 to 03:21 — when the woman in that room disappeared off to do something, or have a shower, or perhaps just change her clothes, because she was in a different outfit when she returned. And Jess found herself thinking that even if she — Georgia

— had alerted the authorities then, taken that opportunity to tell someone what had happened, even anonymously, they still might have been able to do something to try to save her father, and her mother might not have spent the rest of her life in a coma. There had been moments, growing up, when Jess had found herself wondering if Georgia was a victim too. What she had seen this afternoon banished that suspicion for good. It had been more and more frustrating, each time she had watched the video, how little actual footage of Georgia there was, how she always seemed to be captured from behind or speaking from just out of shot, how you never got a clear view of her face or her expression. But even so, even in all that footage, there was not one moment at which she could be seen or heard expressing any concern about the people in the car, any remorse for what she and Jackson had caused, any worry about anyone other than the two of them in that room.

Even though the dance had now begun, even though the music had started and the dancers were slowly uncoiling from the poses in which they had been frozen, Jess had Georgia's undivided attention. "Listen," she said. "I don't know what this is but if it's part of the performance I think it's in

369

very bad taste. And if it isn't . . ."

She took a step toward Jess but Jess anticipated her attempt to reach up and flip her mask off, to find out whom she was talking to. And as Georgia's hand came up, Jess caught her arm by the wrist, and she gripped it, and she turned it, just a little, like you would at school but harder, much harder, her fingers digging into the soft part of Georgia's forearm, and she kept twisting it.

Inside Georgia's mask she heard a gasp, a sharp inhalation of breath.

"The twelfth of December, 2001. Does that date mean anything to you?"

Georgia's eyes narrowed in her mask's eye slits. She thought or pretended to think for a moment. Then she shook her head.

Two weeks before Christmas. That was when it had happened. They had been at her aunt's house for the afternoon, down the road in the next village. It was only a fifteen-minute drive at that time of night. Jess had been wrangling with them about whether she could have another mince pie when they got home, whether she could stay up for a bit and help decorate the tree with them.

"Try harder," said Jess. "Have a think."

She did not turn Georgia's wrist again, but she slightly increased the pressure from her fingers for a minute, to show she was not teasing, to make it clear this was not part of the performance, that she did not care if there were bruises on Georgia's lily-white arm in the morning or how much it would cost and how much time it would take to digitally remove them for whatever film she was shooting now or next.

"I was in Tahiti," Georgia said, eventually, somewhat hesitantly, after some consideration, after some further application of pressure. Then with greater confidence, more firmly: "That Christmas, 2001, I was filming in Tahiti."

"You were in a black four-by-four, traveling too fast, driven by your husband. On a dark country road, on a dark night."

And the joke was, the awful joke was, if they had just come forward and told the truth this would probably all be in the past now. They would have hired the kind of lawyers only people like the Cranes could afford and the prosecution would have settled for whatever lesser charge they thought they could actually get to stick and after a few years no one would even bring up the crash anymore. Or how much he'd had to drink that night. Or whatever drugs he surely had in his system. Or that he had fled the scene.

Georgia shook her head again, faking ignorance. "I was on the other side of the world," she said, spacing her words carefully, emphasizing each syllable. "We were shooting all through the holidays. I remember because the crew kept blocking off the beach to film and they kept getting complaints. We had a big Christmas lunch at the hotel, a New Year's Eve party. And we didn't wrap — you can check this, this information is out there — until, I don't know, the tenth, the eleventh of January. And Jackson was making a film too, over here, down in Pinewood." Was it Jess's imagination or was there a slight quiver in her voice, when she got to that last part?

"You're a liar." Of course, Jess had checked Georgia's whereabouts that night, just as she had checked Jackson's. But she also knew what she had seen — had always known what she had seen. And now she had the memory stick too.

The music was getting so loud that even as close as they were, Jess needed to shout in her mask to be heard, and as they spoke the twirling dancers flung themselves, flung one another, around the room.

Georgia tried to shake her wrist free of Jess's grasp. Instead, Jess tightened it. Then Georgia did shout, did call out for help,

372

continued trying to shake her arm free and pull away. But over the music — those shrieking fiddles, the stamping of feet — her cries were barely audible even from where Jess was standing, and nobody could see Georgia's expression behind her mask. And still the music grew louder, and still faster spun the dancers. And their expressions were still frozen, their grins as rictus-set as the grins on the faces of the masks surrounding the dance floor.

And that was when Jess realized that Georgia was shouting Jackson's name, that she was looking around the room, scanning the faces, scanning the eyes, calling his name and still trying to pull her arm free and trying with her other hand to push Jess away.

He's dead. That was what Jess wanted to tell Georgia. Jackson Crane was dead and as soon as Jess removed the "Do Not Disturb" notice from the instructions relating to his cabin and somebody found his body the police would be called, and they would search cabin ten and they would search cabin forty-two. And once they had established what was in Georgia's cabin and when they had established what was in Jackson's body, it was clear what conclusions they would come to. And Jess would tell her that, and she would tell her soon, but not yet — not until she had some kind of confession, not until she saw something in Georgia's eyes that showed her she knew exactly what Jess was talking about.

"I saw you with my own eyes, that night in the car. I saw you in the car."

She tried to keep her voice steady but despite herself Jess could feel a note of desperation slipping into it, could feel the first hint of a suspicion that this was not working out according to plan, that her control of the situation was slipping. How long ago they seemed, those childish dreams of confronting Georgia, and Georgia confessing, immediately breaking down and begging her forgiveness.

"It's on tape, you know. Recorded. At Country Home. That was where you were driving to, that night, wasn't it? Where you drove back to. You and Jackson."

Still the music went on, the dancers dripping sweat now, their grins painful even to look at, one of the violinists just sawing away over and over at the same top note.

Jess felt a pressure in her forearm and she looked down and found that Georgia was gripping *it* just as hard as Jess was grasping *her* arm. And Georgia brought her masked face up to Jess's masked face, so close they were staring directly into each other's eyes, so close Jess could make out every vein, every tiny capillary, could see each individual clump of mascara on those famous eyelashes, so close that even over the noise she could hear Georgia's voice clearly as she spoke.

"I have no idea what you are talking about," she said, with equal emphasis on every word.

For a moment there was a flicker of doubt in Jess's mind, and then she reminded herself this was an award-winning actress she was talking to, this person with whom she was now practically wrestling in public, while the dancers spun and swooped and leaped, while the music swirled, while the crowd jostled and whooped and cheered.

Jess tried to pull away. Georgia maintained her grip. Jess glanced down at her arm.

"Look, I don't know anything about any car accident. I've never *heard* anything about any car accident. I don't know what this footage is, or how you've obtained it. And I don't know who the hell you are. But there is something I need to tell you. Okay? Listening? *Listening?*"

Georgia's voice was firm, now. Her gaze was steady. Their masks were practically touching.

"There is a reason we always have separate hotel rooms. My husband and I. There is a reason I never visit him on set, when he's away filming something somewhere — and vice versa. It's not a normal life we lead. It's not a normal marriage. How could it be? You can't have any idea — *I* didn't have any idea — what it's like to live the way he does. The way we do. The pressure. The temptation. The adulation. The scrutiny. Do you understand what I am saying?"

Jess was silent.

"Do you understand?" Georgia asked again. "Jackson fucks other people. He's always fucked other people. And I've always known about it. The affairs. The one-offs. It's not exactly the best-kept secret in the business. But there are rules. There are boundaries."

Jess tried to say several things at once and ended up saying nothing. She could feel Georgia's fingers digging now into her upper arm.

She was not finished.

"I love my husband. He is a flawed person, and ours is not a perfect marriage. We fight, and we argue, but I do love him, and it is a marriage. We have been through a lot. We have put each other through a lot. We have helped each other through a lot. I don't want to believe what you're saying — of course I don't want to believe it — but if it is true and if you can prove it —"

Georgia broke off, a catch in her throat, and glanced away — and once again for a moment Jess really did believe this was all coming as news to her, that she did not know anything about the accident. Which would mean . . . My God, what would it mean?

Georgia's grip on Jess's wrist was unshakeable. She could feel Georgia's fingers digging even more urgently into her flesh.

"There is something else I need to explain to you, though, before I start screaming, really screaming, and security comes, and we get that mask off and find out who you are, and why you're telling me all this, and what you want from me, from us, and whether a single word of what you're saying checks out. My husband has a *type*."

Had a type, Jess found herself mentally correcting the dead actor's wife, automatically, the image of Jackson's body on that bed springing unprompted into her head, and even as she was thinking this, she was trying to understand what Georgia was telling her, to piece together what she had seen, what she thought she had seen, what all this meant . . .

Just as the music climaxed, just as — as one — the dancers fell and swooned and scattered across the floor, just as the audience burst into thunderous applause, the ballroom doors crashed open, and someone screamed, and someone laughed.

And for a moment Jess's brain simply refused to process what she was seeing. And then she began to feel an overwhelming urge either to laugh or to scream.

Standing in the doorway was Jackson Crane.

ADAM

Jesus fucking Christ, thought Adam.

He had seen Jackson Crane in some states before, but never anything like this. He wasn't sure he had ever seen anyone in a state quite like this. His skin looked gray. His hair was a mess. His shirt was buttoned up all wrong, untucked, some of it visibly protruding through the open fly of his trousers. He was wiping at his mouth with his sleeve. He was walking like a man with his shoes on the wrong feet.

"Where is he?" Jackson barked at someone, the nearest person to him, half lunging at them as he did so. They recoiled, shaking their heads, holding their hands up in what they presumably hoped was a placatory manner.

All around Jackson people were stepping backward, discreetly retreating, as he lurched and shuffled across the ballroom.

"Ned Groom," he shouted, his voice so slurred with fury and whatever else it was barely recognizable. "Where is he? Where are ya, Ned?"

Pausing, looking around the room, swaying on unsteady legs, he gathered himself for a moment, then bellowed the question again. Adam would hardly have believed it possible, but the closer you got to Jackson, the worse he looked. The weird way his mouth was twitching, as he waited for someone to reply to him. The bizarre angle at which he was holding his head. Those flared nostrils. The stubble, crusty at the corners of his mouth. Those eyes, like bloodshot marbles.

My God, what had he been doing to himself in that cabin?

Seeing Adam striding toward him, Jackson came to an unsteady halt.

"Ned!" he shouted, extending a quivering arm and a wavering finger in Adam's direction. "There he is. Ned."

Before he had a chance to say anything else, Adam had closed the distance between them and gripped Jackson by one of his elbows and managed to turn him in the direction of the stairs. His first priority was to try to defuse the scene, get Jackson somewhere private. The upstairs lounge ought to be empty at this point, as good a place as any. With surprising force Jackson tried to pull away, pushing at Adam's shoulder with his other hand. Adam braced himself, and resisted.

"He's not here," he hissed. "It's me, not Ned. Adam. His brother."

"Where's Ned?"

"I'll take you to him," Adam lied. "Come on, let's get out of here, Jackson."

"Wanna talk to Ned," Jackson slurred.

You and me both, thought Adam. As the day had progressed, he had alternated between mild concern and intense irritation at Ned's continued absence — both underscored by the absolute certainty that, with his brother not there, anything that went wrong tonight would be blamed on him — on Adam — forever.

Seeing two of the security staff hovering, he gestured to them to keep their distance.

Shrugging Adam's arm irritably from his shoulder, rejecting all assistance, almost missing his step entirely several times, Jackson stumbled his way upstairs.

Adam pointed him in the direction of the

door to the lounge. Obviously under the impression he would find Adam's brother in there, Jackson gave a grunt and headed toward it.

Behind them the hubbub was beginning to pick up again. Laughter. Cries of delight and surprise. They had been a masterstroke, the masks, the hoods, he thought. Everywhere you looked people were trying to guess who was who, some lifting up their masks occasionally for a moment to prove or disprove a guess, to reveal perhaps an unexpected familiar face or the instantly recognizable face of someone you had never met before.

Personally, if one more member assumed he was his brother and slapped him on the shoulder to congratulate him on his party, he was inclined to ditch the bloody mask entirely. Even Annie had sidled up to him as they filed into the ballroom to pass him an old-fashioned, whispering as she did so something about it being a shame for the man of the hour to be without a drink on a night like this, or something equally obsequious. It occurred to him she'd not yet realized Ned was nowhere to be seen.

He drained the dregs of it through his straw, placed it on an oak console table, then hurried down the corridor after Jackson Crane.

Jackson turned to face him as he entered the room.

"Right, then," he said, in what appeared to be an attempt at a British accent. Then, lapsing again into his normal voice: "Where's Ned?"

Adam pushed his mask back on his head.

"Listen, mate, I can understand why you're upset. But rather than causing a big scene tonight I think you might actually be better off having a little lie down, know what I mean?"

Adam indicated with a tilt of his head the big leather couch in the middle of the room.

Jackson took a finger and poked Adam with it, in the lapel, hard.

"Listen, *mate*" — again with the accent thing — "I'm not a guy you fuck with. You try to fuck with me, you get fucked, you understand?"

Adam said he understood, half his brain wondering if it was an actual line from one of Jackson's films or whether it just sounded like one. Something that had always worked in Ned's favor, in situations like this, Adam suspected, was how rarely someone like Jackson Crane ever found themselves having to deal with anything like this on their own — without a team of people around

382

them to convey "how Jackson feels" or "what Jackson would like," without someone else at the end of a line to make the calls to ensure something happens. It was no wonder, then, that without his supporting cast of yes-men and fixers, he seemed to be slipping into the language of characters he'd played, just as it was no wonder people like him always went along so meekly in the end with what Ned demanded of them — separated from their phones, their lackeys, presented with an ultimatum, faced with the consequences of their actions going public.

Naturally, they usually liked to let off a little steam first.

"So where is your brother?" Jackson demanded.

"As far as I know? London. Can't tell you any more than that, I'm afraid — mainly because I don't fucking know."

Jackson narrowed his eyes — no mean feat, given the puffy slits they'd been to begin with.

Adam held his hands up.

"Honestly, mate, as far as I can tell, he's not on the island. He sent an email saying he'd been called away to London. That's literally all I know."

Jackson took a couple of steps forward and

all at once his face was right in Adam's, and when Adam jerked his head back, a nasty little smile crossed Jackson's face, and he was spitting as he spoke and you could almost feel the waves of rage emanating from him as he hissed directly into Adam's ear that he could tell his brother that he was a fucking dead man. That *anyone* who tried to blackmail Jackson Crane was a fucking dead man.

And with that, Jackson turned on his heel and stormed out of the room, although not without shoulder-barging the doorframe on the way out.

With a deep sigh, Adam sank for a moment into the armchair that sat in front of the curved bay window, pausing only to lift his feet up and then let them drop on the big Louis Vuitton trunk in front of it that served as a coffee table, resting his heels on the copies of Home's in-house magazine, *Home Truths,* fantailed across it. He stared directly out across the pitch-black sea.

Suddenly he felt absolutely spent.

One of the windows of the room was ajar and from the lawn, down below, he could hear the sound of music, a breaking glass, laughter. All in all, apart from Ned's absence and Jackson's coked-up tantrum, it had been a pretty typical Home launch, so far.

It was also going to be his last. That was what Adam had decided. Come what may. Even if it cost him his marriage, even if it broke Laura's heart, he could no longer be part of this. He did not expect to be forgiven. Not by Laura, not by Ned, not by anyone. He did not deserve to be forgiven. He had let himself down and he had let his wife down, not once but over and over and over. He had allowed terrible things to be done at Home, and said nothing. He had done terrible things himself.

He had burned the original Home Club down. Torched the fucking place. Well, Adam and two other guys from the club, both of whom had been paid well for their work and their silence. Adam? He had done it for nothing. He had done it for love. All those family memories up in smoke. All those old signed photos from over the decades, all up the stairs. All that history. Adam would never forget how he'd felt the next morning, Ned waking him with a phone call to tell him: "Bad news, mate, I'm afraid. Turns out there was some old thesp fast asleep in the gents last night . . ." And Adam had dropped the phone; it had literally slipped through his fingers, meaning it was not until he picked it up again that he could hear Ned at the other end of the line, howling with laughter. In the years since, he had wondered whether Ned might not have found it almost equally funny if it had been true. Sometimes, with a shudder, he thought about what else he might have done, in those days, if Ned had asked him to, or told him the future of their business depended on it.

He had not been threatening Ned, when he had dropped that remark — was it only the previous afternoon? — about all he had done for the club, although he could see now how Ned had taken it that way. All Adam had been trying to do was point out how many risks he'd taken. How much he'd sacrificed. How much of himself he had allowed to be eroded, corroded.

Christ, he felt knackered. Adam checked his watch. Ten past midnight. Time to muster the energy to do a final round of discreet goodbyes — and then it would be back to his room to call Laura. To call her one last time while she still loved him and thought he was basically a kind and decent and worthwhile human being. Perhaps one of the only people in the world who actually thought that. For now.

Adam reached up and adjusted his mask back onto his face, not without effort. His arms felt like lead; his hands seemed to be

386

hanging loose and heavy from his wrists. Jesus. It was as if not just one leg or one arm but his whole body had gone to sleep; his torso was tingling; his scalp felt stretched too tight over his skull. It was hard to tell whether the lights were fading and brightening or it was just his tired eyes playing up.

Somewhere behind him the door opened and closed and he was going to sit up and turn around and offer a greeting but for some reason his body refused to obey his instructions. He could feel himself sort of sliding down the armchair, and his head lolling back, and when he tried to speak it came out as some sort of weird moan.

And then he sensed someone behind him.

And then he felt something around his neck.

And he tried to speak again, tried to lift his hands up to tug at whatever was around his neck, tried to pull his mask off, tried to say something, but he couldn't, and whatever was around his neck was tightening, and he could already feel his eyes on the verge of popping, and great flashes of light were going off in his brain.

And it dawned on him who they must think he was, this person behind him, smelling of cigarettes, twisting whatever was around his neck tighter and tighter and tighter.

And it occurred to him this must be what it felt like, dying.

And it was only then it dawned on him how often, especially over the past few years, it had been Ned who kept putting temptation in his way. How often, when Adam was drunk, it had been Ned ordering *one more round.* How often it had been Ned who insisted on inviting a beautiful woman over to sit with them and then found some excuse to absent himself. And he knew that did not excuse the things he'd done or the people he had hurt. It didn't even really change how he felt about his brother, in the end, the love he had, which had always been unconditional, which had persisted despite everything he knew about him, and there was actually a trace of genuine pity, in the anger he felt. To live your life as Ned did, like some weird game that no one else was playing.

And above all, in his head, Adam kept telling Laura over and over again how sorry he was, how sorry he was, even though he knew she could not hear him, even though she was miles away and he was here, and he was dying, and what a stupid fucking punch line, he found himself thinking, to the stupid fucking joke he had made of his life.

ANNIE

Someone was running in her direction, their breathing ragged, noisily stumbling over bushes, slipping on gravel. From just outside the walled orchard she heard them race around the corner, skidding, panting as they did so. The footsteps slowed, hesitated, then paced back and forth, clearly trying to remember from the tour on the first day where exactly the little wooden door, half-covered by ivy, was located.

Annie checked her watch. It was ten, fifteen minutes maybe since she'd handed Ned the drink — she'd slipped out immediately afterward, making sure someone on her team saw her doing so, mouthing the word *cigarette* at them, making the universal smoking gesture. The finale of the performance was now in full swing — even from here she could hear the violins screech as the music grew shrill and insistent inside the Manor. She wondered which room they had managed to lead him out to, if anyone else had noticed.

A latch clicked.

She drew back into the shadows as a figure emerged through the ornamental apple trees.

"Annie?"

Shut up, you fool, she thought.

"An-nie!"

It was Freddie. Freddie Hunter, with his mask off, fresh from the scene of a murder, shouting her name. Annie took a step backward, the heel of her boot colliding as she did so with something hard, something heavy — a lump of masonry, she discovered, when she stooped to investigate with her fingers, presumably abandoned by some builder at some point.

"Shh," she hissed, sharply, in the direction of Freddie's outline. "Keep your voice down. There are people smoking down by the fire pit on the other side of that wall — they might be able to hear us."

"Annie," he said again, turning in her direction.

Stop saying my name, she thought.

"I'm not going to do it. I can't do it. I won't do it."

Freddie spoke with the quivering defiance of a man who has just, belatedly, discovered his moral backbone.

Behind her back, with one hand, Annie hefted the weight of the broken cinder block. She was not going to use it unless it was necessary, she promised herself. Not unless it was absolutely necessary.

"Where's Keith?" she asked.

He ignored this. Freddie was carrying his cloak and mask in the crook of one arm, his usually vertically waxed hair all out of place, the fingers of his free hand repeatedly combing through it, his face a fuzzy shape in the moonlight.

"He's a human being. You can't just kill another living human being because it's convenient."

She looked around — no sign of Keith. Freddie looked like a deer caught in headlights, ready to bolt at any second. She needed to keep him talking, to work out if he'd blabbed the plan to anyone after wimping out on it, if Keith at least had followed through.

"Your fuckups, your little hotel room meetings to sell stories, that's what we're all trying to cover up here though, isn't it? Your grubby little secret," she spat. "What I don't understand, Freddie, is this: you're a wealthy man. You're successful. Why do it to your friends?"

He shook his head, rubbed his face in both hands.

"I didn't want to. I've never wanted to. There was a . . . journalist. A friend, I thought. A lover, once upon a time. We did things. Together. With other people. Lots of other people. Consensual things, but things that would see my career on TV finished so fast your head would spin. You can probably imagine. They've got the footage. Phone footage, stuff shot secretly when I was wasted, when I . . . when my attention was elsewhere. Photos too. And every so often they need a front-page scoop and can't be bothered to go digging for one. So I get a call. And because I'm paranoid now, about being recorded, I always insist we meet on neutral ground, somewhere private, somewhere safe. Somewhere phones aren't allowed."

"Home," Annie said.

"Yeah," said Freddie, wiping his mouth with his cloak, the whiteness of his shirt under his tuxedo jacket practically all that was visible of him. "Home. Oh, the irony."

"And Ned? What happened just now, with Ned?"

Annie took a few steps closer to Freddie, her fingers tightening on the masonry block behind her back. If he had told Ned anything, she had decided, he was a dead man. If he said anything about going to the police . . .

"I didn't see."

"You didn't see?"

392

"Jackson turned up, all weird and crazy-eyed, demanding to see Ned. We followed them both out of the ballroom, trailed behind them upstairs. Keith and I were waiting outside the room while Jackson was screaming at him, hoping he might do the job for us. Then I realized: I just couldn't do it. I wanted to — but I couldn't. I just couldn't. Even if it all comes out, every story I've sold, every friendship I've tainted, even if Kyra never talks to me again, I'd still rather live with the shame of that than the guilt of knowing I've killed a man."

This struck Annie, at that moment, as pretty much the epitome of selfishness.

It's not all about you, she was tempted to say. This was *her* career, *her* life, perhaps even her freedom on the line. Conspiracy to murder. Incitement to violence. She could just see the tabloid headlines already. In her head it felt like she was trying to play chess, very fast, a bit drunk, even though she was stone-cold sober. If Keith had managed to overpower Ned, if the GHB had kicked in, then maybe, just maybe, everything was going to turn out okay. If Ned managed to fight Keith off, even for long enough to shout for help, they were all fucked.

Someone was coming, stomping noisily through the bushes, scrabbling around on the far side of the wrong wall for the orchard door, swearing to themselves. Freddie flinched, looked up, and in an instant was through the door and gone.

In the dark, the pale trunks of the apple trees all around were ghostly. Somewhere in the branches over Annie's head a pigeon was cooing to itself, *brrrrp brrrrp.*

Tell me Keith hasn't lost his nerve, she thought to herself. Tell me Keith Little isn't about to start bleating on about his conscience too.

Having finally rounded the corner and found the door in the wall, Keith staggered through.

"Over here," she hissed, under her breath. The shape stopped, turned in her direction.

"Annie?"

"Keith?"

"My God, Annie, my fucking God."

"What happened?"

With her free hand, Annie reached her phone out of her pocket, switched the flashlight on, held it up so Keith could see where he was stepping.

"What happened?" she asked again.

In answer, he held up his hands, and in the stark light of the phone she could see his torn palms, the deep bloody tracks in his hands, the paths the cord tie of his cloak

394

had worn in his flesh. His skin was strangely greenish in the light, like the skin of a man at the bottom of the sea, the blood absolutely black.

"You did it," she said.

His face looked not just haggard but hollow, great dark shadows in the indentations of his cheeks. He stared at her.

"He's dead?" she prompted.

He continued to stare at her. Had she detected just the slightest hint of a nod, or was that just the hand that was holding the flashlight quivering? The blood was literally dripping from Keith's hands, trickling stickily down to the ends of his fingers. He barely seemed even to notice.

"You did it," she prompted again. "Keith?"

She was tempted to click her fingers, clap her hands, slap him. Something, anything, to break this stare, snap him back to reality.

"It wasn't him."

"What do you mean?"

"It wasn't Ned. I don't know what happened. We followed him, like you told us. Jackson Crane had been shouting his name, for fuck's sake, in the ballroom. And then from the back, when I went into the room upstairs after Jackson stormed out, he was slumped on the armchair and from behind it could *only* have been Ned, his silhouette, his outline, the slope of the man's shoulders. But it wasn't Ned."

"It wasn't Ned."

"It was Adam. You made me strangle Adam Groom. And because that spineless fuck Freddie ran off down the corridor like a little girl, I had to hide the body myself." Keith looked at his hands as if they had somehow done all this independently of his brain.

Oh fuck, she thought, the pieces of her mental chess game scattering, the whole board cartwheeling through the air. Oh fuck, she thought, as Keith stepped forward and began shaking her by the elbows and asking her what the fuck he should do, what the fuck was he going to do. I don't know, she thought. Why do people always think I'm going to sort out their messes? I didn't tell you to kill the wrong person, did I? Get as far the fuck away from here as possible, was her advice, probably.

"Listen," she said, "let's just slow down and take this step by step. Let's not do anything else at all until we've thought it through carefully."

Adam, dead? Adam, dead. Then where the fuck was Ned?

Where the fuck had Freddie gone running off to, for that matter? Jesus. What if he spoke to someone? Told them what she'd asked him to do?

"I've got to get out of here," Keith announced, belatedly, the penny finally dropping as he glanced down at himself, looked at his hands as if he were finally seeing the state of them. "I've got to get off this fucking island."

Then, somewhere quite nearby, they heard the sound of a helicopter preparing to take off.

CONTINUED FROM PAGE 227

It was the helicopter that woke her up, according to Lyra Highway.

"I could hear the noise, going right over our cabin, really low, shaking stuff. And I was wondering if Freddie was leaving in his helicopter, how were me and Mama going to get home? And I was lying in bed thinking about that when I heard all the shouting."

A thoughtful child, Lyra is strikingly similar in appearance to the photographs of Kyra at her age that appear in her mother's memoir. Throughout Kyra's interview she has been a polite presence, asking if she can have a biscuit, asking if she can have another biscuit, asking if she can play something on her iPad, turning the sound on it down when asked to do so. Likewise, throughout Lyra's interview, Kyra is present, making sure the pre-agreed,

398

carefully worded questions are adhered to, ensuring her daughter is not getting upset or anxious and that, as promised, she is allowed to tell the story in her own words. Just as she did to Annie Spark that Sunday morning on Island Home. Just as she did to the police, that afternoon, with her mother and a lawyer present, in a quiet room in the Manor.

"It was two men shouting," she recalls. "One of them was definitely Keith Little, I know his voice. I went to the window — Mama was still asleep, she's hard to wake up sometimes — and opened the curtains and I could see him, coming out of his cabin, with a suitcase under his arm stuffed with things, but the suitcase wasn't closed, and all his things were falling out, and he kept stopping to pick up dropped things and every time he did, he would drop something else. It looked like his hands were hurting him, and someone I couldn't see kept shouting at him to hurry up. And Keith kept shouting back for him to stop shouting." She thinks for a moment, choosing her words carefully. She glances over at her mother, who encourages her to go on. "And to shut the eff up. And then Keith came around the back of the . . ."

"Of the Land Rover," Kyra prompts.

"Of the Land Rover," Lyra continues. "And he opened the back door and sort of poured his stuff in. And then someone started beeping the horn. And then he shouted something again and he climbed in and they drove off with the wheels skidding, like in a film, so fast that I thought they would crash. But I didn't hear a crash." As far as can be established, it was the last time any human being saw Keith Little, or heard Jackson Crane, alive.

Asked if her daughter found the experience traumatic, Kyra Highway says she has so far shown few signs of it. At the Home Group's expense, Lyra has been seeing one of Harley Street's most highly respected child psychiatrists ever since. Of course, says Kyra, they have had several conversations, about death, and dying, and where people go afterward. "She understands that there was an accident, and that is why people must never drink alcohol when they are driving, and you must never get into a car with someone you think might have been drinking. But she doesn't know all the details, *about the rest of it,*" she says, lowering her voice.

The body of Adam Groom was discovered by a cleaner inside a Louis Vuitton trunk in an upstairs lounge of the Manor at 11:00 a.m. on Sunday, October 31, exactly twelve hours after the man who murdered him, Keith Little, drowned in a waterlogged car on the causeway — driven by Jackson Crane, the man last seen, disheveled and screaming barely coherent threats, being led out of the ballroom by Groom just a few hours before that.

It was a murder so savage that one expert described it, at Adam Groom's autopsy, as a crime of fury. A merciless, senseless, sustained, and brutal attack. A catalog of horrifying details. The cord drawn back and forth across his neck so frequently, so forcefully, that his windpipe was not just crushed but severed in places. The inner membranes of his eyes ruptured by the internal pressure of his strangulation. The missing nails on his fingers torn away as he'd tried to protect himself. The autopsy description of Keith Little's hands likewise lingers in the imagination, his fingers and palms lacerated almost to the bone.

Perhaps only a man whose hands made it impossible for him to drive would have agreed to get into a vehicle that night with Jackson Crane, whose blood-alcohol levels were off the scale, although apparently — according to the toxicology report, leaked to the British tabloid press — this was nothing compared to the cocktail of drugs (Xanax, zaleplon, temazepam, zolpidem, ketamine, cocaine) in his bloodstream. A cocktail so potent it was remarkable he could walk or speak, let alone get behind the wheel of a motor vehicle and attempt to operate it.

All night long, as one man lay dead, folded into vintage luggage, as two more were en route to their deaths by drowning on the causeway, and one was already floating, facedown, in the Blackwater Estuary, the party on the island continued.

CHAPTER NINE:
SUNDAY MORNING

JESS

It was impossible.

At first, despite the evidence of her eyes, her ears — her nose, as he had stumbled past her — Jess was unable to believe it. Jackson Crane, the man she had dosed with enough sleeping pills to kill a horse, who had washed them down with at least a bottle of whiskey, whose graying, unmoving, seemingly unbreathing body she had looked down upon in the mess of his bed, was still alive.

Admittedly, he had looked better. Georgia, standing next to Jess, had given an audible gasp when she had recognized him, visibly stiffening as he made his lurching, reeking way across the dance floor of the ballroom, bellowing.

There was at least a minute or two when Jess had assumed he was bellowing about having been spiked, having been poisoned.

Then she realized he was shouting for Ned. Did he even know how long he had been passed out for? Did he have any idea how close to death he had come? Or was this just a typical weekend in the life of Jackson Crane, more or less how rough he always woke up looking and feeling? He called Ned's name again, loud enough this time to pierce the hubbub even at the farthest reaches of the room.

Some of the people near Jess and Georgia tittered, but nervously, and they stopped immediately as his glare swung in their direction.

For a moment his eyes rested on Jess directly.

Then someone — Ned, presumably — took him by the elbow and steered him up the stairs, and someone at the other end of the room dropped or upended a whole tray of drinks, to scattered, ironic cheers.

And even in the state of mind she was in, even with all the things going through her head, Jess thought Georgia Crane's response interesting: she did nothing. Once, when he stumbled, Georgia flinched and took half a step in his direction, then very visibly stopped herself. Her hands, clenched at her sides, were shaking. Her eyes, when Jess glanced up at her face, were cold with fury.

No, perhaps something even stronger than fury. Perhaps something more like hate.

She didn't know, Jess found herself thinking, in wonder. She knew about the cheating, sure, but not about the accident. And Jess tried to imagine what that felt like. And for a moment she wanted to rush to Georgia, to comfort her.

Before she had even had a chance to think about what she was doing, where she was going, Jess found herself pushing through the crowd in the other direction, barging her way to the opposite side of the room from the staircase up which Jackson had just exited, shoving against backs, crashing into people's chests. Someone shouted something she did not hear. Someone pushed her back, hard.

Then she was running full tilt down one of the corridors of the Manor, people turning to watch her go. And as she ran, she realized she was crying, sobbing, the sounds echoing strangely in the mask she was still wearing, her cloak flying out behind her and tugging at her throat.

And then she was running down a path through the woods. In the distance, through a screen of thin trees, a group of people were visible standing around a bonfire. One of them threw something onto it and sent a cloud of sparks swirling upward. Someone laughed. She kept running.

It was impossible.

Jackson Crane was alive.

Among the many jostling feelings inside her — the anger, the fear, the horror, the disappointment — there was one, quiet but persistent, that took her by surprise. It was relief. Relief that she had failed. Relief that her plan had misfired so completely. Relief that she was not a murderer. That she was not a killer. Because Jess now had in her possession the evidence that Jackson Crane was.

There was a point up ahead where the path crossed over a little stream, a hump-backed wooden bridge over the water. At the top of the bridge she stopped, removed her mask, fiddled loose the knot that held her robe on, and let them both fall down into the darkness, the cloak a deeper patch of shadow for a moment on the surface of the water, the whiteness of the mask disappearing as the waters closed over it. Somewhere up ahead on one of the roads a Land Rover screeched past, its headlights sending the shadows of the trees moving, the music on its radio distantly audible. Jess rubbed her eyes. She wished it were possible somehow to reach inside her head and rub her brain.

Even now, when she pictured the face next to Jackson's in the front of the vehicle he had been driving that night, it was Georgia's face she pictured. Even now. Which meant that all these years, whenever she had thought she was recalling the night of her parents' death, refusing to forget what she had seen, refusing to believe she had forgotten a single detail of that moment, her brain had been at work, embroidering, reordering.

The lights in the corridors of the staff accommodations were turned down, the corridors themselves deserted, the blue light of someone's television showing under their shut door the only sign that anyone was awake. Just as well, probably, given how spattered with mud Jess was, how incapable she felt of any kind of normal human interaction right now. Back in her room she locked the door, pulled the curtains closed, sat in the darkness on the corner of her bed, and brought out her phone.

The second time she'd watched the footage on Jackson Crane's memory stick, once she had realized exactly what it was she was seeing, she had begun to film it on her mobile — holding the phone as steadily as she could, using her other arm for additional support, walkie-talkie turned off, terrified any minute that footsteps would come crunching up the drive to the cabin, that someone would start knocking on the door.

Once she had finished, she had removed the memory stick from the side of the TV, wiped it down, and placed it on Jackson Crane's bedside table. Let the police make of that what they would, she thought. The proof at last that what she had been saying all those years ago had been the truth. The proof that Jackson Crane was a murderer and his wife had gone along with it.

Or was it?

It is bizarre, the relationship between our eyes and our brain.

Now that she had been told the dark-haired woman was not Georgia Crane, it was amazing that she had ever believed it was. For one thing, this was a much taller woman than Jackson's slight wife. And her hair was much longer than she had ever seen Georgia Crane wear her hair — it went all the way down her back. She didn't walk like Georgia, move like Georgia, had none of the delicate, fluttering hand gestures Georgia used for emphasis. Her chin, when her face was briefly visible in profile, was even at a distance far more prominent.

Jess paused the footage with her thumb. She peered at it more closely. She pressed play again.

Even on her phone, even in this footage in which the woman was so often so frustratingly just out of shot or visible only so fleetingly, it was all the ways that this woman was clearly *not* Jackson Crane's wife that kept leaping out at her. Georgia Crane was an outspoken supporter of PETA. This woman was wearing what looked very much like a real fur coat. Georgia Crane would never have worn a pair of big hoop earrings like that, unless for some film role. Georgia Crane's stunt double this woman might have been. Georgia Crane she was not.

Which meant all this time Jess had been directing her hate at the wrong woman.

A type, Georgia had said. My husband has a type.

The footage came to an end. Jess pressed play again. Again the couple burst into the room, Jackson first, the woman following. Again Jackson made his way straight to the liquor cabinet, made a drink for himself, and didn't offer to make a drink for her. Again Jess watched her pace, toss her hair, ignore Jackson as he ranted and burbled and snarled, slumping ever deeper in his armchair, spilling ever more drink down his chin.

"Who are you?" Jess muttered aloud, under her breath.

There was still, Jess's brain kept telling her, something familiar about the way this woman was behaving, something familiar in the way that, as she talked to him, she gathered up her thick hair in one hand and turned it and then let it fall against her back. Her nods. Her shakes of the head. The peculiar combination of subservience and arrogance in her manner. These were not Georgia Crane's gestures, but they were gestures Jess had seen before, did recognize. She racked her brains. She was also tall, this woman, strikingly tall. A model? Some kind of athlete? Another actress? Was it on TV she'd seen these gestures, this person, before? That didn't feel quite right. She paused the footage. She turned the volume up. She scrolled it back a few seconds. She pressed play again. Jackson Crane said something over his shoulder. The woman emitted a familiar, mirthless, single-note laugh.

My God. Of course. How had Jess not seen it before? She had watched and re-wound, watched and rewound this footage, strained her ears to catch each muffled com-

410

ment, obsessively paused and restarted it, rewound and replayed it once more. But she had seen just what she had expected to see, wanted to see. Over and over again her brain had refused to process the evidence of her eyes and ears, refused to acknowledge what was now so glaring, now so obvious.

The woman in the footage, the woman who had been in the car that night, who was in the room with Jackson Crane, was Annie Spark.

NIKKI

It was now almost twenty-four hours since Ned had disappeared into the water, the waves tonight just as rough as they'd been when Nikki had stood in this same spot that short time ago — was it really only a day? — and watched as Ned Groom flailed helplessly around in them.

It is quite a difficult thing to process, watching someone die.

Having stood back passively as a man you knew could not swim tumbled backward into the darkness. Having observed as the phone he'd been holding in his hand hit the wooden deck, watched coolly as his cigar spiraled separately to extinction in the waves. Heard his grunt as he hit the water. Waited for him to resurface. Wondered

411

briefly if he was going to resurface. Jumped a little as his spluttering head broke the water. Briefly wavered, wondering why he was not shouting for help — could he tell you wouldn't give it? Watched as he huffed and floundered and swore, down there in the water below you, trying to get his arms around one of the slick wet piles, scratching at them, getting pulled away by the rising and falling of the waves, getting slammed into them. Going under. Resurfacing. Going under. Cursing you. Going under. Spitting and swearing. Staying under. Staying under.

Had Nikki intended to kill Ned, when she set out to talk to him that night? She had not. Had she meant to push him into the waves? She didn't think so. Yet her mind had been sharp enough — perhaps the cocaine helped? — to pick up the phone that had fallen from his hand before the screen locked, click on the little envelope icon. Three words, sent to his PA — sent to herself — in the small hours of the morning could maybe buy her some time to think. *Gone to London.* It might put off questions she hadn't yet worked out how to answer. To give her just a little time to come to terms with what she had done.

Perhaps Nikki hadn't intended to kill Ned,

but she had nonetheless done so.

To get to the jetty you walked to the end of the rear lawn of the Manor; passed through a gate in the hedge into a rose garden, through yet another gate (this one marked Private); and made your way carefully down a long stepped stone path to the beach. Often, over the past few weeks, Ned would retire down here at the end of the night, to admire the yacht he'd bought and restored at great expense, to pace the jetty, to stare out across the waves. He often called her to demand she join him — even if she was already in bed. *Coat on, Nikki — I've got some notes for you to take down.* So she had known where he'd be heading, when he left the party on Friday night. For one last drink, a cigar to round the evening off. To reflect on his triumph. She had known too that he'd do so alone.

Hearing her footsteps approaching across the wooden boards, he'd looked up with a frown of irritation. Nor did this dissipate immediately when he saw who it was. "Had enough of the party, Nikki?"

Running all the way down both sides of the jetty was a row of sunken uplights, illuminating the drifts of spray from the waves. Between the boards you could look down and see the swirl and surge of the water.

"I want to know why you did it."

Had he snorted? In her head, as she tried to remember the sequence of events now, he had definitely snorted.

"Are you pissed? Not like you, that. Did what?"

"You knew, didn't you? All along. You knew how old I was when I started on the coat check. The kind of girls Ron Cox went for. The kind of girls he groomed."

He gave a little nod of recognition, an almost imperceptible shrug.

"It all looked pretty consensual from where I was sitting."

"I was fifteen years old, Ned. There's a word for what he did."

Ned brought his cigar to his lips, inhaled.

"You set the whole thing up, didn't you? And then you filmed it so that you could blackmail him: nice-guy director cheats on his wife with a child. He'd been a member a while before I ever met him — so you already had him on film sleeping with other girls, but you couldn't easily prove *they* were underage. And there's only so much an everyday adulterer is, presumably, prepared to pay to hush it all up. Having him sleep with me made it so much worse for

him, didn't it? And so much better for you."
She gave a short laugh.

"You must have thought you'd won the
lottery when you found out I was pregnant.
What a stroke of luck! I was so much more
valuable then — you used me to make him
give you the money for Manhattan Home,
didn't you? Your lawyer sent me over the
contract — signed and dated by Ron three
days after I told you I was pregnant. I was
worth a lot, I suppose, because the lawyer
also told me the loan was simply canceled a
few months after, that you never had to pay
those millions back. That's a pretty big gift.
And he kept on giving you cash every now
and again, when you asked for it, didn't he,
until his dementia meant you could no
longer put the squeeze on him. That part I
understand."

Ned offered no response.

"What I don't understand is why you gave
him my baby, Ned. Whose idea was that?
What was the point?"

"The point?"

"Tell me, Ned. Because that's what I am
really struggling with. I mean, there are bits
of it I've figured out. I know why you
needed to get me over to the States, for
instance. I know why you needed me to
have, and then give up, the baby there — to

415

sign the papers while I wasn't in the UK. It wasn't just because that would make it more convenient for Ron, was it?"

Ned said nothing, waited for her to continue.

"It was the law over there, it was on your side, on his side — you knew that, because you were a lawyer. Family law, wasn't it, your specialty? And closed adoption meant that once I'd agreed to it, there was no way I could ever legally find Kurt, or he could ever legally find me. You couldn't have done that here. The law wouldn't have allowed it."

There was in Ned's expression a hint, Nikki felt, of grudging admiration.

"You're right," he said. "You're absolutely right. They're a nightmare in England, those adoption agencies — all those checks, making sure everyone agrees, making sure everyone understands. It's the Wild West over there in comparison. We just did the whole thing through an old associate, a lawyer friend. But *you* signed the papers. Nobody made you do that. You said you never wanted to find your baby. And you never have tried to find him, have you? The thought of looking for you never seems to have occurred to him either. The law in New York was changed just last year actually, so

416

he could access his original birth certificate now, the one with your name in it, if he'd wanted to. It was a smart thing that Ron did, not telling those kids who were biologically his."

He glanced at the end of his cigar then back up at her.

"So the truth is, Nikki, yes, I did set it up. I never broke my word, you know. I promised I would give you a way of giving him a better life than you could offer him, and I did. Not doing badly, is he? Haven't heard him complaining much, the past twenty-whatever years."

"I still don't understand why," she said. "At first I thought it might be some mad coincidence, when he told us his birthday. Then I saw his birthmarks, at the pool, and I knew that it wasn't. But what I can't understand is, Ron was paranoid about birth control when I was with him, so why would he want to secretly adopt our son?"

Ned rocked on his heels, took a swig of his drink, lifted his cigar to his lips.

"DNA," he said.

"DNA?"

"If you've lived your life the way Ron Cox has lived his, it must have been a pretty scary time when all that paternity-testing stuff started coming in, back in the late eighties. It stung a few of my clients, cited in some *very* expensive divorces." He made a whistling sound.

"It was a new reality to adjust to for men like Ron. Not the prospect of child support — it's the reputational aspect that's the issue. The damage that a scandal might do to the brand. And you've got to remember how much your brand is worth, when you're someone like Ron Cox. When you're a director whose name people know, whose movies they go to see, in their millions, a guy who's known as a family entertainer, a *family guy* — there's a lot of money at stake. A lot of money. And it's not just your brand either. Marianne's got her things going on, her public persona to protect. And they've got this setup, the ranch, those kids — their kids, adopted kids — already. It's always been her dream to have this big family . . ."

Her voice a mere croak, she asked if Marianne had known about Kurt, who his father really was.

Ned snorted softly, exhaling two plumes of smoke from his nose. "Not unless Ron told her, God rest her soul. Or she figured it out. Jesus, the state of the guy's brain these days, he probably doesn't know himself which kids are his and which aren't."

Nikki could remember trying to process

418

this and feeling she was never quite going to manage it. She could remember the crash of the waves, the sound of distant voices, distant laughter.

Ned held up his hands — cigar in one, crystal glass in the other. "Look, don't blame me. It was a favor, really. A favor to Ron. He was giving me, giving Home, a lot of money to keep it all quiet. He asked me to arrange it and I arranged it. I mean he paid, of course. And it wasn't cheap, the agency, convincing them to adapt their . . . their processes."

"I don't understand," she said. "Why do Ron a favor, when you already had him over a barrel?"

Ned smiled patiently.

"Because that's how this works. That's how this all works. Give and take. You scratch my back . . . Sometimes you help someone out of a situation. Sometimes you call in a favor in return."

"Sometimes you engineer a situation . . ." said Nikki, understanding.

"Exactly."

There is perhaps no rage so compelling as the rage we feel on behalf of other people — or that we convince ourselves we are feeling on behalf of other people.

The final straw was the smirk Ned was

419

wearing. Pleasantly drunk, on a night when a dream had come to glorious fruition, he could not keep that pleased-with-himself smile from his face, reflecting on how clever he had been, how deftly it had all been taken care of. My God, she thought to herself, he's been waiting years to gloat about it like this.

"He was evidence," Nikki said softly. "Kurt. To Ron."

"Exactly," said Ned, and made a gesture like someone dinging a little invisible bell with his finger. He finished his glass with a gulp. "I might have had his balls in a vice, but that doesn't mean I couldn't do the guy a favor. A little gesture of goodwill, you might call it. What he didn't want was you popping up too, some hysterical girl, five years down the line, ten years down the line, and making a fuss and having the physical evidence to prove it was all true."

"And me, Ned. Why did you keep me around, once you'd got what you wanted?" she asked.

Ned had actually laughed out loud. "A good PA is hard to find, Nikki. And you are a really bloody good PA. You're polite, you're efficient, you're beautiful but you have so little ego it's like you've made yourself invisible, unlike Annie fucking

420

Spark. And most importantly, I have never met anyone who asked fewer questions. I would have thought at some point in the past quarter fucking century you might have worked out that we've been blackmailing members almost since the day I inherited the business. But no. It doesn't even appear to have entered your pretty little head. Stupid or just naive? I never could work it out. But I know you won't tell anyone, because who would believe *you*, my right-hand woman, weren't in on it?"

It was the laugh that echoed in her head, the tone of his words as much as the words themselves. She thought about all that Ned had done for her over the decades, all that he had done to keep her close, to make her feel part of something, loyal to Home, loyal to him. A father figure for the girl who didn't have her own. She thought about all she had done, and given up, in return. Still he was smirking and it suddenly hit her that it was because he genuinely could not conceive — and did not care, not one iota — how all of this might make her feel, that after all these years he not only thought of her solely in terms of her value to him, to Home, but also seemed to find it hard to imagine that she might object to that, or see herself differently. That was as galling as anything — the knowledge that he had played games not just with her life, and her son's life, but with their very ideas of themselves too, their sense of who they were.

There was simply nothing to say. She turned and started to walk toward the shore, glancing back once she was halfway down the jetty to see Ned looking out over the water once more, admiring his boat.

He was a big man, but he'd had a few drinks, and of course he wasn't expecting it. Not from her: his pliant, stupid, naive PA. (She had surprised herself too, when she turned and charged at him.) She had a ten- or fifteen-foot run-up, to build momentum. Nikki could not remember now, when she looked back, whether she had said or shouted anything as she did it. But she would never forget the moment of impact, her hands against his back, the couple of surprised steps forward he had taken. The second push, with all her force, before he had quite regained his balance. His stumble. His trip — the heel of his shoe catching on something, perhaps. The long, long time — some trick of the brain, surely — he seemed to hang in the air, frozen, falling. The thump with which his body hit the water.

God forgive me, Nikki thought, looking down at the waves, replaying it all again in

her head: the push, the fall, the desperate
final scrabbling that followed. She had killed
him.

She had killed him and she did not regret
it at all.

ANNIE

"Everything all right, Annie?"

That was what people kept asking, as they
passed, as she hurried by. As she made her
way — almost blindly, stumbling, on the
brink of panic — through the woods, along
the paths, back toward the Manor.

"Having a wonderful time!" she shouted
back, hoping no one noticed the strain in
her voice. Or just: "Fantastic!" or "Brilliant,
darling!"

Presumably she didn't look all right,
though, or people would not be asking.

Keith had killed the wrong man. And she
had no idea where Ned Groom was.

Keith had killed the wrong man and now
he was loose somewhere on the island with
his hands all fucked up and Freddie Hunter
was flying off alone in his helicopter. They
would blame her, of course. If they got
caught, if they got accused, they would both
try to pin it all on her in a minute. Unless . . .

She reached the firepit on the front lawn,

from which two members were attempting to light a joint, their masks pushed back onto the tops of their heads.

"How's it going, Annie?"

"Brilliant! Amazing! Don't set yourselves on fire."

Everyone laughed. A minute later she could hear one of the men behind her howling and jumping around and yelling about his scorched knuckles.

With any luck, she thought, they would burn the whole island down.

Annie forced herself to slow her pace as her feet crunched onto the gravel directly outside the Manor. She could hear the band who had struck up after the grand finale, the noise of dozens of simultaneous shouted conversations floating out through open windows. A waitress was working her way around the path, picking up empty glasses. She and Annie nodded at each other as they passed.

The Manor might have been in the direction Annie was heading, but it wasn't her destination. She checked to see if anyone was watching, then took a sharp turn left, down the slope toward the cabins.

Practically the first cabin she passed was Freddie Hunter's — and as she stepped up onto its deck, she realized the door was ajar.

Inside, all the signs of hasty packing. Annie checked each of the rooms in turn. On the floor of the bathrooms was a tangle of towels and bathrobes. On the bed his mask and robe. No wash kit by the sink. No clothes anywhere. No suitcase. He had packed it all up and fucked off. She checked under the bed. She checked the side of all three of the flatscreen wall-mounted TVs in the cabin — lounge, bedroom, bathroom (an unlikely place, admittedly, to watch your own blackmail showreel). With her sleeves pulled down over her fingers, she opened and closed every drawer in both the bedside tables, all of the slide-out drawers in the base of the wardrobe, even the drawers on the desk and the table in the corner with a lamp on it. The memory stick was gone too.

"Fuck," said Annie.

Of course the memory stick was gone; Freddie Hunter was not an absolute fool. Still, it would be useless to him — he didn't know it, but it self-erased in seventy-two hours. That was Ned's insurance policy — he had handed them all their own blackmail tapes knowing they'd be blank by the time they set foot back on the mainland, so that even if they were desperate enough to involve the police (and they'd have to be desperate, of course), Ned could protest his innocence.

But if Keith hadn't stashed the body properly — and given the state he was in she wouldn't have trusted the man to tie his own shoelaces — someone would surely sound the alarm. And if that happened soon, the police might arrive in time to view the footage. (Although perhaps, Annie speculated, that might work in her favor: it would certainly establish a motive for Keith extracting his revenge on the Grooms.) However, finding the memory sticks and copying the clips onto her laptop were Annie's only chance of establishing a meaningful hold over either man.

Shit shit shit. They were all going to be questioned. Everyone on the island, probably. It was going to be a PR disaster for Home as well as everything else.

On the other hand, she thought, with an audible laugh that sounded a lot more hysterical than she had expected, she pitied the poor detective tasked with cross-referencing every party guest's account of the weekend. If you asked them where they were and what they were doing even at this exact moment, half of them wouldn't know — or they'd certainly need to have a little think about it first.

The wind slammed the cabin's front door

and Annie let out an actual scream. This was pointless — Freddie had obviously taken it with him.

Keith's cabin was her next stop. She knocked, received no answer, hammered on the door, still received no answer. She looked around. Nobody. She turned her master key, reached for the handle — and discovered it sticky to the touch.

"Fuck," said Annie.

She turned the handle, pushed the door open, wiped the handle with a tissue, then did the same to her hand.

Fuck fuck fuck.

Not only had he arrived here before her, from the looks of it he was long gone too. The room? It looked like a murder scene. There was a bloody handprint on the mirror over the bed, blood all over the sheets, blood smeared over the towels bundled on the bed. There was blood on the mask on the floor, blood coating the strap at the back where he'd pulled it off. One of the bathroom sinks was a mess.

Oh Keith, she thought to herself. Oh Keith, when the police see this, you're going to have a lot of explaining to do.

His bags were gone — the bag with all his cameras, the shoulder bag he'd turned up with that had all his clothes inside.

She checked the sides of the wall-mounted TV in the bedroom, the one in the bathroom, the one in the living room. Nothing. She pulled her sleeves down over her fingers and checked all the drawers again. Nothing.

Then she looked under the bed — and saw bundled up, dark and hard to spot, pushed against the wall, the skinny jeans Keith had been wearing that afternoon. Annie got down on her knees and tried to retrieve them. They were just out of reach. Checking for blood on the floor, she lay down on her front and stretched for them again. This time she managed to get her fingertips on them, to shuffle them across the floorboards just enough to get a proper grip. Kneeling again, she dragged the tangled item out from under the bed. She checked the back pockets, patted the front pocket, peered into the watch pocket.

There was something in there. Grasping it between thumb and forefinger, heart pounding, she extracted it.

It was a memory stick.

Got you now, she thought.

The jeans went back under the bed. The memory stick went into her jacket pocket. As she was pulling her sleeves over her hands to close the front door of Keith's cabin without touching it, her phone rang.

It was, Annie felt, a tribute to her considerable reserves of self-control that she did not scream.

"This is Annie," she said.

She cleared her throat. She coughed into her hand.

"This is Annie," she repeated at a slightly more natural pitch.

"No," she said, shaking her head, "I'm sorry, I haven't seen Adam. I haven't seen him all evening to be honest."

She was pacing away from Keith's cabin, now, back toward her own. A golf cart rattled past, its four occupants swaying wildly along with each bump of the vehicle. Someone shouted something. She waved a couple of fingers of the hand that was holding the phone.

She halted, abruptly.

"I'm sorry. Say that again?"

She checked the time. It was past midnight.

"Well how long have they been there? How long? *How* long? Well who are they? What on earth do they want?"

A group of about thirty locals from Littlesea had been standing irritably in the Boathouse for an hour now, insisting that Adam Groom had personally invited them to have a drink and watch the fireworks, and were refusing to leave. The staff behind the desk had tried calling Adam. They had left several messages on Annie's phone too. Ned was unavailable, Nikki had said. *"Canapés,"* someone could be heard saying in the background. *"Tell her we were promised canapés. This is an absolute disgrace."*

And it was at that moment — as Annie tried to resist giving in to the hysteria that had been threatening to bubble up in her for quite some time now, tried to swallow the laugh in case she was unable to stop, while the voice at the other end of the line kept asking what she should do — that the very first firework flared overhead.

CONTINUED FROM PAGE 261

One of the biggest questions facing Annie Spark in her first seven days as interim CEO of the Home Group was what to do about the other eleven Home clubs around the world. Island Home was a crime scene. The brand itself was a global news story, its founder still missing. Ought the company to close the others too, out of respect for the dead? In the end, Spark reflects, the choice was an instinctive one. "To keep the Home fires burning, so to speak," she says, "was the least we could do for our members. They needed to know that whatever happened, we were still there for them. We needed places where our people could come together, grieve together, be together." Her decision may also have been a pragmatic one — according to a junior on Spark's team who has asked not to be named, they received more applications for membership in that week than they'd had in the entire year preceding it.

Sitting on an elegant brocade armchair in a quiet corner of the main bar of Manhattan Home, dressed head to toe in black with her dark hair scraped back into a neat ponytail, lipstick an uncharacteristic nude, she cuts a significantly less flamboyant, undoubtedly more serious, figure than she once did. Her task now, she says, is remaining true to Ned's vision. "Ned is irreplaceable, of course. But he would not want Home to die with him. This club has risen from the ashes once. It is my job to make sure — for the members' sake as well as Ned's — that we do so again. I think he'd be proud."

She grows thoughtful. "I hope he would anyway," she says, almost to herself. "I'm sorry." She takes a moment, a deep breath. "It's still hard to talk about. I think a lot of us, we're still coming to terms with it, the idea that he isn't coming back. There are still times — when we're sitting here, for instance — when part of you expects him to come walking in through those doors, laughing, cracking jokes. I guess that's the thing: if you're a big personality, a larger-than-life human being, you really leave a big hole behind you when you go."

It is the death of Ned Groom that remains the final tantalizing mystery of that weekend. All eyewitness accounts of Ned at the party describe him as being in good spirits, ebullient, slightly intoxicated at most. He was a man at the height of his success, the peak of his career, in good health, both physical and mental, very comfortable financially. "Gone to London," he wrote, in that last, cryptic, mystifying email — but all the evidence suggests he never left the island alive. Was there some kind of accident? Did he for some reason enter the water, fully clothed, not a strong swimmer, intentionally? Was he murdered? We may never know. Perhaps, were Keith Little or Adam Groom or Jackson Crane still alive, one of them might be able to shed some light on the loss. There are certainly those who believe that one or more of those men was with Ned at the time of his death, or caused it. Theories abound on the internet, as elaborate as they are ingenious. But the truth is, life is always both more and less complicated than fiction.

The classic murder mystery ends with a neat set of motives, a culprit, and a comeuppance. Perhaps that is why we read them. Perhaps that is why we love them.

433

Because real life offers us so few of these consolations, so few of these satisfactions. Maybe one day a clue will be uncovered or a confession will come to light to offer us the sense of closure the books and the movies have taught us to expect, and to believe we deserve.

For now, however, there are still some secrets Island Home insists on keeping.

EPILOGUE
A FUNERAL

ANNIE

It had worked out rather neatly, thought Annie, placing the copy of *Vanity Fair* into the pocket behind the driver's seat, checking the clock on the dashboard as she did so, and calculating the remaining time to their destination. Ned dead. Adam dead. Keith dead. Jackson dead. It was no wonder so many of the articles about Island Home made references to Shakespearean tragedy.

Not that she recognized it at the time, but all that first week, before Ned's body had been found, Annie had felt like a sleepwalker. One of the symptoms of shock, after all, is that you don't realize you are in shock. As acting CEO of Home — who else was going to do it? — she was issuing instructions, managing damage limitation. Taking phone calls from the press, reassuring members, telling the police over and over again what her movements had been, what she had seen, what she had heard. Unpacking how Ned had been acting, the toll the opening of Island Home, delayed and over budget, must have taken on him. Guessing where he might have gone, if he was hiding. Did she think he might have taken his own life? In all honesty, before he was found floating lifeless in the North Sea, she'd had absolutely no idea where he was or what could have happened.

Answering questions about Keith, his state of mind that night. Explaining Jackson's movements that weekend, as far as she understood them. Describing Adam, what he was like as a person, who could have held a grudge and why.

After a while, she had given her version of events so many times it had started to feel like the truth. She had even thought about starting to introduce some inconsistencies so it would not look like she was sticking strictly to a carefully devised mental script.

It was only after a week — when one of them asked her if she thought it possible that Jackson Crane or Keith Little had murdered Ned and disposed of the body — that she'd realized the police did not have a clue where to even start. After a brief flurry of interest in his helicopter, they had seemed to forget about Freddie Hunter as a suspect entirely.

She'd been very lucky. Keith leaving the memory stick in his cabin, rather than taking it with him for the police to find on his body. Freddie keeping his mouth shut. Ned murdered — she did not for one second believe it had been an accident — without a single drop of blood staining her own hands.

It really did feel as though, if you wanted something enough, the universe arranged it.

How strange it had felt, at first, walking into Home and feeling the atmosphere change and realizing she was the person changing it. After all those years second-guessing Ned, trying to read the weather, now *she* was the weather. Acting CEO of the Home Group, only awaiting a few formalities before the final rubber stamp made the position permanent.

She resisted the temptation to retrieve the magazine and read the article again. News is what someone, somewhere, wants suppressed — isn't that what they said? Everything else is just PR. And really, she couldn't have hoped for a better puff piece — mostly because she had all but written it herself. Ned had always teased her about that. "You writers," he would say, scanning his daily press cuttings, "must be the laziest people in the whole bloody world."

He wasn't wrong.

The *Vanity Fair* journalist, in his bobbly V neck, with his thinning hair, his rheumy eyes, about a decade older than his byline picture would have suggested, had turned up with the air of a man determined to get to the bottom of things, ready to investigate and judge, dissect and pontificate. Instead he had soaked up every word she told him, believed it, transcribed it, then paraphrased it in print. Two weeks after the interview he had emailed asking about the possibility of free membership.

As she watched the countryside skim bleakly past the car window, she wondered if there would be any journalists there today, hovering ghoulishly outside the church. A field full of crows rose and scattered. Where *was* this place? When she had agreed to come to Adam's funeral — after some careful consideration of how it might look had she not — Annie had known it would not be on anything like the same scale as Ned's, but she had at least assumed it would be in London. My God. Was this where they had grown up, Ned and Adam? No wonder they never talked about it. What would they have said? There was literally nothing here — miles and miles of flat brownish fields.

She steeled herself, knowing she would have to talk to everyone, look sad, sound sad. And it *was* sad, she supposed, for Laura and for Mr. and Mrs. Groom. But nobody else missed him much — Adam with his banter, Adam with his wandering hands, Adam with his casual sexism and his everyday laziness. It *was* a shame he was dead, she supposed, but it was not her fault. Not really. Not exactly. And overall, it was better for the business. What would Home have been like with Ned's brother in charge?

"Nearly there," her driver noted, pointing out the road sign they were passing.

As for Island Home itself, it was still closed to members, operating on a skeleton staff, everyone else laid off. The police had given them the all clear to reopen months ago, and bookings had gone through the roof when they'd started to take them again for the following year. But Annie wanted to at least appear respectful and, more important, to attempt to get into the bunker beneath Ned's cottage. There had to be thousands of hours of footage down there. Filmed over decades. Ned had ensured that the door was so well disguised, the police hadn't even realized it was there — why would they even think to look? — just as he'd ensured the cameras wired into every

439

cabin went completely undetected. It was not just the members under threat if they'd been spotted.

Because somewhere in that bunker there was footage of her too, from the weekend Jackson Crane had invited her to a cottage at Country Home. Footage of them fucking. Footage of the glossy black old-fashioned phone beside the bed ringing and Jackson breaking off to have a conversation with Georgia, in Tahiti, and Annie lying very still and very quiet. Footage of them discussing where to go for dinner, and Jackson insisting he wanted to drive over to a local village and have a pint in a real English pub. Footage of them drinking another bottle of wine in bed. Of him downing a whiskey chaser. Footage of Jackson indignant at the suggestion they should call the idea off, or get a cab. Footage of them returning later that evening, stumbling in, the full horror of the situation just starting to sink in. Footage of her on the phone, nodding along as Ned talked her through what to do — where to drive Jackson's four-by-four to, which part of the lake in the grounds of Country Home was deep enough to drive it into, what route to take to get there, what to do with the hand brake and the windows, how to wedge the pedal down with a brick. Footage she did not know at the time was being captured, that once she had realized, she then spent years wishing he would delete. Footage that would destroy what was left of the late Jackson Crane's reputation and everything she had worked for in one fell swoop.

The trouble was, only Ned had known the combination to the door. She had tried his birthday, tried his parents' birthdays, even tried Adam's birthday. She had tried the date of the Covent Garden Home relaunch and the date England had last won the World Cup. She had tried 000 000. She had tried 007 007. The tumblers had turned. The locks had not opened. The walls of the vault were ten feet thick. The door itself was the same. You could not get in there with a drill. You could not get in there with a bulldozer. The place was literally designed to resist the blast from a nuclear bomb. She'd briefly considered drafting in some sort of help, but where would she have found it and how would she have been sure she could trust them?

That was what made her heart race out of nowhere, forced her to take deep breaths until it passed. Not memories of that night with Jackson, and what they had done — she had long since developed ways of not thinking about that at all. Not guilt about Adam's death. Not sorrow about Ned's. It was the realization, which had only sunk in slowly in the days, the weeks, after their deaths, that, with a few exceptions, she had very little idea exactly which of their members Ned had been blackmailing, for what, or for how long. Some she suspected, of course. Some she could guess. But in order for Home to survive, in order for Home to flourish, the truth was that they were going to have to acquire a whole new generation of wealthy members. They would have to let the wankers in — tech millionaires, hedge funders, rich-kid influencers, and bullshit wellness gurus — and accumulate a whole new catalog of dirty secrets, recorded in the secret little Home Cinemas in every club, which thankfully had been easier to access and understand. Probably a whole new *type* of secret, given the sort of people she was hoping to attract to Home. It would take months. It could take years.

That was the thought that woke Annie up at night — in Ned's bed, in one of Ned's suites, the only rooms in the clubs that were not extensively bugged — and sent her to splash water on her face in Ned's sink and look at herself in Ned's mirror and ask herself if she could do this, if she was strong enough to do this. If she was brave enough to do this, if she was merciless enough to do this. And, to harden her resolve, she thought of them, all those members, all those disgusting members, all the things they got up to when they thought no one was looking, all the things they thought would never catch up with them. And she told herself yes, she could do this. She was even going to enjoy doing it because, as Ned always said, all you need to do is present them with something you know they can't resist, somewhere they think they can get away with it.

All Annie needed to do was give them enough velvet rope to hang themselves with.

LAURA

It was going to be a very different funeral from Ned's, that was for sure. No press, few celebrities, hardly anyone even from Home. Just a few old school friends, two or three colleagues, some mates from university, one or two of Laura's friends, for support — and Adam's parents, of course. Their second funeral in a month. It was typical early March weather: slanting rain and a damp chill in the air. In the doorway of the chapel, Adam's father Richard was greeting the mourners as they arrived. He looked older, thinner. As they were shaking hands, Laura leaned in for a hug and through his jacket she could feel the bones of his shoulders, sense he did not really know what to do with his free arm, whether to put it around her or leave it dangling at his side. Eventually he compromised, resting it briefly, awkwardly, across the small of her back.

"How are you doing?" he had asked her, his voice almost catching as he did so.

As well as could be expected, she told him.

Four and a half months. That was how long the police, the coroner, had held on to the bodies. First for the postmortems, then for the inquests. Four and a half months it had taken for the whole process to be concluded. If you could call what they had reached a conclusion, even then, when it came to her husband. As for the ligature marks around Adam's neck — discreetly covered up, when she had been down to Essex to identify the body — it was apparent immediately that they had been caused by the length of cord discovered wrapped around it, later identified as the belt rope from Keith Little's cloak, just as those deep, livid, pale-lipped wounds pictured in her husband's autopsy report had matched perfectly the ones that had been found on the deceased artist's hands when the police divers had removed him from the car. As far as who had killed Adam went, it seemed an open-and-shut case. What nobody seemed to be able to explain was *why* Keith had done it. No one who had attended the party that weekend had seen them argue, heard of any disagreement. Nobody could explain why the toxicology report had shown all that GHB in her husband's body. Nobody could explain how Keith had even recognized him, with everyone wearing masks and capes. Sometimes, she felt convinced there was some enormous conspiracy going on, with Keith as the fall guy, or Adam, or both of them. Frequently, she cursed herself for not having been there, for having said to Adam years ago that she wasn't interested in coming along to Home launches and parties, hanging around while he was working, feeling awkward. In her dreams Adam would be there, sitting in their living room or at the kitchen table, and she would ask him what had happened, and he would just smile or shrug, as if to say, *Don't you know this is just a dream, your dream, I can't tell you anything you don't already know,* and it would come crashing down on her, even in her dream, that this was a mirage and she was never going to really see him like this and she was never going to be able to talk to him outside her head ever again.

Rather than wooden pews, there were rows of colored plastic chairs, the stackable kind that always reminded Laura of school assembly. About half the chairs were occupied.

His mother, hunched up in a warm coat, was standing alone near the front row and Laura went over to offer her condolences. She seemed literally to have shrunk since the last time Laura had seen her: Laura was not a tall person but when she put her arms around Jan, Adam's mother barely came up to her chest. Jan then took a step back to look her up and down.

"You look well, Laura," she informed her daughter-in-law, sounding thoughtful. "Really well."

As ever with Jan, Laura immediately found herself wondering whether she was being paranoid, or if the slight hint of implied criticism she had detected in the other woman's tone was deliberate. She couldn't help it. There was just something about Adam's mother that Laura had always found terrifying. The very first time she'd met her, the first time Adam had taken her home for the weekend, Jan had welcomed her at the front door, given her a stiff hug, held her at arm's length, inspected with seeming admiration the brand-new Whistles coat Laura had bought for the occasion, and then told Adam brightly that if his girlfriend *was* planning to come along to church on Sunday morning, they would need to find her a Remembrance Day poppy. If Jan really was fond of her, as Adam had always claimed, Laura dreaded to think what Jan's manner had been like with those girlfriends of Adam's she hadn't approved of. Even now, even here, the instant Laura started talking to Jan she could hear her voice becoming fake and overenthusiastic, feel her face arranging itself into a fixed, ingratiating grimace.

It reminded her of how she had so often felt around Ned. My God, how hard had she tried to get Ned to like her, when she and Adam had first got together? The amount of time she had spent trying to pretend she liked him. Ned, with his perpetual watchful smirk. Ned with those jokes of his, which always served the purpose of reminding someone of their place in the pecking order. Ned who, in every single conversation she had ever had with him, found a way of making it obvious how much more important what he did was than what she did; who, whenever she and he and

Adam were talking, managed to insert some in-joke she would not get, or launch without explanation or apology into a discussion of someone she didn't know. And always afterward if she brought it up, Adam would spring to his brother's defense — so after a while she stopped bringing it up.

Something that had driven her wild, in her grief, was the way that people only ever talked about Adam in passing, that the newspapers and the magazine pieces always had Keith (WHAT DROVE AN ARTIST TO MURDER?) or Jackson Crane as the focus, or Ned and the clubs. What about Adam? she always wanted to ask them. What about Adam, her husband, with his little quirks, his little kindnesses? His attentiveness, when someone else was speaking. His ease, in talking to people, in finding a way of connecting with them, whatever the situation. His ability to see the funny side of things. To make her laugh, even when she hadn't wanted to.

Keep it together, she told herself, her hands tightening in her lap. She sniffed hard, a sharp ache in her throat.

Of all the people he had worked with at Home, of all the members he had spent so much time with, it was only Nikki, Freddie Hunter, and Annie Spark who had reached

out to her after Adam's death, done anything to acknowledge her loss. Nikki with a
big bunch of lilies and a thoughtful card
and a very touching long message this
morning to apologize for not being there.
Freddie Hunter with a lovely mention in his
opening monologue, his first night back on
TV several weeks after the incident. Annie
with a kind offer to do what she could to
keep the press away from Laura, and this
funeral.

Freddie and Annie were both here today,
sitting on opposite sides of the chapel, near
the back. Freddie had nodded at her and
smiled as she came in. Annie had given her
a little wave.

At no point in the elegy was the precise
manner of Adam's death commented on.
That was understandable. Instead, the vicar
used vague, generic words like *unexpected*
and *tragic* and *heartbreaking*. He might also
have said *unexplained* and *incomprehensible.*
The whole thing had been impossible for
anyone to unpick. It had winded Laura,
perhaps forever. There were experiences she
and Adam had shared that she was now the
only person to remember (that night in
Rome, that terrible restaurant, the waiter
with the dripping nose; that summer morning they had swum in the ocean, off Cape

449

Cod; the first time they had made love), private jokes to which only she knew the punch line. Now and then she still, after all these months, found herself making a mental note of something to tell Adam, found herself thinking of something she wanted to ask him, then realizing with a sudden jolt of the heart that she couldn't. A couple of times she had come across a bookmark in a book or something in a drawer that he had been the last person to touch and use and it would feel as though her heart were breaking afresh all over again.

For about the first quarter of the ceremony, she felt herself continually on the brink of tears, a raw ache in her gullet and a tissue twisted up in her hand. Then the vicar started telling everyone what the Bible had to say about things and she had tuned out for a bit. It was Adam's father who delivered the first part of the eulogy, his soft voice almost drowned out by the drumming of rain on the chapel roof, the wind rattling the windows. When it came time to talk about Adam's childhood, Richard's voice failed him completely, and he stood there gulping and rubbing at his throat, trying to gather himself and remember where he'd got up to. When she looked across at Adam's mother, she saw her head was down and her shoulders were shaking.

Laura delivered the second part of the eulogy.

Halfway through it, Annie's phone started ringing.

JESS

Sometimes in the middle of the night, Jess awoke and for a moment imagined she was back on the island. With a start she would sit up, feel in the wrong place for her bedside lamp, grope around under her pillow for her phone, start to panic, her heart thumping, a rising sensation in her throat. And then she would remember. And then her panic would start to subside. And then she would reach across to the correct side of the bed and turn her bedside light on and she would find herself in her own bed, in her own room, home.

It felt as if it had all been some kind of dream — or a lingering nightmare.

They had been extraordinarily understanding at the Grange when she'd asked for her old job back — or rather, dropped them a tentative line asking if they needed her to help with the handover or work out her notice period fully, letting them know she was unexpectedly available. As it turned out, they hadn't even got around to advertising the position and had sounded delighted to hear she had changed her mind about leaving, was sorry she had done so abruptly. Of course, it had been a little strange at first, being back. Naturally, with all those stories in the papers people were bound to ask her questions. It was only to be expected they would want to talk about it. The truth was, she didn't really have anything to tell them that they hadn't read about already. She had not seen Jackson Crane getting into the car that night. She had never met Keith Little. She had never been formally introduced to Ned Groom. She had only met Adam Groom properly twice. As for when Island Home would reopen, if it ever would, their guess was as good as hers.

All Jess's team on the Island had received an email from Annie Spark, acting CEO of the Home Group while its management and ownership were ironed out, thanking them for their outstanding work, especially everything they had done to keep people calm, and explaining that while they would find a bonus in their next paycheck, that paycheck would also be their final one. With no members staying on the island for the foreseeable future, no housekeeping team would be needed — nor any chefs, bartenders, waiters, or drivers. In fact, just a few security staff and some of the gardeners had been kept on. The email had both opened and ended with a reminder that all the legal documentation everyone who worked at Home had signed about talking to the press remained in force.

The team would certainly have had a lot to say. The start of that Sunday had been absolute carnage. Housekeeping had been hard at work on constant rotation, sweeping up broken champagne flutes, trying to get flattened canapés out of carpets. As each new shift started, the last handed over with stories of what it was like out there, of the things they had seen. One member, still in his mask but wearing nothing else, asleep in his Jacuzzi. One member still wandering up and down the perimeter of the lake looking for a missing shoe, muttering to themself. A cabin door kicked off its hinges, by someone unable at five in the morning to find their key. Another cabin's sprinkler system set off when a dropped cigarette set smoldering the tufted Moroccan rug.

Everywhere you looked in the Manor, guests had been slumbering, snoring, sprawled out, wrapped in their cloaks. At five in the morning a small group had decided to go for a swim in the lake — and then run screaming back into the house, muddy and freezing. At six in the morning there had been a hog roast on the lawn, people squatting on their haunches to watch the sun come up. At eight, security had announced that one of the branded Land Rovers was missing. At nine the first members had sat down to breakfast at Poseidon. At nine thirty the screaming had started.

It was Bex who had found Adam's body. She was tidying up with another girl in the upper lounge of the Manor, had noticed the rug was rucked up and had tried to lift the Louis Vuitton coffee-table trunk. Puzzled as to why it was so heavy, she had cleared various glasses off it and located the catch and flipped it and lifted the lid and inside it there he was. Still in his cape from the night before. Still with the rope around his neck.

By ten o'clock, when the first police boat arrived, with at least an hour and a half before the causeway was passable again, people were already queueing at the Boathouse to get off the island, screaming at the reception staff, demanding — in one woman's words — to be evacuated.

It wasn't until about eleven that people had started talking about Ned Groom as if he were not just absent but missing. At least that was when Jess became aware of the staff

454

speculating about where he was, calls going back and forth between the different Homes. Annie screaming at people to find Ned and get him on the phone. Annie suddenly the person in charge, the person to whom everyone seemed to be deferring. Annie Spark, the woman who had been in the car with Jackson Crane that night, all those years ago. Annie Spark, who had come storming into Jess's office before his body had even been formally identified, while the emergency services were still working out how they were going to get the Land Rover out of the sea, and had demanded the key for Jackson's cabin.

It was not hard to guess why she wanted it.

Four memory sticks. That was how many there must have been. One for each of the four members (excluding Georgia Crane) invited to that special dinner on the very first night of the launch party: one for Kurt Cox, one for Jackson Crane, one for Freddie Hunter, and one for Keith Little. No wonder they'd been so concerned when Kyra Highway turned up unannounced.

Jess had handed it over, of course, the cabin key. She had even offered to accompany her, to drive her over in a buggy. Annie had dismissed the offer with a swish of her hand, a minutely brief, cold, and patronizing smile.

What Annie did not know, of course, was that the footage she was so keen to get her hands on before the police or anyone else did was also recorded now on Jess's phone.

What Annie must have thought, when she got to Jackson's cabin and saw that memory stick there on the bedside table where Jess had left it, was that she had once again got away with it, the murder of Jess's parents. That she had got her hands on the only piece of hard evidence linking her to their deaths. It was hard even to imagine the relief she must have felt. How could she possibly have envisaged that she was still in so much danger?

For months now Jess had been torn between going to the police straightaway or letting something slip anonymously to the press first. It would have been easy enough to do the latter, given the number of journalists who had tried to contact her in the aftermath of what had happened. The *Sun* had left her voice mails, the *Daily Express,* the *Mail,* all of them. Later on, a journalist from *Vanity Fair* had sent her a series of long emails.

It wasn't revenge that she wanted. She had already tasted revenge on the island.

In some ways, perhaps, it felt the perfect and appropriate punishment, letting Annie go on with her life, letting her carry on running Home, giving interviews — and knowing that at any moment, practically at the press of a button, you could bring her life, the whole company, tumbling down.

Jess had waited a long time for justice to be served. She could wait a little longer, now.

Because one thing she did not want was for her story, the story of her parents, the truth about Jackson and Annie and what they had done, to get lost in the media cacophony about the deaths on the island, to become some sort of footnote to the deaths of Ned Groom and Jackson Crane and Keith Little, the murder of Adam Groom, part of that whole macabre hullabaloo.

But even a story as big as the deaths on Island Home could not hold the public's attention forever. Not in the era of the twenty-four-hour news cycle. Not in a world as turbulent as ours.

By the end of the month Freddie Hunter was back on TV, clips of his return circulating on YouTube, his earnest and tearful eulogy for Ned much praised, his smile as broad as ever — even though he didn't seem to be doing his helicopter karaoke sections anymore. His very first guest? Kyra Highway, "an old friend" as he introduced her, promoting her new album of Christmas songs, including a duet with her daughter — and at the end of the show Lyra herself had been beckoned out from the wings and they had all sung it together, all in their Santa hats, beaming merrily, collapsing into seemingly unforced laughter as the credits rolled.

On the surface of things, then, whatever he had done, whatever Home had footage of him doing, Freddie had got away with it.

There was just one moment, though, on his show, when the conversation had turned a little serious, when they'd talked about the island, and Kyra had mentioned Adam's name and, for a second, just a second, Freddie's smile had grown very forced indeed, and if you paused the footage at that very moment, you could see in his eyes, flicking left, what looked to Jess like genuine terror — and you found yourself wondering exactly what he knew about Adam's death, and what he knew but had left out in that much-praised eulogy for Ned.

She did find herself thinking about Georgia Crane, and all she'd been through, and the decisions she'd obviously made — and the toll they might be taking. To be told your husband is a killer, and then to learn your husband is dead in the space of a few short hours. To be forced to undertake the work of mourning in public. To be forced to defend your dead, murdering husband from accusations of complicity in the death of Adam, the death of Ned. She was, of course, a very wealthy woman now, Georgia Crane. Even with all the money she had given away to charity, to worthy causes. Even with all the money it would cost her to run for political office, as she had recently suggested she was considering doing.

"You can call, you should all feel you can call," Annie had told them. "I am sorry we can't keep you all on, but I'm here if you need me, you all have my mobile number."

They did. Jess did. How many times before had she thought about calling it? Every time she was alone in a bedroom at the Grange, every time she was out for drinks and someone else left their phone on the table. She had imagined calling Annie's number and saying something cryptic, something damning, perhaps saying nothing at all while Annie panicked and threatened and begged and pleaded.

It wasn't until her father's birthday — the day that would have been her father's birthday — that she actually did it. Jess took the afternoon off from the hotel, as usual, visited her father's grave, laid some flowers too on her mother's, crossed the road to a phone booth, fed it with coins, and dialed Annie's number.

Annie answered on the third or fourth ring but didn't immediately say anything. Had she been in a meeting, or at some sort of lunch event? Jess could hear her apologizing to people, people muttering, then what sounded like high heels on flagstones. "Hello?" she said brightly. Jess stayed silent. "Can I help you?" Annie asked, still friendly. Jess did not speak. "Who is this?" Jess did not answer. "Is anyone there? I can't hear you. Hello? Listen, it might be my reception."

"I've seen it," Jess said slowly. "I've seen what you did."

There was a long pause.

When she eventually spoke again, Annie's voice was almost a whisper: "What do you want from me?"

But the truth was there was no longer anything Jess wanted from Annie, nor was there any way of taking back what she'd done. The footage itself she had already uploaded to YouTube just before going out, emailed it as an attachment to the police.

460

What happened next was in the hands of the law, and the media. What happened next was the rest of Jess's life.

"It's over," she said, and hung up.

NIKKI

And just like that, it was over. Without even a thank-you or a sorry. After twenty-five years. Just a quick, blunt phone call from Annie to say that "obviously" under the circumstances Nikki's services would no longer be required. A phone call, and an extraordinarily large lump sum payment that had landed, without fanfare, in her bank account.

Nikki could not have been more relieved. Every time she thought of Home, every time she thought of Ned, she could feel a sort of existential shudder go through her.

Some people asked her what she was going to do next. Surely the offers of work must have been rolling in — members had always been trying to poach her before. Surely she was just playing hard to get and weighing up offers. And it was true, one or two had gently sounded her out at Ned's funeral — an event she had forced herself to attend, for appearance's sake, just as she had forced her face to remain neutral through all those heartfelt tributes to him.

461

What Nikki kept telling them, those people with their questions, their offers, was that she was just not sure she was ready to jump into another position like that with someone else right now. And so the offers kept escalating, the terms getting more and more generous. And still Nikki kept politely declining, or deferring a decision. And people kept asking what she was doing with herself, and didn't it all seem terribly quiet after her glamorous life with Ned? And the truth was she was just pottering around the house, mostly, or in the garden, and seeing people for dinner, and reading, and thinking about Kurt.

Her son.

Sometimes, when she was sitting in front of the TV in the evening or cooking herself dinner or running in the park, she would look at her watch and work out the time in LA and wonder what he was doing, Kurt, how he was processing what he had learned on the island. And it did cross her mind to call him, tell him the truth, the whole truth. And she found herself asking herself whether that would be a kindness or just selfish, whether if she were he, she would want to know, and whether she could really trust the promptings of her own heart. And still the job offers came in. From London.

From New York. From LA.

A good PA is hard to find.

It had always been one of their traditions, at Home, to throw a viewing party the night of the big awards ceremonies. The Oscars. The Emmys. The Grammys. The Brits. Everyone in one of the screening rooms with popcorn, sunk deep into those enormous leather sofas, applauding or laughing at the clips, catcalling, all stamping their feet and cheering whenever anyone that was in the room got mentioned, all throwing their popcorn at the screen and booing whenever the wrong person won. And it was fun, and funny, to see the people you knew up there, pretending to smile, pretending happily to clap whenever someone else beat them to an award, and know exactly what they were actually thinking and what they would say the next time you saw them. It was fun, and funny, seeing if any of the winners would mention Ned, mention Home, watch him growl and pretend to sulk if they did not.

She hadn't been intending to watch any of the awards this year. Why would she? She wasn't in that world anymore. But occasionally, after her bath, as she was getting ready to go up to bed, she would just flick the TV on, and one night when she did so, it was one of the awards shows she happened to catch, right at the end of a video-montage tribute to Jackson Crane, Georgia Crane in the front row, brushing away a single tear, receiving a consoling hand on her bare shoulder from the actor next to her. Then the announcer said something about Ron Cox. If the remote control had been closer to hand, Nikki would have switched the TV off before she even recognized the man in the tuxedo approaching the stage, taking the steps up to the stage two at a time, making his way to the podium, clapping the announcer on the back as they ceded the podium to him.

It was Kurt Cox.

There was a hushed silence, a couple of swallowed coughs as he unfolded a piece of paper and retrieved from the pocket of his tuxedo jacket a pair of reading glasses, made some crack about them. Then his face grew serious, and he began to speak about his father: "A man known to many of you personally, and to millions more through his films."

He was dead. Ron Cox was dead and Nikki hadn't even noticed, had missed the news somehow. How odd it felt, his absence from the world, the man whom she had once thought she had loved.

Kurt was talking now, with feeling, about the kindness his father had shown to him growing up, about being taken onto the set of all those much-loved wonderful movies, being the first to watch them sometimes, his dad noting his reactions, asking his opinions. He spoke about the generosity of his father, his charity work, his love of his family — second only to which came his love of golf. Laughter had rippled around the room. That was the father he knew, he said.

But there was also the man that some of *them* knew. That some of them had helped enable. Accusations that had been hushed up, and hushed up, and hushed up again, but that everyone in this room, in Hollywood, knew about. About the girls, young girls, threatened into silence or paid off, the vast machinery of fear and manipulation and exploitation on which his father's career had depended. And at first the camera kept cutting back and forth to faces in the audience. Angry faces. Frightened faces. And you could see the host standing in the corner of the stage, not knowing what to do or say, voices no doubt screaming in his ear. You could hear Kurt speeding up as he spoke — he even made some reference about needing to get this said before they cut him short and went to a commercial break. And he was talking now about how women who tried to tell the truth were ground down, gaslit. How talk-show hosts made jokes about them, how the media dug dirt on them, how they were advised to settle out of court. And how that was wrong. How what his father had done was wrong, using his wealth and his power first to pressure girls and then to silence them. And that was what he had wanted to say about his father and other men like him sitting in this room. That now he knew, although he had loved the man with all his heart, he could not stand here on this stage and let his father's memory be buffed and burnished like a gold statuette.

That was when they finally turned up the music to drown out Kurt's mic and started playing the preplanned showreel of all the most heartwarming moments from all of Ron Cox's most heartwarming movies.

For a long time after she had turned the television off, Nikki just sat there, occasionally dabbing at her face with the sleeve of her sweater, occasionally digging a little ball of tissue out of her pajama pocket to blow her nose. She didn't need to look online to know what people would already be talking about, nor what they would be saying about

Ron Cox, about Kurt. She could imagine there would be people defending Ron, and accusing Kurt, and all the people who always had opinions about things would be racing to be the first person off the mark with their hot take, and already the battle lines would be forming.

She put her phone down, walked to the window, and looked out into the darkness, at the bare tree at the end of the lawn silhouetted against the orange-lit sky, the moon behind the clouds.

And she stood there for a long time, thinking. About Ron. About Ned. About all the things she had done in her life and all the things she had still to do. About all the ways one person can shape and twist and hurt another. About the difficulties, perhaps even the impossibility, of ever fully putting some things right. About the past and about the present and the future. About a decision, and a phone call, to the young man that she was proud to have given birth to, that it had finally come time to make.

ACKNOWLEDGMENTS

The past couple of years have not been the easiest time for anyone trying to do anything, and it certainly wasn't an easy time to write a book. The fact that we managed it is down to the support of our friends, family, and each other — as well as to brilliant teams on both sides of the Atlantic.

We'd both like to thank our supersmart and ever-kind and supportive agents, Emma Finn at C&W and Hillary Jacobson at ICM: we cannot tell you how much we appreciate your wisdom and cheerleading. We also thank Luke Speed (thank you for answering our endless questions about everything; we think you are great!) and Anna Weguelin at Curtis Brown; Kate Burton, Jake Smith-Bosanquet, Matilda Ayris, and the lovely rights team at C&W.

At Harper, thank you to Doug Jones, our editor, Sarah Stein (one day we will go for those pancakes!), Hayley Salmon, Katherine

Beitner, and the sales, production, publicity, and marketing teams, and the art team who created a brilliantly atmospheric cover for *The Club*. At Mantle, we thank our editor, Sam Humphries, as well as Samantha Fletcher, Alice Gray, the sales, production, marketing, and publicity teams. Our early blurbers, thank you — Harriet Tyce, Cesca Major, Holly Watt, Charlotte Philby, and Eliza-Jane Brazier. We really appreciate it!

To the Book of the Month team, and complete legends Richard Madeley and Judy Finnegan and the WH Smith team, thank you for selecting our debut novel, *People Like Her,* to be a pick.

Collette would like to thank the wordy women on the other end of Whatsapp through successive lockdowns and beyond — Holly Watt, Rebecca Thornton, Alice Wignall, Celia Walden. Also Sebastian Isaac, Richard Acton, and Robert Boon for their professional expertise. Catherine Jarvie and Karolyn Fairs for being our trusted first readers, as always. Lesley McGuire, Sagar Shah, Eleanor O'Carroll, and Tanya Petsa for just general everything; Amy Little (we survived!), Graham Banton, and the tribe of Banton boys for sanity-saving Sunday walks. Alicia Clarke and Annick Wolfers for their camera skills. The wonderful women of Churchill & Partners — Beverley Churchill, Shelley Landale-Down; Jo Lee and Dan Henshaw.

For their help, advice, support, and encouragement over the years, Paul would like to thank: Cara Harvey, Sarah Jackson, Julia Jordan, Louise Joy, Eric Langley, David McAllister, Adrian Poole, Peter Robinson, Claire Sargent, Oli Seares, Katy Stewart-Moore, Jane Vlitos, John Vlitos, as well as my friends and colleagues in the School of English Literature, Film, and Creative Writing at the University of Surrey.

And of course our daughter, who is already in training to join the family band.

ABOUT THE AUTHOR

Ellery Lloyd is the pseudonym for the London-based husband-and-wife writing team Collette Lyons and Paul Vlitos. Collette is a journalist and editor, the former content director of *Elle* (UK), and editorial director at Soho House. She has written for *The Guardian, The Telegraph,* and the *Sunday Times.* Paul is the author of two previous novels, *Welcome to the Working Week* and *Every Day Is Like Sunday.* He is the subject leader for English literature, film, and creative writing at the University of Surrey.